THERE IS A GRAVEYARD
THAT DWELLS IN MAN

This Graveyard is for Ania, a Blythe Spirit amongst our Blithe Cats, with All my Love and Always Yours,

David+++

There Is A Graveyard That Dwells In Man

Selected By David Tibet

There Is A Graveyard That Dwells In Man
Edited by David Tibet
ISBN: 9781907222610

First Published by Strange Attractor Press 2020
Texts Copyright © 2020 The Authors & Their Estates
Introduction Copyright © 2020 David Tibet
Artwork by David Tibet & Ania Goszczyńska
Layout by Maia Gaffney-Hyde

Transcription by Bea Turner. Proofing by Richard Bancroft. Strange Attractor
and David Tibet send them Love and Thanks for all their invaluable help.

Strange Attractor Press BM SAP,
London, WC1N 3XX, UK
www.strangeattractor.co.uk

Distributed by The MIT Press, Cambridge, Massachusetts.
And London, England.

Printed and bound in the United Kingdom by TJ International

Contents

23. He that is not with me, is against me: and hee that gathereth not with me, scattereth. 24. When the vncleane spirit is gone out of a man, he walketh through drie places, seeking rest: and finding none, he sayth, I will returne vnto my house whence I came out. 25. And when hee commeth, hee findeth it swept and garnished. 26. Then goeth he, and taketh to him seuen other spirits more wicked then himselfe, and they enter in, and dwell there, and the last state of that man is worse then the first.

St. Luke XI: 23—26

43. When the vncleane spirit is gone out of a man, hee walketh thorow dry places, seeking rest, and findeth none. 44. Then he saith, I will returne into my house from whence I came out; And when he is come, he findeth it emptie, swept, and garnished. 45. Then goeth he, and taketh with himselfe seuen other spirits more wicked then himselfe, and they enter in and dwell there: And the last state of that man is worse then the first. Euen so shal it be also vnto this wicked generation.

St. Matthew XII: 43—45

A Rainbow Rag To An Astral Bull
David Tibet

𒈗 𒂊 𒅆 𒆠 𒀀 𒈪 𒌝 𒂊 𒀀 𒈪
𒈦 𒈪 𒂊 𒀀 𒅆 𒆠 𒉌 𒀀 𒁲 𒌋 𒀀 𒌋 𒀭 𒁲
𒅆 𒆠 𒅗 𒆤 𒈝 𒁲 𒈦 𒂊 𒁲 ᐸ 𒈪 𒂠 𒈝 𒁲

šiptu alsīkunūši ilū mušīti

ittīkunu alsi mušītu kallatu kuttumtu

alsi barārītu qablītu u namārītu

INCANTATION: I summon you, Gods of the Night
With you I summon Night, the covered bride
I summon Twilight, Midnight, and Dawn

Maqlû ("Burning"), Tablet 1, lines 1-3

In my introduction to *The Moons At Your Door*, the first volume in this series of anthologies of the short stories—all, it has to be said, either supernatural or weird in their nature—that have most inspired and influenced me in all my work, I wrote at some length about what brought me to those Moons that I saw at play around me.

Whether those Moons arose, or descended, for me, they waited patiently outside my door. On opening that door, I ran inside, so fast and inwards, to escape their greetings. But inside, inwards, I saw that there was a Graveyard there, the source of those Moons—and this Graveyard is the source of that pull to the dark and that call to the twilight that dwells within us all.

In this brief essay, I would like to consider the Graveyard that dwells in me—and in us all—and to which we will all journey at the Anointed God's appointed hour, hand in grave, grave in hand, a doomed Puss-In-Boots.

For when I look back at all my obsessions, all my enthusiasms, I feel them as strongly and as vividly now as when I first encountered them, and I run—so fast—after them still. They are so real to me, as real as rainbows, and quite as ungraspable.

I just need to hear the name "Stenbock" and I see myself in the company of Count Eric. When I look at the inscribed copies I own of his works, I see him clearly as he writes his Greek and as he thinks on other loves, his head dropping like a flower as his own chosen flowers overwhelm his blood. His writing is real, the images are real, and my dreams are the real.

Just so, in all of those artists whose works so move me, whose rainbow is so deep inside me, I see their escape from, and their return to, that twilit grave from which they ran, as if by running so fast they could shield their eyes to not notice how quickly their steps returned them to that same.

This obsession that I have, and which so many of us share, is a fire from a falling star—even if I do not quite remember when the spark first lit me, or when I first saw that bright dead star fall. And these sparks, these fires, sometimes come to us because they have already chosen us, knowing our face for far longer than we have known their name.

Under the firelight of this star, as an example of the Graveyard that dwells in us all, I would like to detail my obsession with Borley Rectory, known as "the most haunted house in England", after the psychic investigator Harry Price's book of the same name, published by Longmans, Green and Co. in London in 1940.

I don't remember exactly when I first read about Borley, but it would certainly have been in Malaysia sometime between 1970 and 1973, in some lurid book promising, and delivering, lurid contents.

As soon as I read the name, the name read me and the name goaded me into a long, long journey to find anything and everything about it and under it and over it and in it—its very essence, if you will. The most haunted house haunted me. And since it was burnt down in 1939, and then demolished in 1944, its intangibility made it all the more tangible to me. We can now read, in *The Borley Rectory Companion* (The History Press, London 2009), that indispensable book Paul Adams co-authored with Eddie Brazil and the late Peter Underwood, that:

> "Items known to have come from inside the Rectory are incredibly rare. Steuart Kiernander rescued a tangle of bell-wires and one of the Bull wine bottles from the Rectory ruins following a visit in the 1940s; he gave them as a souvenir to Peter Underwood, who was also presented with a miniature blue-and-white plate by Ethel Bull and a wooden inkwell by Alfred Bull, made by his brother the Revd Harry; both these latter items were later stolen from the collection and their whereabouts today are unknown."

Even though I was not aware of the utter scarcity of items physically connected to Borley Rectory when I first read about it fifty, or so, years ago, I now feel that Borley already knew my name, and that she had numbered me amongst her elect. Anyway, I started collecting anything I could find about Borley Rectory, starting with paperbacks in any edition at all, and moving on to first editions in hardback, and then first editions in dust-jackets, and then again those same books written, and inscribed, by Harry Price, the author who first brought the case to the public, and so sensationally did so. But no matter how scarce the book, no matter how fulsomely inscribed by, and to, those who had been part of the story, I had to acquire an actual physical link to the Rectory and to the story that had so taken me—something which I could truly call as real as rainbows—that connection which takes me back to that Graveyard which dwells in the heart of every story. The photographs I saw in books of the "tangled bell-wires", or of a wine-bottle, or a bell, were filled with such ephemeral beauty, which filled me with such sweet melancholy—and such beauty and such melancholy I wished to hold and to know.

Whether I inadvertently summoned the *ilū mušīti*—those gods of the night upon which the first three lines of Tablet I of *Maqlû*, written in the Neo-Assyrian form of Akkadian, so sparingly yet eloquently call—or whether Borley herself, who had no doubt long known those gods' true night names, asked them to find me, I found that to those who wait, all things come, for better or worse.

And so Borley came to me, like a dream, in a rush and a skip, with her bag of twilight tricks. And this is how it happened: I had noticed an item offered online for auction that was described as a silver-bottomed hip-flask, with missing cap, and the words "REV H BULL BORLEY RECTORY" engraved on the silver, along with a Cross. This was indeed a Rainbow Rag to me in my vocation as Astral Bull. I asked the seller, a young man named Sam, about the provenance of the hip-flask. In fact it turned out to be a container for Holy Water... and following on from this, I was to see more of Borley than I had ever dreamt.

In my first conversation with Sam, which swept between Nick Drake, Marc Bolan, and Keith Emerson, we discovered that we got on very well and soon became good friends.

And such was the beginning of my acquisition of the largest collection in existence of Borley Rectory memorabilia—which also included items from the equally-haunted Borley Church (or equally-unhaunted, if you wish to split ghosts)—and had previously belonged to Sam's wealthy, eccentric, and recently departed, great-uncle, an enthusiastic collector of esoteric curiosities, and who had been especially interested in Borley Rectory, time-travel, and early DNA research.

So now, when I look at the walls of my study, on which hang the paintings of Borley Rectory and of Borley Church painted by the Reverend Harry Bull, or at the furniture on which he has carved his name and the legend "BORLEY RECTORY REV H BULL" and a Cross, or the cheap metal tin on which he has engraved the motto "MEMENTO MORI" with a Death's Head and a Crow and Cross, or the holograph notes he has left regarding two experiences he had of the ghostly sad nun who haunted the Rectory, or listen to the plaintive melody that comes from the music box that he owned—I am there in the Rectory with him, and the Rainbow is real, and the Rectory is the real. I open a box Harry owned, and wonder what made him place in it a small number of animal bones in a small oval tin. I have several of his pocket-watches, on all of which all the hands have stopped as surely as time itself stopped in Borley. On the back of each one is again engraved his, and the Rectory's, name next to the usual simple Cross. I don't know whose dark black hair is curled in the velvet-covered locket which bears the inscription "Harry 2nd Feb 1900"— Harry's? His father's? His wife's? His lover's—is she the unidentified woman who sits smiling in a photograph that I found in the little hidden drawer in one of the several wooden boxes I acquired?

Each such object I hold in my hand, or each such story I read in a book, or that I hear from the long-dead voice of some long-dead face, who hid behind her and his own many masks, is a Graveyard.

Amongst the graves and the tombs and the chipped angels and the shining words that shine from under the worn Biblical verses and the sugar-sweet hopes and prayers beautiful and hopes sentimental, each of these stories come—voices in sounds or in words or in stone, spinning in the airs, as dark as moths and as bright as butterflies, spinning on to where they return, and where we shall meet them again too—that Graveyard of many colours and of many births in which there is no end, and which is itself only a mask, and behind which the Aleph waits.

David Tibet, Hastings, All Hallows' Eve, 2019!

A Black Solitude
HR Wakefield

I have no explanation of this story, in fact, one of my reasons for telling it lies in the hope that some reader of it may provide one. I rather dislike being left in such an elucidatory void. I got permission to tell it from Lady Foreland; she is sure the Chief would not have minded. I shall probably tell it very badly, for I am an organizer of writers by profession, not a writer myself. The "Chief", was Lord Foreland, the first and greatest of the newspaper peers; none of his many successors can hold a candle—or should it be a telephone?—to him. I was his personal, private secretary for six years. I got the job directly after the Kaiser War when I was twenty-two. I was a callow, carefree, confident youth in those days, still housing a number of small pieces of shrapnel, but otherwise healthy enough, and very proud of serving such a celebrity.

The events in this narrative occurred at Caston Place, the Chief's most renowned country house. This was a famous specimen of early Tudor manor house, in Surrey, charming rather than beautiful, perhaps; though never have I seen such exquisitely mellow brick. The grounds were unarguably lovely. The great lawn—finest turf in the world—lined by Lebanon cedars, the flower, rock, water and kitchen gardens, all showpieces and deservedly so, the best private golf-course in the Islands, snipe in the water, meadows down by the strolling, serpentine Wear. Well, if I were a millionaire, that's the sort of cottage I would choose. The interior, too, after the Chief's purse had mated with "Ladyship's" taste, had been most delicately modernized without a trace of "vulgarized." I was there about thirty week-ends in the year and I grew to love it. It was a great old gentleman, an eternally young old gentleman and it died, like so many other gentlemen of my times, in the wars. And also, like many such gentlemen, it had a secret which died with it. My little bedroom was almost at the end of the east wing. It had once been, I fancy, the dressing-room of the big bedroom next door to it. To my surprise I found that this big bedroom was never used, even when the most lavish house-parties came for the weekend. It was not kept locked, but no one ever slept there.

One day I went in and inspected it. By any standards I had known up till then it was a *vast* room, and somehow vaguely unprepossessing. It had very dark oak panelling and a great oak bed. Two full length portraits flanked the fireplace.

The owners of Caston had fallen on sufficiently mediocre days not to be able to afford to live in it, though the rent the Chief paid for it must have gone far to reconcile them to such exile. Portraits of their forebears—the majority third-rate daubs to be accurate— liberally littered the walls. The Chief told me there'd always been a "sticky" streak in the family (though the latest generation were tame enough) with a notorious name for cruelty, improvidence and various and versatile depravities. These portraits certainly, for the most part, bore this indictment out. They were a baleful-looking crew, men, women and children, and their decorative value exceptionally meager. But the two in the room, as I will call it from henceforth, struck, it seemed to me, a new and noxious low. They were man and wife, I suppose, and fitting mates. They were both in the middle forties, I should say, period, early Stuart, judging from their garb. The husband had a very nasty pair of close-set beady eyes and his lower lip—a family stigmata this—was fleshy, puffy and pouting, the lip of an insatiable and unscrupulous egoist and sensualist. He carried his head bunched forward and his chin down, as though staring hard at the artist and giving him the toughest piece of his mind. The lady was a blonde, and sufficient in herself to give blondes a bad name. She had the lightest blue eyes I ever saw in a face, almost toneless. They were big, too far apart and as hard staring as her spouse's. Her mouth was just one long, hard, thin line of scarlet. Her expression was ruthless and contemptuous, as though telling the painter he was an incompetent—which was true—and informing him it would be a case of "off with his head" if he didn't hurry up. I remember thinking that if he'd ever seen the colour of his fee, he was lucky. When I looked at them I found them staring back at me and I felt I would *not* let them stare me down. I thought how lowering it might be to find those four evil eyes on one when one woke up in the morning, and that it might not be too jocund to turn the light out knowing they were there. (In some frail moods it is difficult to differentiate entirely man and his effigy. And that goes, if you know what I mean, for *dead* men—and women—too.) These twain looked, if I may so put it, as though at any moment they might step down from their frames and beat me up.

Well, here was a small mystery and I made up my mind to solve it. It wasn't as if Caston was over-supplied with bedrooms. Those old houses are smaller than they look, in this sense, that many of their rooms are, to our ideas, ludicrously large, and there are too few of them. I knew Ladyship could have put the room to very good purpose if she'd so chosen. Why didn't she so choose? It was puzzling. I was new to the job, and it was not part of it to ask possibly awkward domestic questions. So I waited my chance and presently it came.

One day, when I was on my own down at Caston making arrangements for a big staff party the chief was throwing, I took a stroll round the grounds with Chumley, the butler and a great character. The very first time I stayed at Caston, the Chief sent for Chumley and in his presence said to me, "This is my butler, the best butler in England, and a very great rogue. Owing to his defalcations and the house property he has purchased therefrom, he is also a very rich man. No doubt eventually he will go to America, the devil, the spiritual home of the best British butlers. Never, my boy, let me catch you giving him a tip."

"Well, sir" I said, "*may he* give *me* one sometimes?" The Chief was in a good humour, luckily, and passed this rather saucy remark. In fact, he said it showed I had a promising eye to the main commercial chance. (After the Chief died he *did* go to America and some years later he sent me his photograph seated at the wheel of a Rolls-Royce, a cigar in his mouth and an Alsatian sitting beside him. An eagle amongst doves!) Well, on this occasion we were strolling about on the lawn and I asked him, glancing up at its windows, why the room was never occupied. "His Lordship's brother, Sir Alfred, had an unpleasant experience there," he replied, "but please do not say I told you."

"I don't quite know, but he started screaming out one night and went straight back to London first thing in the morning. He never came here again and died very soon after."

"And it has never been used since?"

"Only on one occasion, sir; the editor of the *Evening Sentinel* slept there later on and he looked very *green* at breakfast the next morning. I think he must have said something to his Lordship, for he gave me orders the room wasn't to be used again."

"Was that Mr. Spenland, the present editor?"

"No, sir, Mr. Cocks, the former editor: He also died soon—within a week, as I remember it."

"Odd, Chumley!"

"Possibly, sir, but keep what I've told you under your hat, if I may use that expression. I made some inquiries in the village and they weren't surprised at all. Until his Lordship took the house the end of that wing was blocked up and never used."

"Why?"

"Hard to say, sir. Not considered lucky, I gathered."

"That's nice for me, sleeping there!"

"Have you been bothered, sir?"

"I don't think so. I get some funny dreams, but that's the food and drink, I expect. Not what I'm used to. But how d'you mean, not lucky?"

"They kept a tight mouth about that, but Morton, the game-keeper, told me there's supposed to be somebody or something still living on in that room."

"*What* a yarn!"

"Yes, sir," agreed Chumley doubtfully. "None of the maids will go in there alone after dark."

"Just because they've heard tales about it!"

"I suppose so, though one of them got a fright some years back. Anyway, don't tell his Lordship I said anything. He's a bit touchy about it; he likes all his possessions to be *perfect*." A very shrewd remark!

"No, all right," I promised, and we resumed discussing the business of the hour.

That night, just before going to bed, I paid a visit to the room. I had been busy with mundane and concrete matters. I had dined well, so it was with a very disdainful and nonchalant air that I climbed the stairs. At once, it is no use denying it, my psychic outlook changed. I suddenly realized that Caston when empty, was a very quiet, brooding place, and that I had never quite liked being alone in it, it was a bit "much" overpowering for a "singleton."

The weather had soured during the evening, clouding over with a falling glass and a fitful rising summer wind. My little enclave at the end of the passage seemed peculiarly aloof and dispiriting. Chumley's enigmatic remarks recurred to me with some force at that moment and with a heightened significance. I thought of those two dead men, the one who'd screamed and the other who'd looked "green"—what a word!—at breakfast. However, you know the feeling. I didn't want to open that door, and yet I knew if I didn't I should have kicked myself for a craven and never—or at least not for a long time—got it out of my system. My year at the War had taught me that each time one funks one finds it harder not to do it next time. All of which may sound much ado about precious little, but you weren't standing facing that door at midnight on July 20th, 1923! Well, with a small whistle of defiance I turned the handle of that door and flipped on the lights. Anti-climax, of course! Just a huge old room like any other of its kind. And yet was it quite normal? Well, there was that commonplace feeling everyone has experienced that someone had been in there a moment before, that the air was still warm from that someone's presence; perhaps rather more than that; perhaps, quite absurd, of course, that one was being observed by someone unseen. My eyes ran round the room swiftly and then settled on those criminal types athwart the fireplace. They had their eyes on me pretty starkly. "Avaunt!" they seemed to be saying, or whatever was the contemporary phrase for "Beat it!" I stared back at them. "Not till I'm ready!" I replied out loud in a would-be jocular way. There was an odd echo in that room. It seemed to swing round the walls and come back to hit me in the face. Then I heard a scraping noise from the chimney, Jack-daws nesting in it, no doubt second-brood; my voice had disturbed their slumbers. I moved further into the room. The rustling in the chimney grew louder. "Well, good night, all!" I said facetiously, but there was no echo. I tried again; no echo at all. That was a puzzle. I shifted my position and said good night to them once more. This time the echo nearly blew my head off and something tapped three times on one of the windows. I suddenly felt that uncontrollable atavistic dread of ambush and glanced sharply round behind my back. "I'm not afraid of you," I said loudly. "Do your worst!" But somehow I knew it was time to go. I paced back slowly and deliberately, turned out the light, banged the door and went to bed.

What a history that room must have had, I thought, to have been blocked off from the world like that for years. And now the ban was up once more. Strong medicine there of some sort! What sort? And there was only some thin panelling and plaster between me and it. I kept my ears pricked, for I was a bit on edge, my subconscious was alert and receptive.

I went to bed and presently to sleep. Sometime in the night I awoke hearing something, which, my subconscious told me, I had heard several times before, but now, *consciously* for the first time; it was a kind of *crack* like the flipping of giant fingers, twice repeated. A displeasing, staccato, urgent and peremptory sound, the source of which I quite failed to trace.

Now the Chief, like most self-made men, especially in his profession, had some queer "old friends," many of whom had been associated with him in his days of struggle, but had, for the most part, been left far behind in the success marathon. The Chief had not a trace of snobbery about these; so long as he liked them and they amused him they remained his friends, rich or poor, success or duds and, in several cases, reputable or not. Perhaps the queerest of all these was one Apuleius Charlton. This person was generally deemed a very dubious type and a complete back-number, the last belated survivor of the Mauve decade, with a withered green carnation in his frayed buttonhole and trailing thin clouds of obsolete diabolism. Incidentally, he belonged to a cadet branch of a very "old family." As a sinister monster of depravity I found him sheer Disney and so did the Chief, but he had unarguably superior brains, a kind of charm, and an ebullient personality. In fact, *personality* is quite too flaccid a word; he was *sui generis*, the sole member of his species. There was a strong tinge of Casanova about him; he shared his brazen candour, occasional brilliant insight, his refusal to accept the silly laws of God and man as binding upon himself, his essential spiritual loneliness. He was a big hefty creature, an athlete by right of birth, with a huge domed head, large watery eyes and jet-black hair, the fringe of which he tortured into twin spiral locks. Between them was a small, red magical mark, a three-pronged "moon" swastika. He had been everywhere in the world, I think, and his travel tales were legion and sensational and owing something, no doubt, to an ebullient imagination. He was

7

then barred from a number of countries, rather unhumorously, for while his bark was Cerberian, his bite was vastly over-rated. He had, no doubt, acquired certain monies by various modes of false pretenses, but never a sizable hoard; and those he diddled were, I am sure, consummate mugs who just asked to be "taken." He said so himself and I believed him.

He had written copiously on many subjects with an air of complete confidence and authority, and in his youth had been a goodish minor poet of the erotic, adjectival Swinburne school, but somehow he never had any real money. That was his incurable malady. There are a number of such vagrant oddities in the world, lone wolves, or rather, I think, they remind me of great ostracized, solitary birds, forever winging their way fearlessly and hopefully from one barren place to another, wiry, wary, and shunned by the timourous and "respectable" flock. He had written stuff for the Chief's publication before his name became so odoriferous, climbed with him in several parts of the world, for he was brilliant and scientific mountaineer, and gone with him on esoteric drinking bouts in the wine countries, for he knew his epicurean tipples and taught the Chief to judge a vintage. Lastly, and immensely most important to himself, he was a magician with a cult or mystery of his very own invention and a small band of very odd initiates indeed. Hence the swastika and much ponderous and eleusinian jewelry on convenient parts of his person, including a perfectly superb jade ring. I know jade and this piece was incomparably fine. (You will hear of it again.) For this aspect of his ego the Chief, not necessarily rightly, expressed the most caustic contempt, telling him the only reason why he and his rival Merlins and Fingals shrouded their doings in veils of secrecy—and this went for Masons, Buffaloes, Elks, and all other mumbo-jumbo practitioners—was that they had nothing to conceal except the most puerile and humiliating drivel worthy of their Woolworth regalia, and they were ashamed to disclose such infantile lucubrations and primitive piffle. All the same some people were definitely scared of old Apuleius, and no doubt he had a formidable and impressive side. He was sixty odd at this time and very well preserved in spite of his hard boozing, addiction to drugs and sexual fervour, for it was alleged that joy-maidens or Hierodoules were well represented in his mystic entourage. (If I were a Merlin, they would be in mine!)

Of course he never figured in house parties, but the Chief had him down to Caston now and again and, I know, sent him a most welcome cheque at regular intervals.

In November of this same year, the Chief and his Lady went away for a month's holiday to the Riviera, and just before he met old Apuleius in the street looking a bit down at heel and told him he could doss down at Caston while he was away, that I would look after him, and that the cellar was at his disposal, but that this invitation did *not* extend to his coterie, particularly the Hierodoules! Poor Apuleius leaped at this timely and handsome offer and the day after the Chief's departure he appeared at the house bearing his invariable baggage, one small, dejected cardboard suitcase—at least, it looked like cardboard. I was on holiday, too, or rather half-holiday, for I got six to a dozen telegrams a day from the Chief and had made a rash promise to begin the cataloguing of his library. (I may say he had two other secretaries to do the donkey-work.) But I had plenty of spare time to shoot, golf and catch some of the nice little trout in the stream. So there were old Apuleius and I almost alone for a month and all the best at our disposal. He treated me always with some pleasing but quite unnecessary deference, for I was the Czar's little shadow and a lad worth cultivating. Beside he liked me a little and he didn't like anyone very much. I resolved covertly to examine this psychological freak, because I never could decide how much of a charlatan he was and how much he believed in his own bunkum. Such characters are very dark little forests and it's a job to blaze any sort of trail through them.

He arrived, very sensibly, just in time for lunch and did himself extremely well. He was in great spirits and splendid form talking with vast verve and rather above my jejune head. I quite forget what it was all about. He slept for a while after lunch and then began a prolonged prowl around the establishment, which he had never properly inspected before. I went with him, for the unworthy reason that the house was full of small, highly-saleable articles and he had a reputation for sometimes confusing meum with tuum when confronted with such. At length we reached my little enclave and there facing him was the room. "What's that?" he asked, staring hard at the door. "Oh, just a bedroom," I replied. Suddenly he moved forward quickly, opened the door, and drew a quick, dramatic breath. At once he seemed transformed. You have seen the life come to a drowsy cat's eyes when it hears the rustle of a mouse. You may have noted the changed demeanour of some oafish and lugubrious athlete when he spies a football or a bag of golf clubs. Just such a metamorphosis occurred in Apuleius when he opened that door. He became intent, absorbed, *professional*. I felt compensatingly insignificant and meager.

"Nobody sleeps here?" he said.

"No," I replied.

"Not twice anyway," he said sharply.

"Why?" I asked.

He went up to the criminal types and scrutinized them carefully. And then he pointed out to me some things I had not noticed before, a tiny figure of a hare with a human and very repulsive face at the right-hand side of the gentleman, a crescent moon with something enigmatic peering out between its horns on the same side of the lady. "As I expected," he observed in his most impressive manner, and left it at that.

"Well, what about it?" I asked impatiently.

"That would take rather a long time to explain, my dear Pelham," he replied, "and with all respect, I doubt if you would ever quite understand. Let me just say this. Such places as these are as rare as they are perilous. In a sense this is a timeless place. What once happened here didn't change, didn't pass on, it was *crystallized*. What happened herein eternally repeats itself. Here time, as it were, was trapped and can't move on. Man is life and life is change so such places are deadly to man. If man cannot change, he dies. Death is the end of a stage in a certain process of change. Only the dead can live in this room."

"And do they?" I asked, bemused by this rigamarole.

"In a sense, yes."

The effusion didn't commend itself to me. (Besides it was still daylight.) I countered with vivacity. "Well," I said, "you may be right, but the moment anyone begins philosophizing about time I get a bellyache. It is one of the prevailing infirmities of third-rate minds. Personally I believe it to be no more a genuine mystery than say, money, with which it is vulgarly identified. All this pother about both is due to a confusion of thought based on a confusion of terms. The word 'time' is habitually used in about sixteen different senses. If I were asked to define metaphysics, I should describe it as an acrimonious and sterile controversy about the connotation of certain abstract terms. But I'll give you this, the room has a bad name." (There was no getting round that, and he'd instantly spotted it. How?)

"It should not even be *entered* after dark," he said, "save by those who—well—understand it and enter it fore-armed."

"You say something happened here and eternally reacts itself. What?"

"Those two," he replied, pointing to the types, "made an experiment which in a sense succeeded."

"And that was?"

"Once again I am in a difficulty. These dark territories are such new ground to you. You must understand there are no such entities as good and evil, there are merely forces, some beneficent, some injurious, indeed, fatal, to man. He exists precariously poised between these forces. Those two, as it were, allied themselves with the forces noxious to man; what used to be called selling oneself to the devil. These things are beyond you, my dear Pelham, and

11

I should not pursue them. It is one of the oldest mysteries of the world, the idea that if one can become all evil, drink the soma of the fiend, one immortalizes oneself; one becomes impervious to change and so to death. Actually, it is not so. It cannot be done. One cannot defeat death, but one can become what is loosely called an evil spirit, a focus for a concentration of destructive energy, and, in that limited sense, undying."

"Of course, you're right, that's all cuneiform to me," I replied staring up at the ambitious pair. "But what's the result? What happens then?"

"Well, those two made that attempt. I can tell that for certain reasons, and achieved that limited success. They practised every conceivable wicked and unspeakable thing. This room was their laboratory, their torture-chamber; it reeks of it. When they died, they became chained to this room. It is their *Hell*, if you like so to put it."

"In what state are they?" I asked not knowing whether to laugh or cry. "I mean are they conscious? Do they know, for example, you are discussing them?"

"To begin with 'they' is a misnomer. 'They' are *one*; male and female principles have been fused and the feminine predominates, for it is the more primitive, potent and dangerous. The resultant 'It' is not conscious in our sense of the word, it has no illusion of *will*. It is a state we cannot understand and so cannot describe. It has been absorbed into the very soul of that power which is inimicable to man and is endowed with its venom. But it cannot roam; it is anchored to this room. To destroy man is It's delight. In that It finds It's *orgasm*. What occurs in this room is the eternal generation, condensation and release of murderous energy. After dark, for it cannot be released in daylight, this whole room will be soaked in and embued with that energy."

"How does It destroy?"

"It can do so simply by fear and fear can kill. Once in India I passed through a cholera-infected area. The very road was thick with bodies, but more of them had died from sheer fear than the disease. It would kill *you* by fear, but It could not so kill me. It would have to—well—*overpower* me to destroy me. I am coming here tonight."

"I shouldn't!" I said hastily. "I'm not sure the Chief would permit it. If anything happened to you, he'd be furious."

"It will not. I know the only safeguards against and antidotes to these forces. So leave me now. I will start to prepare my defences. I will see you at dinner."

So I went off to do some work, completely baffled and somewhat uneasy in mind.

At dinner Apuleius was preoccupied and portentous, and actually drank nothing but water, a sure sign he was taking life seriously. I was preoccupied too. I knew perfectly well the Chief would have shoved down a formidable foot on the whole thing, but I wasn't the Chief, Apuleius had been given the run of the house and I had no authority to control his movements within it. All the same, looking back on it, I think I acted feebly and that I should have exercised a veto however arbitrary, and kept him out of that room that night. All I did was to employ persuasion, and quite ineffectually. "My dear Pelham," he propounded, "this is a challenge I must accept. I have devoted much of my life to this crusade of safeguarding man from those black forces which, unknown to the blind and unpercipient, are forever striving and with ever increasing success to break down his resistance and shatter him. If I fully succeed tonight I shall cleanse that room and make it harmless, white and habitable again. I shall be very thankful if I can do the Chief this service."

"But supposing they are too strong for you?" I protested. "That energy may be more virulent and vicious than you reckon on."

"That is a risk I must take. So far I have always conquered them, and I can rally mighty forces to my aid. In this sign,"—and he touched the swastika on his forehead—"I shall conquer once again. Have no fears."

I must say he looked impressive, exalted, when he said this.

After dinner he again disappeared for a while and I tried to do some more work, but of all jobs cataloguing a library is the most soporific. I dozed off and presently woke to find him standing before me. He had repainted the swastika, which gleamed somberly.

"I am ready," he declared, "and now I will rest for a while. I will enter that room at five minutes to midnight."

"What kind of ordeal do you think awaits you?" I asked. "Or do you mind telling me?"

"The moment I enter that room I shall pronounce certain formulae, what you would loosely call incantations. I shall then, to use a military metaphor, entrench myself within a defensive ring and concentrate my whole spirit on rallying to my side the powers of white, the forces of salvation. They will come to me. Already the black forces will be concentrating upon me, the tension will increase every moment. Sometime the black will strike and the white will lash back, the grapple will be joined. When those dark forces have done their worst and been repelled, white will have been re-established in that room, the sting of evil, of destruction and of black will have been drawn. I shall be exhausted and soon pass into a coma from which I shall awake refreshed, hale and with added powers. And then we will enjoy our holiday together, my dear Pelham, and drink deep, having cleansed this lovely house of its ancient doom."

"I wish I could be with you in that struggle," I said doubtfully.

"It is unthinkable," he replied forcibly. "It has taken me forty years to learn how to conduct this fearful quarrel. I could not extend that which protects me to you. You would be inevitably destroyed."

"Just killed?" I asked repressing a nervous and blasphemous itch to laugh.

"More than that, though that for certain. You might never be seen again."

Now I will be frank, it did seem to me that already there was a tension, a sense of malaise in that great room where we were sitting. The wind had risen to half-a-gale and the rain had come with it. The old house seemed like a ship heaving at its moorings. The windows shook, the curtains stirred, the wind went roaring by. And really for the first time I knew old Apuleius to be a strange and formidable fellow and no figure of fun, and that that shining emblem on his brow might have more than a derisory significance. I grew very restless, the current stirring my nerves seemed to have had its voltage raised. I should have liked to have gone out into that storm and walked the tension down. Odd, distorting little pictures formed and vanished in my mind's eye; masks of evil, a flaming body hurtling through the sky, a ring of sultry fire, a dark stream of birds, a bloody sword. I shook myself and fetched a drink. Apuleius was sitting down now, motionless, his chin on his breast, his hands gripping the arms of his chair. And presently the clock chimed three times, it was a quarter to midnight.

"No drink, Apuleius?" I asked, to break the silence.

"No," he replied. "Alcohol relaxes, and I require the utmost stiffening of my spirit. If I had known what was before me I would not have drunk at lunch."

"Then put it off till you've prepared yourself properly!"

"No," he replied, "it must be tonight."

"Look here," I urged, "you realize there will only be a thin wall between us. If you're in any trouble bang on that wall and I'll come fighting."

"Have no fear," he said, "all will be well."

"Yes, but if it isn't will you bang on that wall?"

"In the last extremity I will, but it will not be necessary. And now the time has come."

We got up together. I took the tantalus of whiskey with me and a syphon. I had no intention of sleeping and I felt like some Scotch courage. The gale was now at its height, screaming wickedly round the house; a fit night for black and white, I thought, as we mounted the lightly creaking stairs. We parted without a word at the door of my room and Apuleius went on. Just before he opened that door he raised himself to his full height, touched the mark on his forehead, turned the handle and strode in. To this day I can see him there in my mind's eye as clearly as I did twenty-three long years ago. Then he disappeared, and I went in and closed my door. I sat down in an armchair, knocked back a big drink and tried to read. But I was half-listening all the time and couldn't concentrate. What was happening on the other side of that thin wall? I cursed the wind which waxed and waxed in venom drowning all small sounds. I could hear their straining timber roar as the great cedars fought the gale. The room seemed charged with a heightening tension. I had felt something like it before in the dynamo room of a great power station, when those smooth spinning cylinders seemed to charge and shake the air with the huge power they so nonchalantly and quietly engendered, a power that in its essence remains a mighty mystery to this day.

I tried to visualize what Apuleius was doing. Sitting inside his magic circle, I supposed, murmuring his protective runes, straining to keep back that which strove to pass the barrier. I concentrated all my will upon it and presently I had the strangest illusion of my life. It was as though I was seeing into that room as though the wall had become almost transparent and I was gazing through its thinning veil. Apuleius was sitting there in the middle of the room surrounded by a faintly illuminated ring. His eyes were staring, his face contorted into an odious rictus, his mouth moving convulsively. On the carpet just outside the ring huge shadows were crouching, other shadows of dubious and daunting shape were leaning down the walls. All seemed to have their heads pointing at him. All the time the lighted ring grew slowly dimmer. Suddenly there came, repeated over and over again, that horrid cracking of giant fingers, the lights in my room flickered, reddened and sparked. And then there was a dazzling flash of lightning and a blast of thunder which went roaring down the gale. I could stand no more and leapt to my feet.

Suddenly I heard Apuleius scream, once quickly, the second a piercing, drawn-out cry of agony. And then came a frenzied beating on the wall. I dashed out into the passage and flung open the door of the room. It was dimly lit, it was quiet, it was empty, the only movement, the slight stirring of the long, dark window curtains. I ran along to his room. Save for the little cardboard suitcase it was empty too. I shouted for him until Chumley came to investigate whether I had really gone crazy, or was merely very tight. He was wearing, I noted, a mink-collared dressing-gown over a pair of the Chief's most scintillating monogrammed silk pajamas.

And on that mildly farcical note I will end the story of that night. For Apuleius was never seen again. Of course, most of the few people who cared in the least whether he was alive or dead believed he'd done a bunk for reasons not unconnected with the constabulary. He was soon forgotten for he had long ceased to hit even the tiniest headlines. He had disappeared before and now he'd done it again. Good riddance! When the Chief heard my story he flew into a considerable fury though not with me, for he was a fair man and agreed it was not my function to control his guest and a man more than twice my own age. He wanted to believe the done-a-bunk theory naturally enough, but he realized it was dead against the weight of evidence. He had the room locked up and gave orders no one was to enter it without his or Ladyship's permission in the future.

The years passed and so presently did the Chief, no doubt to put some ginger into celestial or infernal journalism. I got a very nice job in his organization for life, I hoped, but then came the war and I transferred my talents temporarily to the M.O.I. In 1941 I was for a time bomb-jolly through being flung out of bed and hard up against a wall when my Kensington house was next door to a direct hit. I had still kept in touch with Ladyship, then living very sensibly in a safe area, and one morning in June, 1944, she rang me up to say she had just heard Caston had been damaged by a fly-bomb and would I go down and see what had happened.

Poor sweet old place! The doodle had dived clap in the middle of the courtyard which had, of course, enclosed the blast—and that was that. Those Tudor houses were lightly built of delicate brick and lots of glass, so Caston was no more. Center block pulverized, right wing still collapsing by stages when I arrived. My old left wing just a great mountain of debris, bricks, beds, furniture, pictures, clothes—an incredible chaos spangled everywhere with that lovely old glass. The rescue squads were digging in the center wing for the bodies of the caretaker and his wife. A bulldozer and cranes rolled up while I was there. I climbed up the monstrous and pathetic pile feeling sad and full of memories. On the summit I picked up a piece of canvas and, turning it over I was being regarded by the palest eyes which ever stared from a woman's face above a long, thin streak of scarlet. I threw it down again, *that* was not the sort of souvenir I relished. As I did so, I saw something glitter from between two broken bricks. I pulled it out and there was a sea-green jade ring on the splintered bone of a fleshless finger. I got the rescue men to dig around there, but we found nothing more.

That ring is on the desk beside me as I write these words. It is lovely beyond all telling. How it happened to be where I found it is, as I have told you, a matter for you to decide.

The Death Mask
HD Everett

"Yes, that is a portrait of my wife. It is considered to be a good likeness. But of course she was older-looking towards the last."

Enderby and I were on our way to the smoking-room after dinner, and the picture hung on the staircase. We had been chums at school a quarter of a century ago, and later on, at college; but I had spent the last decade out of England. I returned to find my friend a widower of four years' standing. And a good job too, I thought to myself when I heard of it, for I had no great liking for the late Gloriana. Probably the sentiment, or want of sentiment, had been mutual: she did not smile on me, but I doubt if she smiled on any of poor Tom Enderby's bachelor cronies. The picture was certainly like her. She was a fine woman, with aquiline features and a cold eye. The artist had done the features justice—and the eye, which seemed to keep a steely watch on all the comings and goings of the house out of which she had died.

We made only a brief pause before the portrait, and then went on. The smoking-room was an apartment built out at the back of the house by a former owner, and shut off by double doors to serve as a nursery. Mrs Enderby had no family, and she disliked the smell of tobacco. So the big room was made over to Tom's pipes and cigars; and if Tom's friends wanted to smoke, they must smoke there or not at all. I remembered the room and the rule, but

I was not prepared to find it still existing. I had expected to light my after-dinner cigar over the dessert dishes, now there was no presiding lady to consider.

We were soon installed in a couple of deep-cushioned chairs before a good fire. I thought Enderby breathed more freely when he closed the double doors behind us, shutting off the dull formal house, and the staircase and the picture. But he was not looking well; there hung about him an unmistakable air of depression. Could he be fretting after Gloriana? Perhaps during their married years, he had fallen into the way of depending on a woman to care for him. It is pleasant enough when the woman is the right sort; but I shouldn't myself have fancied being cared for by the late Mrs Enderby. And, if the fretting was a fact, it would be easy to find a remedy. Evelyn has a couple of pretty sisters, and we would have him over to stay at our place.

"You must run down and see us," I said presently, pursuing this idea. "I want to introduce you to my wife. Can you come next week?"

His face lit up with real pleasure.

"I should like it of all things," he said heartily. But a qualification came after. The cloud settled back over him and he sighed. "That is, if I can get away."

"Why, what is to hinder you?"

"It may not seem much to stay for, but I—I have got in the way of stopping here—to keep things together." He did not look at me, but leaned over to the fender to knock the ash off his cigar.

"Tell you what, Tom, you are getting hipped living by yourself. Why don't you sell the house, or let it off just as it is, and try a complete change?"

"I can't sell it. I'm only the tenant for life. It was my wife's."

"Well, I suppose there is nothing to prevent you letting it? Or if you can't let it, you might shut it up."

"There is nothing *legal* to prevent me - !" The emphasis was too fine to attract notice, but I remembered it after.

"Then, my dear fellow, why not? Knock about a bit, and see the world. But, to my thinking, the best thing you could do would be to marry again."

He shook his head drearily.

"Of course it is a delicate matter to urge upon a widower. But you have paid the utmost ceremonial respect. Four years, you know. The greatest stickler for propriety would deem it ample."

"It isn't that. Dick, I—I've a great mind to tell you rather a queer story." He puffed hard at his smoke, and stared into the red coals in the pauses. "But I don't know what you'd think of it. Or think of me."

"Try me," I said. "I'll give you my opinion after. And you know I'm safe to confide in."

"I sometimes think I should feel better if I told it. It's—it's queer enough to be laughable. But it hasn't been any laughing-matter to me."

He threw the stump of his cigar into the fire, and turned to me. And then I saw how pale he was, and that a dew of perspiration was breaking out on his white face.

"I was very much of your opinion, Dick: I thought I should be happier if I married again. And I went so far as to get engaged. But the engagement was broken off, and I am going to tell you why.

"My wife was some time ailing before she died, and the doctors were in consultation. But I did not know how serious her complaint was till the last. Then they told me there was no hope, as coma had set in. But it was possible, even probably, that there would be a revival of consciousness before death, and for this I was to hold myself ready.

"I dare say you will write me down a coward, but I dreaded the revival: I was ready to pray that she might pass away in her sleep. I knew she held exalted views about the marriage tie, and I felt sure if there were any last words she would exact a pledge.

"I could not at such a moment refuse to promise, and I did not want to be tied. You will recollect that she was my senior. I was about to be left a widower in middle life, and in the natural course of things I had a good many years before me. You see?"

"My dear fellow, I don't think a promise so extorted ought to bind you. It isn't fair!"

"Wait and hear me. I was sitting here, miserable enough, as you may suppose, when the doctor came to fetch me to her room. Mrs Enderby was conscious and had asked for me, but he particularly begged me not to agitate her in any way, lest pain should return. She was lying stretched out in the bed, looking already like a corpse.

"'Tom,' she said, 'they tell me I am dying, and there is something I want you to—promise.'

"I groaned in spirit. It was all up with me, I thought. But she went on. 'When I am dead and in my coffin, I want you to cover my face with your own hands. Promise me this.'

"It was not in the very least what I expected. Of course I promised.

"'I want you to cover my face with a particular handkerchief on which I set a value. When the time comes, open the cabinet to the right of the window, and you will find it in the third drawer.'

"That was every word she said, if you believe me, Dick. She just sighed and shut her eyes as if she was going to sleep, and she never spoke again. Three or four days later they came again to ask me if I wished to take a last look, as the undertaker's men were about to close the coffin.

"I felt a great reluctance, but it was necessary I should go. She looked as if made of wax, and was colder than ice to touch. I opened the cabinet, and there, just as she said, was a large handkerchief of very fine cambric, lying by itself. It was embroidered with a monogram device in all four corners, and was not of a sort I had ever seen her use. I spread it out and laid it over the dead face; and then what happened was rather curious. It seemed to draw down over the features and cling to them, to nose and mouth and forehead and the shut eyes, till it became a perfect mask. My nerves were shaken, I suppose; I was seized with horror, and flung back the covering sheet, hastily quitting the room. And the coffin was closed that night.

"Well, she was buried, and I put up a monument which the neighbourhood considered handsome. As you see, I was bound by no pledge to abstain from marriage; and, though I knew what would have been her wish, I saw no reason why I should regard it. And, some months after, a family of the name of Ashcroft came to live at The Leasowes, and they had a pretty daughter.

"I took a fancy to Lucy Ashcroft the first time I saw her, and it was soon apparent that she was well inclined to me. She was a gentle, yielding little thing; not the superior style of woman. Not at all like—"

(I made no comment, but I could well understand that in his new matrimonial venture Tom would prefer a contrast.)

"—but I thought I had a very good chance of happiness with her; and I grew fond of her: very fond of her indeed. Her people were of the hospitable sort, and they encouraged me to go to The Leasowes, dropping in when I felt inclined: it did not seem as if they would be likely to put obstacles in our way. Matters progressed, and I made up my mind one evening to walk over there and declare myself. I had been up to town the day before, and came back with a ring in my pocket: rather a fanciful design of double hearts, but I thought Lucy would think it pretty, and would let me put it on her finger. I went up to change into dinner things, making myself as spruce as possible, and coming to the conclusion before the glass that I was not such a bad figure of a man after all, and that there was not much grey in my hair. Ay, Dick, you may smile: it is a good bit greyer now.

"I had taken out a clean handkerchief, and thrown the one carried through the day crumpled on the floor. I don't know what made me turn to look there, but, once it caught my eye, I stood staring at it as if spellbound. The handkerchief was moving—Dick, I swear it—rapidly altering in shape, puffing up here and there as if blown by wind, spreading and moulding itself into the features of a face. And what face should it be but the death-mask of Gloriana, which I had covered in the coffin eleven months before.

"To say I was horror-stricken conveys little of the feeling that possessed me. I snatched up the rag of cambric and flung it on the fire, and it was nothing but a rag in my hand, and in another moment no more than blackened tinder on the bar of the grate. There was no face below."

"Of course not," I said. "It was a mere hallucination. You were cheated by an excited fancy."

"You may be sure I told myself all that, and more; and I went downstairs and tried to pull myself together with a dram. But I was curiously upset, and, for that night at least, I found it impossible to play the wooer. The recollection of the death-mask was too vivid; it would have come between me and Lucy's lips.

"The effect wore off, however. In a day or two I was bold again, and as much disposed to smile at my folly as you are at this moment. I proposed, and Lucy accepted me; and I put on the ring. Ashcroft *père* was graciously pleased to approve of the settlements I offered, and Ashcroft *mère* promised to regard me as a son. And during the first forty-eight hours of our engagement, there was not a cloud to mar the blue.

"I proposed on a Monday, and on Wednesday I went again to dine and spend the evening with just their family party. Lucy and I found our way afterwards into the back drawing-room, which seemed to be made over to us by tacit understanding. Anyway, we had it to ourselves; and as Lucy sat on the settee, busy with her work, I was privileged to sit beside her, close enough to watch the careful stitches she was setting, under which the pattern grew.

"She was embroidering a square of fine linen to serve as a tea-cloth, and it was intended for a present to a friend; she was anxious, she told me, to finish it in the next few days, ready for despatch. But I was somewhat impatient of her engrossment in the work; I wanted her to look at me while we talked, and to be permitted to hold her hand. I was making plans for a tour we would take together after Easter; arguing that eight weeks spent in preparation was enough for any reasonable bride. Lucy was easily entreated; she laid aside the linen square on the table at her elbow. I held her fingers captive, but her eyes wandered from my face, as she was still deliciously shy.

"All at once she exclaimed. Her work was moving, there was growing to be a face in it: did I not see?

"I saw, indeed. It was the Gloriana death-mask, forming there as it had formed in my handkerchief at home: the marked nose and chin, the severe mouth, the mould of forehead, almost complete. I snatched it up and dropped it over the back of the couch. 'It did look like a face,' I allowed. 'But never mind it, darling; I want you to attend to me.' Something of this sort I said, I hardly know what, for my blood was running cold. Lucy pouted; she wanted to dwell on the marvel, and my impatient action had displeased her. I went on talking wildly, being afraid of pauses, but the psychological moment had gone by. I felt I did not carry her with me as before: she hesitated over my persuasions; the forecast of a Sicilian honeymoon had ceased to charm. By-and-by she suggested that Mrs Ashcroft would expect us to rejoin the circle in the other room. And perhaps I would pick up her work for her—still with a slight air of offence.

"I walked round the settee to recover the luckless piece of linen; but she turned also, looking over the back, so at the same instant we both saw.

"There again was the Face, rigid and severe; and now the corners of the cloth were tucked under, completing the form of the head. And that was not all. Some white drapery had been improvised and extended beyond it on the floor, presenting the complete figure laid out straight and stiff, ready for the grave. Lucy's alarm was excusable. She shrieked aloud, shriek upon shriek, and immediately an indignant family of Ashcrofts rushed in through the half-drawn *portières* which divided the two rooms, demanding the cause of her distress.

"Meanwhile I had fallen upon the puffed-out form, and destroyed it. Lucy's embroidery composed the head; the figure was ingeniously contrived out of a large Turkish bath-sheet, brought in from one of the bedrooms, no-one knew how or when. I held up the things protesting their innocence, while the family were stabbing me through and through with looks of indignation, and Lucy was sobbing in her mother's arms. She might have been foolish, she allowed; it did seem ridiculous now she saw what it was. But at the moment it was too dreadful: it looked so like—so like! And here a fresh sob choked her into silence.

"Peace was restored at last, but plainly the Ashcrofts doubted me. The genial father stiffened, and Mrs Ashcroft administered indirect reproofs. She hated practical joking, so she informed me; she might be wrong, and no doubt she was old-fashioned, but she had been brought up to consider it in the highest degree ill-bred. And perhaps I had not considered how sensitive Lucy was, and how easily alarmed. She hoped I would take warning for the future, and that nothing of this kind would occur again.

"Practical joking—oh, ye gods! As if it was likely that I, alone with the girl of my heart, would waste the precious hour in building up effigies of sham corpses on the floor! And Lucy ought to have known that the accusation was absurd, as I had never for a moment left her side. She did take my part when more composed; but the mystery remained, beyond explanation of hers or mine.

"As for the future, I could not think of that without a failing heart. If the Power arrayed against us were in truth what superstition feared, I might as well give up hope at once, for I knew there would be no relenting. I could see the whole absurdity of the thing as well as you do now; but, if you put yourself in my place, Dick, you will be forced to confess that it was tragic too.

"I did not see Lucy the next day, as I was bound to go again to town; but we had planned to meet and ride together on the Friday morning. I was to be at The Leasowes at a certain hour, and you may be sure I was punctual. Her horse had already been brought round, and the groom was leading it up and down. I had hardly dismounted when she came down the steps of the porch; and I noticed at once a new look on her face, a harder set about that red mouth of hers which was so soft and kissable. But she let me put her up on the saddle and settle her foot in the stirrup, and she was the bearer of a gracious message from her mother. I was expected to return to lunch, and Mrs Ashcroft begged us to be punctual, as a friend who had stayed the night with them, would be leaving immediately after.

"'You will be pleased to meet her, I think,' said Lucy, leaning forward to pat her horse. 'I find she knows you very well. It is Miss Kingsworthy.'

"Now Miss Kingsworthy was a school friend of Gloriana's, who used now and then to visit us here. I was not aware that she and the Ashcrofts were acquainted; but, as I have said, they had only recently come into the neighbourhood as tenants of The Leasowes. I had no opportunity to express pleasure or the reverse, for Lucy was riding on; and putting her horse to a brisk pace. It was some time before she drew rein, and again admitted conversation. We were descending a steep hill, and the groom was following at a discreet distance behind, far enough to be out of earshot.

"Lucy looked very pretty on horseback; but this is by the way. The mannish hat suited her, and so did the habit fitting closely to her shape.

"'Tom,' she said; and again I noticed that new hardness in her face. 'Tom, Miss Kingsworthy tells me your wife did not wish you to marry again, and she made you promise her that you would not. Miss Kingsworthy was quite astonished to hear that you and I were engaged. Is this true?'

"I was able to tell her it was not; that my wife had never asked, and I had never given her, any such pledge. I allowed she disliked second marriages—in certain cases, and perhaps she had made some remark to that effect to Miss Kingsworthy; it was not unlikely. And then I appealed to her. Surely she would not let a mischief-maker's tittle-tattle come between her and me?

"I thought her profile looked less obdurate, but she would not let her eyes meet mine as she answered: 'Of course not, if that was all. And I doubt if I would have heeded it, only that it seemed to fit in with—something else. Tom, it was very horrible, what we saw on Wednesday evening. And—and—don't be angry, but I asked Miss Kingsworthy what your wife was like. I did not tell her why I wanted to know.'

"'What has that to do with it?' I demanded—stoutly enough; but, alas! I was too well aware.

"'She told me Mrs Enderby was handsome, but she had not very marked features, and was severe-looking when she did not smile. A high forehead, a Roman nose, and a decided chin. Tom, the face in the cloth was just like that. Did you not see?'

"Of course I protested. 'My darling, what nonsense! I saw it looked a little like a face but I pulled it to pieces at once because you were frightened. Why, Lucy, I shall have you turning into a spiritualist if you take up these fancies.'

"'No,' she said, 'I do not want to be anything foolish. I have thought it over, and if it happens only once I have made up my mind to believe it a mistake and to forget. But if it comes again—if it goes on coming!' Here she shuddered and turned white. 'Oh Tom, I could not—I could not!'

"That was the ultimatum. She liked me as much as ever; she even owned to a warmer feeling; but she was not going to marry a haunted man. Well, I suppose I cannot blame her. I might have given the same advice in another fellow's case, though in my own I felt it hard.

"I am close to the end now, so I shall need to tax your patience very little longer. A single chance remained. Gloriana's power, whatever its nature and however derived, might have been so spent in the previous efforts that she could effect no more. I clung to this shred of hope, and did my best to play the part of the light-hearted lover, the sort of companion Lucy expected, who would shape himself to her mood; but I was conscious that I played it ill.

"The ride was a lengthy business. Lucy's horse cast a shoe, and it was impossible to change the saddle on to the groom's hack or my own mare, as neither of them had been trained to the habit. We were bound to return at a foot-pace, and did not reach The Leasowes until two o'clock. Lunch was over: Mrs Ashcroft had set out for the station driving Miss Kingsworthy; but some cutlets were keeping hot for us, so we were informed, and could be served immediately.

"We went at once into the dining-room, as Lucy was hungry; and she took off her hat and laid it on a side-table: she said the close fit of it made her head ache. The cutlets had been misrepresented: they were lukewarm; but Lucy made a good meal off them and the fruit-tart which followed, very much at her leisure. Heaven knows I would not have grudged her so much as a mouthful; but that luncheon was an ordeal I cannot readily forget.

"The servant absented himself, having seen us served; and then my troubles began. The tablecloth seemed alive at the corner which was between us; it rose in waves as if puffed up by wind, though the window was fast shut against any wandering airs. I tried to seem unconscious; tried to talk as if no horror of apprehension was filling all my mind, while I was flattening out the bewitched damask with a grasp I hardly dared relax. Lucy rose at last, saying she must change her dress. Occupied with the cloth, it had not occurred to me to look round, or keep watch on what might be going on in another part of the room. The hat on the side-table had been tilted over sideways, and in that position it was made to crown another presentation of the Face. What it was made of this time I cannot say; probably a serviette, as several lay about. The linen material, of whatever sort, was again moulded into the perfect form; but this time the mouth showed humour, and appeared to relax in a grim smile.

"Lucy shrieked, and dropped into my arms in a swoon: a real genuine fainting-fit, out of which she was brought round with difficulty, after I had summoned the help of doctors.

"I hung about miserably till her safety was assured, and then went as miserably home. Next morning I received a cutting little note from my mother-in-law elect, in which she returned the ring, and informed me the engagement must be considered at an end.

"Well, Dick, you know now why I do not marry. And what have you to say?"

Lost Keep
LA Lewis

Peter Hunt was barely seventeen when news reached him of his Aunt Kate's death in a North London Hospital, and, knowing that she was almost penniless, he entertained no expectation of benefits as her only surviving relative. It was with some surprise, therefore, that he read in the Matron's letter of the despatch of a small, locked box, recently brought from a safe-deposit to her bedside, to which she had evidently attached great importance. By the same post there also arrived a package from his Aunt herself addressed in the weak, spidery calligraphy of extreme age, enclosed a key and a brief note which read: "To my nephew, Peter Hunt. Open the box and make what use Fate wills of its contents."

The box arrived by delivery van in the evening of the same day, and was carried upstarts by Peter himself to his mean back bedroom in a Tilbury lodging-house. It was not very heavy, and any hope of hoarded coin vanished as soon as he lifted it, though there remained, of course, the slender chance of banknotes or bearer bonds. He cut the cords with which its lock had been reinforced and, taking the key from his pocket, opened it. It contained three objects only—a small-scale model of a stone fortress mounted on a pedestal shaped to resemble a rocky hill, a folded sheet of paper, and something which looked like a silver-framed magnifying glass, except that its lens was opaque—almost black, in fact—and nearly impervious to light.

Peter drew the miniature towards him—it was not more than three inches high—and examined it as closely as the poor light from the dirty window would allow. It was too early to use the gas. The meter was always ravenous for his pennies.

Even to his untutored eyes the workmanship of the model was exquisite, the degree of finish seeming to represent a lifetime's labour. Every single stone block—and there were thousands—in the structure of the building had been faithfully reproduced, and even such details as patches of lichen had not been overlooked. With luck the thing should be worth several pounds as a curiosity. Perhaps he would have it valued by Christie's; it wouldn't do to trust "Uncle" Abe at the corner shop. He pushed it aside and reached for the folded paper, recognising his father's characteristic handwriting as he smoothed it out. It related to the contents of the box, and read as follows—

"I, Vernon John Hunt, having been given by the doctors three months to live, have determined to put in writing what is known of 'Lost Keep' of which this scale model has been handed down from parent to child for many generations.

"Tradition has it that the miniature was made under pain of death by an Italian craftsman condemned by an early ancestor to imprisonment in the original stronghold until such time as he should complete the task. That he did complete it the miniature itself testifies, but history does not relate whether his release followed or whether, with the callousness of Feudal days, he was left to rot in his prison. There is, I regret to say, some ground for the latter supposition, for he is credited in the Latin manuscript, now destroyed, with having laid some kind of curse on this piece of craftsmanship. A peculiarity of the whole matter is that there have been so many female heirs that the name of the original title-holders is forgotten, the heirloom having passed haphazard from male to female issue and so transferred itself to various different families. Even the locality of the original site is unrecorded—hence its name of 'Lost Keep'—and the curse of the modeller is concerned with this fact. The old fortress, if it still stands, may be in Iceland, Scandinavia, Russia, or, for that matter, any part of the world; but, translating from the Latin script, it is supposed to be rediscoverable by any one who has *'the wit or fortune to combine glass and facsimile with understanding.'* Whoever solves the riddle, however, is threatened with *'greater temptations of the Devil than have beset any other of Adam's descendants,'* and, if he succumbs, will find *'death in the home of his fathers at the hand of his son.'* Doubtless each successive holder of the heirloom has attacked the problem, though there is no rumoured instance of its solution. I in my turn have wasted hours in speculation as to the purpose of the dark glass shaped so like a lens, yet so obviously useless as such, and have examined every point of the model's surface with a normal reading-glass for signs of engraved lettering, but have learned no more than to marvel at the delicacy of the work. On the latter count the model would probably be of considerable value among collectors, but its secret, if it really possesses one, is well hidden.

"So, being under sentence of death, I entrust this sole heirloom of a family whose fortunes are at ebb to my sister Kate, requesting her to hold it for my son Peter until her death or his majority."

The document was neither dated nor signed.

Peter leaned back and looked with a distaste that familiarity had never conquered round the shabby room. So his *father* had believed the model to be of value too? So much the better. He'd have no false sentiment about parting with it since he'd never even heard of it till to-day, and he'd certainly get it valued at an early opportunity. It ought to fetch enough to pay for a course of night classes at a technical school, or—with great luck—a real college career for which he could drop his present uncongenial job as warehouse packer and fit himself to enter those higher spheres that his hereditary instinct craved. Meanwhile his day's work was finished and he could not afford to go out looking for amusement. He might as well have a shot at the dark glass problem.

Picking the apparently useless thing up, he studied it closely. It certainly *looked* like a lens, being a circle of some vitreous composition thick at the centre, thin at the sides, and mounted in a metal ring. Lighting the gas-jet—an old-fashioned fish-tail burner—he held the thing to the light, but through its opacity could distinguish only a shapeless blurr. Perhaps distance, either from the eyes or the object to be focused, would sharpen its outline. He experimented thus, standing at arm's length from the jet, and gradually advancing the glass towards the flame. At really close quarters it *did* seem to let through a little more light, and he was so occupied with this discovery that he never thought of the effect which the accompanying heat might have on the glass until a sharp snap followed by a tinkle on the linoleum informed him that he had cracked it.

With a muttered expletive the boy turned it over, and at once noticed an interesting fact. The glass appeared to be built up in layers, and the heat had split off a piece of the outer one, revealing a second and seemingly undamaged surface beneath.

He pursed his lips in a whistle. The discovery might have some bearing on the apparent uselessness of the object. It was a natural conclusion that a perfect lens might be hidden under the dark covering, though the purpose of all the secrecy and mystery woven around glass and miniature was more than Peter could guess. He found his pen-knife, and, carefully inserting it under the broken edge, split off another fragment. Once started, the remainder came away so easily that in a few minutes he had completely exposed the underlying surface the layer on the other side flaking away with equal facility after a light rap with the handle of the knife. The now transparent lens—tinted, as far as he could judge against the twilight with his back to the gas, a kind of smoky blue—possessed an astounding power of magnification when he tried it on the back of his hand. The hand, as such, in fact, completely disappeared, and the circle of glass showed only a portion of the skin enlarged to a degree which he would have thought only a microscope could achieve. As he watched, the enlarging process seemed to continue as though concentric rings of the tissue were rolling out from the centre and vanishing through the rim. He had a sickening sensation of being about to sink bodily into the glass, and, hastily shutting his eyes, put it down on the table. The queer sensation passed off rapidly, but left him with a mixed feeling of giddiness, excitement, and fear. There was something uncanny about the lens—*damned* uncanny—but his faults did not include cowardice, and he resolved to complete his experiments single-handed. With this decision he proceeded to lock the door, and, pulling the table as near as he could to the gas-jet, sat down to test the effect of the lens on the miniature.

The grey, perpetual twilight had neither brightened nor darkened by one iota when Peter completed his seventh circuit of the mighty battlements. Dizzily far below him the waves of an apparently tideless sea broke and hissed back along the same bank of shingle, neither advancing nor retiring, each followed by an interminable succession of troughs and crests sweeping in from a vague horizon that seemed infinitely distant from the high eminence upon which he stood. But for their maddeningly regular beat no sound whatever broke the silence, no breeze moved the cold and stagnant air, and throughout the gigantic mass of masonry he was the only thing that lived. Above him the sky was a leaden monotony broken at one place alone by a mere pin-point of light which appeared to be a far-off beacon. It shone where the diminishing thread of a titanic causeway merged into the sky-line.

Peter drew a clammy hand across his eyes and leaned wearily against the ramparts. *Was he mad?* Or had some unbelievable miracle literally transported him in a flash of time from his dingy back-room to this far distant and eerie place? That he was not dreaming his sore knuckles proved, where he had struck them hard against unyielding stone in the panic frenzy of his incredible translation. He said aloud, "O God!" in a meaningless sort of way, and repeated it several times, partly for the love of any sound other than that of the waves, and partly to focus his attention. Though he could not then have put it into words, the panorama, to his rather limited mind accustomed to concrete surroundings, savoured alarmingly of the Abstract.

Resolutely directing his gaze at the nearest buttress of the ramparts, he went over in his mind, perhaps for the twentieth time, the series of his sensations from the moment when he had held the lens over the model. Through the glass the tiny castle had appeared to grow and grow in swiftly overlapping rings from its centre, there had been a feeling of suction as though he were being dragged violently towards it, and then a moment—or an hour—of complete black-out from which he had emerged to a realization of standing in an immense copy of the miniature courtyard looking up at the terrific mass of the Keep. Appalled by its sickening height and crushed by his own proportional sense of smallness, he had nevertheless been impelled to enter the open door and climb endlessly up flight after flight of stone steps till he came out weak and trembling on the roof. And then the feverish pacing of its periphery, a prey to wonder, fear, and a horrible giddiness each time he looked down towards the sea. And all the time the grey, unnatural twilight had persisted, tormenting him with the half-knowledge that he was not even on the Earth at all, but in some incredible place utterly divorced from all things human and alive.

It was healthy, physical hunger that eventually restored his mental balance to something near normality. In whatever nightmare realm he had landed himself, it clearly contained no possible source of food, and he must find his way out before starvation overtook him. The castle was sea-girt, and the interminable causeway that stretched from the shore towards the horizon was the only apparent means of exit. He felt a trifle fortified at the prospect of escape, and eagerly began the long descent of the stairways.

"The glass," Mrs. Stebbings repeated defiantly, "ain't here, and I ain't took it. Them bits in the 'earth might be it—broke—but that don't tell me where young 'Unt 'as 'opped orf to." She tossed her head. "And 'im owing me a week's rent," she added with meaning. The Police Sergeant turned from his inspection of the broken lock and gave her an expressionless glance. "That's all right," he replied, "I'm not accusing you of taking it, but it certainly isn't in this room. No doubt Hunt has it with him—that's to say if there is a glass as this writing states.

"Now, Mrs. S." he went on pacifically, "please see if your other lodger is in the house. We shall want him to confirm your account of breaking into this room—not that we doubt your word," he added hastily, "just as a matter of form." As the landlady's footsteps died away on the rickety stairs he turned to the constable who accompanied him.

"Another mare's nest, I fancy," he remarked, "lodger owes week's rent and can't pay, so leaves quietly. Can't smuggle his stuff out 'cause she's too sharp-eyed. Clothes aren't worth much, anyway. Hard on the lady, of course, but scarcely one of the cases where we call in the Yard." He paused, and looked thoughtfully around him. "All the same," he continued, "it is a bit queer how he got out with the door locked inside. The window's too big a drop, the roof's out of reach, and there are no marks on the key to show he turned it from outside with forceps."

"How long's he been missing?" asked the Constable. The Sergeant consulted his watch. "About forty-two hours. She saw him coming upstairs with a parcel—probably this," he indicated the box and model on the table, "about five p.m. on Saturday, left him to sleep, as she supposed, all yesterday, and got the other fellow to break the lock when he didn't come down to breakfast this morning, and she found the door fastened. Yes, it looks like a case of convenient disappearance, seeing that he's not turned up at his job. Well, she ought to get her rent and a bit over on the price of this miniature if he doesn't come back to claim it after a reasonable interval. But I doubt if she'll see Master Hunt again in *this* house," he concluded.

"For God's sake water—and food," said a hoarse, feeble voice behind them, and they swung round in amazement to see the missing lodger, pale and haggard, sprawled across the bed!

That familiarity breeds contempt is a proverb of some antiquity and more than a little justification, and although contempt was the last sentiment Peter Hunt felt with regard to Lost Keep it was not long before his initial fear of the unknown was transmuted into a complacent acceptance of his heritage and of the supernatural powers it conveyed. His circumstances at the age of thirty differed vastly from those in which the arrival of the remarkable miniature had found him. He now possessed a house in Park Lane, a country-seat down in Dorset, three cars, a large staff of servants for the upkeep of his establishments, and, above all, a very charming but neglected wife among whose many contributions to his well-being was a son and heir also named Peter, but generally known as Pete for purposes of distinction.

It was in the library of his Park Lane mansion that Peter was sitting one August evening when a telephone call informed him that Lord Knifton proposed calling on him for a private interview in half an hour's time, and Peter's thin lips twisted into a grimace of satisfaction as he hung up the receiver. Knifton was his co-director in many of the big commercial enterprises from which his income was derived, and he had lately been behaving in a most obstructive way by refusing to approve certain conversion schemes which he—Peter—had evolved for their joint enrichment at the expense of the shareholders. He was one of the few financial magnates sufficiently powerful to interfere seriously with Peter's activities, and the time had come when one or the other must definitely take second place. Well, Knifton might indulge in whatever ideals he chose, but Peter *knew* which of them that one would be.

He opened the draw of his desk and took out the miniature fortress. The hard circle of the lens pressed comfortably against his abdomen in the inner pocket where it always reposed. A thousand Kniftons could not dominate the master of Lost Keep.

With half an hour's leisure, Peter's thoughts wandered back to the day when he had discovered the trick of the model and so nearly lost his life in the discovery. Even now he shuddered to recall that unending march along the rocky causeway that seemed to lead on eternally towards an horizon that never grew a mile nearer. How that unchanging grey twilight had mocked him with its denial of Time after he had dropped his watch into the sea and had no means of counting the passage of the hours. The sullen waves had lapped on with changeless rhythm either side of him, raising and lowering their fringe of decaying weed with never a variation in the limit of their lift—until he had screamed aloud at their inexorable monotony. He remembered how he had tramped on mile after mile towards the ever-receding sky-line till sheer exhaustion had dropped him in his tracks, and how, as he fell, his hand doubled under him, had come in contact with the lens which he then recollected having slipped into his pocket just as unconsciousness was claiming him in the Tilbury bedroom. With tired fingers he had drawn it out and held it, by some inner prompting, between his dim eyes and the distant beacon, to find himself, an instant later, lying across his bed with two policemen in the room and the tread of his landlady's feet ascending the stairs. Even then, with no formulated ideas of the value of his discovery, instinct had warned him to slip the lens again into his pocket, and to their excited queries about where he had been and the manner of his return he had reiterated foolishly that he had been asleep. They had given him water—that of the strange ocean had been too brackish to drink—and bread, which he had devoured wolfishly, but to all their questions he had answered, "I don't know. I was asleep," until they finally left him, evidently much mystified, and whispering together.

It was during the ensuing night that, unable to sleep for thinking about the model fortress, he began to realize the almost unlimited possibilities it contained. In whatever uncharted spot the original was situated, he felt sure that its whereabouts remained undiscovered by man, and it followed logically that he would have unquestioned dominion there. True, there were no inhabitants upon whom to exercise it—but suppose he could find a way of transporting other people to the place? He had assured himself that the whole thing was not feverish delirium by making several more brief visits to the Keep, always being careful to maintain a tight hold on the lens when the period of black-out arrived. Reference to the alarm clock by his bed showed him that, whatever might be the distance from the model to the real fortress, the transit occupied no measurable time at all; and this fact alone, should he choose to defy mankind, would provide a perfect *alibi*, since no jury would admit that he could travel hundreds—maybe thousands—of miles in a fraction of a second. Any breach of law or convention would have to be carried out at the *real* place at a time when he was known to be at home, and this arrangement would safeguard him against its very discovery. He reverted to the problem of getting his victims— veritable slaves they would be—to the island of his sovereignty, and concluded that the lens was large enough for two people to look through it at once, if it were held at the right distance.

Peter awoke from a half-dream and smiled at the model. To this day he had never come an inch nearer to solving the location of Lost Keep itself, but the miniature had served him well, and he loved those early memories. How scornfully disbelieving his foreman had been when he had hinted at the acquisition of something with magical properties! It had required a lot of restraint and tact to persuade him round to the lodging-house for a demonstration after he had brusquely sacked Peter for failing to be at work on that memorable Monday, but Peter had feigned cheerful indifference, supporting his attitude with talk of a quite mythical better job waiting for him, and the mention of a bottle of whiskey, bought out of his slender savings, had clinched the matter. After a few drinks Peter had brought out the miniature, and, inviting the foreman to sit beside him and concentrate upon it, had focused it with the lens. The usual enlargement of the image and the subsequent black-out had duly occurred, but this time, on coming to his senses in the great courtyard, he had seen beside him another figure—a figure with dropped jaw and blank eyes staring up at the colossal pile overhanging them. He had thereupon directed the lens at the beacon and translated himself back to Tilbury—alone.

It was only fair to himself, Peter always reflected at this point, to remember that he had been in ignorance of the man's alcoholic heart. He had intended only to punish him by leaving him marooned for a day, and it was with no little horror—for his autocratic power was still new—that he found him lying dead at the gateway on the following morning. Assurance of immunity, however, had gone far to overcome any remorse he had felt, and the six pounds odd which he had found in the man's pockets had consoled him in his unemployment. Those six pounds had, in fact, been the foundation of his present fortune, for from that chance windfall the acquisition of other and larger sums had been a rational and easy step, and he had found that anything he carried on his person was translated with him on his journeys between Lost Keep and the everyday world. Other advantages, too, were afforded by his unique possession; there had been, for instance, women who had denied him.

On one thing Peter had always congratulated himself. He had never allowed any of his bond-slaves to escape from Lost Keep. Once, indeed, he had been tempted to bring back a girl, for whom he had felt an unusually lasting passion, into the warm world of sunlight and blue skies, but he had realized in time the danger of having his secret betrayed, and had left her to pine in the cold, grey twilight where none it seemed could survive more than a few months. He had taken her food and drink in plenty, for it had hurt him to visualize her in the agonies of starvation, but he had seen the lovely face grow wan, and the eyes lose a spark more of their lustre on each successive visit, and at the end he stayed away for many days rather than face more of her pleadings for release.

Peter shook himself, and glanced at the clock. Knifton was nearly due. He had been sitting dreaming in his shirt-sleeves, for the evening was oppressively hot, and now he rose and donned a heavy silk dressing gown that was hung over the back of his chair. It was a highly coloured affair, the fabric of which had been especially woven for him in a unique pattern of interlacing circles.

Lord Knifton was a man some fifty years of age, who possessed both personality and tact. Though he frankly disagreed with many of Peter's principles, and never hesitated to tell him so, when their joint affairs were involved, he had considerable respect for his business acumen, and liked him well enough socially. Thus it was that, on being shown into the library, he made no immediate attempt to introduce the subject of their recent dispute, but shook hands and accepted a cigar while chatting of generalities. He soon noticed the model fortress and remarked upon its brilliant workmanship.

"Yes," Peter agreed, "a marvellous example of miniature craft—but its wonders show up better when viewed through this glass. Just sit still and keep the model in focus. Don't look away even if it makes your head swim for a second. There's no danger to the eyes, and you'll find the effect amazing." He leaned over the back of Lord Knifton's chair, and held the lens so that both could see the fortress through it.

"And now, Knifton," he said stridently, "I've got you just where I want you."

His companion rubbed his eyes and looked about his in bewilderment. A moment ago he had been sitting in Hunt's luxuriously furnished library on a hot August night, looking at a miniature on the desk. Now, by some miracle, he found himself in a gigantic, stone-flagged court, high-walled, and fronted by a fortress of staggering dimensions, while, under a dead grey sky that cast no shadows, the windless air struck coldly through his thin evening suit. The stench of a charnel-house assailed his nostrils, and he saw with revulsion that the ground was strewn with human remains in all stages of decomposition from bare, bleached skeletons to gory carcasses of the freshly slain, and the less recently alive—hideously distended.

He cried out sharply, and recoiled several paces, slewing round with upraised arms as he collided with someone behind him.

"Only your host," said the voice of Peter Hunt, with a chilly suavity from which all trace of friendliness had vanished, "please make yourself quite at home. It is your home, now, you know—that is, until you realize that I'm bound to win in the end, and sign this concession you so smugly discountenanced yesterday."

He produced an impressive looking document, stiff with seals, and opened it with a flourish, then, seeing that his guest remained tongue-tied, went on bitingly, "Framing a spate of questions, I suppose? What's this place? How did I get here? And so forth. Well, you may save your breath. *Where* you are I know no better than you. What I do know is, that I have been absolutely monarch of it for many years. Peter Hunt of Park Lane, pillar of Society, political leader, supporter of the Constitution, deferring to the wishes of a dozen pettifogging public bodies—and enjoying the farce because I know that I can, at will, take any man to whose opinion I pretend to bow, and bring him here and *rule* him as *you* can rule a dog!" He laughed unpleasantly. "You damned fool! Do you think it's for the money that I want your signature? I can get enough to pay the National Debt by bringing the rich to Lost Keep and stripping them of their wealth. There's one in there," he muttered, as a despairing moan echoed from behind a barred grating in the stonework, "he's trying to decide whether it's worth while to sign a cheque and write home to say how much he's enjoying his holiday—in Portugal! No, my esteemed and scrupulous partner, one grows weary of ruling over subjects a few at a time in this gloomy place. I want to come out into the open and rule a country—and when this concession goes through I can do it!"

At last Lord Knifton spoke, and in his tones were neither fear not anger. Only an abiding sorrow.

"Peter Hunt," he replied solemnly, "by some diabolical means which I do not even wish to fathom you wield a power that no man is ready to possess. I can only say: God take that power from you before more evil is done!"

As he spoke a swift shadow blotted out half the sky, and Hunt threw back his head in amazement. In the whole course of his association with this weird retreat he had never known anything to break the canopy of twilight, and his hands fell nervelessly to his sides as there burst on his vision a mass of shining metal, so huge as almost to dwarf the Keep, miraculously suspended in space above it. For a few seconds its great spatulate point hovered over the turrets. Then, it darted down and rushed at them, its lower edge grinding and roaring along the paving stones.

"Uncle, you promised to show me your new microscope. May I see it now?" Pete demanded with a sidelong glance at his mother.

"But it's bedtime, dear," said Lydia Hunt, "and you can see Uncle Harry's reading. Run upstairs now like a good boy and you shall see it tomorrow."

Pete drooped a pathetic lower lip. He was a sunny-natured child, though a trifle spoilt.

"Oh, but Uncle *did* promise. He *said* to-day, and I've been looking forward to it all school-time. I told the other chaps in our form about it, and they'll want to hear what I've seen with it to-morrow. Won't you show me something to-night *please*, Uncle Harry?"

Lydia's brother looked up from his evening paper with a whimsical smile. "Well," he laughed, "I've promised to take it round to Dr. Pruden's to-morrow to check over some of his cultures, so perhaps the boy had better see it to-night. It won't take long. All right, Pete. The 'mike's' in Daddy's library, and I believe he's got Lord Knifton there with him, but we'll see if they'll let us have it."

Pete clutched one of his hands with the enthusiasm of the ten-year-old, and danced across the hall at his side. They came to the library door and knocked, but there was no reply. Pete pushed it open and looked in. "Come on, Uncle Harry," he cried, "they must have gone out. Where's the microscope?"

His uncle crossed over to a cupboard, lifted out something large and shiny, and stood it on the desk. It was an expensive instrument, covered with exciting little brass knobs, and Pete's eyes gleamed when they saw it. "Coo, what a beauty!" he exclaimed rapturously, "wish I had one!... Oh, and look, Uncle! Here's daddy's model fortress! I've never seen it properly before. Can we look at *that* through the microscope?"

"No, of course not, you silly kid. They're for examining very tiny things like grains of dust, and you have to put them between the glass plates so as to light them from behind. If you just stood the end of the barrel against a lump of solid stuff you'd see nothing at all. Now then, here's a slide," he went on, handing the boy two little oblongs of glass, "just get a wee flake of dirt on the tip of that silver paper-knife and park it between these. Then I'll show you how the world looks to an influenza germ."

Pete giggled, and scraped up a speck of dust from the courtyard of the model fortress, wiped the paperknife on the slide, and obediently passed it across. His uncle fitted it into a frame at the lower end of the barrel, bent down to the eye-piece and began manipulating the brass knobs. Pete watched him, fascinated, and chafed at the time it took to get the adjustment right. He was on the point of asking how soon he might be allowed to have a look when he heard his uncle give a low whistle.

"Pete," he said, in a funny unsteady voice, and without lifting his head from the eye-piece, "go and ask Mummy to come here, will you. And then hang on in the drawing-room till we call you, there's a good chap. I've got something I want her to see first, and after that you shall have the microscope to yourself till you go to bed."

Though crestfallen at this further delay, Pete understood from the tone that it was not the time to argue, and presently Mrs. Hunt had taken his place by the desk. Her brother rose, and gave her a strange searching glance.

"Take a look at that, old girl," he suggested, indicating the microscope, "and tell me if I'm dreaming." Lydia sat down in the chair. "Why, Harry," she exclaimed, "they're miniature skeletons! But how on earth can they be modelled so perfectly on such a scale?"

Her brother shook his head. "Pete certainly scraped that bit of dust off the miniature," he answered.

"But they are *not* models! Take a grip on yourself and shift the slide from right to left. This is the button that operates it!"

Lydia obeyed the instruction and then broke out again in a tone of astonishment: "But it's unbelievable! A pigmy race no bigger than bacilli, and shaped in the exact pattern of humans!... Why," she added, "there are even buckles and bits of cloth just like we wear. But they *must* be models!"

"Move the slide a bit further," said Harry quietly, and then gipped her by the shoulders as she thrust her chair backwards from the desk with a cry of horror, cheeks blanched and eyes dilated.

"Harry! Harry!" she gasped, "I can't bear it! It's Peter and Lord Knifton! That dressing-gown. There's not another like it in the world!... Oh, that horrible mess of blood... And the limbs were—were still *twitching*! What does it *mean*?"

Lydia drained the tumbler and straightened up in the chair.

"You mean that the original castle really exists and that, in some beastly fashion, its happenings are mirrored in the model?... Then tell me, Harry. How can we find the real place? There may still be life in them. We must send help. We *must*!"

Her brother sighed. "There is no journey to make. How such a thing can be, God knows—but that thing is Lost Keep, and there they are locked—*multum in parvo*—Ugh! It makes me sick!"

Suddenly Lydia was galvanized into action. She began to turn out the drawers of the desk, scattering their contents on the carpet. "The lens, Harry. The lens!" she cried hysterically. "We can go ourselves and find out!"

Harry took her gently by the arm, "No, dear," he replied with finality, "Peter has the lens."

The Slype House
AC Benson

In the town of Garchester, close to St. Peter's Church, and near the river, stood a dark old house called the Slype House, from a narrow passage of that name that ran close to it, down to a bridge over the stream. The house showed a front of mouldering and discoloured stone to the street, pierced by small windows, like a monastery; and indeed, it was formerly inhabited by a college of priests who had served the Church. It abutted at one angle upon the aisle of the church, and there was a casement window that looked out from a room in the house, formerly the infirmary, into the aisle; it had been so built that any priest that was sick might hear the Mass from his bed, without descending into the church. Behind the house lay a little garden, closely grown up with trees and tall weeds, that ran down to the stream. In the wall that gave on the water, was a small door that admitted to an old timbered bridge that crossed the stream, and had a barred gate on the further side, which was rarely seen open; though if a man had watched attentively he might sometimes have seen a small lean person, much bowed and with a halting gait, slip out very quietly about dusk, and walk, with his eyes cast down, among the shadowy byways.

The name of the man who thus dwelt in the Slype House, as it appeared in the roll of burgesses, was Anthony Purvis. He was of an ancient family, and had inherited wealth. A word must be said of his childhood and youth. He was a sickly child, an only son, his father a man of substance, who lived very easily in the country; his mother had died when he was quite a child, and this sorrow had been borne very heavily by his father, who had loved her tenderly, and after her death had become morose and sullen, withdrawing himself from all company and exercise and brooding angrily over his loss, as though God had determined to vex him. He had never cared much for the child, who had been peevish and fretful; and the boy's presence had done little but remind him of the wife he had lost; so that the child had lived alone, nourishing his own fancies, and reading much in a library of curious books that was in the house. The boy's health had been too tender for him to go to school; but when he was eighteen, he seemed stronger, and his father sent him to a university, more for the sake of being relieved of the boy's presence than for his good. And there, being unused to the society of his equals, he had been much flouted and despised for his feeble frame; till a certain bitter ambition sprang up in his mind, like a poisonous flower, to gain power and make himself a name; and he had determined that as he could not be loved he might still be feared; so he bided his time in bitterness, making great progress in his studies; then, when those days were over, he departed eagerly, and sought and obtained his father's leave to betake himself to a university of Italy, where he fell into somewhat evil hands; for he made a friendship with an old doctor of the college, who feared not God and thought ill of man, and spent all his time in dark researches into the evil secrets of nature, the study of poisons that have enmity to the life of man, and many other hidden works of darkness, such as intercourse with spirits of evil, and the black influences that lie in wait for the soul; and he found Anthony an apt pupil. There he lived for some years till he was nearly thirty, seldom visiting his home, and writing but formal letters to his father, who supplied him gladly with a small revenue, so long as he kept apart and troubled him not.

Then his father had died, and Anthony came home to take up his inheritance, which was a plentiful one; he sold his land, and visiting the town of Garchester, by chance, for it lay near his home, he had lighted upon the Slype House, which lay very desolate and gloomy; and as he needed a large place for his instruments and devices, he had bought the house, and had now lived there for twenty years in great loneliness, but not ill-content.

To serve him he had none but a man and his wife, who were quiet and simple people and asked no questions; the wife cooked his meals, and kept the rooms, where he slept and read, clean and neat; the man moved his machines for him and arranged his phials and instruments, having a light touch and a serviceable memory.

The door of the house that gave on the street opened into a hall; to the right was a kitchen, and a pair of rooms where the man and his wife lived. On the left was a large room running through the house; the windows on to the street were walled up, and the windows at the back looked on the garden, the trees of which grew close to the casements, making the room dark, and in a breeze rustling their leaves or leafless branches against the panes. In this room Anthony had a furnace with bellows, the smoke of which discharged itself into the chimney; and here he did much of his work, making mechanical toys, as a clock to measure the speed of wind or water, a little chariot that ran a few yards by itself, a puppet that moved its arms and laughed—and other things that had wiled away his idle hours; the room was filled up with dark lumber, in a sort of order that would have looked to a stranger like disorder, but so that Anthony could lay his hand on all that he needed. From the hall, which was paved with stone, went up the stairs, very strong and broad, of massive oak; under which was a postern that gave on the garden; on the floor above was a room where Anthony slept, which again had its windows to the street boarded up, for he was a light sleeper, and the morning sounds of the awakening city disturbed him.

The room was hung with a dark arras, sprinkled with red flowers; he slept in a great bed with black curtains to shut out all light; the windows looked into the garden; but on the left of the bed, which stood with its head to the street, was an alcove, behind the hangings, containing the window that gave on the church. On the same floor were three other rooms; in one of these, looking on the garden, Anthony had his meals. It was a plain panelled room. Next was a room where he read, filled with books, also looking on the garden; and next to that was a little room of which he alone had the key. This room he kept locked, and no one set foot in it but himself. There was one more room on this floor, set apart for a guest who never came, with a great bed and a press of oak. And that looked on the street. Above, there was a row of plain plastered rooms, in which stood furniture for which Anthony had not use, and many crates in which his machines and phials came to him; this floor was seldom visited, except by the man, who sometimes came to put a box there; and the spiders had it to themselves; except for a little room where stood an optic glass through which on clear nights Anthony sometimes looked at the moon and stars, if there was any odd misadventure among them, such as an eclipse; or when a fiery-tailed comet went his way silently in the heavens, coming from none might say whence and going none knew whither, on some strange errand of God.

Anthony had but two friends who ever came to see him. One was an old physician who had ceased to practise his trade, which indeed was never abundant, and who would sometimes drink a glass of wine with Anthony, and engage in curious talk of men's bodies and diseases, or look at one of Anthony's toys. Anthony had come to know him by having called him in to cure some ailment, which needed a surgical knife; and that had made a kind of friendship between them; but Anthony had little need thereafter to consult him about his health, which indeed was now settled enough, though he had but little vigour; and he knew enough of drugs to cure himself when he was ill. The other friend was a foolish priest of the college, that made belief to be a student but was none, who thought Anthony a very wise and mighty person, and listened with open mouth and eyes to all that he said or showed him. This priest, who was fond of wonders, had introduced himself to Anthony by making believe to borrow a volume of him; and then had grown proud of the acquaintance, and bragged greatly of it to his friends, mixing up much that was fanciful with a little that was true. But the result was that gossip spread wide about Anthony, and he was held in the town to be a very fearful person, who could do strange mischief if he had a mind to; Anthony never cared to walk abroad, for he was of a shy habit, and disliked to meet the eyes of his fellows; but if he did go about, men began to look curiously after him as he went by, shook their heads and talked together with a dark pleasure, while children fled before his face and women feared him; all of which pleased Anthony mightily, if the truth were told; for at the bottom of his restless and eager spirit lay a deep vanity unseen, like a lake in woods; he hungered not indeed for fame, but for repute—*monstrari digito*, as the poet has it; and he cared little in what repute he was held, so long as men thought him great and marvellous; and as he could not win renown by brave deeds and words, he was rejoiced to win it by keeping up a certain darkness and mystery about his ways and doings; and this was very dear to him, so that when the silly priest called him Seer and Wizard, he frowned and looked sideways; but he laughed in his heart and was glad.

Now, when Anthony was near his fiftieth year, there fell on him a heaviness of spirit which daily increased upon him. He began to question of his end and what lay beyond. He had always made pretence to mock at religion, and had grown to believe that in death the soul was extinguished like a burnt-out flame. He began, too, to question of his life and what he had done. He had made a few toys, he had filled vacant hours, and he had gained an ugly kind of fame—and this was all. Was he so certain, he began to think, after all, that death was the end? Were there not, perhaps, in the vast house of God, rooms and chambers beyond that in which he was set for awhile to pace to and fro? About this time he began to read in a Bible that had lain dusty and unopened on a shelf. It was his mother's book, and he found therein many little tokens of her presence. Here was a verse underlined; at some gracious passages the page was much fingered and worn; in one place there were stains that looked like the mark of tears; then again, in one page, there was a small tress of hair, golden hair, tied in a paper with a name across it, that seemed to be the name of a little sister of his mother's that died a child; and again there were a few withered flowers, like little sad ghosts, stuck through a paper on which was written his father's name—the name of the sad, harsh, silent man whom Anthony had feared with all his heart. Had those two, indeed, on some day of summer, walked to and fro, or sate in some woodland corner, whispering sweet words of love together? Anthony felt a sudden hunger of the heart for a woman's love, for tender words to soothe his sadness, for the laughter and kisses of children—and he began to ransack his mind for memories of his mother; he could remember being pressed to her heart one morning when she lay abed, with her fragrant hair falling about him. The worst was that he must bear his sorrow alone, for there were none to whom he could talk of such things, The doctor was as dry as an old bunch of herbs, and as for the priest, Anthony was ashamed to show anything but contempt and pride in his presence.

For relief he began to turn to a branch of his studies that he had long disused; this was a fearful commerce with the unseen spirits. Anthony could remember having practised some experiments of this kind with the old Italian doctor; but he remembered them with a kind of disgust, for they seemed to him but a sort of deadly juggling; and such dark things as he had seen seemed like a dangerous sport with unclean and coltish beings, more brute-like than human. Yet now he read in his curious books with care, and studied the tales of necromancers, who had indeed seemed to have some power over the souls of men departed. But the old books gave him but little faith, and a kind of angry disgust at the things attempted. And he began to think that the horror in which such men as made these books abode, was not more than the dark shadow cast on the mirror of the soul by their own desperate imaginings and timorous excursions.

One day, a Sunday, he was strangely sad and heavy; he could settle to nothing, but threw book after book aside, and when he turned to some work of construction, his hand seemed to have lost its cunning. It was a grey and sullen day in October; a warm wet wind came buffeting up from the west, and roared in the chimneys and eaves of the old house. The shrubs in the garden plucked themselves hither and thither as though in pain. Anthony walked to and fro after his midday meal, which he had eaten hastily and without savour; at last as though with a sudden resolution, he went to a secret cabinet and got out a key; and with it he went to the door of the little room that was ever locked.

He stopped at the threshold for a while, looking hither and thither; and then he suddenly unlocked it and went in, closing and locking it behind him. The room was as dark as night, but Anthony going softly, his hands before him, went to a corner and got a tinder-box which lay there, and made a flame.

A small dark room appeared, hung with a black tapestry; the window was heavily shuttered and curtained; in the centre of the room stood what looked like a small altar, painted black; the floor was all bare, but with white marks upon it, half effaced. Anthony looked about the room, glancing sidelong, as though in some kind of doubt; his breath went and came quickly, and he looked paler than was his wont.

Presently, as though reassured by the silence and calm of the place, he went to a tall press that stood in a corner, which he opened, and took from it certain things—a dish of metal, some small leathern bags, a large lump of chalk, and a book. He laid all but the chalk down on the altar, and then opening the book, read in it a little; and then he went with the chalk and drew certain marks upon the floor, first making a circle, which he went over again and again with anxious care; at times he went back and peeped into the book as though uncertain. Then he opened the bags, which seemed to hold certain kinds of powder, this dusty, that in grains; he ran them through his hands, and then poured a little of each into his dish, and mixed them with his hands. Then he stopped and looked about him. Then he walked to a place in the wall on the further side of the altar from the door, and drew the arras carefully aside, disclosing a little alcove in the wall; into this he looked fearfully, as though he was afraid of what he might see.

In the alcove, which was all in black, appeared a small shelf, that stood but a little way out from the wall. Upon it, gleaming very white against the black, stood the skull of a man, and on either side of the skull were the bones of a man's hand. It looked to him, as he gazed on it with a sort of curious disgust, as though a dead man had come up to the surface of a black tide, and was preparing presently to leap out. On either side stood two long silver candlesticks, very dark with disuse; but instead of holding candles, they were fitted at the top with flat metal dishes; and in these he poured some of his powders, mixing them as before with his fingers. Between the candlesticks and behind the skull was an old and dark picture, at which he gazed for a time, holding his taper on high. The picture represented a man fleeing in a kind of furious haste from a wood, his hands spread wide, and his eyes staring out of the picture; behind him everywhere was the wood, above which was a star in the sky—and out of the wood leaned a strange pale horned thing, very dim. The horror in the man's face was skilfully painted, and Anthony felt a shudder pass through his veins. He knew not what the picture meant; it had been given to him by the old Italian, who had smiled a wicked smile when he gave it, and told him that it had a very great virtue. When Anthony had asked him of the subject of the picture, the old Italian had said, "Oh, it is as appears; he hath been where he ought not, and he hath seen somewhat he doth not like." When Anthony would fain have known more, and especially what the thing was that leaned out of the wood, the old Italian had smiled cruelly and said, "Know you not? Well, you will know some day when you have seen him;" and never a word more would he say.

When Anthony had put all things in order, he opened the book at a certain place, and laid it upon the altar; and then it seemed as though his courage failed him, for he drew the curtain again over the alcove, unlocked the door, set the tinder-box and the candle back in their place, and softly left the room.

He was very restless all evening. He took down books from the shelves, turned them over, and put them back again. He addressed himself to some unfinished work, but soon threw it aside; he paced up and down, and spent a long time, with his hands clasped behind him, looking out into the desolate garden, where a still, red sunset burnt behind the leafless trees. He was like a man who has made up his mind to a grave decision, and shrinks back upon the brink. When his food was served he could hardly touch it, and he drank no wine as his custom was to do, but only water, saying to himself that his head must be clear. But in the evening he went to his bedroom, and searched for something in a press there; he found at last what he was searching for, and unfolded a long black robe, looking gloomily upon it, as though it aroused unwelcome thoughts; while he was pondering, he heard a hum of music behind the arras; he put the robe down, and stepped through the hangings, and stood awhile in the little oriel that looked down into the church. Vespers were proceeding; he saw the holy lights dimly through the dusty panes, and heard the low preluding of the organ; then, solemn and slow, rose the sound of a chanted psalm on the air; he carefully unfastened the casement which opened inward and unclosed it, standing for a while to listen, while the air, fragrant with incense smoke, drew into the room along the vaulted roof. There were but a few worshippers in the church, who stood below him; two lights burnt stilly upon the altar, and he saw distinctly the thin hands of a priest who held a book close to his face. He had not set foot within a church for many years, and the sight and sound drew his mind back to his childhood's days. At last with a sigh he put the window to very softly, and went to his study, where he made pretence to read, till the hour came when he was wont to retire to his bed. He sent his servant away, but instead of lying down, he sate, looking upon a parchment, which he held in his hand, while the bells of the city slowly told out the creeping hours.

At last, a few minutes before midnight, he rose from his place; the house was now all silent, and without the night was very still as though all things slept tranquilly. He opened the press and took from it the black robe, and put it round him, so that it covered him from head to foot, and then gathered up the parchment, and the key of the locked room, and went softly out, and so came to the door. This he undid with a kind of secret and awestruck haste, locking it behind him. Once inside the room, he wrestled awhile with a strong aversion to what was in his mind to do, and stood for a moment, listening intently, as though he expected to hear some sound. But the room was still, except for the faint biting of some small creature in the wainscot.

Then with a swift motion he took up the tinderbox and made a light; he drew aside the curtain that hid the alcove; he put fire to the powder in the candlesticks, which at first spluttered, and then swiftly kindling sent up a thick smoky flame, fragrant with drugs, burning hotly and red. Then he came back to the altar; cast a swift glance round him to see that all was ready; put fire to the powder on the altar, and in a low and inward voice began to recite words from the book, and from the parchment which he held in his hand; once or twice he glanced fearfully at the skull, and the hands which gleamed luridly through the smoke; the figures in the picture wavered in the heat; and now the powders began to burn clear, and throw up a steady light; and still he read, sometimes turning a page, until at last he made an end; and drawing something from a silver box which lay beside the book, he dropped it in the flame, and looked straight before him to see what might befall. The thing that fell in the flame burned up brightly, with a little leaping of sparks, but soon it died down; and there was a long silence in the room, a breathless silence, which, to Anthony's disordered mind, was not like the silence of emptiness, but such silence as may be heard when unseen things are crowding quietly to a closed door, expecting it to be opened, and as it were holding each other back.

Suddenly, between him and the picture, appeared for a moment a pale light, as of moonlight and then with a horror which words cannot attain to describe, Anthony saw a face hang in the air a few feet from him, that looked in his own eyes with a sort of intent fury, as though to spring upon him if he turned either to the right hand or to the left. His knees tottered beneath him, and a sweat of icy coldness sprang on his brow; there followed a sound like no sound that Anthony had ever dreamed of hearing; a sound that was near and yet remote, a sound that was low and yet charged with power, like the groaning of a voice in grievous pain and anger, that strives to be free and yet is helpless. And then Anthony knew that he had indeed opened the door that looks into the other world, and that a deadly thing that held him in enmity had looked out. His reeling brain still told him that he was safe where he was, but that he must not step or fall outside the circle; but how he should resist the power of the wicked face he knew not. He tried to frame a prayer in his heart; but there swept such a fury of hatred across the face that he dared not. So he closed his eyes and stood dizzily waiting to fall, and knowing that if he fell it was the end.

Suddenly, as he stood with closed eyes, he felt the horror of the spell relax; he opened his eyes again, and saw that the face died out upon the air, becoming first white and then thin, like the husk that stands on a rush when a fly draws itself from its skin, and floats away into the sunshine.

Then there fell a low and sweet music upon the air, like a concert of flutes and harps, very far away. And then suddenly, in a sweet clear radiance, the face of his mother, as she lived in his mind, appeared in the space, and looked at him with a kind of heavenly love; then beside the face appeared two thin hands which seemed to wave a blessing towards him, which flowed like healing into his soul.

The relief from the horror, and the flood of tenderness that came into his heart, made him reckless. The tears came into his eyes, not in a rising film, but a flood hot and large. He took a step forwards round the altar; but as he did so, the vision disappeared, the lights shot up into a flare and went out; the house seemed to be suddenly shaken; in the darkness he heard the rattle of bones, and the clash of metal, and Anthony fell all his length upon the ground and lay as one dead.

But while he thus lay, there came to him in some secret cell of the mind a dreadful vision, which he could only dimly remember afterwards with a fitful horror. He thought that he was walking in the cloister of some great house or college, a cool place, with a pleasant garden in the court. He paced up and down, and each time that he did so, he paused a little before a great door at the end, a huge blind portal, with much carving about it, which he somehow knew he was forbidden to enter. Nevertheless, each time that he came to it, he felt a strong wish, that constantly increased, to set foot therein. Now in the dream there fell on him a certain heaviness, and the shadow of a cloud fell over the court, and struck the sunshine out of it. And at last he made up his mind that he would enter. He pushed the door open with much difficulty, and found himself in a long blank passage, very damp and chilly, but with a glimmering light; he walked a few paces down it. The flags underfoot were slimy, and the walls streamed with damp. He then thought that he would return; but the great door was closed behind him, and he could not open it. This made him very fearful; and while he considered what he should do, he saw a tall and angry-looking man approaching very swiftly down the passage. As he turned to face him, the other came straight to him, and asked him very sternly what he did there; to which Anthony replied that he had found the door open. To which the other replied that it was fast now, and that he must go forward. He seized Anthony as he spoke by the arm, and urged him down the passage. Anthony would fain have resisted, but he felt like a child in the grip of a giant, and went forward in great terror and perplexity. Presently they came to a door in the side of the wall, and as they passed it, there stepped out an ugly shadowy thing, the nature of which he could not clearly discern, and marched softly behind them. Soon they came to a turn in the passage, and in a moment the way stopped on the brink of a dark well, that seemed to go down a long way into the earth, and out of which came a cold fetid air, with a hollow sound like a complaining voice. Anthony drew back as far as he could from the pit, and set his back to the wall, his companion letting go of him. But he could not go backward, for the thing behind him was in the passage and barred the way, creeping slowly nearer. Then Anthony was in a great agony of mind, and waited for the end.

But while he waited, there came some one very softly down the passage and drew near; and the other, who had led him to the place, waited, as though ill-pleased to be interrupted; it was too murky for Anthony to see the new-comer, but he knew in some way that he was a friend. The stranger came up to them, and spoke in a low voice to the man who had drawn Anthony thither, as though pleading for something; and the man answered angrily, but yet with a certain dark respect, and seemed to argue that he was acting in his right, and might not be interfered with. Anthony could not hear what they said, they spoke so low, but he guessed the sense, and knew that it was himself of whom they discoursed, and listened with a fearful wonder to see which would prevail. The end soon came, for the tall man, who had brought him there, broke out into a great storm of passion; and Anthony heard him say, "He hath yielded himself to his own will; and he is mine here; so let us make an end." Then the stranger seemed to consider; and then with a quiet courage, and in a soft and silvery voice like that of a child, said, "I would that you would have yielded to my prayer; but as you will not, I have no choice." And he took his hand from under the cloak that wrapped him, and held something out; then there came a great roaring out of the pit, and a zigzag flame flickered in the dark. Then in a moment the tall man and the shadow were gone; Anthony could not see whither they went, and he would have thanked the stranger; but the other put his finger to his lip as though to order silence, and pointed to the way he had come, saying, "Make haste and go back; for they will return anon with others; you know not how dear it hath cost me." Anthony could see the stranger's face in the gloom, and he was surprised to see it so youthful; but he saw also that tears stood in the eyes of the stranger, and that something dark like blood trickled down his brow; yet he looked very lovingly at him. So Anthony made haste to go back, and found the door ajar; but as he reached it, he heard a horrible din behind him, of cries and screams; and it was with a sense of gratitude, that he could not put into words, but which filled all his heart, that he found himself back in the cloister again. And then the vision all fled away, and with a shock coming to himself, he found that he was lying in his own room; and then he knew that a battle had been fought out over his soul, and that the evil had not prevailed.

He was cold and aching in every limb; the room was silent and dark, with the heavy smell of the burnt drugs all about it. Anthony crept to the door, and opened it; locked it again, and made his way in the dark very feebly to his bed-chamber; he had just the strength to get into his bed, then all his life seemed to ebb from him, and he lay, and thought that he was dying. Presently from without there came the crying of cocks, and a bell beat the hour of four; and after that, in his vigil of weakness, it was strange to see the light glimmer in the crevices, and to hear the awakening birds that in the garden bushes took up, one after another, their slender piping song, till all the choir cried together.

But Anthony felt a strange peace in his heart; and he had a sense, though he could not say why, that it was as once in his childhood, when he was ill, and his mother had sate softly by him while he slept.

So he waited, and in spite of his mortal weakness that was a blessed hour.

When his man came to rouse him in the morning, Anthony said that he believed that he was very ill, that he had had a fall, and that the old doctor must be fetched to him. The man looked so strangely upon him, that Anthony knew that he had some fear upon his mind. Presently the doctor was brought, and Anthony answered such questions as were put to him, in a faint voice, saying, "I was late at my work, and I slipped and fell." The doctor, who looked troubled, gave directions; and when he went away he heard his man behind the door asking the doctor about the strange storm in the night, that had seemed like an earthquake, or as if a thunderbolt had struck the house. But the doctor said very gruffly, "It is no time to talk thus, when your master is sick to death." But Anthony knew in himself that he would not die yet.

It was long ere he was restored to a measure of health; and indeed he never rightly recovered the use of his limbs; the doctor held that he had suffered some stroke of palsy; at which Anthony smiled a little, and made not answer.

When he was well enough to creep to and fro, he went sadly to the dark room, and with much pain and weakness carried the furniture out of it. The picture he cut in pieces and burnt; and the candles and dishes, with the book, he cast into a deep pool in the stream; the bones he buried in the earth; the hangings he stored away for his own funeral.

Anthony never entered his workroom again; but day after day he sate in his chair, and read a little, but mostly in the Bible; he made a friend of a very wise old priest, to whom he opened all his heart, and to whom he conveyed much money to be bestowed on the poor; there was a great calm in his spirit, which was soon written in his face, in spite of his pain, for he often suffered sorely; but he told the priest that something, he knew not certainly what, seemed to dwell by him, waiting patiently for his coming; and so Anthony awaited his end.

The Small People
Thomas Ligotti

Coming of age in this world has always been a strange process. I'm sure you understand, Doctor. There are so many adjustments that need to be made before we are presentable in company. One doesn't understand all the workings, all the stages of development in the process of becoming who we are and what we are. It can be so difficult. Others expected me to be complete at a certain age, ready to jump up and take my place when called to do so. "Time to wake up," they said. "Time to do this or time to do that," they said. "It's show time," they said. And I had better be willing and able when the time came.

Please excuse my outburst, Doctor. I'm doing my best. I know my lines. I've told this story before, as you know. And I do want to be good this time. My parents were always scolding me to be good about one thing or another. "You came from a good family," they frequently said to me, as if saying I was biologically their own could make it so. Now, I cannot deny that their criticism of certain attitudes I held was unmerited. My mother and father resorted to using the words *shameful little bigot* quite a bit. "How could we have raised such a shameful little bigot?" she would say to him or he would say to her. "He doesn't get it from my side of the family," one of them would shout. And then the other, right on cue, would respond, "Well, he doesn't get it from mine either." There it was again—the genetic issue, which might have upset me had I been older and wise to the fact that my status in the family was but a legal fiction. In light of later events, of course, biology was the least of our differences. This is a very delicate topic for me, as you know.

Moving on, my parents would then fight, if only for the sake of appearances, speaking the same lines they'd spoken before. Back and forth, back and forth they'd go at each other. Then finally they'd come back around to their little boy, who was such a shameful little bigot. Obviously, it wasn't in their interest to acknowledge the truth—that foremost I was afraid, not bigoted. Calling me bigoted was simply a tactic for confusing the issue. But any hatred I displayed was epiphenomenal to my fear. Every child has his fears, and the worst of mine was a fear of *them*. Not my mother and father. Well, I was afraid of them, too—that's not unusual. But as a child I didn't hate them. I hated those others—*the small people*.

One time my parents and I were on vacation. My father was at the wheel. He was smiling slightly and staring with concentration. That was how he always looked, even when he wasn't driving—always smiling slightly and always staring with concentration. Next to him my mother sat quietly. The sun was shining on her smooth face. She had such a smooth face, Doctor, and big eyes. I was sitting in the middle of the back seat, minding my own business and taking in the wide spaces of the scenery, not focusing on anything in particular. Then I saw the sign just off the right side of the road. It had one of those simple faces on it, and written below were the words: SMALL COUNTRY. My whole body tightened, as it always did when I saw one of those road signs. The arrow at the bottom of the sign pointed straight up, so that drivers would know they were in range of small country.

I slid over to the right side of the car and began to survey the landscape. A short distance from the road we were on was another road, a smaller road. It meandered through an open plain slightly below us. I shifted my eyes toward the front seat and saw my father looking in the rearview mirror at me. But I didn't care. This was the closest I had ever been to small country, and I wanted to see all I could, which for a long while wasn't anything except that empty plain with that small road passing through it. Such is the perversity born of fear. At the same time that I wanted to see something, I was terrified of what I might see. I felt as if I were having one of those dreams where you're alone but still feel the presence of something unimaginably awful that might appear all of a sudden. It was at the height of this nightmarish sensation that I saw the little car turning a bend in the small road. About the same time, our road—the big road—started curving toward the other. The closer the little car came to us, the more I felt the urge to dive to the floor of our car. But then I would have missed seeing them.

Their car, the little car, looked like a toy. It wasn't exactly its size that demoted it from a properly motorized conveyance to a plaything, because the pretend car wasn't so near our real car that I could compare the two. It was the flagrant actuality that everything about it was toy-like, as if it were made of molded plastic and rolling along on teetering wheels. And it bore none of the details on it of a real car, at least that I could tell. Structurally, it had a simple square body painted bright red. That had to be the color, of course, just so that it would stand out in the scene, and I could be all the more afraid than if its color had been white or yellow or some shade of blue. But I stopped attending to the car once I saw what was inside.

Until then, I scarcely had a glimpse of any small people. My strange fear of them originated mostly from the simple face on the road signs that alerted people, real people, of their impending entry into small country. The mere idea of the smalls was enough to make me anxious about something I couldn't name. And after looking into that red plastic toy, I was sorry I hadn't thrown myself down onto the floor of our car, even knowing that my parents would have called me a shameful little bigot for the rest of the vacation.

After our cars passed each other, my father looked in the rearview mirror and said to me, "So, did you see them?" I didn't say anything. I was defiantly silent.

"Your father asked you a question," said my mother. "You should answer him." But I maintained my silence. And if I had spoken, I wouldn't have said anything about what I saw in that car. I wasn't even afraid at that point. I was bitter and resentful that my father could have asked me in such a bland tone of voice if I saw them. I wanted to scream at both my parents, scream murderously and also with some puzzlement, a plea for understanding. How could people, big people, have such a complacent attitude toward the smalls? How could they give certain presents to children for their birthday or any time presents were in order when those presents might look like that little car and the small people inside it? They were travesties of real people, that's all they were—two older small people, like a father and mother, in the front seat, and two young small people, whose gender I couldn't tell at a distance, sitting rigidly in the back. How could there even exist certain toys, for instance an imitation baking oven—a play version of the real thing, yet one that quite probably replicated the actual baking ovens used by the small people? Even if the resemblance wasn't one-to-one between the two miniature ovens, the thought could still enter a child's head, "This oven must be something like those the small people have in their kitchens." Who could be so stupid or malicious that they could ignore the possibility of such a thing— that an object some children might have in front of them, or even in their little hands, could have a counterpart in small country? It was too monstrous to contemplate that at a certain age children can and do become cognizant of the likeness of their toys to entities in the small country world, including the small people who live there, if they are even alive. Why didn't they react, as I had, with fear and hatred once they came of a certain age?

Naturally, I knew that for practical reasons the world of the smalls and the real world were securely set apart, just as borders between many places of divergent laws and customs were partitioned and even guarded with powerful weapons against each other. But it wasn't the same between the smalls and everyone else. This was something I felt deep inside me, though I risked being stigmatized as a shameful little bigot not only by my parents but also by most anyone wherever I went.

For the rest of our vacation that year, I was miserably anxious as well as miserably hateful. From the moment my father asked me if I saw what was in that little toy car, my hatred for the small people that grew out of my fear of them reached its zenith and held there. Of course, I had seen them, idiot father of mine. Why did he ridicule me, taking their side? At one point, all of the occupants of the little car suddenly swiveled their heads toward us, then abruptly swiveled them back to their previously fixed positions. To my mind, they did this as if to say, "We know you are looking at us. Now we are looking at you. Now you know that we knew you were looking at us. And henceforth there will be no escaping this mutual knowledge." Those damn swivel-heads, I thought, even though I could only imagine what went on in their heads, because in fact they appeared to have nothing going on inside them. They were just hollow, empty things.

Not long after this encounter, my father pointed out the window. By the side of the road was another sign with one of those simple faces on it. Below that face were the words: LEAVING SMALL COUNTRY.

"All clear," my father said with a vexing condescension in his voice and a slight smile on his face.

"Oh, leave the boy alone," my mother said, but only as a sort of warning that my father was taking things too far. Right then, I could have thrown a fit the likes of which my parents had never seen or suspected of me. Nor was it wholly improbable that I might have leapt into the front seat and steered our car into the roadside ditch, which was of some depth. I might have killed us all, or perhaps only my father and mother. But then, in a flash of mentation, it occurred to me that with the demise of my parents I would likely fall under the care of another couple whose attitude toward my fear and hatred of the small people probably would not have differed from theirs. Certainly my disposition was not in line with that of the larger share of humanity. In good faith, I have to admit as much, Doctor. I know you must be aware of the torment an individual suffers when he begins to wonder if he is the one on the wrong side of reality. Perhaps it was a defensive tactic of my mind, then, that though I was still afflicted by fright and hatred when it came to the small people, I also felt for the first time a curiosity about them. Surely that signaled a healthier perspective, and I welcomed it.

My newfound curiosity waxed and waned for about a year or so. It either intensified or abated depending on how often I awoke sweating with sick horror after dreaming about the small people. I finally acted on my curiosity only after I had a dream in which real people, including myself, were somehow changed either into small people or *half-small people*. The latter particularly disturbed me. Yes, I thought, *now is the time*. And so I began my quest to get to the bottom of the mystery that, at least for me, surrounded the small people.

The library seemed the natural starting point to research my subject. In no time at all, it seemed, I could find out all I needed to know about the small people. And possibly what I learned would terminate, or at least temper, my fear of them, and even alleviate, or dissolve entirely, my hatred of their kind. But I was only a child with a rudimentary conception of how things truly were in this world at its deepest level. I found out soon enough, though, that I had misled myself.

I was ahead of my class in school and knew my way around a library better than most children my age. Thus, you can imagine my devastation when I failed to unearth any substantive information about the small people. How could there be such a gap in what would seem a vital realm of study—what conspiracy of silence, what code of secrecy was in effect that I could find hardly a mention of these creatures, not even in the form of records or statistics relating to them? Yet ultimately I was forced to conclude that nothing was being hidden from me as well as the rest of the world on the subject I attempted to investigate. At least, it wasn't being hidden deliberately, consciously. That would have been an impossible task. Some blabbermouth is always around who is unable to keep what he knows to himself—chatterboxes without whom the details of humanity's most lurid episodes would be lost, let alone something as conspicuous as the small people. No, Doctor, only one thing could keep them out of the limelight—pure neglect, a protective disinterest, as the old philosophers of the human psyche might have seen it: the mind's looking away when unsettling facts come into view, facts that one would rather not focus on for long. Where the small people were concerned, there was nearly a blackout of intelligence.

I'm not saying that no one has ever ruminated on the phenomenon of the small people. No doubt everyone has pondered their existence at some time or another. But such considerations have never been sustained long enough to create a body of inquiry and knowledge. Before pen could be put to paper or an expedition launched, some negating incuriosity set in that dissipated any spur to action, or any action that resulted in authoritative books and peer-reviewed essays in specialized journals—all that might comprise a modest shelf even in the middling libraries of our world. If you should say that even highly arcane matters, not to mention anything right before our eyes, have evaded the closest research, I would have to respond, perhaps a bit vigorously—*false*. Question: How could we know we were keeping certain truths from ourselves regarding how things truly are in this world at its deepest level? Answer: Because we have done it before. Do I really need to give particulars? And many continue the charade long after some voice indicates beyond credible doubt what is true and what is not. *The time has not come yet*, I thought. And perhaps it never would.

In point of fact, though, I must admit to having heard vague mutterings about the small people when I was at the library that day. For instance, I came across a history book—that is, a book concerned with *our* history—and in its index there was a reference to a footnote in which the author alluded to the small people. In that footnote were written the words: "Of course they have no recorded history of their own." Naturally, this scrupulous scholar adduced his source for this assertion in the usual style, and it made me so happy to read the arid citation "See Paulson," or maybe it was "Hayworth," possibly "Heywood." Whomever I was told to see, I sought out. But nothing was contained there—nothing to corroborate that the small people had no recorded history of their own. Why would a scholar of any standing slip up that way, leading the reader to a source that did not support what he had written? Mistakes do happen, no doubt about that. But how could it be that they happened whenever someone wrote something about the small people, as I discovered they always did? All day long, one book led me to another and each left me empty-handed. Was I being diverted here and there by falsehoods, or were bits of truth being parcelled out in such a way that no complete picture formed of the small people, or none that could be placed beside the one we had of ourselves in the great photo-album of humankind—a portrait that itself began to seem incomplete to a child who believed until then that we knew everything that had anything to do with our world? The big world, that is.

During the hours I spent that day in the library, I went from basement to belfry, only to find myself cornered by the walls of one dead end after another. With studious intent I walked into a repository of learning with the light of a beautiful morning shining upon me and my self-appointed mission. But great clouds rolled in, thunder shook the walls, rain tapped louder and louder against the windows and lightning flashed outside them. By degrees, the neat hallways of the library I had entered turned to dank and dripping stonework corridors of a Gothic castle through which I wandered in search of a way out. I trembled as if trapped in one of those dreams of mine where I feel surrounded by unseen horrors. At last, all I wanted was to wake up. But I couldn't awake, not until I had some answers. Abandoning the library in disgust, I returned home and moped about for weeks in a stupor of desperation and nervous suspicion.

Not long after that inauspicious day of wasted labor, something happened that helped me come back to myself, such as I was, while also advancing my obsession with the swivel-heads. Until then, I was no expert at making friends. How unexpected it was, then, that I should make a friend when I needed one most. I was so surprised because nothing in my life had ever worked out that way. For once, I actually gained an advantage over my circumstances.

It was after school, after the time between leaving home to go to school in the morning and leaving school in the afternoon to go back home, where I waited for it to be time for dinner, time for doing homework, and then other times until it was time to go to bed before it was time to wake up again and face another round of times to do things. In any case, on the day in question I made friends with this other boy. The reason for this fortuitous bond was that he spoke the following words: "Damn those small people." I asked him why he said that. I also asked if he was afraid of the small people as I was afraid of them. He said he wasn't afraid of the small people, but I didn't believe him because of the way he said this. His eyes looked away from me, and he started to fidget. His voice became very quiet, too, until he stopped talking altogether and just stared at the ground. Then he looked up at me, shaking off the fear that possessed him, and said in a boisterous voice, "I'm not afraid of those dummy-things. I just hate them."

I smiled and said, "I call them swivel-heads. And I hate them, too."

Immediately we became friends and began spending time together every day after school, that is, until it was time for us to go home for dinner and then go through all the other times there were. We played games the way young people do, or are supposed to do at that stage of development. We wrestled quite a bit, but there wasn't anything mean or crazy about it. We also talked a lot about the small people. One theme of conversation to which we often returned involved catching one of the smalls and what we'd do when we did.

"I'd twist its arms until they were backwards." To me, that seemed like something you could actually do to the small people, even if my only basis for this conviction was a brief sighting of them while on vacation a few years before.

"Then it would have to do everything turned around, like eating with its back to the dinner table, if they even eat. It would have to reach for its food without being able to see it," my friend speculated, warming to his vision. I pictured the scene for a moment.

"Yeah," I said.

We laughed quite a bit about small people whose arms and also legs we had twisted backwards, as well as other things we would do if we caught one of them. Eventually, we became so exhausted from laughing that we were out of breath and had to sit quietly for a while. That was when my friend smiled at me in a certain way. Not smiling slightly like my father did, but smiling as if he was thinking something very particular, looking at me with a questioning expression on his face. And right then I had the feeling I could read his mind and he could read mine. From that moment, we became more serious in our talks about the swivel-headed dummy-things. My friend also shared with me a secret. What he told me was that his father—maybe his mother, too—also hated the small people. "My grandfather hated them even more. He thought all sorts of things about them and what he called their *powers*." Then my friend confided that his father always knew the location of small country, and their family moved every so often to avoid it. "We're going to be moving again pretty soon. Dad says that the smalls are too close already... and they're getting closer every day. He even let me know where new small country is going up, so I won't get too near it."

Not long after that day, I asked my parents if I could sleep over at my friend's house. He did the same, asking his parents if he could sleep over at my house. Our ruse worked, and on the night we were supposed to sleep over at each other's houses we instead met at a pre-arranged location—the lavatory hut in the old park on the edge of town. When I entered the small wooden building, my friend was already studying a wrinkled piece of notebook paper on which he had drawn a map. "Here's where the small country is going to be," he said, pointing to a place a few miles outside the town's limits. "It's secluded right now, my dad said." According to my friend, however, it wouldn't be long before the signs were put up and everyone would know it was there. "Not that they could do anything about it," my friend said.

"Yeah," I replied, knowing that whoever complained would be called a shameful bigot or some roughly equivalent term of reproach. As my friend and I sat cross-legged on the floor of the lavatory hut, it became increasingly apparent that neither of us was entirely dedicated to our plan of stealing our way into the presently secluded region of small country and capturing one of its residents. And the longer we waited, the more our project deteriorated into something ill-conceived and probably unfeasible. Ultimately, though, our doubts were overcome by our hatred.

"The small people," my friend said. That was all—just three words spoken in a tense, quiet voice. Yet those words gave vent to a rage at something that had seized his life. I looked at him and saw all second thoughts written on his face transform into a spirit of determination. No doubt he saw my own features overtaken by the same spirit.

We entered the secluded small country by way of a little road that was in the process of construction. Some small children were loitering in the area. Construction sites are always a temptation for children, though these small children weren't behaving in the usually rambunctious manner one might expect if they had been real children. They didn't see us, or so we assumed. But it wasn't long before they started to walk away from the hidden spot where my friend and I were observing them. It was probably time for them to be somewhere, I thought—time to do whatever the smalls did at that hour, for by then it was almost full evening. They moved with rigid, mechanical motions, and we shadowed them easily. We could have caught up to them and grabbed one, pulled it back over into big country—normal country, I mean, the real world where real people live. But I don't think I could have brought myself to do that, as much as my friend and I had talked about it. I looked at him, and he shook his head, so I knew he felt the same. At that point, I'm not sure that either of us knew what we wanted to do. Again, our plans were coming apart.

We kept following the smalls, though. I noticed that even if they weren't moving very fast, they did seem to be moving as fast as they could, as if they were hurrying to get somewhere. Their arms and legs shifted around in the manner of prosthetic limbs, making them look almost crippled, though not crippled so that you felt sorry for them, I should say, but maimed in a way that made you want to keep your distance, as if they could infect you with some dreadful condition. Eventually, we saw lights ahead. With an artificial radiance, they flooded the darkness on the other side of a hill that the small children were approaching. And when they got to the top of the hill, they paused for a moment, their silhouettes outlined against the sky by the lights shining on them from below. For a moment, it was a rather picturesque tableau. But soon the small children did something with their heads, raising them up with a slow mechanical motion by elongating their necks, like a telescope sliding open a little. Then they swiveled those heads around without moving their bodies—turning them just enough so that it seemed they were looking at me and my friend. Both of us dropped to the ground as if we had been shot. In the darkness,

I heard my friend whisper, "Those rotten, horrible smalls. You can never know what they're going to do. I hate them so much."

"Yeah," I murmured in soft response.

When we looked up from the ground, the small children were gone, no doubt having moved down the other side of the hill. It couldn't have been a very steep incline there, or so I calculated. Otherwise, the smalls—with their awkward, practically disabled bodies—wouldn't have been able to negotiate the descent. But when my friend and I ran up to the hilltop, moving in a crouched position, we saw that it was almost a straight drop over the edge. And the small children were now walking like broken robots down below us. Their destination looked like a little toy town that was evidently under construction. "See," my friend said. "My dad knew it. Pretty soon all of this land around here will be small country."

They were moving around like mad in a kind of pit. Stretching out for about a mile was a half-built town that was almost a double of the town where my friend and I lived. The smalls were hopping around in a frenzy to finish it, as if they were on a tight schedule. "Maybe they have to complete the place before a certain time," my friend conjectured. "Why else would they be working at night?" *Or maybe that's just the way they are*, I thought. All kinds of small building machinery were positioned along the town's main street, though none of it was in motion. Small people who looked as if they were directing operations stood with their stubby arms outstretched, pointing in all directions or inspecting unrolled building plans held tightly by their tiny digits. Everyone seemed busy with some project—putting up storefronts that had little detail or identifying features, working on skeletal frameworks that maybe were going to be houses, or carrying around what appeared to be prefabricated parts that would ultimately be integrated into the toy town. On several street corners small people were yelling through staticky bull horns. But they didn't seem to be addressing anyone in particular, and what they were shouting wasn't distinguishable as anything but gibberish. As a matter of fact—just pure, natural fact—when I considered the scene before me from its smallest to its most prominent features, the whole enterprise of the small people's town-building seemed to be nothing but an act. They weren't building anything with point and purpose at its core, anything that was more than a spectral illusion—they were putting on a show. Whether or not this was intentional on their part intrigued me for some reason.

Once I had thrown off the strangeness of the spectacle, I could see how rickety, how shoddy everything was. All the buildings were crooked or unevenly sized with respect to the town as a whole. The windows were more trapezoidal than square or rectangular, and the shutters attached to some windows hung loosely, flapping against the walls behind them. A light breeze could have caused the town to collapse and blow away, which may have accounted for the disappearance and emergence of so much small country within real landscapes. I knew that all towns, and even cities, in the big world would eventually go to ruin in time, however sturdy they might appear for however long a period. Thousands of years of towns and cities in the past had proven that. And thousands or millions of years awaited the dissolution of the world as it now stood. But this town was not made to last. It was as if the small people knew there was no point in bothering with permanence. As I said, that explained a lot to me about small country—how it was always moving from one location to another, as my friend's father was aware so that he could move his family away from wherever it rose up after a period of seclusion. But there was also something more. They sought no permanent standing in the world. For them, existence was all chaos, nonsense, and emptiness. I knew the same had been written about our world, the supposedly real world. But that was opinion, speculation. And only very few had claimed as much. Yet the small people as a lot seemed to embrace these objectionable qualities as truths. Now it became more explicable to me that they should be passed over in the archives of human thought. Theirs was not a lone voice speaking out of time. Theirs was a society subsisting, even thriving, on the brink of nonexistence—an enigma that repulsed wholesome deliberation by real people. And their habitats were all but ruins upon inauguration.

No one in the big world, or very few, mentioned that the fully extinct leavings of towns like this remained after the smalls relocated, because once a place had become small country it was left alone, as if it was not fit to be reclaimed by real humans, as if the earth in these places had been polluted by an alien occupancy, and only pestilence abided there. You know this as well as I do, Doctor. But nobody writes about this fact, and its corollary that one day there will be no room left for a real world to be built—the unreal was moving in. I believed I realized this truth at a deep level within me during the one brave day I spent at a middling library. And now I was shaken by it to my marrow.

Maybe there are grubby pamphlets passed around among people like my friend's father, crumpled pages whose possession would cause someone to be branded as a shameless little bigot, you might say—an outcast. So anything that appears in print or otherwise about the small people is labeled as pernicious ravings and propaganda. There are means for hushing up what people would prefer not to delve into. But I've already gone into that.

Gazing at the new small town going up, such as it was, was to witness the intrusion of an unnatural colony of beings into the anatomy of our world—not a different race or group, but something that did not belong, neither here nor anywhere conceivable by human senses or cognition. It was something unknown that had taken form, or was in the process of taking form, coming of age in a world it was displacing. That night with my friend brought so many things home to me. A new phase in my feeling about the smalls had begun fermenting within my being. "None of it is real," my friend said. "I don't know what it is." A creeping sense of something hitherto concealed overcame me, as I'm sure it did him. Fear had now gotten the better of both hatred and curiosity. Beside me, my friend whispered: "Let's get out of here." In sync, we jumped to our feet. When we turned about, though, I almost lost consciousness. For behind us was a regiment of small people standing in a semi-circle. How long had they been there? To me, that was more frightening than discovering their presence—being watched without knowing it by a group of smalls.

They didn't speak a word—neither to us nor among one another. Nothing shocked me about that, but it did add to the disorienting unreality of the situation. For a time, they stayed in place. Paradoxically, they appeared gigantic, that is, gigantic for toys, given their toy-like aspect. For instance, their clothes seemed to be painted on them, not worn by them. And their faces were so smooth, gleaming in the moonlight without any of the characteristic qualities of flesh. Despite their masculine semblance, their faces were beardless. They were also unwrinkled, unworn by time and somehow immortal. This was how they had always been, created somehow but not developed in stages from birth to their present age. There had been no process of coming of age for them, I thought later—no birth or death or all the things in between that trouble our own existence, or at least troubled us when we attended to them. There was only going through the motions, a pretense of life. In a way, they were a mirror of us—of what we wanted for ourselves. They marked time and nothing else. Time to do this. Time to do that. Time to make another town. Time to relocate, having poisoned a new landscape with small country.

During the stand-off between the smalls and my friend and me, an uncanny stillness prevailed. But then their heads swiveled simultaneously. Each turned toward another. They didn't seem to be exchanging glances, though, or even looking directly into one into another's glassy, empty eyes—not as my friend and I looked to each other with the same thought in our minds. We couldn't run around them, because they surrounded us. And we didn't want to jump down the steep incline at our backs and land in the small town. So we began to move slowly through their ranks, not knowing what to expect. While we had come there to harm them, our taste for that was now lost. It seemed to us, as we later talked of it that night, that we could not understand them at all or what malevolence they might harbor toward us.

Very slowly, then, we moved between them, and they didn't attempt to block our path. However, they did do something, or seemed to do something. This was to lightly press their bodies against ours as we passed. That turned out to be worse than any brute physical encounter we could have had with them—their touch. For they were not stiff and rigid as we expected, not the hard, plastic toys we might have neatly torn apart, bloodlessly dislodging their seemingly prosthetic limbs. Instead, we found that they were soft, very soft. Their shapes felt as if they were giving way as they lightly pressed themselves against us. But they were also swivel-headed dummy-things—freakish unrealities like their town and maybe everything having to do with small country. Did they even exist as our minds conjured existence, both our own and that of all else within our perception? What were these things that seemed to be all appearance and no substance? Fortunately, such questions did not paralyze us.

Once my friend and I were on the other side of the smalls, we ran without pause to where we commenced our terribly misconceived incursion into small country. The rest of the night we spent shivering with cold and fear in the lavatory hut at the old park on the edge of town. The only time we spoke was in the morning. Just before we parted for our respective homes, my friend looked at me with an abysmal expression on his face and said, "My dad will kill me if he ever finds out what we did."

"Yeah," I said, drawing out at length that single, stupid syllable, exhaling it in a dead voice.

Not long after our misadventure, my friend moved away with his family. And before the end of that school year, those signs went up with the simple faces on them. They first appeared at the edge of town and then proceeded for some miles along the open road beyond. I made a point of going around and finding all the signs I could, noting which direction their arrows pointed to indicate small country. I saw that people still went to the old park. They must have been aware that small country wasn't far away, but that made no difference to them, not as it did to me.

A few weeks before it was time for the new school year to begin, I received a letter from my friend. It was hand delivered to me by my mother, who first took a moment to interrogate me about any packs of cigarettes I might have hidden in the basement, which was where I happened to be at the time, lying on an old sofa we had down there. After that night in small country, my friend and I tried smoking cigarettes for a while. I think we both wanted to do something we'd never done before, something to make us feel we had changed and were no longer those kids who talked so much about the smalls. I kept the last pack of cigarettes we shared, and my mom found them. I hadn't even smoked since my friend moved away. I was elated when I got his letter, which was only a single page. But I read that page countless times, savoring its words and even reciting them in my friend's voice. There was nothing more in the letter than my friend's banal depiction of the new place he was living and the school he would be attending. That was enough to relieve the sense of demoralization I felt since he had been gone. I wrote back to him, of course, and that initiated an exchange of letters between us, and even some phone calls. I told him that I still had the last pack of cigarettes we shared, even though my mother had taken them. What I never asked him was whether he had made any new friends.

In mid-winter, I opened the latest missive from my friend after a hiatus during which he had answered none of my letters. What I read in it revived a kaleidoscope of memories and emotions, none of them welcome to my still delicate state of mind. The news my friend related was that his father had disappeared about a month before. One day, he didn't return from work, and his family had heard nothing from him since. My friend didn't write a word about any particular suspicions he had, and that I also nurtured. He did say that the police had come to his house. As a rule, his mother wouldn't have allowed them into their home to poke around. His father had never trusted the police or any other persons of officialdom, and neither did his mother. But in this circumstance, that rule went out the window.

The police didn't find anything that interested them in the house, but when they looked around the garage they turned up a lock box hidden underneath a workshop table. My friend's mother gave them permission to open it, and inside they discovered, as my friend quoted them, "stacks of literature." Then he wrote, "Both my mom and I were fairly certain that what they called literature wasn't pornography or anything of the kind. It was stuff about them." That was the first reference to the small people I could recollect appearing in our correspondence to each other. Naturally, this was a subject that we didn't want to linger over. My friend continued regarding what was hidden in his dad's lock box that the police pried open: "Some of it was in envelopes with postmarks from all over the world." The police rummaged through the material until my friend's mother told them there wasn't anything in there that would help them find her husband. "The cops didn't say a word after that," my friend wrote. "I thought they might. It seemed to me they should have, the way they were looking at each other. But they just piled the envelopes and stuff back in the box and shoved the box back underneath my dad's workshop table. Then they left, and we haven't heard from them since, the bastards."

For a few days, I didn't know what to write in response to my friend's letter. I considered phoning him, but I didn't think that was a prudent action to take. Finally, I composed a short letter of vague condolences and hopes that his dad had business he thought it best not to share with him and his mother. My letter was a mass of circumlocutions that I was sure my friend would understand. To my grief, I never received a response to that letter, and it was almost spring before I could admit to myself that I would never hear from him again.

I said that my friend avoided mentioning the smalls in our letters. However, as I later pored over our correspondence I saw that he had written something to me that I blocked from recall. The erasure of his words from my memory was understandable, for what he wrote was simply too strange to reflect upon for very long. If you'll remember, Doctor, I posed the following question: "How could we know we were keeping certain truths from ourselves regarding how things are in this world at its deepest level?" And the answer I gave to my own question was this: "Because we had done it before." Well, that's exactly what I had done when I read what my friend wrote to me in one of his letters. Here is my recitation of it from memory: "My dad got drunk last night and told me things I had never heard from him before. I didn't understand most of it. What I do remember was his repeating what he called a spectral link between the smalls and some people in the real world. Then he went on about people who looked and acted like humans but were not human. Maybe he said they were not *completely* human. He did have a term for them. It was *half-small people.*"

You might be able to comprehend, Doctor, how disquieted I was to see written in my friend's hand certain words that, at least in concept, had occurred to me only in a dream. I hated to think that there was a *spectral link* between myself and the smalls, and though I have spoken of peculiar truths regarding how things really are in this world at its deepest level, truths that we keep ourselves from knowing, I concluded with stark lucidity that there was absolutely *no* spectral link between myself and the smalls—not as I understood my friend's father to have used these words. If anything, it was exactly the opposite. The small people were drastically alien to me. I was derided by my parents as a shameless little bigot because of my fear of them and my hatred of them, feelings that I had not known to exist in anyone else besides my friend, and vicariously through him with his father—and his mother, too, it seemed, whom I believe had also gone the way of the rest of my friend's family. But where they had gone I couldn't bring myself to ponder.

While continuing to be afraid of the smalls and to hate them, these emotions were now transferred with a rabid vehemence toward the half-smalls, whom my friend added sometimes devolved—or whatever the proper term might be—in both appearance and nature into small people through and through. Following this transformation, which they might not even know was possible or considered desirable—there was nothing for them to do except move into small country and live among their kind, that is, if they didn't regard this prospect as so repellent that they took other measures rather than losing the sense of *who* they were, or thought they were, and *what* they were, or thought they were. With its small people, this world just seemed a preposterous mess to me, and now it was revealed to be even worse than I knew. Why couldn't things be different? What would it take for our lives to make some kind of sense? Maybe that's just not possible, I thought. Maybe any world would be just as preposterous. Yet the existence of the half-smalls nevertheless still inspired in me a crawling fear, a new unseen horror, as I've mentioned having this sensation in dreams, along with a hatred of them for having what I thought was a weakness connecting them in some spectral manner with the small people. At least the latter were something of a phenomenally known quantity to my mind, however little I understood about them. But the halfers were something else— interlopers in a world where they didn't belong, the source of all questions about who or what human beings might be as a life form. For as tiresome as it has become, the question of what it means to be human continues to fervently preoccupy us— because without that definition we cannot positively know if our laborious self-perpetuation is worth the candle we keep lit in the blackness of the universe. We cannot decide whether we should continue or terminate the human race, if there is anything that might be called the human race, since we are as fragmented in the aggregate as we are as individuals—things of parts and not the integrated organisms we represent to ourselves. All the same, as naïve and arrogant as this may sound, I felt that my sensibility enabled my insight into this immemorial affair. I thought of this sensibility as a type of instinct that actually *forced* me to see things as they were and not as I was supposed to see them so that I could get by in life.

From this point on, as I walked the streets of the town where I lived, I could see only how contrary everything was to the picture of it I was psychologically strong-armed into having. Now the place where I grew up was no more than another preposterous mess. The town's motto on the sign as you entered Main Street was: "A Good Place to Live"—not exactly a boastful statement. In actuality, though, it was pretty crummy. Not crummy *in itself*, I should say, because I had never lived in any other towns. They might be as crummy as my native town. The whole planet might be crummy for all I knew then. When I looked closely at the city hall, for instance, I could see it was wobbly. Maybe at one time I would have thought nothing of walking through the wide front doors of the place. Now that my eyes could see that they tilted quite visibly, I wouldn't have entered its space on a dare. Or take the post office. If my mother had ordered me in her most calmly intimidating voice to go buy her some stamps, I wouldn't do it. Not one foot would I set inside, because its bricks were set together all wrong. One of them could slide a little, I gauged, and the walls might come crashing down in a flash and bury me alive as I was standing in line to buy some rotten stamps which had images on them that were so faded and cock-eyed I couldn't tell anymore what they were supposed to represent. Once they were printed with images of monuments in one place or another where my family went on vacation, as I remembered in my mind's eye, but from then on they appeared all bent up and sagging. And they were all supposed to be *so grand*. Taken in total, the whole world was supposed to be *so grand*. But it wasn't, not from my perspective, which was no longer so muddled I couldn't see things for what they were and not how I was supposed to see them. In my view, all the earth and anything that stood upon it was just like the town where I lived—not a *good* place but a *crummy* place. Even new places that people were always rushing around to build were crummy from the start—wobbly and tilted, bent and sagging. All the energy and hustling that went into building a car wash or a row of stores that seemed shoot up overnight like mushrooms—it was just so useless. Everything was supposed to amount to something, as testified by the ubiquitous Grand Openings of some place wherever you looked. But nothing amounted to anything. It was all just trying to be what it wasn't—real, that is, authentic in every sense of the word, and not fatally bogus.

I could see the same thing in people that I did in the flimsy material world, this junkyard of cast-off ectoplasm. They didn't meet expectations either, though, as I said, no one yet has been able to say definitely who or what we are. And I don't think anyone will ever be able to do so. I don't think they want to. What I do think they want is to say that humans, real humans, are this and that and the other thing—that there are millions of qualities humans have that nothing else has, and they say all this to keep us confused, to keep themselves confused, about what humans really are, except that they're not small people. But now I was fixated on the half-smalls. Now my sensibility, my special instinct, had become sufficiently honed to discern who was what. Not that I expected any consolation from such knowledge—it was simply something to do while I decided what to do with myself.

At first, as I walked around town during the summer after I stopped receiving letters from my friend, I wasn't sure exactly how my sensibility was functioning. I would get a feeling, like a tingling inside me, when I saw certain people strolling down the sidewalk or sitting at picnic tables outside the frozen custard stand that did land-office business throughout the summer months. I'm sure you get the picture, Doc. It was show time and nothing but. No doubt some clickety-clack version of it was being enacted by the smalls, as I was now with some confidence able to imagine after beholding one of their own towns in its construction stage, a poor excuse for even the crummiest human town, if one wants to get into degrees of crumminess, that is.

All things considered, my wits were in relatively fair working order, and my sensibility was becoming more and more sharply attuned. Occasionally, the tingling sensation I felt in the proximity of certain persons caught me off guard and pierced my spine with anxiety, but for the most part I was in control. Within the span of about a week, I not only felt something about those people but also began to see little things about them, things you wouldn't notice without an exacting gaze. After my confrontation with the small people and detecting the smoothness of their faces, which were bereft of the character bestowed by time, unwrinkled and unworn, I saw a family resemblance in the same people who set off that tingling inside me. I wished my friend could have been there, because I was sure he would have seen the same thing about them—that they were halfers.

Some days I'd walk from one end of town to the other, and I'd pick out the real people from the half-small people. As I passed by each person I would check off their identities in my mind— halfer, real, halfer, real, and so on. Mr. So-and-so—halfer. The old woman who walks her dog in the park every day—real. Schoolteachers—halfers every one. Cops, too, all halfers, which made me think of my friend's family and the investigating officers who found the literature under his father's workshop table. The girl who sat next to me in math class—real. I was glad about that. The middle-aged lady in the window at the beauty shop— everyone thought she had a facelift done, but she was a halfer. With children it was more of a challenge sorting out the real ones from the halfers. Most of them I let pass as real. There was one group of kids, though, all spindly specimens with empty stares. They had to be half-smalls.

All told, I judged about half the people in town as real and half as halfers. I had gotten to be quite proficient at spotting our citizens as one or the other—too good, in the end. I really should have shut off my thoughts sometimes, but I couldn't do that.

It was Saturday, and my dad was off work for the weekend. My family always barbequed hamburgers and hot dogs on those days and ate them together around a plastic table in the backyard. We don't tend to see our parents the way we do others. We're too close to them. Even if they make you miserable and call you a shameful little bigot, they're still your parents—special circumstances notwithstanding. But after all the time I spent around town separating the real people from the half-smalls, I scrutinized everyone the same. More to the point, I felt that tingling inside me. Being with both my mother and father for an extended period of time on a Saturday afternoon, and sitting with them around a plastic table in the backyard, I was tingling like mad. My father was smiling slightly and staring with concentration as he always did. But I never noticed that he was really staring at nothing in particular - that he was more or less gawking with bottomless eyes. And though the sun was shining on my mother's smooth face, her big eyes weren't squinting. Furthermore, they didn't look right or left, up or down. They were just big eyes like a big doll would have. The longer I sat with my parents eating hamburgers, hot dogs, and potato salad with no egg whites, because from the first time I ate potato salad with egg whites I refused to eat it again that way, the more I tingled inside. My parents did what they had to do in order to be real parents to me. But we weren't biologically related, as I'm sure it says in your file on me. I was adopted as an infant, and now I knew that I was only a prop, something to aid them in not being found out for what they were.

Before they told me, I already knew somehow that I was adopted. And I was never happy about that. But on that Saturday as I sat eating dinner with my parents around a plastic table, I praised whatever there was to praise that I was adopted, or else I would have been a halfer, too, if in fact that's the way it works. Nevertheless, I was pleased not to be their real offspring. I couldn't be sure, of course, if reals could give birth to halfers or the other way around, since I didn't know how the spectral link between the small people and the real people worked. My friend was taken from me before I could learn more about that, and maybe about other things. I hated that—I hated it with all my being. And what happened, as I mentioned, was that all my hate for the small people transferred to the half-smalls. Now I wondered if the reason for that transference wasn't due to my subliminal recognition of having parents who belonged to that weird species.

Retrospectively, it made all the sense in this clockwork world that my father and mother were halfers—the way they reproached me so often about being a shameful little bigot when in truth I was not a bigot but a real person who was afraid of the small people and couldn't accept the arrangement the big world had with them. Maybe real parents would have understood that, I don't know. I wanted to think so. I wanted to think that there was something sensible, or at least something of marginal value about the tick-tock world I had been born into. But the two halfers sitting with me at that plastic table only berated me as a shameless little bigot, certainly because they wanted to stifle my sensitivity to how things were in the world at its deepest level and to muddle my brain as I came of age, going through all the adjustments in the process so that that I could be presented in company— that is, so that I would be a sightless moron like everyone else, everyone except people like the only friend I ever had in my life. In a split-second, as I sat munching my hamburger or hot dog and watching my mother and father that day, I was hopelessly possessed by hatred for them.

That night I lay awake in my bed for a long time, earnestly trying to arrive at some way to live with the household status quo, just as real humans had arranged at some time in the past to live with the small people, though no book I could find would pinpoint when that was or how it was done. But there was no way I could do that—no way at all. It must have been around the middle of the night—I didn't plan a specific time—that I entered mother and father's bedroom. They were lying on their backs in bed, the moonlight glowing on my father's slightly smiling face and concentrating stare as well as on my mother's smooth face and big eyes, which were open. Both their eyes were open. I don't know why. Maybe they didn't sleep. It wasn't as if I was the sort of person to peek into his parents' bedroom to see what they were doing.

"Dad, Mom," I said, just to get their attention. They didn't even sit up in bed, though. Maybe they were sleeping, in their own way. "Listen," I continued. "I want to tell you something. What I want to tell you is..." Then, with all the lung power I could summon, I screamed: "I'm a shameful little bigot. I hate the small people. I hate them for all I'm worth. But more than I hate the small people, I hate you."

Then I jumped on the bed and was all over them with the knives I'd gotten from the kitchen. *Push, push, push. Chop, chop, chop.* They didn't make a sound the whole time. I can tell you one thing—halfers aren't soft like the smalls. I really had to work on those things that called themselves my parents.

I wasn't exactly amazed that I never saw the inside of a courtroom, knowing as I did what I knew. I didn't know, however, what would ensue in the aftermath of my deed—that I would be locked up in this place. Whatever it is, it isn't a prison, not with the superlative educational facilities you've provided, allowing my mind and sensibility to flourish. If our positions were reversed, that would be my scheme—cultivate me like a plant, breed me into something that could express its view of the world at its deepest level. You were ready for me from the very first, so I have to assume I'm not the only one to do what I did, and for the reason I did it. That's right, isn't it, Doctor? But I've been here so long. How many more doctors must I see who want to hear my story? Are you in training or something? I'm as sane as your shoes, we both know that, even though I should have gone mad long ago from my dreams alone. Why can't we make a deal, come to an arrangement? I'm practically an old man. My coming of age came and went. I'd kill myself if I thought you'd let me. That's not what you want, though, is it? Could you please give me an answer just once?

Everything is such a mystery with you people—halfers I used to think, but I don't know anymore. I lost my instinct for that the moment I stepped into this place. Did you do that? And what about the tingling? That hasn't happened in who knows how long. It would be nice to see a clock or a calendar every so often. Don't you care about time, whatever you are? How about space, existence, all the commotion of reality? I've known it was all just a preposterous mess for ages now. I also learned that I should be on the outside, and the rest of this ludicrous world, or most of it, should be in here for study and rehabilitation, adjustment and readjustment, if that's the point. What are you trying to accomplish? Whatever it is, you seem to be doing a terrible job of it. Is everything still as crummy as I remember it? Your world, whichever one it may have been, was an offense to my eyes. And it didn't have to be that way. But maybe that's the way you wanted it—a nightmare from morning stool to bedtime stories.

Oh, here they come—the big boys. You can tell them to take their hands off me. Big boys with big hands. But are they really big, or only half big? I believe an autopsy could establish the facts, if you'd allow me the pleasure. My parents were half-smalls. The alignment of their bones was human enough, but their organs seemed all of a piece. It could have been they were starting to convert, I don't know. So what's inside of the small people, Doctor? My guess is that they're composed of some doughy substance inside and out—a flabby clay that can be molded into any form, having no identity of its own. Is this really our world, the real world, or is it theirs? Did the right hand of evolution know what the left hand was doing? And what about the spectral link? I have my theories. I've had lots of time to think about that, for what it's worth—thinking. Give me a hint, something to mull over. I just need a speck of hope to keep me from going to pieces—a little truth to hang onto. Answer me, Doctor, before I'm dragged off. Who are you? What are you? Answer me. For the love of all that is real—Who am I? What am I?

The Shrine of Death
Lady Dilke

Ah! Life has many secrets!—These were the first words that fell on the ears of a little girl baby, whose mother had just been brought to bed. As she grew up she pondered their meaning, and, before all things, she desired to know the secrets of life. Thus, longing and brooding, she grew apart from other children, and her dreams were ever of how the secrets of life should be revealed to her.

Now, when she was about fifteen years of age, a famous witch passed through the town in which she dwelt, and the child heard much talk of her, and people said that her knowledge of all things was great, and that even as the past lay open before her, so there was nothing in the future that could be hidden from her. Then the child thought to herself, "This woman, if by any means I get speech of her, can, if she will, tell me all the secrets of life."

Nor was it long after, that walking late in the evening with other and lesser children, along the ramparts on the east side of the town, she came to a corner of the wall which lay in deep shadow, and out of the shadow there sprang a large black dog, baying loudly, and the children were terrified, and fled, crying out, "It is the witch's dog!" and one, the least of all, fell in its terror, so the elder one tarried, and lifted it from the ground, and, as she comforted it—for it was shaken by its fall, and the dog continued baying—the witch herself came out of the shadow, and said, "Off with you, you little fools, and break my peace no more with your folly." And the little one ran for fear, but the elder girl stood still, and laying hold of the witch's mantle, she said, "Before I go, tell me, what are the secrets of life?" And the witch answered, "Marry Death, fair child, and you will know."

At the first, the saying of the witch fell like a stone in the girl's heart, but ere long her words, and the words which she had heard in the hour of her birth, filled all her thoughts, and when other girls jested or spoke of feasts and merriment, of happy love and all the joys of life, such talk seemed to her mere wind of idle tales, and the gossips who would have made a match for her schemed in vain, for she had but one desire, the desire to woo Death, and learn the secrets of life. Often now she would seek the ramparts in late evening, hoping that in the shadows she might once more find the witch, and learn from her the way to her desire; but she found her not.

Returning in the darkness, it so happened, after one of these fruitless journeys, that she passed under the walls of an ancient church, and looking up at the windows, she saw the flickering of a low, unsteady light upon the coloured panes, and she drew near to the door, and, seeing it ajar, she pushed it open and entered, and passing between the mighty columns of the nave, she stepped aside to the spot whence the light proceeded. Having done so, she found herself standing in front of a great tomb, in one side of which were brazen gates, and beyond the gates a long flight of marble steps leading down to a vast hall or chapel below; and about the gates in a silver lamp, a light was burning, and as the chains by which the lamp was suspended moved slightly in the draught from the open door of the church, the light which burnt in it flickered, and all the shadows around shifted so that nothing seemed still, and this constant recurrence of change was like the dance of phantoms in the air. And the girl, seeing the blackness, thought of the corner on the ramparts where she had met the witch, and almost she expected to see her, and to hear her dog baying in the shadows.

When she drew nearer, she found that the walls were loaded with sculpture, and the niches along the sides were filled with statues of the wise men of all time; but at the corners were four women whose heads were bowed, and whose hands were bound in chains. Then, looking at them as they sat thus, discrowned but majestic, the soul of the girl was filled with sorrow, and she fell weeping, and, clasping her hands in her grief, she cast her eyes to heaven. As she did so, the lamp swayed a little forwards, and its rays touched with light a figure seated on the top of the monument. When the girl caught sight of this figure she ceased weeping, and when she had withdrawn a step or two backwards, so as to get a fuller view, she fell upon her knees and a gleam of wondrous expectation shone out of her face; for, on the top of the tomb, robed and crowned, sat the image of Death, and a great gladness and awe filled her soul, for she thought, "If I may but be found worthy to enter his portals, all the secrets of life will be mine." And laying her hands on the gates, she sought to open them, but they were locked, so after a little while she went sadly away.

Each day, from this time forth, when twilight fell, the girl returned to the church, and would there remain kneeling for many hours before the shrine of Death, nor could she by any means be drawn away from her purpose. Her mind was fixed on her desire, so that she became insensible to all else; and the whole town mocked her, and her own people held her for mad. So then, at last, they took her before a priest, and the priest, when he had talked with her awhile, said, "Let her have her way. Let her pass a night within the shrine; on the morrow it may be that her wits will have returned to her."

So a day was set, and they robed her in white as a bride, and in great state, with youths bearing torches, and many maidens, whose hands were full of flowers, she was brought through the city at nightfall to the church; and the gates of the shrine were opened, and as she passed within, the youths put out their torches and the maidens threw their roses on the steps beneath her feet.

When the gates closed upon her, she stood still awhile upon the uppersteps, and so she waited until the last footfall had ceased to echo in the church, and she knew herself to be alone in the long desired presence. Then, full of reverent longing and awe, she drew her veil about her, and as she did so, she found a red rose that had caught in it, and, striving to dislodge it, she brought it close to her face, and its perfume was very strong, and she saw, as in a vision, the rose garden of her mother's house, and the face of one who had wooed her there in the sun; but, even as she stood irresolute, the baying of a hound in the distant street fell on her ears, and she remembered the words of the witch, "Marry Death, fair child, if you would know the secrets of life," and casting the rose from her, she began to descend the steps.

As she went down, she heard, as it were, the light pattering of feet behind her; but turning, when she came to the foot, to look, she found that this sounds was only the echoing fall from step to step of the flowers which her long robes had drawn after her, and she heeded them not, for she was now within the shrine, and looking to the right hand and to the left, she saw long rows of tombs, each one hewn in marble and covered with sculpture of wondrous beauty.

All this, though, she saw dimly; the plainest thing to view was the long black shadow of her own form, cast before her by the light from the lamp above, and as she looked beyond the uttermost rim of shadow, she became aware of an awful shape seated at a marble table whereon lay an open book. Looking on this dread shape, she trembled, for she knew that she was in the presence of Death. Then, seeing the book, her heart was uplifted within her, and stepping boldly forwards, she seated herself before it, and as she did so, it seemed to her that she heard a shiver from within the tombs.

Now, when she came near, Death had raised his finger, and he pointed to the writing on the open page, but, as she put her hands upon the book, the blood rushed back to her heart, for it was ice-cold, and again it seemed to her that something moved within the tombs. It was but for a minute, then her courage returned, and she fixed her eyes eagerly upon the lines before her and began to read, but the very letters were at first strange to her, and even when she knew them she could by no means frame them into words, or make any sentence out of them, so that, at the last, she looked up in her wonderment to seek aid. But he, the terrible one, before whom she sat, again lifted his finger, and as he pointed to the page, a weight as of lead forced down her eyes upon the book; and now the letters shifted strangely, and when she thought to have seized a word or a phrase it would suddenly be gone, for if the text shone out plain for an instant, the strange shadows, moving with the movements of the silver lamp, would blot it again as quickly from sight.

At this, distraction filled her mind, and she heard her own breathing like sobs in the darkness, and fear choked her; for ever, when she would have appealed for help, her eyes saw the same deadly menace, the same uplifted and threatening finger. Then, glancing to left and right, a new horror took possession of her, for the lids of the tombs were yawning wide, and whenever her thoughts turned to flight, their awful tenants peered at her from above the edges, and they made as though they would have stayed her.

Thus she sat till it was long past midnight, and her heart was sick within her, when again the distant baying of a hound reached her ears; but this sound, instead of giving her fresh courage, seemed to her but a bitter mockery, for she thought, "What shall the secrets of life profit me, if I must make my bed with Death?" And she became mad with anger, and she cursed the counsels of the witch, and in her desperation, like a creature caught in the toils, she sprang from her seat and made towards the steps by which she had come. Ere she could reach them, all the dreadful dwellers in the tombs were before her, and she, seeing the way to life was barred for ever, fell to the ground at their feet and gave up her spirit in a great agony. Then each terrible one returned to his place, and the book which lay open before Death closed with a noise as of thunder, and the light which burnt before his shrine went out, so that all was darkness.

In the morning, when that company which had brought her came back to the church, they wondered much to see the lamp extinguished, and fetching a taper, some went down fearfully into the vault. There all was as it had ever been, only the girl lay face downwards amongst the withered roses, and when they lifted her up they saw that she was dead; but her eyes were wide with horror. And so another tomb was hewn in marble, and she was laid with the rest, and when men tell the tale of her strange bridal they say, "She had but the reward of her folly. God rest her soul!"

The Inmost Light
Arthur Machen

I

One evening in autumn, when the deformities of London were
veiled in faint blue mist, and its vistas and far-reaching streets
seemed splendid, Mr Charles Salisbury was slowly pacing down
Rupert Street, drawing nearer to his favourite restaurant by slow
degrees. His eyes were downcast in study of the pavement, and
thus it was that as he passed in at the narrow door a man who had
come up from the lower end of the street jostled against him.

"I beg your pardon—wasn't looking where I was going. Why,
it's Dyson!"

"Yes, quite so. How are you, Salisbury?"

"Quite well. But where have you been, Dyson? I don't think I
can have seen you for the last five years?"

"No; I dare say not. You remember I was getting rather hard up
when you came to my place at Charlotte Street?"

"Perfectly. I think I remember your telling me that you owed
five weeks' rent, and that you had parted with your watch for a
comparatively small sum."

"My dear Salisbury, your memory is admirable. Yes, I was
hard up. But the curious thing is that soon after you saw me I
became harder up. My financial state was described by a friend as

'stone broke'. I don't approve of slang, mind you, but such was my condition. But suppose we go in; there might be other people who would like to dine—it's a human weakness, Salisbury."

"Certainly; come along. I was wondering as I walked down whether the corner table were taken. It has a velvet back you know."

"I know the spot; it's vacant. Yes, as I was saying, I became even harder up."

"What did you do then?" asked Salisbury, disposing of his hat, and settling down in the corner of the seat, with a glance of fond anticipation at the menu.

"What did I do? Why, I sat down and reflected. I had a good classical education, and a positive distaste for business of any kind: that was the capital with which I faced the world. Do you know, I have heard people describe olives as nasty! What lamentable Philistinism! I have often thought, Salisbury, that I could write genuine poetry under the influence of olives and red wine. Let us have Chianti; it may not be very good, but the flasks are simply charming."

"It is pretty good here. We may as well have a big flask."

"Very good. I reflected, then, on my want of prospects, and I determined to embark in literature."

"Really; that was strange. You seem in pretty comfortable circumstances, though."

"Though! What a satire upon a noble profession. I am afraid, Salisbury, you haven't a proper idea of the dignity of an artist. You see me sitting at my desk—or at least you can see me if you care to call—with pen and ink, and simple nothingness before me, and if you come again in a few hours you will (in all probability) find a creation!"

"Yes, quite so. I had an idea that literature was not remunerative."

"You are mistaken; its rewards are great. I may mention, by the way, that shortly after you saw me I succeeded to a small income. An uncle died, and proved unexpectedly generous."

"Ah, I see. That must have been convenient."

"It was pleasant—undeniably pleasant. I have always considered it in the light of an endowment of my researches. I told you I was a man of letters; it would, perhaps, be more correct to describe myself as a man of science."

"Dear me, Dyson, you have really changed very much in the last few years. I had a notion, don't you know, that you were a sort of idler about town, the kind of man one might meet on the north side of Piccadilly every day from May to July."

"Exactly. I was even then forming myself, though all unconsciously. You know my poor father could not afford to send me to the University. I used to grumble in my ignorance at not having completed my education. That was the folly of youth, Salisbury; my University was Piccadilly. There I began to study the great science which still occupies me."

"What science do you mean?"

"The science of the great city; the physiology of London; literally and metaphysically the greatest subject that the mind of man can conceive. What an admirable salmi this is; undoubtedly the final end of the pheasant. Yet I feel sometimes positively overwhelmed with the thought of the vastness and complexity of London. Paris a man may get to understand thoroughly with a reasonable amount of study; but London is always a mystery. In Paris you may say: 'Here live the actresses, here the Bohemians, and the Ratés'; but it is different in London. You may point out a street, correctly enough, as the abode of washerwomen; but, in that second floor, a man may be studying Chaldee roots, and in the garret over the way a forgotten artist is dying by inches."

"I see you are Dyson, unchanged and unchangeable," said Salisbury, slowly sipping his Chianti. "I think you are misled by a too fervid imagination; the mystery of London exists only in your fancy. It seems to me a dull place enough. We seldom hear of a really artistic crime in London, whereas I believe Paris abounds in that sort of thing."

"Give me some more wine. Thanks. You are mistaken, my dear fellow, you are really mistaken. London has nothing to be ashamed of in the way of crime. Where we fail is for want of Homers, not Agamemnons. *Carent quia vate sacro*, you know."

"I recall the quotation. But I don't think I quite follow you."

"Well, in plain language, we have no good writers in London who make a speciality of that kind of thing. Our common reporter is a dull dog; every story that he has to tell is spoilt in the telling. His idea of horror and of what excites horror is so lamentably deficient. Nothing will content the fellow but blood, vulgar red blood, and when he can get it he lays it on thick, and considers that he has produced a telling article. It's a poor notion. And, by some curious fatality, it is the most commonplace and brutal murders which always attract the most attention and get written up the most. For instance, I dare say that you never heard of the Harlesden case?"

"No; no, I don't remember anything about it."

"Of course not. And yet the story is a curious one. I will tell it you over our coffee. Harlesden, you know, or I expect you don't know, is quite on the out-quarters of London; something curiously different from your fine old crusted suburb like Norwood or Hampstead, different as each of these is from the other. Hampstead, I mean, is where you look for the head of your great China house with his three acres of land and pine-houses, though of late there is the artistic substratum; while Norwood is the home of the prosperous middle-class family who took the house 'because it was near the Palace', and sickened of the Palace six months afterwards; but Harlesden is a place of no character. It's too new to have any character as yet. There are the rows of red houses and the rows of white houses and the bright green Venetians, and the blistering doorways, and the little backyards they call gardens, and a few feeble shops, and then, just as you think you're going to grasp the physiognomy of the settlement, it all melts away."

"How the dickens is that? The houses don't tumble down before one's eyes, I suppose!"

"Well, no, not exactly that. But Harlesden as an entity disappears. Your street turns into a quiet lane, and your staring houses into elm trees, and the back-gardens into green meadows. You pass instantly from town to country; there is no transition as in a small country town, no soft gradations of wider lawns and orchards, with houses gradually becoming less dense, but a dead stop. I believe the people who live there mostly go into the City. I have seen once or twice a laden 'bus bound thitherwards. But however that may be, I can't conceive a greater loneliness in a desert at midnight than there is there at midday. It is like a city of the dead; the streets are glaring and desolate, and as you pass it suddenly strikes you that this too is part of London. Well, a year or two ago there was a doctor living there; he had set up his brass plate and his red lamp at the very end of one of those shining streets, and from the back of the house, the fields stretched away to the north. I don't know what his reason was in settling down in such an out-of-the-way place, perhaps Dr Black, as we will call him, was a far-seeing man and looked ahead. His relations, so it appeared afterwards, had lost sight of him for many years and didn't even know he was a doctor, much less where he lived.

"However, there he was settled in Harlesden, with some fragments of a practice, and an uncommonly pretty wife. People used to see them walking out together in the summer evenings soon after they came to Harlesden, and, so far as could be observed, they seemed a very affectionate couple. These walks went on through the autumn, and then ceased; but, of course, as the days grew dark and the weather cold, the lanes near Harlesden might be expected to lose many of their attractions. All through the winter nobody saw anything of Mrs Black, the doctor used to reply to his patients' inquiries that she was a 'little out of sorts, would be better, no doubt, in the spring'. But the spring came, and the summer, and no Mrs Black appeared, and at last people began to rumour and talk amongst themselves, and all sorts of queer things were said at 'high teas', which you may possibly have heard are the only form of entertainment known in such suburbs. Dr Black began to surprise some very odd looks cast in his direction, and the practice, such as it was, fell off before his eyes. In short, when the neighbours whispered about the matter, they whispered that Mrs Black was dead, and that the doctor had made away with her. But this wasn't the case; Mrs Black was seen alive in June. It was a Sunday afternoon, one of those few exquisite days that an English climate offers, and half London had strayed out into the fields, north, south, east, and west to smell the scent of the white May, and to see if the wild roses were yet in blossom in the hedges. I had gone out myself early in the morning, and had had a long ramble, and somehow or other as I was steering homeward I found myself in this very Harlesden we have been talking about. To be exact, I had a glass of beer in the 'General Gordon', the most flourishing house in the neighbourhood, and as I was wandering rather aimlessly about, I saw an uncommonly tempting gap in a hedgerow, and resolved to explore the meadow beyond. Soft grass is very grateful to the feet after the infernal grit strewn on suburban sidewalks, and after walking about for some time I thought I should like to sit down on a bank and have a smoke. While I was getting out my pouch, I looked up in the direction of the houses, and as I looked I felt my breath caught back, and my teeth began to chatter, and the stick I had in one hand snapped in two with the grip I gave it. It was as if I had had an electric current down my spine, and yet for some moment of time which seemed long, but which must have been very short, I caught myself wondering what on earth was the matter. Then I knew what had made my very heart shudder and my bones grind together in an agony. As I glanced up I had looked straight towards the last house in the row before me, and in an upper window of that house I had seen for some short fraction of a second a face. It was the face of a woman, and yet it was not human. You and I, Salisbury, have heard in our time, as we sat in our seats in church in sober English fashion, of a lust that cannot be satiated and of a fire that is unquenchable, but few of us have any notion what these words mean. I hope you never may, for as I saw that face at the window, with the blue sky above me and the warm air playing in gusts about me, I knew I had looked into another world—looked through the window of a commonplace, brand-new house, and seen hell open before me. When the first shock was over, I thought once or twice that I should have fainted; my face streamed with a cold sweat, and my breath came and went in sobs, as if I had been half drowned. I managed to get up at last, and walked round to the street, and there I saw the name 'Dr Black' on the post by the front gate. As fate or my luck would have it, the door opened and a man came down the steps as I passed by. I had no doubt it was the doctor himself. He was of a type rather common in London; long and thin, with a pasty face and a dull black moustache. He gave me a look as we passed each other on the pavement, and though it was merely the casual glance which one foot-passenger bestows on another, I felt convinced in my mind that here was an ugly customer to deal with. As you may imagine, I went my way a good deal puzzled and horrified too by what I had seen; for I had paid another visit to the 'General Gordon', and had got together a good deal of the common gossip of the place about the Blacks. I didn't mention the fact that I had seen a woman's face in the window; but I heard that Mrs Black had been much admired for her beautiful golden hair, and round what had struck me with such a nameless terror, there was a mist of flowing yellow hair, as it were an aureole of glory round the visage of a satyr. The whole thing bothered me in an indescribable manner; and when I got home I tried my best to think of the impression I had received as an illusion, but it was no use. I knew very well I had seen what I have tried to describe to you, and I was morally certain that I had seen Mrs Black. And then there was the gossip of the place, the suspicion of foul play, which I knew to be false, and my own conviction that there was some deadly mischief or other going on in that bright red house at the corner of Devon Road: how to construct a theory of a reasonable kind out of these two elements. In short, I found myself in a world of mystery; I puzzled my head over it and filled up my leisure moments by gathering together odd threads of speculation, but I never moved a step towards any real solution, and as the summer days went on the matter seemed to grow misty and indistinct, shadowing some vague terror, like a nightmare of last month. I suppose it would before long have faded into the background of my brain—I should not have forgotten it, for such a thing could never be forgotten—but one morning as I was looking over the paper my eye was caught by a heading over some two dozen lines of small type. The words I had seen were simply, 'The Harlesden Case', and I knew what I was going to read. Mrs Black was dead. Black had called in another medical man to certify as to cause of death, and something or other had aroused the strange doctor's suspicions and there had been an inquest and post-mortem. And the result? That, I will confess, did astonish me considerably; it was the triumph of the unexpected. The two doctors who made the autopsy were obliged to confess that they could not discover the faintest trace of any kind of foul play; their most exquisite tests and reagents failed to detect the presence of poison in the most infinitesimal quantity. Death, they found, had been caused by a somewhat obscure and scientifically interesting form of brain disease. The tissue of the brain and the molecules of the grey matter had undergone a most extraordinary series of changes; and the younger of the two doctors, who has some reputation, I believe, as a specialist in brain trouble, made some remarks in giving his evidence which struck me deeply at the time, though I did not then grasp their full significance. He said: 'At the commencement of the examination I was astonished to find appearances of a character entirely new to me, notwithstanding my somewhat large experience. I need not specify these appearances at present, it will be sufficient for me to state that as I proceeded in my task I could scarcely believe that the brain before me was that of a human being at all.' There was some surprise at this statement, as you may imagine, and the coroner asked the doctor if he meant to say that the brain resembled that of an animal. 'No,' he replied, 'I should not put it in that way. Some of the appearances I noticed seemed to point in that direction, but others, and these were the more surprising, indicated a nervous organisation of a wholly different character from that either of man or the lower animals.' It was a curious thing to say, but of course the jury brought in a verdict of death from natural causes, and, so far as the public was concerned, the case came to an end. But after I had read what the doctor said I made up my mind that I should like to know a good deal more, and I set to work on what seemed likely to prove an interesting investigation. I had really a good deal of trouble, but I was successful in a measure. Though why—my dear fellow, I had no notion at the time. Are you aware that we have been here nearly four hours? The waiters are staring at us. Let's have the bill and be gone."

The two men went out in silence, and stood a moment in the cool air, watching the hurrying traffic of Coventry Street pass before them to the accompaniment of the ringing bells of hansoms and the cries of the newsboys; the deep far murmur of London surging up ever and again from beneath these louder noises.

"It is a strange case, isn't it?" said Dyson at length. "What do you think of it?"

"My dear fellow, I haven't heard the end, so I will reserve my opinion. When will you give me the sequel?"

"Come to my rooms some evening; say next Thursday. Here's the address. Goodnight; I want to get down to the Strand." Dyson hailed a passing hansom, and Salisbury turned northward to walk home to his lodgings.

II

Mr Salisbury, as may have been gathered from the few remarks which he had found it possible to introduce in the course of the evening, was a young gentleman of a peculiarly solid form of intellect, coy and retiring before the mysterious and the uncommon, with a constitutional dislike of paradox. During the restaurant dinner he had been forced to listen in almost absolute silence to a strange tissue of improbabilities strung together with the ingenuity of a born meddler in plots and mysteries, and it was with a feeling of weariness that he crossed Shaftesbury Avenue, and dived into the recesses of Soho, for his lodgings were in a modest neighbourhood to the north of Oxford Street. As he walked he speculated on the probable fate of Dyson, relying on literature, unbefriended by a thoughtful relative, and could not help concluding that so much subtlety united to a too vivid imagination would in all likelihood have been rewarded with a pair of sandwich-boards or a super's banner.

Absorbed in this train of thought, and admiring the perverse dexterity which could transmute the face of a sickly woman and a case of brain disease into the crude elements of romance, Salisbury strayed on through the dimly lighted streets, not noticing the gusty wind which drove sharply round corners and whirled the stray rubbish of the pavement into the air in eddies, while black clouds gathered over the sickly yellow moon. Even a stray drop or two of rain blown into his face did not rouse him from his meditations, and it was only when with a sudden rush the storm tore down upon the street that he began to consider the expediency of finding some shelter. The rain, driven by the wind, pelted down with the violence of a thunderstorm, dashing up from the stones and hissing through the air, and soon a perfect torrent of water coursed along the kennels and accumulated in pools over the choked-up drains. The few stray passengers who had been loafing rather than walking about the street had scuttered away, like frightened rabbits, to some invisible places of refuge, and though Salisbury whistled loud and long for a hansom, no hansom appeared. He looked about him, as if to discover how far he might be from the haven of Oxford Street, but strolling carelessly along, he had turned out of his way, and found himself in an unknown region, and one to all appearance devoid even of a public-house where shelter could be bought for the modest sum of twopence. The street lamps were few and at long intervals, and burned behind grimy glasses with the sickly light of oil, and by this wavering glimmer Salisbury could make out the shadowy and vast old houses of which the street was composed. As he passed along, hurrying, and shrinking from the full sweep of the rain, he noticed the innumerable bell-handles, with names that seemed about to vanish of old age graven on brass plates beneath them, and here and there a richly carved penthouse overhung the door, blackening with the grime of fifty years. The storm seemed to grow more and more furious; he was wet through, and a new hat had become a ruin, and still Oxford Street seemed as far off as ever; it was with deep relief that the dripping man caught sight of a dark archway which seemed to promise shelter from the rain if not from the wind. Salisbury took up his position in the driest corner and looked about him; he was standing in a kind of passage contrived under part of a house, and behind him stretched a narrow footway leading between blank walls to regions unknown. He had stood there for some time, vainly endeavouring to rid himself of some of his superfluous moisture, and listening for the passing wheel of a hansom, when his attention was aroused by a loud noise coming from the direction of the passage behind, and growing louder as it drew nearer. In a couple of minutes he could make out the shrill, raucous voice of a woman, threatening and renouncing and making the very stones echo with her accents, while now and then a man grumbled and expostulated. Though to all appearance devoid of romance, Salisbury had some relish for street rows, and was, indeed, somewhat of an amateur in the more amusing phases of drunkenness; he therefore composed himself to listen and observe with something of the air of a subscriber to grand opera. To his annoyance, however, the tempest seemed suddenly to be composed, and he could hear nothing but the impatient steps of the woman and the slow lurch of the man as they came towards him. Keeping back in the shadow of the wall, he could see the two drawing nearer; the man was evidently drunk, and had much ado to avoid frequent collision with the wall as he tacked across from one side to the other, like some bark beating up against a wind. The woman was looking straight in front of her, with tears streaming from her eyes, but suddenly as they went by the flame blazed up again, and she burst forth into a torrent of abuse, facing round upon her companion.

"You low rascal, you mean, contemptible cur," she went on, after an incoherent storm of curses, "you think I'm to work and slave for you always, I suppose, while you're after that Green Street girl and drinking every penny you've got? But you're mistaken, Sam—indeed, I'll bear it no longer. Damn you, you dirty thief, I've done with you and your master too, so you can go your own errands, and I only hope they'll get you into trouble."

The woman tore at the bosom of her dress, and taking something out that looked like paper, crumpled it up and flung it away. It fell at Salisbury's feet. She ran out and disappeared in the darkness, while the man lurched slowly into the street, grumbling indistinctly to himself in a perplexed tone of voice. Salisbury looked out after him, and saw him maundering along the pavement, halting now and then and swaying indecisively, and then starting off at some fresh tangent. The sky had cleared, and white fleecy clouds were fleeting across the moon, high in the heaven. The light came and went by turns, as the clouds passed by, and, turning round as the clear, white rays shone into the passage, Salisbury saw the little ball of crumpled paper which the woman had cast down. Oddly curious to know what it might contain, he picked it up and put it in his pocket, and set out afresh on his journey.

III

Salisbury was a man of habit. When he got home, drenched to the skin, his clothes hanging lank about him, and a ghastly dew besmearing his hat, his only thought was of his health, of which he took studious care. So, after changing his clothes and encasing himself in a warm dressing-gown, he proceeded to prepare a sudorific in the shape of hot gin and water, warming the latter over one of those spirit-lamps which mitigate the austerities of the modern hermit's life. By the time this preparation had been exhibited, and Salisbury's disturbed feelings had been soothed by a pipe of tobacco, he was able to get into bed in a happy state of vacancy, without a thought of his adventure in the dark archway, or of the weird fancies with which Dyson had seasoned his dinner.

It was the same at breakfast the next morning, for Salisbury made a point of not thinking of anything until that meal was over; but when the cup and saucer were cleared away, and the morning pipe was lit, he remembered the little ball of paper, and began fumbling in the pockets of his wet coat. He did not remember into which pocket he had put it, and as he dived now into one and now into another, he experienced a strange feeling of apprehension lest it should not be there at all, though he could not for the life of him have explained the importance he attached to what was in all probability mere rubbish. But he sighed with relief when his fingers touched the crumpled surface in an inside pocket, and he drew it out gently and laid it on the little desk by his easy-chair with as much care as if it had been some rare jewel. Salisbury sat smoking and staring at his find for a few minutes, an odd temptation to throw the thing in the fire and have done with it struggling with as odd a speculation as to its possible contents, and as to the reason why the infuriated woman should have flung a bit of paper from her with such vehemence.

As might be expected, it was the latter feeling that conquered in the end, and yet it was with something like repugnance that he at last took the paper and unrolled it, and laid it out before him. It was a piece of common dirty paper, to all appearance torn out of a cheap exercise book, and in the middle were a few lines written in a queer cramped hand. Salisbury bent his head and stared eagerly at it for a moment, drawing a long breath, and then fell back in his chair gazing blankly before him, till at last with a sudden revulsion he burst into a peal of laughter, so long and loud and uproarious that the landlady's baby in the floor below awoke from sleep and echoed his mirth with hideous yells. But he laughed again and again, and took the paper up to read a second time what seemed such meaningless nonsense.

"Q. has had to go and see his friends in Paris," it began. "Traverse Handel S. 'Once around the grass, and twice around the lass, and thrice around the maple-tree.'"

Salisbury took up the paper and crumpled it as the angry woman had done, and aimed it at the fire. He did not throw it there, however, but tossed it carelessly into the well of the desk, and laughed again. The sheer folly of the thing offended him, and he was ashamed of his own eager speculation, as one who pores over the high-sounding announcements in the agony column of the daily paper, and finds nothing but advertisement and triviality.

He walked to the window, and stared out at the languid morning life of his quarter; the maids in slatternly print dresses washing door-steps, the fish-monger and the butcher on their rounds, and the tradesmen standing at the doors of their small shops, drooping for lack of trade and excitement. In the distance a blue haze gave some grandeur to the prospect, but the view as a whole was depressing, and would only have interested a student of the life of London, who finds something rare and choice in its every aspect. Salisbury turned away in disgust, and settled himself in the easy-chair, upholstered in a bright shade of green, and decked with yellow gimp, which was the pride and attraction of the apartments.

Here he composed himself to his morning's occupation—the perusal of a novel that dealt with sport and love in a manner that suggested the collaboration of a stud-groom and a ladies' college. In an ordinary way, however, Salisbury would have been carried on by the interest of the story up to lunch-time, but this morning he fidgeted in and out of his chair, took the book up and laid it down again, and swore at last to himself and at himself in mere irritation.

In point of fact the jingle of the paper found in the archway had "got into his head", and do what he would he could not help muttering over and over, "Once around the grass, and twice around the lass, and thrice around the maple-tree." It became a positive pain, like the foolish burden of a music-hall song, everlastingly quoted, and sung at all hours of the day and night, and treasured by the street boys as an unfailing resource for six months together. He went out into the streets, and tried to forget his enemy in the jostling of the crowds and the roar and clatter of the traffic, but presently he would find himself stealing quietly aside, and pacing some deserted byway, vainly puzzling his brains, and trying to fix some meaning to phrases that were meaningless. It was a positive relief when Thursday came, and he remembered that he had made an appointment to go and see Dyson; the flimsy reveries of the self-styled man of letters appeared entertaining when compared with this ceaseless iteration, this maze of thought from which there seemed no possibility of escape. Dyson's abode was in one of the quietest of the quiet streets that lead down from the Strand to the river, and when Salisbury passed from the narrow stairway into his friend's room, he saw that the uncle had been beneficent indeed.

The floor glowed and flamed with all the colours of the East; it was, as Dyson pompously remarked, "a sunset in a dream", and the lamplight, the twilight of London streets, was shut out with strangely worked curtains, glittering here and there with threads of gold. In the shelves of an oak armoire stood jars and plates of old French china, and the black and white of etchings not to be found in the Haymarket or in Bond Street, stood out against the splendour of a Japanese paper. Salisbury sat down on the settle by the hearth, and sniffed the mingled fumes of incense and tobacco, wondering and dumb before all this splendour after the green rep and the oleographs, the gilt-framed mirror, and the lustres of his own apartment.

"I am glad you have come," said Dyson. "Comfortable little room, isn't it? But you don't look very well, Salisbury. Nothing disagreed with you, has it?"

"No; but I have been a good deal bothered for the last few days. The fact is I had an odd kind of—of—adventure, I suppose I may call it, that night I saw you, and it has worried me a good deal. And the provoking part of it is that it's the merest nonsense—but, however, I will tell you all about it, by and by. You were going to let me have the rest of that odd story you began at the restaurant."

"Yes. But I am afraid, Salisbury, you are incorrigible. You are a slave to what you call matter of fact. You know perfectly well that in your heart you think the oddness in that case is of my making, and that it is all really as plain as the police reports. However, as I have begun, I will go on. But first we will have something to drink, and you may as well light your pipe."

Dyson went up to the oak cupboard, and drew from its depths a rotund bottle and two little glasses, quaintly gilded.

"It's Benedictine," he said. "You'll have some, won't you?"

Salisbury assented, and the two men sat sipping and smoking reflectively for some minutes before Dyson began.

"Let me see," he said at last, "we were at the inquest, weren't we? No, we had done with that. Ah, I remember. I was telling you that on the whole I had been successful in my inquiries, investigation, or whatever you like to call it, into the matter. Wasn't that where I left off?"

"Yes, that was it. To be precise, I think 'though' was the last word you said on the matter."

"Exactly. I have been thinking it all over since the other night, and I have come to the conclusion that that 'though' is a very big 'though' indeed. Not to put too fine a point on it, I have had to confess that what I found out, or thought I found out, amounts in reality to nothing. I am as far away from the heart of the case as ever. However, I may as well tell you what I do know. You may remember my saying that I was impressed a good deal by some remarks of one of the doctors who gave evidence at the inquest.

"Well, I determined that my first step must be to try if I could get something more definite and intelligible out of that doctor.

Somehow or other I managed to get an introduction to the man, and he gave me an appointment to come and see him. He turned out to be a pleasant, genial fellow; rather young and not in the least like the typical medical man, and he began the conference by offering me whisky and cigars. I didn't think it worth while to beat about the bush, so I began by saying that part of his evidence at the Harlesden Inquest struck me as very peculiar, and I gave him the printed report, with the sentences in question underlined.

"He just glanced at the slip, and gave me a queer look. 'It struck you as peculiar, did it?' said he. 'Well, you must remember that the Harlesden case was very peculiar. In fact, I think I may safely say that in some features it was unique—quite unique.' 'Quite so,' I replied, 'and that's exactly why it interests me, and why I want to know more about it. And I thought that if anybody could give me any information it would be you. What is your opinion of the matter?'

"It was a pretty downright sort of question, and my doctor looked rather taken aback.

"'Well,' he said, 'as I fancy your motive in inquiring into the question must be mere curiosity, I think I may tell you my opinion with tolerable freedom. So, Mr., Mr Dyson? if you want to know my theory, it is this: I believe that Dr Black killed his wife.'

"'But the verdict, I answered, 'the verdict was given from your own evidence.'

"'Quite so; the verdict was given in accordance with the evidence of my colleague and myself, and, under the circumstances, I think the jury acted very sensibly. In fact, I don't see what else they could have done. But I stick to my opinion, mind you, and I say this also. I don't wonder at Black's doing what I firmly believe he did. I think he was justified.'

"'Justified! How could that be?' I asked. I was astonished, as you may imagine, at the answer I had got. The doctor wheeled round his chair and looked steadily at me for a moment before he answered.

"'I suppose you are not a man of science yourself? No; then it would be of no use my going into detail. I have always been firmly opposed myself to any partnership between physiology and psychology. I believe that both are bound to suffer. No one recognises more decidedly than I do the impassable gulf, the fathomless abyss that separates the world of consciousness from the sphere of matter. We know that every change of consciousness is accompanied by a rearrangement of the molecules in the grey matter; and that is all. What the link between them is, or why they occur together, we do not know, and most authorities believe that we never can know. Yet, I will tell you that as I did my work, the knife in my hand, I felt convinced, in spite of all theories, that what lay before me was not the brain of a dead woman—not the brain of a human being at all. Of course I saw the face; but it was quite placid, devoid of all expression. It must have been a beautiful face, no doubt, but I can honestly say that I would not have looked in that face when there was life behind it for a thousand guineas, no, nor for twice that sum.'

"'My dear sir,' I said, 'you surprise me extremely. You say that it was not the brain of a human being. What was it, then?'

"'The brain of a devil.' He spoke quite coolly, and never moved a muscle. 'The brain of a devil,' he repeated, 'and I have no doubt that Black found some way of putting an end to it. I don't blame him if he did. Whatever Mrs Black was, she was not fit to stay in this world. Will you have anything more? No? Goodnight, goodnight.'

"It was a queer sort of opinion to get from a man of science, wasn't it? When he was saying that he would not have looked on that face when alive for a thousand guineas, or two thousand guineas, I was thinking of the face I had seen, but I said nothing. I went again to Harlesden, and passed from one shop to another, making small purchases, and trying to find out whether there was anything about the Blacks which was not already common property, but there was very little to hear. One of the tradesmen to whom I spoke said he had known the dead woman well; she used to buy of him such quantities of grocery as were required for their small household, for they never kept a servant, but had a charwoman in occasionally, and she had not seen Mrs Black for months before she died.

"According to this man Mrs Black was 'a nice lady', always kind and considerate, and so fond of her husband and he of her, as everyone thought. And yet, to put the doctor's opinion on one side, I knew what I had seen. And then after thinking it all over, and putting one thing with another, it seemed to me that the only person likely to give me much assistance would be Black himself, and I made up my mind to find him. Of course he wasn't to be found in Harlesden; he had left, I was told, directly after the funeral.

"Everything in the house had been sold, and one fine day Black got into the train with a small portmanteau, and went, nobody knew where. It was a chance if he were ever heard of again, and it was by a mere chance that I came across him at last. I was walking one day along Gray's Inn Road, not bound for anywhere in particular, but looking about me, as usual, and holding on to my hat, for it was a gusty day in early March, and the wind was making the tree-tops in the Inn rock and quiver. I had come up from the Holborn end, and I had almost got to Theobald's Road when I noticed a man walking in front of me, leaning on a stick, and to all appearance very feeble.

"There was something about his look that made me curious, I don't know why, and I began to walk briskly with the idea of overtaking him, when of a sudden his hat blew off and came bounding along the pavement to my feet. Of course I rescued the hat, and gave it a glance as I went towards its owner. It was a biography in itself; a Piccadilly maker's name in the inside, but I don't think a beggar would have picked it out of the gutter. Then I looked up and saw Dr Black of Harlesden waiting for me. A queer thing, wasn't it? But, Salisbury, what a change! When I saw Dr Black come down the steps of his house at Harlesden he was an upright man, walking firmly with well-built limbs; a man, I should say, in the prime of his life. And now before me there

crouched this wretched creature, bent and feeble, with shrunken
cheeks, and hair that was whitening fast, and limbs that trembled
and shook together, and misery in his eyes. He thanked me for
bringing him his hat, saying, 'I don't think I should ever have got
it, I can't run much now. A gusty day, sir, isn't it?' and with this he
was turning away, but by little and little I contrived to draw him
into the current of conversation, and we walked together eastward.
I think the man would have been glad to get rid of me; but I didn't
intend to let him go, and he stopped at last in front of a miserable
house in a miserable street. It was, I verily believe, one of the most
wretched quarters I have ever seen: houses that must have been
sordid and hideous enough when new, that had gathered foulness
with every year, and now seemed to lean and totter to their fall. 'I
live up there,' said Black, pointing to the tiles, 'not in the front—in
the back. I am very quiet there. I won't ask you to come in now, but
perhaps some other day—' I caught him up at that, and told him I
should be only too glad to come and see him. He gave me an odd
sort of glance, as if he were wondering what on earth I or anybody
else could care about him, and I left him fumbling with his latch-
key. I think you will say I did pretty well when I tell you that within
a few weeks I had made myself an intimate friend of Black's. I shall
never forget the first time I went to his room; I hope I shall never
see such abject, squalid misery again.

"The foul paper, from which all pattern or trace of a pattern had
long vanished, subdued and penetrated with the grime of the evil
street, was hanging in mouldering pennons from the wall. Only at
the end of the room was it possible to stand upright, and the sight
of the wretched bed and the odour of corruption that pervaded the
place made me turn faint and sick. Here I found him munching
a piece of bread; he seemed surprised to find that I had kept my
promise, but he gave me his chair and sat on the bed while we
talked. I used to go to see him often, and we had long conversations
together, but he never mentioned Harlesden or his wife. I fancy
that he supposed me ignorant of the matter, or thought that if I

had heard of it, I should never connect the respectable Dr Black of Harlesden with a poor garreteer in the backwoods of London. He was a strange man, and as we sat together smoking, I often wondered whether he were mad or sane, for I think the wildest dreams of Paracelsus and the Rosicrucians would appear plain and sober fact compared with the theories I have heard him earnestly advance in that grimy den of his. I once ventured to hint something of the sort to him. I suggested that something he had said was in flat contradiction to all science and all experience. 'No,' he answered, 'not all experience, for mine counts for something. I am no dealer in unproved theories; what I say I have proved for myself, and at a terrible cost. There is a region of knowledge which you will never know, which wise men seeing from afar off shun like the plague, as well they may, but into that region I have gone. If you knew, if you could even dream of what may be done, of what one or two men have done in this quiet world of ours, your very soul would shudder and faint within you. What you have heard from me has been but the merest husk and outer covering of true science— that science which means death, and that which is more awful than death, to those who gain it. No, when men say that there are strange things in the world, they little know the awe and the terror that dwell always with them and about them.' There was a sort of fascination about the man that drew me to him, and I was quite sorry to have to leave London for a month or two; I missed his odd talk. A few days after I came back to town I thought I would look him up, but when I gave the two rings at the bell that used to summon him, there was no answer. I rang and rang again, and was just turning to go away, when the door opened and a dirty woman asked me what I wanted. From her look I fancy she took me for a plain-clothes officer after one of her lodgers, but when I inquired if Mr Black were in, she gave me a stare of another kind. 'There's no Mr Black lives here,' she said. 'He's gone. He's dead this six weeks. I always thought he was a bit queer in his head, or else had been and got into some trouble or other. He used to go out every morning from ten till one, and one Monday morning we heard him come in, and go into his room and shut the door, and a few minutes after, just as we was a-sitting down to our dinner, there was such a scream that I thought I should have gone right off. And then we heard a stamping, and down he came, raging and cursing most dreadful, swearing he had been robbed of something that was worth millions. And then he just dropped down in the passage, and we thought he was dead. We got him up to his room, and put him on his bed, and I just sat there and waited, while my 'usband he went for the doctor. And there was the winder wide open, and a little tin box he had lying on the floor open and empty, but of course nobody could possible have got in at the winder, and as for him having anything that was worth anything, it's nonsense, for he was often weeks and weeks behind with his rent, and my 'usband he threatened often and often to turn him into the street, for, as he said, we've got a living to myke like other people—and, of course, that's true; but, somehow, I didn't like to do it, though he was an odd kind of a man, and I fancy had been better off. And then the doctor came and looked at him, and said as he couldn't do nothing, and that night he died as I was a-sitting by his bed; and I can tell you that, with one thing and another, we lost money by him, for the few bits of clothes as he had were worth next to nothing when they came to be sold.' I gave the woman half a sovereign for her trouble, and went home thinking of Dr Black and the epitaph she had made him, and wondering at his strange fancy that he had been robbed. I take it that he had very little to fear on that score, poor fellow; but I suppose that he was really mad, and died in a sudden access of his mania. His landlady said that once or twice when she had had occasion to go into his room (to dun the poor wretch for his rent, most likely), he would keep her at the door for about a minute, and that when she came in she would find him putting away his tin box in the corner by the window; I suppose he had become possessed with the idea of some great treasure, and fancied himself a wealthy man in the midst of all his misery. Explicit, my tale is ended, and you see that though I knew Black, I know nothing of his wife or of the history of her death.—That's the Harlesden case, Salisbury, and I think it interests me all the more deeply because there does not seem the shadow of a possibility that I or anyone else will ever know more about it. What do you think of it?"

"Well, Dyson, I must say that I think you have contrived to surround the whole thing with a mystery of your own making. I go for the doctor's solution: Black murdered his wife, being himself in all probability an undeveloped lunatic."

"What? Do you believe, then, that this woman was something too awful, too terrible to be allowed to remain on the earth? You will remember that the doctor said it was the brain of a devil?"

"Yes, yes, but he was speaking, of course, metaphorically. It's really quite a simple matter if you only look at it like that."

"Ah, well, you may be right; but yet I am sure you are not. Well, well, it's no good discussing it any more. A little more Benedictine? That's right; try some of this tobacco. Didn't you say that you had been bothered by something—something which happened that night we dined together?"

"Yes, I have been worried, Dyson, worried a great deal. I—But it's such a trivial matter—indeed, such an absurdity—that I feel ashamed to trouble you with it."

"Never mind, let's have it, absurd or not."

With many hesitations, and with much inward resentment of the folly of the thing, Salisbury told his tale, and repeated reluctantly the absurd intelligence and the absurder doggerel of the scrap of paper, expecting to hear Dyson burst out into a roar of laughter.

"Isn't it too bad that I should let myself be bothered by such stuff as that?" he asked, when he had stuttered out the jingle of once, and twice, and thrice.

Dyson had listened to it all gravely, even to the end, and meditated for a few minutes in silence.

"Yes," he said at length, "it was a curious chance, your taking shelter in that archway just as those two went by. But I don't know that I should call what was written on the paper nonsense; it is bizarre certainly, but I expect it has a meaning for somebody. Just repeat it again, will you, and I will write it down. Perhaps we might find a cipher of some sort, though I hardly think we shall."

Again had the reluctant lips of Salisbury slowly to stammer out the rubbish that he abhorred, while Dyson jotted it down on a slip of paper.

"Look over it, will you?" he said, when it was done; "it may be important that I should have every word in its place. Is that all right?"

"Yes; that is an accurate copy. But I don't think you will get much out of it. Depend upon it, it is mere nonsense, a wanton scribble. I must be going now, Dyson. No, no more; that stuff of yours is pretty strong. Goodnight."

"I suppose you would like to hear from me, if I did find out anything?"

"No, not I; I don't want to hear about the thing again. You may regard the discovery, if it is one, as your own."

"Very well. Goodnight."

IV

A good many hours after Salisbury had returned to the company of the green rep chairs, Dyson still sat at his desk, itself a Japanese romance, smoking many pipes, and meditating over his friend's story. The bizarre quality of the inscription which had annoyed Salisbury was to him an attraction, and now and again he took it up and scanned thoughtfully what he had written, especially the quaint jingle at the end. It was a token, a symbol, he decided, and not a cipher, and the woman who had flung it away was in all probability entirely ignorant of its meaning; she was but the agent of the 'Sam' she had abused and discarded, and he too was again the agent of someone unknown; possibly of the individual styled Q, who had been forced to visit his French friends. But what to make of 'Traverse Handel S.' Here was the root and source of the enigma, and not all the tobacco of Virginia seemed likely to suggest any clue here. It seemed almost hopeless, but Dyson regarded himself as the Wellington of mysteries, and went to bed feeling assured that sooner or later he would hit upon the right track. For the next few days he was deeply engaged in his literary labours, labours which were a profound mystery even to the most intimate of his friends, who searched the railway bookstalls in vain for the result of so many hours spent at the Japanese bureau in company with strong tobacco and black tea. On this occasion Dyson confined himself to his room for four days, and it was with genuine relief that he laid down his pen and went out into the streets in quest of relaxation and fresh air. The gas-lamps were being lighted, and the fifth edition of the evening papers was being howled through the streets, and Dyson, feeling that he wanted quiet, turned away from the clamorous Strand, and began to trend away to the north-west. Soon he found himself in streets that echoed to his footsteps, and crossing a broad new thoroughfare, and verging still to the west, Dyson discovered that he had penetrated to the depths of Soho. Here again was life; rare vintages of France and Italy, at prices which seemed contemptibly small, allured the passer-by; here were cheeses, vast and rich, here olive oil, and here a grove of Rabelaisian sausages; while in a neighbouring shop the whole Press of Paris appeared to be on sale. In the middle of the roadway a strange miscellany of nations sauntered to and fro, for there cab and hansom rarely ventured; and from window over window the inhabitants looked forth in pleased contemplation of the scene. Dyson made his way slowly along, mingling with the crowd on the cobble-stones, listening to the queer babel of French and German, and Italian and English, glancing now and again at the shop-windows with their levelled batteries of bottles, and had almost gained the end of the street, when his attention was arrested by a small shop at the corner, a vivid contrast to its neighbours. It was the typical shop of the poor quarter; a shop entirely English. Here were vended tobacco and sweets, cheap pipes of clay and cherry-wood; penny exercise books and pen-holders jostled for precedence with comic songs, and story papers with appalling cuts showed that romance claimed its place beside the actualities of the evening paper, the bills of which fluttered at the doorway.

Dyson glanced up at the name above the door, and stood by the kennel trembling, for a sharp pang, the pang of one who has made a discovery, had for a moment left him incapable of motion. The name over the shop was Travers. Dyson looked up again, this time at the corner of the wall above the lamp-post, and read in white letters on a blue ground the words 'Handel Street, W.C.', and the legend was repeated in fainter letters just below. He gave a little sigh of satisfaction, and without more ado walked boldly into the shop, and stared full in the face of the fat man who was sitting behind the counter. The fellow rose to his feet, and returned the stare a little curiously, and then began in stereotyped phrase—

"What can I do for you, sir?"

Dyson enjoyed the situation and a dawning perplexity on the man's face. He propped his stick carefully against the counter and leaning over it, said slowly and impressively—"Once around the grass, and twice around the lass, and thrice around the maple-tree."

Dyson had calculated on his words producing an effect, and he was not disappointed. The vendor of miscellanies gasped, open-mouthed like a fish, and steadied himself against the counter. When he spoke, after a short interval, it was in a hoarse mutter, tremulous and unsteady.

"Would you mind saying that again, sir? I didn't quite catch it."

"My good man, I shall most certainly do nothing of the kind. You heard what I said perfectly well. You have got a clock in your shop, I see; an admirable timekeeper, I have no doubt. Well, I give you a minute by your own clock."

The man looked about him in a perplexed indecision, and Dyson felt that it was time to be bold.

"Look here, Travers, the time is nearly up. You have heard of Q, I think. Remember, I hold your life in my hands. Now!"

Dyson was shocked at the result of his own audacity. The man shrank and shrivelled in terror, the sweat poured down a face of ashy white, and he held up his hands before him.

"Mr Davies, Mr Davies, don't say that—don't for Heaven's sake. I didn't know you at first, I didn't indeed. Good God! Mr Davies, you wouldn't ruin me? I'll get it in a moment."

"You had better not lose any more time."

The man slunk piteously out of his own shop, and went into a back parlour. Dyson heard his trembling fingers fumbling with a bunch of keys, and the creak of an opening box. He came back presently with a small package neatly tied up in brown paper in his hands, and still, full of terror, handed it to Dyson.

"I'm glad to be rid of it," he said, "I'll take no more jobs of this sort."

Dyson took the parcel and his stick, and walked out of the shop with a nod, turning round as he passed the door. Travers had sunk into his seat, his face still white with terror, with one hand over his eyes, and Dyson speculated a good deal as he walked rapidly away as to what queer chords those could be on which he had played so roughly. He hailed the first hansom he could see and drove home, and when he had lit his hanging lamp, and laid his parcel on the table, he paused for a moment, wondering on what strange thing the lamplight would soon shine. He locked his door, and cut the strings, and unfolded the paper layer after layer, and came at last to a small wooden box, simply but solidly made. There was no lock, and Dyson had simply to raise the lid, and as he did so he drew a long breath and started back. The lamp seemed to glimmer feebly like a single candle, but the whole room blazed with light—and not with light alone, but with a thousand colours, with all the glories of some painted window; and upon the walls of his room and on the familiar furniture, the glow flamed back and seemed to flow again to its source, the little wooden box. For there upon a bed of soft wool lay the most splendid jewel, a jewel such as Dyson had never dreamed of, and within it shone the blue of far skies, and the green of the sea by the shore, and the red of the ruby, and deep violet rays, and in the middle of all it seemed aflame as if a fountain of fire rose up, and fell, and rose again with sparks like stars for drops. Dyson gave a long deep sigh, and dropped into his chair, and put his hands over his eyes to think. The jewel was like an opal, but from a long experience of the shop-windows he knew there was no such thing as an opal one-quarter or one-eighth of its size. He looked at the stone again, with a feeling that was almost awe, and placed it gently on the table under the lamp, and watched the wonderful flame that shone and sparkled in its centre, and then turned to the box, curious to know whether it might contain other marvels. He lifted the bed of wool on which the opal had reclined, and saw beneath, no more jewels, but a little old pocket-book, worn and shabby with use. Dyson opened it at the first leaf, and dropped the book again appalled. He had read the name of the owner, neatly written in blue ink:

STEVEN BLACK, M.D.,
Oranmore,
     Devon Road,
       Harlesden.

It was several minutes before Dyson could bring himself to open the book a second time; he remembered the wretched exile in his garret; and his strange talk, and the memory too of the face he had seen at the window, and of what the specialist had said, surged up in his mind, and as he held his finger on the cover, he shivered, dreading what might be written within. When at last he held it in his hand, and turned the pages, he found that the first two leaves were blank, but the third was covered with clear, minute writing, and Dyson began to read with the light of the opal flaming in his eyes.

V

"Ever since I was a young man"—the record began—"I devoted all my leisure and a good deal of time that ought to have been given to other studies to the investigation of curious and obscure branches of knowledge. What are commonly called the pleasures of life had never any attractions for me, and I lived alone in London, avoiding my fellow-students, and in my turn avoided by them as a man self-absorbed and unsympathetic. So long as I could gratify my desire of knowledge of a peculiar kind, knowledge of which the very existence is a profound secret to most men, I was intensely happy, and I have often spent whole nights sitting in the darkness of my room, and thinking of the strange world on the brink of which I trod. My professional studies, however, and the necessity of obtaining a degree, for some time forced my more obscure employment into the back-ground, and soon after I had qualified I met Agnes, who became my wife. We took a new house in this remote suburb, and I began the regular routine of a sober practice, and for some months lived happily enough, sharing in the life about me, and only thinking at odd intervals of that occult science which had once fascinated my whole being. I had learnt enough of the paths I had begun to tread to know that they were beyond all expression difficult and dangerous, that to persevere meant in all probability the wreck of a life, and that they led to regions so terrible, that the mind of man shrinks appalled at the very thought. Moreover, the quiet and the peace I had enjoyed since my marriage had wiled me away to a great extent from places where I knew no peace could dwell. But suddenly—I think indeed it was the work of a single night, as I lay awake on my bed gazing into the darkness— suddenly, I say, the old desire, the former longing, returned, and returned with a force that had been intensified ten times by its absence; and when the day dawned and I looked out of the window, and saw with haggard eyes the sunrise in the east, I knew that my doom had been pronounced; that as I had gone far, so now I must go farther with unfaltering steps. I turned to the bed where my wife was sleeping peacefully, and lay down again, weeping bitter tears, for the sun had set on our happy life and had risen with a dawn of terror to us both. I will not set down here in minute detail what followed; outwardly I went about the day's labour as before, saying nothing to my wife. But she soon saw that I had changed; I spent my spare time in a room which I had fitted up as a laboratory, and often I crept upstairs in the grey dawn of the morning, when the light of many lamps still glowed over London; and each night I had stolen a step nearer to that great abyss which I was to bridge over, the gulf between the world of consciousness and the world of matter. My experiments were many and complicated in their nature, and it was some months before I realised whither they all pointed, and when this was borne in upon me in a moment's time,

I felt my face whiten and my heart still within me. But the power to draw back, the power to stand before the doors that now opened wide before me and not to enter in, had long ago been absent; the way was closed, and I could only pass onward. My position was as utterly hopeless as that of the prisoner in an utter dungeon, whose only light is that of the dungeon above him; the doors were shut and escape was impossible. Experiment after experiment gave the same result, and I knew, and shrank even as the thought passed through my mind, that in the work I had to do there must be elements which no laboratory could furnish, which no scales could ever measure. In that work, from which even I doubted to escape with life, life itself must enter; from some human being there must be drawn that essence which men call the soul, and in its place (for in the scheme of the world there is no vacant chamber)—in its place would enter in what the lips can hardly utter, what the mind cannot conceive without a horror more awful than the horror of death itself. And when I knew this, I knew also on whom this fate would fall; I looked into my wife's eyes. Even at that hour, if I had gone out and taken a rope and hanged myself, I might have escaped, and she also, but in no other way. At last I told her all. She shuddered, and wept, and called on her dead mother for help, and asked me if I had no mercy, and I could only sigh. I concealed nothing from her; I told her what she would become, and what would enter in where her life had been; I told her of all the shame and of all the horror. You who will read this when I am dead— if indeed I allow this record to survive,—you who have opened the box and have seen what lies there, if you could understand what lies hidden in that opal! For one night my wife consented to what I asked of her, consented with the tears running down her beautiful face, and hot shame flushing red over her neck and breast, consented to undergo this for me.

I threw open the window, and we looked together at the sky and the dark earth for the last time; it was a fine star-light night, and there was a pleasant breeze blowing, and I kissed her on her lips, and her tears ran down upon my face. That night she came down to my laboratory, and there, with shutters bolted and barred down, with curtains drawn thick and close, so that the very stars might be shut out from the sight of that room, while the crucible hissed and boiled over the lamp, I did what had to be done, and led out what was no longer a woman. But on the table the opal flamed and sparkled with such light as no eyes of man have ever gazed on, and the rays of the flame that was within it flashed and glittered, and shone even to my heart. My wife had only asked one thing of me; that when there came at last what I had told her, I would kill her. I have kept that promise."

There was nothing more. Dyson let the little pocket-book fall, and turned and looked again at the opal with its flaming inmost light, and then with unutterable irresistible horror surging up in his heart, grasped the jewel, and flung it on the ground, and trampled it beneath his heel. His face was white with terror as he turned away, and for a moment stood sick and trembling, and then with a start he leapt across the room and steadied himself against the door. There was an angry hiss, as of steam escaping under great pressure, and as he gazed, motionless, a volume of heavy yellow smoke was slowly issuing from the very centre of the jewel, and wreathing itself in snakelike coils above it. And then a thin white flame burst forth from the smoke, and shot up into the air and vanished; and on the ground there lay a thing like a cinder, black and crumbling to the touch.

Paymon's Trio
Colette de Curzon

I had always been fond of music: it was a kind of passion in me,
around which I centred my whole existence, and in the beauty of
which I derived all the pleasures I required from life. I was well up
in anything and everything connected with music, from the earliest
and from the most primitive of rondos to the latest symphonies
and concertos. I played the violin passing well, though my talent
and ability of execution fell far short of my desires. I had played
second violin in various concerts, provincial ones, of course, for a
natural reticence and shyness prevented me from daring to launch
my meagre talent into higher spheres. Besides which, the violin for
me was not a profession: it was merely a friend in whom I confided
all the thoughts and emotions of my soul, which I could not have
expressed in any other way. For even the most retired of men needs
to express himself in one way or another.

I had always connected music with the beautiful side of life. In
this, for my fifty-odd years, I was strangely naïve. The experience I
went through for a long time shook the rock-solid foundation of my
innocent belief. It will, no doubt, be hard for anyone reading this
story to believe it all, or even any part of it; but I am here to testify
that every word of it is true, I and my two very dearest and noblest
of friends, for we all three went through the same experience, and
all three unanimously declare that every word of it is solid fact. A

few years have elapsed since the evil day that brought a passing shadow on my life's passion, but the memory of it is still fresh in my mind.

I will start at the beginning and try to impart all its vividness up to you.

It was on a raw November's evening, with bleary dusk swiftly descending on windswept London, as I was returning from Hyde Park, where I had taken my dog, Angus, for his afternoon exercise, that I suddenly remembered that I had gone out for a double purpose: the first already mentioned, and the second a half-hearted quest for a second-hand copy of Burton's *Anatomy of Melancholy.* To say that I was interested in that work would be a great exaggeration. I had heard various reports about it that did not rouse my enthusiasm, but as it had got a new vogue at the moment and was much talked of, I wished to acquaint myself of its content, so as to know, roughly, at any rate, what it was about.

I prided myself of being erudite—such puny little accomplishments are very satisfactory—and my total ignorance concerning Burton's work was a serious lapse in my literary learning. So, *Melancholy* bound, I made my way down some narrow side streets, ill-lit by bleary lampposts, where I knew I would find a number of barrows of second-hand books, and where I hoped to find the work in question. The first two barrows revealed a great deal in the nature of melancholy, but not Burton's. At the third, which was overshadowed by the towering bulk of a surly woman vendor, who eyed me as suspiciously as though I were a notorious nihilist, I found the book I was looking for. Or books—for it was in three volumes. But they were firmly wedged behind a tall black volume which I found necessary to remove in order to reach them.

I daresay I was clumsy, or perhaps Angus chose that particular moment to tug on his leash and jerk my arm. At any rate, Angus or no Angus, my hand slipped from the black book which, having been dislodged, fell with a thud on to the muddy pavement, its binding being badly stained in the process. I remember thinking, in spite of my vexation, that the fat woman was no doubt proud of having suspected me of evil intentions from the start, for I was certainly proving myself to be no ordinary customer.

I picked up the book, and seeing how badly damaged it was, I thought it only civil of me to buy it of her, though many of her books were in more distressing conditions. She accepted my offer grudgingly, and had the impudence to charge me an extra 6d on the original two shillings. Being hardly in a position to argue, I allowed her to engulf my half crown and departed with my new acquisition under my arm... and the *Anatomy* still skulking dismally in its barrow.

When I got home to my flat—which I shared with my most faithful and congenial of friends, Arnold Barker, with whom I had seen two wars and a prison camp in Germany—I naturally inspected the book I had just purchased. Arnold was out at the time, so that I had the flat all to myself. I dreaded so the fearful trash which would have disgraced my library—some cheap romance that would make me shudder. But the binding at once calmed my fears: no romantic author would have chosen thick black leather to garb his story. The title in gold print was hardly discernible.

I opened the book and felt a little shiver of pleasant anticipation run down my spine. In bold black lettering, ornamented with fantastic arabesques *à la* Cruikshank, the title displayed itself to my eyes: *Le Dictionnaire Infernal* by J Collin de Plancy, 1864. It was in French, which pleased me all the more, as my knowledge of that language was more than fair, and it was full of weird, humoristic and infinitely varied engravings by some artist of the middle of the last century.

I perused it avidly and rapidly acquainted myself of its contents. An Infernal Dictionary it was, written in a semi-serious, semi-comical style, giving full details concerning the nether regions, rites, inhabitants, spiritualism, stars reading, fortune telling etc, which, as the author informed us from time to time, all had to be taken *cum granu salis*. I hasten to say that I in no way dabbled in demonology, but this book, though certainly dealing with the black arts, was harmless to so experienced a reader as myself. And I looked forward to several days of pleasant entertainment with my unusual discovery. I pictured Arnold's face as I would show him my find, for the occult had always fascinated him.

I skimmed the pages once more, smoothing out those which had been crushed in the fall—or perhaps before—when my fingers encountered a bulky irregular thickness in the top cover of the book. The fly leaf had been stuck back over this irregularity, and gummed down with exceedingly dirty fingers.

To say that I was puzzled would of course be true. But I was more than puzzled: I was very intrigued. Without a moment's hesitation, I slipped my penknife along the gummed fly leaf and cut it right out; a thin piece of folded paper slipped out and fell onto the carpet at my feet. What made me hesitate just then to pick it up? Nothing apparently, and yet fully ten seconds elapsed before I took it in my hand and unfolded it. And then my enthusiasm was fired, for the folded sheets—there were three of them—were covered with music: music written in a neat, precise hand, in very small characters, and which to my experienced eyes appeared very difficult to decipher.

Each sheet contained the three different parts of a trio—piano, violin and cello. That was, as far as I was able to see—for the characters being very small and my eyes not so good as they had been, I could not read very much of it. I was, however, thrilled; childishly, I must confess, I hoped—even grown men can be foolish—that this might be some unknown work from a great composer's hand. But on second perusal, I was quickly disillusioned. The author of this music had signed his name: P Everard, 1865, which told me exactly nothing, for P Everard was quite unknown to me.

The only thing that intrigued me considerably was the title of the trio. Still in the same neat hand, I saw the skilfully-drawn figure of a naked man seated on the back of a dromedary, and read, '*In worship of Paymon*' underlining the picture.

It may have been a trick of the light, or my imagination, but the face of the man was incredibly evil, and I hastily looked away from it.

Well, this was a find! However obscure the composer, it was interesting to find a document dating back to the nineteenth century, so well-preserved and under such unusual circumstances. Perhaps its very age would make it valuable? I would have to interview some authorities on old manuscripts and ascertain the fact. In the meanwhile, the temptation being very great, I set about playing the violin part on my fiddle. My fingers literally ached to feel the polished wood of my instrument between them and I was keenly interested at having something entirely new to decipher.

Propping up the violin part on my stand—the paper, though thin, was very stiff and needed no support—I attacked the opening bars. They were incredibly difficult and at first I thought I would not be able to play them, although I can say without boasting that I am more than a mere amateur in that respect. But gradually I got used to the peculiar rhythm of the piece and made my way brilliantly through it. Strangely enough, however, I felt intense displeasure at the sounds that were springing from my bow. The melody was beautiful, worthy of Handel's *Messiah*, or Berlioz's *L'Enfance du Christ*, for it was religious. Yes, religious: and at the same time it seemed only to be a parody of religion, with an underlying current of something infinitely evil that distorted its purity.

How could music express that, you may wonder. I do not know, but I felt in every fibre of my body that what I was playing was 'impure' and I hated as much as I admired the music I was rendering.

As I attacked the last bar, Arnold Barker's startled voice broke in my ear. "Good God, Greville, what on earth is that you're playing? It's terrible!"

Arnold, in all his six-foot-three of ageing manhood, brought me out of my trance with his very material and down-to-earth remark. I was grateful to him. I lowered my fiddle.

"Well, I daresay it could be better played," said I, "but it is amazingly difficult."

"I don't mean you played it badly," Arnold hastily interposed. "Not by a long chalk. But... but... it's the music. It's wonderful, but extraordinarily unpleasant. Who on earth wrote it?" He took off his mist-sodden coat and hat, and picked up one of the two remaining sheets of music.

As he scanned it, I explained my little adventure, and how I had come into possession of the unusual manuscript.

The book did not appear to rouse much interest in him: his whole attention was centred on the sheet of paper he was holding. As I was finishing speaking, he said, "This appears to be the piano part: I suppose I could try my hand at it, and accompany you. Though, as you say, it appears to be extraordinarily difficult... the rhythm is unusual."

He was puzzled as I had been, and I watched him as he seated himself at the piano and played the first opening bars. He was a born pianist: these short competent hands, as they stretched nimbly over the keys, were sufficient proof of that. The only defect in his talent that had prevented him from making a career of it was his deplorable memory and total incapacity to play anything without the music under his eyes. Now, he did not appear to find his part difficult—not as I had done. Of course, the piano, in this trio, merely featured as an accompaniment, a subdued monotone which now and then picked up the main theme of the piece and exercised variations upon it.

Arnold played the piece half-way through, then stopped abruptly. "Of course my part is rather dull," said he. "It needs the violin and the cello to bring it out. But, well... I don't mind admitting that I don't like it. It's... uncanny..."

I nodded in agreement.

"What do you make of the man's name?"

"Nothing."

"As far as I can tell, the name Everard has never become famous in the music world, and yet the man was gifted, for this piece has rare qualities. It reminds one of some strains of *The Messiah*, and yet... well, there's just that something in it that makes it all wrong."

"It's peculiar," I admitted. "Extraordinary luck my finding it as I did. I suppose it has been in the binding of that book since the date when it was written. But why was it... well... I should say 'concealed'? I can't think. And what about that dedication, at the top of the first sheet? Who is Paymon?"

Arnold bent closer to the picture, and I noticed him suck in his breath as in some surprise. He straightened himself up and cast me rather a furtive look. "I don't know," he mused. "Paymon... and 'in worship' too. Somebody this fellow Everard must have been frightfully fond of. But have you noticed the expression on the man's face? It's rather unpleasant."

"*Evil* is more like it—the man was an artist as well as a musician. It's very odd. I will have to take this manuscript to old Mason's tomorrow and see what he can make of it. It may have worldwide interest for all we know."

But, the following day being a Sunday, I did not care to trouble my old friend with my mysterious manuscript, and I spent my time, much to my reluctance, practising my part of the trio. It held an extraordinary fascination for me, and yet repelled me in every note I drew across the strings. When I looked at that small, hideous picture, I felt as though a cunning little devil had got inside my fingers and compelled me to play against my will, with the notes dancing and jumbling before my eyes, and the weird strains of the music filling my head and making me loathe myself for yielding to that strange force.

Late in the afternoon, Arnold, who had been strangely moody as he listened to me from the depths of his favourite armchair, rose to his feet and came over to where I was playing. "Look here, Greville," said he. "There is something definitely wrong with that music. I feel it, and I know you do too. I can't analyse it, but it is there all the same. We ought to get rid of it somehow. Take it to Mason's and tell him to do what he likes with it, or burn it or something, but don't keep it."

I was stubborn. "It may have its value, you know," I remonstrated. "And, after all... it's really beautiful." And I wondered at myself for praising something which I loathed with all my heart.

"Yes, it's beautiful. But it's bad. Don't lie to yourself—you think so too. I have been watching you all the time you were playing, and by Heaven, if anyone seemed to be in absolute terror of something, that person was you. That thing's infernal—I've a good mind to destroy it here and now!"

He seized the three sheets that were lying on the violin stand and made as though to throw them into the fire. But I stayed his hand and murmured quite feverishly (and quite, it seemed, against my will), "No! Not just yet. After all, it's a trio, and we have only played two parts of it. If we could get Ian McDonald to come round this evening with his cello, we could play the whole thing together—just once, to hear it as it should be played. And then... well... we can destroy it."

"Ian? That boy will be scared stiff!"

"Scared? Of what? Of a few notes on a sheet of paper eighty-five years old? You're being foolish, Arnold. We both are. There's nothing wrong with the music at all. It's weird, uncanny perhaps, but that's all that's to be said against it. So is *Peer Gynt* for that matter, and yet no-one would dream of being scared by it, as we are by this trio..."

Arnold still looked very doubtful, so I pressed my point.

Why, I wonder now... why was I so eagerly enthusiastic about my find, when deep down in my mind I felt a lurking fear of it, as of an evil thing that polluted whatever it touched? I detested it, and yet that little naked figure on the dromedary's back held my senses in a kind of spell and made me talk as I was now doing: without my being able to control my thoughts and voice as I wished.

"After all," I argued, "this is *my* discovery, and it's only natural that I should wish to know what the whole effect of the trio is like. As we've played it—you and I—it was, well, lop-sided. It needs the cello to complete it. And, you said yourself when you first heard it that it was beautiful!"

"And ghastly," Arnold added sulkily, but he was clearly mollified. He perused his part of the trio once more.

On the three sheets was repeated the detestable little figure, and I noticed that Arnold kept his hand carefully over the wicked face, and on replacing the sheet on the music stand, he averted his eyes. So, that drawing held that strange influence over him, too? Perhaps... perhaps... there was something after all.

But Arnold prevented any further speculation.

"All right," he said, in a resigned voice. "I'll go round and collect young Ian. But remember, I take no responsibility."

"Responsibility? What responsibility?" I asked.

Arnold looked embarrassed. "Oh, I don't know. But if... well... if this blasted trio upsets the lot of us, I want you to know that I wash my hands of the whole thing from this very minute."

"Don't be a damned idiot, Arnold," I said with some heat. "I never knew you to be so ridiculously impressed by a piece of music. You're as silly as a five year old child!"

Even as I spoke, I felt my inner thoughts battling against the words I uttered.

The little man on the paper seemed to grin at me, and I suddenly felt physically sick. I turned to stop Arnold, but he had already left the room, even as I opened my mouth to speak to him. I heard the clang of the front door as he slammed it. I regretted my insistence. I hated myself for having persuaded Arnold to fetch Ian, and, obeying a sudden impulse, I seized the papers and prepared to throw them into the smouldering fire in the chimney. The little man's eyes on the paper followed mine as I moved, as though daring me to carry out my intention. I stopped and stared at the grinning face... and I replaced the sheets on the music stand, with a thrill of unpleasant fear running down my spine.

Arnold was away some time. When he came back, he had brought Ian with him and between them they carried the latter's cello—a very beautiful instrument in a fine leather case. Ian, compared to both of us, was a mere child: he was barely twenty-eight, with a gentle, effeminate face and a weak body that was greatly at a disadvantage beside Arnold's towering strength and healthy vitality. But he was a fine fellow for all his physical deficiencies, and in spite of the difference in our ages, we were all three the best of friends, brought together by our common interest in music. Ian played in various concerts and was an excellent cellist.

I greeted him warmly, for I was very fond of him, and before showing him the music, made him feel quite at home. But Arnold had probably put him on his mettle, for almost at once, he asked me *what this blessed trio was about*, and why we were so eager to play it, and why we made such mysteries about it?

"Arnold told me it was beautiful and awful all at the same time, and quite a difficult piece even from my point of view, which I presume must be taken as a compliment. I don't mind admitting I'm keen to play it."

Arnold grunted his disapproval from behind the thick clay pipe he always smoked, and I felt a guilty qualm in my mind that for some reason made me hesitate. As Ian looked a little surprised, I overcame my reluctance and, taking up the old manuscript, handed it to him. He looked at it carefully for several minutes without uttering a word, then he handed back the piano and violin parts, keeping the cello part, and remarked, 'It ought to be deuced good, you know. Yes, that is quite a find you've made there, Greville, quite a find. But what an unpleasant little picture that is at the top. It is quite out of keeping with the music, I've a feeling."

"I don't know about that," Arnold murmured. "I can't say that I agree."

Ian looked up in some surprise, and I, sensing some embarrassing question concerning the music, rose to my feet and said, "Well, since we are all ready, there's no sense in wasting time talking. Let's get to work."

There was little time wasted in preparing our instruments for the trio. Ian was eager and in some excitement; I was, for some strange reason, peculiarly nervous; Arnold, I noticed with a little irritation, was moody, and placed himself at the piano with a good deal of ill grace. Why did he accept to play his part so grudgingly, I wondered as I tuned my fiddle. After all, this was just a piece of music like any other. In fact, it was more beautiful than many I had heard and played myself. Surely his musician's enthusiasm would be fired at being given such scope to express itself! For this trio, in its way, was a masterpiece.

I ran a scale and looked at the little man; the name Paymon in that neat, precise hand danced before my eyes and made me blink. I would have to stop my eyes wandering to the picture if I wanted to play my part properly. But wherever I looked, the man on his dromedary seemed to follow me and leer at my futile efforts to evade him. I glanced at Ian and noticed that he was looking a little annoyed.

"This damn little picture is blurring my eyes," he complained rather crossly. "It seems to be everywhere!"

"I noticed that myself," I admitted.

"I can't get it out of the way: the best thing to do is to cover it up."

I gave them a small sheet of paper each and we all three pinned the sheets down upon our respective pictures. I felt a certain amount of relief at not seeing that ugly face and, tapping my stand with my fiddle bow, said, "Are you fellows ready?"

Two silent nods, and we began.

And now, how can I describe what happened, or how it happened? It is fixed in my mind and yet I cannot find words suitable to impart to you the horror of our experience. I think the music was the worst part of it all. As we played, I could hardly believe that this... this hellish sound was really being created by our own fingers. Hellish. Demonic. Those are the only words for it, and yet in itself, it was none of those things. But there was something about it that conveyed that ghastly impression, as though the author had composed it with the wish to convey profane emotions to its executants. I confess that I was frightened—really and truly afraid—possessed of such fear as I have never experienced before or since: fear of something awful and all-powerful which I did not understand. I played on, struggling to drop my fiddle and stop, but compelled by some force to continue.

And then, when we were half-way through, a strangled cry from Ian broke the horrible spell. "Oh God, stop it, stop it! This is awful!"

I seemed to wake as from a dream. I lowered my violin and looked at the young man. He was as white and trembling, with dilated eyes staring at the music before him. He looked, with his thin face and yellow hair, like a corpse.

I murmured hoarsely, "Ian, what is the matter?"

He did not answer me. With one hand, he still held his cello; with the other—the right one—he made a sign of the cross and murmured, "Christ—oh, Christ, have mercy on us!" and sank in a dead faint onto the carpet.

In two seconds, galvanised into action, we were beside him and, Arnold supporting his head and shoulders, I administered what aid I could to him, though my intense excitement made me of little use. He was very far gone, and it took us nearly twenty minutes to revive him. When he opened his eyes, he looked at us both, a prey to abject terror, then, clutching at my coat in fear, he murmured, "The music... the music... it's possessed. You must destroy it at once!"

We exchanged glances, Arnold and I. Arnold seemed to say, "I told you so" and I accepted the rebuke meekly. But I obeyed.

This music was evil, and had to be destroyed. I rose to my feet and went to the music stand. Then I suddenly felt the blood draining from my face and leaving my lips dry. For the music lay on the carpet—clawed to pieces. Only the grinning man on his dromedary was intact...

It was some weeks later, when we had somewhat recovered from our experience, that I ventured to open the book I had recently bought and which had been the cause of so much trouble. I had the name Paymon on the brain, and quite by chance, I opened the Infernal Dictionary at the letter P. I had no intention of looking for the name Paymon. I did not, of course, think it existed in any dictionary. I merely turned the pages over and looked at the illustrations. At the sixth or seventh page of that letter, my attention was attracted by the only picture in the column—that of a hideous little man, seated on the back of a dromedary. The name Paymon was written beneath it, along with a small article, concerning the illustration.

I read avidly. '*Paymon: one of the gods of Hell. Appears to exorcists in the shape of a man seated on the back of a dromedary. May be summoned by libations or human sacrifices. Is very partial to music.*'

One, Two, Buckle My Shoe
Nugent Barker

"AND now," said Harlock solemnly, pushing back his chair, "and now to business."

We rose to our feet at the far end of the studio, and watched him delicately pinching out the half-burnt candles on the shining dinner table. It was a scene that we had all been waiting for, from past experience—a transformation from the choice and orderly to the grotesque, for it left us standing in the large and leaping firelight.

Sitting at the chimney-side, ready to have our breaths caught by Harlock while we filled our chairs with comfort, we were in another room altogether. Witticisms lay behind us, arguments had been thrashed out and buried, the bowl, for the time being, had flowed; and towering shadows, the perfect background for ghost-stories, had taken their place.

We waited for our host's thin, fire-crimsoned face to reveal to us that his mounting list of horrors was about to be capped by an effort supremely terrifying for a Christmas occasion... but the slow, grim smile never came. He kicked the pine logs into a fiercer blaze; then fell to groping in the remotest corner of his studio.

When he returned, bringing from the shadows an unframed canvas, we supposed that the supreme effort had surely arrived: the story was to be too disturbing for even the remotest of smiles. He stood the canvas on a chair at one end of the fireplace, so that we all had a fairly good view of it. The quality of the painting and the subject of the picture appeared to give to each other a dark and sinister life under the shifting light of the flames; but it was not until the clock had struck, bringing him up with a start, that Harlock began to tell us the following story:

"I found it in a corner of a shop in Fulham Road. It's a good piece of painting, as you can see—even by firelight; but that was not the reason why I bought it. The reason was not so—so aesthetic as that. I bought it because I knew the subject, and because I knew why the painter had painted it. *His* reason was not aesthetic, either—the man is quite unknown to me, by the way—and I don't expect he cared how little he got for his picture. He wanted to thrust it out of his sight... and he got rid of it because it had served its turn—the painting of it had prevented him from going mad."

Harlock put his finger-tips together.

"I myself had done the same thing, you see. But I never sold my picture. I never tried. Perhaps my professional instinct is not so developed as his. As soon as I had painted it, from memory, putting in that finishing touch, that pinpoint of light in the landscape, I took a knife, and slashed the thing to pieces.

"No doubt," he continued, hesitatingly, looking round briefly at our row of faces, "you are wondering why, having got rid of it in such a deliberate manner, I bought its counterpart the moment I saw one in a shop. The reason is very simple. I was overjoyed at finding that another person besides myself had been to the place... I always think of it as the loneliest *inhabited* house in England. The atrocious puffball weed told me that the house was indeed the very same. Without doubt, *he* had tasted the cheese and cider there... had stayed there half the night... had handled the same set of instruments..."

Harlock stared into the heart of the fire.

"Very vividly," he continued, in a thoughtful voice, "I remember that slow and oddly clear September evening when, having walked for the better part of a day, I found myself, with the sea waves at my back, staying inland at a house, a cottage, a habitation—call it what you like—that sprawled beneath a thin protection of stunted and ragged trees at the back of a field of washed-out poppies, under a rising moon. A solitary light was shining below the thatched eaves, and I walked towards it over the poppy field.

"A nice sort of place to come upon when you're tired and hungry and have lost your way! Look for yourselves. Did you ever see a more god-forsaken spot, such ragged trees, such a sprawling and shapeless dwelling? And yet, you know, because of its very shapelessness it *had* a shape—the picture has caught it perfectly, and so did mine. Can you imagine such a ridiculous combination of things as a bloated pancake with a blanket of heavy thatch on the top of it? That's how it looked, in detail, when I was right up to it. All the straw colour had been soaked out by the sea-wind. And look at that feathery, puff-ball weed! It shows like a ground-mist in the picture, doesn't it? Up to the thatched eaves in many places; even higher. Heaven knows how I found the door at last, and the courage to thump it. I shall never forget that dead and dismal thumping on the door. Then I tried the latch, and found myself at once in a room that seemed to spread over the whole house. For all I knew, it *was* the house. The endless sagging beams helped to make it look like that, I think. And at first I could see nothing else in particular—nothing but the lamp on the huge round table, and a multitude of tiny windows with that weed shining beyond them. Then I saw some plates and dishes on the wall, the swinging of a pendulum—and after that... I always wish I had never seen the large and pale and flabby woman who was moving towards me from the far end of the room. She was unspeakably large. I stood my ground, staring, and I believe I counted the thumping clicks of the pendulum clock; they must have been, at any rate, the only links between myself and the busy world outside. They pulled me together at last, I suppose, for suddenly I blurted out that I had lost my way and had seen her light; and as she approached the table, smiling at me enormously, she sucked in her tiny lips until they almost disappeared. But the horridest thing about her was that she seemed to have earth in her hair."

Here Harlock paused; but only a stranger would have broken the silence. "I have never seen a fatter woman," our host continued. "She panted at the slightest exertion—gently enough—it was the only sound that ever came from her—but sufficiently to show me that she was certainly flesh and blood. Otherwise I might have had my doubts about her. For even at a distance the house had looked haunted. Something in the very set of the trees—the flock of feathers on the evening light—and the soughing of the sea... And because of her shortness of breath I began to suspect that her fatness was constitutional. Oh, you mustn't think that I was working it out as clearly as this! It was merely a matter of instinct, I suppose, roused by my hopes of a good square meal. And in the end, of course, I found I was right: my spirits had risen too high. Risen at the prospect of a well-stocked larder, I mean. For she motioned me up to the table, and I sat on a stool, an antique thing, hollowed and polished with years of sitting; and then she took a loaf of bread and half a cheese from a cupboard, and poured me out a bowl of cider, and I wanted to cry. Or very nearly.

"She sat there facing me across the table, large and still and silent in her wan, robe-like dress, while in my hunger I tried to swallow my tough bread and crumbly cheese and to wash them down with hurried gulps of cider from the bowl; and whenever I glanced at her over the rim I saw her horrid smile. My hostess sat with her clasped plump hands on the table, smiling at unknown things. Hostess? What a funny word to use! I watched her get up noiselessly, and then—I wish I could make you hear the sound that followed. She went round the room, swishing the little window-curtains on their metal rings and rods: swish, swish, swish, swish, a ripple passing round the room, blotting out the moonlight, blotting out those pictures of feathery, puff-ball weed.

"She left me abruptly after that—abruptly for her, I mean— and I wondered, with rather mixed feelings, whether she had gone to prepare a room for me—a bed. Perhaps it was because of her unbroken silence, and the even flow of her movements, that I took her hospitality, such as it was, as a matter of course. I don't remember asking myself whether she would expect to be paid for my night's lodging; she and money seemed so utterly unrelated to each other, I suppose. But I do remember that this sudden and welcome change in the evening's entertainment left me somewhat breathless—a bit frightened. Should I run away? While there was time? The same old situation that you come across in books. Such nonsense! But that's exactly how I felt, just then. The cider didn't help me. The cheese was appalling. Dry, crumbly stuff. Sour, too. Tasting rather of earth.

"I was to get many things into my head that night, but never the cider. This woman's flowing bowl was not of that kind. I could have shattered the silence without an effort, if it had been. In the end I made my effort, and succeeded—but what a fool I felt! 'I must do my best,' I thought, 'to keep my spirits up. *I shall see it out!*'—and the sudden sound of my voice startled me and made me laugh. I began at once to examine the room with deep interest. Here and there the ceiling bulged to such an extent that I *knew* I would bump my head against it sooner or later—running from the house in a moment of panic, for instance—it's funny what nerves will do! I liked the clock high up on the wall—and that was scarcely higher than head-level. It was one of those ancient timepieces built when time was really slow, with a round, brass face, a leisurely pendulum, and two brass weights on chains—by which I gathered that the clock would strike at any moment now—it was nearly nine—and I was curious to hear its voice. The plates and dishes on the cloudy dresser gave out a sort of phosphorescent light. They had no other use, I thought, but to be seen and wondered at; for a large oak chest was standing in front of the range. The mouth of the chimney above the chest was hollow, dark, and dead. There was no fireside. No chimney corner. Nowhere to sit and tell stories...

"I never heard it strike," he said, with a kind of regret. "She came back before that happened. I heard the last of its loud ticks as she closed the door upon them; and I felt quite lonely then, lonely and rather bewildered, for while I was following her along the countless passages and ups and downs of her strange residence she looked like a thick mist rolling in front of me... if you can imagine such a silly thing as a solid mist panting for breath."

Harlock turned, and gazed for several moments—with a certain look of distress, I thought—at the picture in the chair. "I want you," he said, "I want you to get the hang of that room she took me to. I mean especially the feeling of it. But to begin with, it was a very big room, and she had lighted it with six or seven candles. Quite a showy display! Three of them were standing on a large, square table in the middle of the floor. The floor itself was covered with some kind of cork matting. She had stood two candles on a chest of drawers. She had even placed a candle on a chair in one of the corners, near the huge, painted, wooden bed. All the furniture was very massive, and painted. After the candles, it was the colour of the room that I noticed chiefly. The walls were panelled—shallow panels from wainscot to cornice—and painted a bluish green—I may as well call it viridian; a very light and faded but still rather shiny viridian. The furniture was of the same colour; so was the bed-linen, and the billowy eiderdown; so were the heavy, shallow window-curtains; and because of this prevalent colouring, and in spite of the size of the furniture, the room looked empty and asleep. I sat on the edge of the high bed, on the top of the thick eiderdown, with the toes of my shoes just touching the floor. My mind was all on the room in which I was sitting. I was trying to get the feeling of it. And do you know what it was? You can't. It was *children*.

"It had been a nursery. But whose children, whose nursery, how can we ever know? Hers? That would be the most natural thing in the world... and the most horrible. And in any case," said Harlock thoughtfully, after a pause, "the question didn't seem to matter very much to me then, and I don't know that it does now. The feeling was there—the feeling of the nursery itself, I mean, of—merely of children long departed. And that also—I remember thinking to myself after a time—didn't matter any longer. The history of the room was over. Over and done with. Or was it, perhaps, only 'over', and not yet 'done with'?

"At this point in my speculations I took off my heavy walking-shoes, and lay flat on the bed, under the thick eiderdown, which I pulled up to my chin. I had left all the candles burning, for I was afraid to sleep. I spent some time tracing with my eyes the very faded pattern on the ceiling, pretending that the pattern was a maze and that I was walking about in it, a game that I never get tired of; but even if I had gone to sleep I suppose the little bell would have woken me. You know how it is, in a strange room—things are watching you all the night, and you awaken early, suddenly, all alert: you wake up to listen for something that you have just heard. For some time I had been listening to the far off flump of the slow waves on the shore; and suddenly I heard the tinkle of a bell on the beach. They had washed up a bell? In a few moments, of course, I knew that it had tinkled in the room. I let the thought sink in. Then I threw off the eiderdown!

"It was only a momentary panic. One of those unreasoning fears that children do have, you know. In fact, as I roved about in my socks, searching for a toy, the room appeared quite friendly. I felt that I had known it all my life—The Viridian Room. I heard the bell tinkling again, jerkily, intermittently. At last I stood in front of a tall cupboard. It wasn't locked. And there were no shelves in it—nothing to throw shadows. On the floor, at the back, I saw the bell shining in the candlelight. It was one of those tiny, round bells that toy reins have on them. I couldn't see why it had rung. By that, I mean, of course, *how* the bell had rung... the material reason... I took it out," said Harlock, "I took it out and tinkled it; and presently I went and looked at the box of chalks on the table.

"It was open. I had seen it all the time—seen it without realising exactly what it was, I mean—seen just its existence, and not its purpose; for who would expect a box like that to contain chalks all of the same colour? After tinkling my bell for some time I dropped it on to the table and sat there facing the open cupboard and toying with my chalks, and presently I wanted a sheet of paper to write on. I found it in the drawer beside me, an exercise-book. I pulled up my chair, spread my elbows, and wrote at once, in viridian green, on a new page:

One, two, buckle my shoe;
Three, four, knock at the door;
Five, six, pick up sticks;
Seven, eight, lay them straight;
Nine, ten, a fine fat hen;
Eleven, twelve, dig and delve.

"You remember that nursery rhyme? Until then I had forgotten it. I used to think it was full of sense, even when taken in a lump; and while I was still sitting at the table, looking across it into the open, lighted cupboard, and thinking over the words that I had just written down, I saw the mouse. At the back of the cupboard, against the wall, I saw a mousehole. Clearly the source of the tinkling! While I watched, two black shiny eyes appeared, and the furry shadow glided along the floor of the cupboard and into the room, where it took to moving in fits and starts.

"'Hi there! What are you up to, you little beggar?' I called out, starting off in pursuit, and brandishing one of my heavy walking-shoes—but not with any serious purpose; you know I would never hit a creature, don't you? I simply followed the mouse across the room as far as the chest of drawers; and there I found a pair of shoes on the floor... kicked off into the corner between the chest and the wall.

"One, two, buckle my shoe."

Harlock had dropped into his gentlest voice.

"They *did* have buckles on them. Buckles as bright as silver. So I put on the shoes, and buckled them up, and found that in them

I could walk as stealthily as a cat. I prowled with such gentleness over the room that I hardly made a candle quiver; and presently I stopped in front of the narrow door, the door that I haven't yet told you about.

"You see it the moment you enter the room—a rather low and narrow door on the far side of the table; but you don't *really* see it until later, when you are standing right in front of it, looking at the little knocker—the kind that you sometimes see on the study door in a vicarage.

"*Three, four, knock at the door.*"

"I knocked at the door.

"'Come in!' called an incredibly high-pitched, thin, and windy voice. I went in, shutting the door behind me."

At this point, Harlock jumped to his feet, and proposed loudly a round of drinks. He switched on a blaze of light, and we heard him boiling his electric kettle behind our backs.

"All that I could see at first," he continued, in a steady voice, a minute or so after he had returned to his chair, and while we were still sipping our whisky toddies in the restored fire-light, "was a regiment of moonbeams slanting into the room through uncurtained lattice windows, and a man facing me across the floor, motionless, waiting—myself, in a mirror. What a fool one feels, when one's two selves are brought thus face to face—each of them scared of the other! The first movement—the sudden tentative trial— and the spell is broken, and you turn eagerly to look for the thing that you *expect* to find. I saw her, at hand, lying on her large bed, slowly kneading the eiderdown beneath her with her fat fingers, pulling in her lips, watching me with her small eyes; and the floor and the bed and the woman were patterned with lattice windows. The bars of shadow and light showed me her rounded, massive bulk to perfection. Five, six, pick up sticks.

"And where do you think I found them? Why, on the bed itself, of course! A couple of bedstaffs. Do you know what a bedstaff is? It's a loose cross-piece of antique bedsteads, often used as a handy weapon. I took them from the head and foot of the bed, and while I was doing so the face of my hostess was twisting about with a kind of cringing, mock terror. Five, six, pick up sticks—seven, eight— lay them straight! I remember that while I was wielding my cudgels I glanced in the mirror and saw the shadows of the window bars slipping along them. Lay them straight, lay them straight! Seven, eight, lay them straight! I laid them good and straight. Once I felt a shiver in my arm—I had hit the ceiling.

"As soon as I had satisfied myself that the flutters of her heart had ceased—I can still feel her wrist between my finger and thumb, you know—I dropped my bedstaffs for good, and hurried off to open one of the two other doors in the room—The Garden Door, I fancied the children had called it. How breathless was the scene through The Garden Door! I held my breath and gazed all over the great neglected garden; then I returned to the woman and picked her up, and I swear she was no heavier than a puff-ball. But what an armful she made! What an armful! What a fine fat hen! I carried her into the garden and over the rank grass and plunged with her into the cluster of weed beyond. I had seen it through The Garden Door, shimmering in the moonlight. The stuff stood higher than my head, and was here in great profusion—a forest of weed. I don't know how long I took to reach my destination. Probably not very long; but when you're pretending to be a pirate—or something of that kind—carrying your booty into the depths of the woods, to bury it, well, you don't care at all how long you take to reach the burial place. I came upon it in a moment, without warning—a sudden breaking from the weed into broad moonlight. 'This is the place,' I remember saying—'this is the spot they have chosen.'

"A spade lay ready to my hand, and fluff from the surrounding weed was drifting and settling all the while on to the tumbled earth.

"Eleven, twelve,
Dig and delve."

"I put down my burden, and took up the spade; and in that spot I dug and delved.

"When I came out of the weed," said Harlock, in his softest voice, "I saw that the feathers were sticking to my clothes like splashes of plaster." The fire had burnt low, we could scarcely see each other's faces, and only his voice was holding our little group together. "And I think it was the sight of those feathers," he said, "that sent me tearing back in a panic over the lawn, slapping my clothes all the time. Escape! I had no other thought but that. The children's rhyme had worked its way with me. Escape from the house and the clump of weed and the infamous thing that I had buried there. I ran through the bedroom and into the viridian nursery and kicked off the buckled shoes—kicked them into the corner, as all the others had done!—and while I was sitting on the bed, putting on my walking shoes, and looking towards the open cupboard, I saw the mouse returning to his hole beside the little bell...

"What was the use of my shutting the cupboard door with a bang? The Viridian Room hardly echoed to it. And even the loudest noise would not have convinced me that in that silent house such a sudden crash must certainly have brought things to an end. I even took steps to prove to my satisfaction that I was right. I ran back into the bedroom, back into all those spears of moonlight; and then—I wish I had never opened the Garden Door again. It was not what I actually saw, but what I knew I would see if I stayed for more than a very few moments... Looking across the wild, moonlit grass, I saw at least a *shaking* in the tops of the weed—and it wasn't the wind, you know—the movement was working its way towards me, slowly, jerkily, inch by inch...

"Fear, of course, won in the end. It sent me racing back into the depths of the house, where I caught my head a whack against the ceiling of the living-room, for the lamp was out. She had put it out.

The clock was thumping loudly; and I was scared to death that she might find me there before I got away.

"I hardly know how I got away in time. Hunting for the door, plunging through the puff-balls, sprinting over the poppy field— have you ever seen poppies by moonlight? Sanity! That's what I was after! Sanity, and the breath of the sea! Well, there was no breath, the wind was dead, there were no waves; but I scooped up the water in my two hands, and cooled the bump on my head... And after that I went back to the foreshore and watched the house until I saw her light gleaming again..."

Harlock stared at the dying fire.

"I suppose I ought to have known it at once," he said, as if to himself. "Especially from a distance. Known that the spot was haunted, I mean. It was there, staring me in the face—the queer shape, the mist of puff-balls, the heavy thatch, the very set of the trees."

Then one of us, softly, as if to take the edge off the silence that followed, ventured a remark.

"I suppose the real ghost was the children."

"*She* was not!" Harlock burst out. "She was something far worse than that!"

Nothing further was said while we watched our host returning his picture to the remote corner.

Liszt's Concerto Pathétique
Edna W. Underwood

It was in the winter of 1906 that the following remarkable incidents were communicated to me, and truly in a most remarkable manner. But who may say what shall be the intermediary link, the invisible tie to connect us with the facts of a vanished past? Who may say what vague but mentally potent beings dwell on the border line separating the real from the unreal, floating up perhaps from unthinkable depths of time and space, there to await the propitious moment for tapping some nerve of consciousness in us and establishing telegraphic communication with the soul? Over these spirit wires of thought and feeling they flash faint messages. They set the nerves a-tingle with the consciousness of an infinity of unknown lives surrounding our own, of invisible electric bodies that shock us into the recovery of forgotten memories, of the realisation of a limitless land that spreads beside us and upon the verge of which we live precariously poised.

On an afternoon in the winter of 1906 I attended a concert given by two well-known pianists. The *pièce de résistance* of the concert—it was for this that I had come—was a two-piano number, the *Concerto Pathétique* of Liszt, that sonorous tone tragedy with its wildly dramatic incidents, interrupted from time to time by a melody of more than mortal sweetness. As I listened, annoyed by the movements of seat companions, the bobbing black heads in front, or the dry winter light that filtered through a window to the right, striking sharply a corsage ornament or a jewel, and projecting into my eyes daggered light as from a crystal ball, suddenly my surroundings vanished, and I found myself alone looking out across a land that I had never seen.

Before me lay a twilight desert, sombre and lonely. Grey sand, uninterrupted by tree or dwelling, as undulating and as barren as the sea, stretched on and on. After a time I discovered that it was not twilight that caused the dimness. Upon the horizon there was nothing to indicate the vanishing of a sun or the future rising of a moon. Within the sky there were no stars. A Cimmerian twilight lay over all. I realised then that it was some place of purgatorial punishment, where sweet light did not come nor green earth growths, nor rain, nor the sound of leaves. It was a place of puzzling incompleteness and fragmentary physical form. There were arms twisted and bony and unattached to bodies, whose bent-fingered hands thirsted for cruelty or itched for gold. There were legs wrinkled and withered with pain and curved fantastically. There were backs bowed by the bearing of burdens, and a multitude of winged and awful faces forming a discordant chromatic scale of miseries, now flashing out leering and wanton smiles, and anon fading away into monotonous greyness.

It was a land of disembodied pain, where the shadow forms of sorrow dwelled. Regret, remorse, shame, misery, and anguish here got themselves clothed in unearthly substances, and strained futilely earthward where repentance lay. Here evil thoughts and desires were at once translated into form, swiftly to fade back again by uncountable disgusting gradations to the insubstantiality of dreams.

Across this desert a woman fled, breathless with haste and terror. She was young, scarcely more than a child, as years count, and she would have been beautiful had not her features been disfigured by grief. Out behind, a long black robe floated like an emblem of evil, giving to her appearance a certain cloistral touch. Closer inspection proved it to be a nun's cloak. It was unfastened and thrown hastily

160

about her where it was held together by one small nervous hand. Her hair, which was pale gold, was short-cropped and curly, and bore the imprint of a close covering. There was something pitiful in these little clustering curls of faded gold, which were down-soft like the hair on a baby's neck. They told of helplessness and youth. Now in places they were darkened by the perspiration of fear. Cloistral life and the nun's hood had bleached her face and given to it a marble pallor, until it seemed to radiate light in the general dimness. Her eyes were a dark ethereal blue. In their depths lay a light made of blended pain, passion, and regret. As the hideous sand monsters drifted toward her, threatening to block her way, then vanished to reshape themselves into still more hideous forms, childishly she opened her mouth to call for help. But no sound issued from her lips, although the little chin quivered piteously. I knew that she was dumb and could not speak.

As she sped on, upbourne by an unnatural energy, there rang out upon the desert air a melody of more than mortal sweetness, the brief and broken fragment of a phrase. As the music died away upon the moonless space, there fell across the sand the pallid cold radiance of a cross, but so far away, so etherealised by space and distance, that it was scarcely more than a shadow's shadow.

At first, I thought that the music was in some inexplicable way related to the beauty of her face—that perhaps they were one. There was a similarity between them. Both set to vibrating the same responsive fibres of the heart. Both were penetratingly sweet, yet touched with sorrow.

Further consideration proved this conjecture to be vain, and that the music came from some alien yet nearby place. I could see by the woman's face that it caused her joy and sorrow, and I felt that it always sang on in her heart, and that her trembling lips tried to frame its sounds. Yet—in some way I could not understand—it kept her forever outside the radiance of the cross.

Again and again it rang out—a melody of more than mortal sweetness. And each time the woman hastened her pace. The face of the desert began to change, and in the distance there was something that lay like the shimmer of light. I watched it as it grew brighter. Colours were distinguishable. It was a garden! Oh, the yearning in her face! Oh, the effort with which she summoned strength to reach it! Her eyes grew black with determination. Her little curls were spotted with moisture. Sweeter and more penetrating became the breath of melody. It winged her feet with courage. It put strength into her heart. Yes, yes, there it lay! A fresh, bright, green garden, where a happy multitude of tiny blue and white flowers grew. Over it iris-winged insects fluttered. The sun shone resplendently. Here was the home of the melody. Its sweetness was that of love and the fullness of life. Now the radiance of the cross no longer touched the sandy waste. It remained high in the air, aloof and far, a wan gold shadow of exquisite remoteness, like the ghost of a vanished joy.

As she drew nearer, more intense became the light that fell upon the garden. It became a blue and dazzling glory, beneath which the tiny flowers expanded and expanded until they were lilies of mammoth size and proportion. Oh, so lustrous, so satin soft, so voluptuously lovely was their texture! A rare fragrance filtered from them through the sand-thick air, a languorous, seductive, benumbing fragrance, like the intangible soul of pleasure. When again the music came, the giant lily buds burst open, disclosing in place of pistil and stamen the white glorious bodies of women, whose hair outfloated in bright crinkles like blown flame, and whose feet trod an amorous measure.

Now I knew whence the music came. It was made by the twining beauty of seductive arms, the swaying of bright torsos, the interlacing of lithe limbs, the argent light struck from bared breasts and brows. It was their white passion, their wanton loveliness, their amorous longing, their electric, vital, and indomitable youth translated into tone.

Far above the desert now, the wan cross hung in dim remoteness, a faint frown of light, withdrawing coldly into the depths of space. The garden glory touched the woman's face. The sand monsters fell back, no longer encumbering her. Happiness and courage shone from her eyes. The journey was nearly over. A step—a dozen steps and she would have gained the garden. She was all but there. She flung away the convent cloak. The sweet wind lifted the little curls upon her brow. A blue lily leaned amorously to meet her, its petals ready to enfold her. The strange light swathed her about like a robe. The melody touched her heart to joy. She was ready to grasp a waiting flower; one white hand reached for it, when a thunder of many wings was heard.

From across the desert, from the sky above, a multitude of blackish green-winged monsters, darkening the air to a dun midnight, dashed down. Their black and sullen bodies, outspread wing on wing, shut out the garden and formed a hideous wall of crawling heads. The great wings surrounded and engulfed her, beating her back—back—back—with lightning-like rapidity. Away, away, away they swept her, so swiftly that the desert was left behind. And still they swept her on and on, across another land—a land of granite, bleak and sterile and black, whose darkness was shivered from time to time by the angry glare of whirling swords that formed the mighty gate of a realm of night. Here the whirring wings uplifted her. She had no more hold upon the earth. Below, above, beside, were depth on depth of overlapping wings. Once, for an instant, the swaying, fluttering band fell back. Sharp sword light streaked her face. I saw its white horror and the little curls a-dance with fear. Then more monsters came rushing. The earth and the air were a-quiver with wings. There was a rush and a roar. There was a noise as of many waters. Then the monsters swept away into the land of darkness beyond, where nothing was distinguishable, where there was no measurement of time or space. Again the granite land was lone and silent, its grey immovableness disturbed only by the swinging gate of swords, which streaked the rocks with floating ribbons of light.

The Room in the Tower
EF Benson

It is probable that everybody who is at all a constant dreamer has had at least one experience of an event or a sequence of circumstances which have come to his mind in sleep being subsequently realised in the material world. But, in my opinion, so far from this being a strange thing, it would be far odder if this fulfilment did not occasionally happen, since our dreams are, as a rule, concerned with people whom we know and places with which we are familiar, such as might very naturally occur in the awake and daylit world. True, these dreams are often broken into by some absurd and fantastic incident, which puts them out of court in regard to their subsequent fulfilment, but on the mere calculation of chances, it does not appear in the least unlikely that a dream imagined by anyone who dreams constantly should occasionally come true. Not long ago, for instance, I experienced such a fulfilment of a dream which seems to me in no way remarkable and to have no kind of psychical significance. The manner of it was as follows.

A certain friend of mine, living abroad, is amiable enough to write to me about once in a fortnight. Thus, when fourteen days of thereabouts have elapsed since I last heard from him, my mind, probably, either consciously or subconsciously, is expectant of a letter from him. One night last week I dreamed that as I was going upstairs to dress for dinner I heard, as I often heard, the sound of the postman's knock on my front door, and diverted my direction downstairs instead. There, among other correspondence, was a letter from him. Thereafter the fantastic entered, for on opening it I found inside the ace of diamonds and scribbled across it in his well-known handwriting, "I am sending you this for safe custody, as you know it is running an unreasonable risk to keep aces in Italy." The next evening I was just preparing to go upstairs to dress when I heard the postman's knock, and did precisely as I had done in my dream. There, among other letters, was one from my friend. Only it did not contain the ace of diamonds. Had it done so, I should have attached more weight to the matter, which, as it stands, seems to me a perfectly ordinary coincidence. No doubt I consciously or subconsciously expected a letter from him, and this suggested to me my dream. Similarly, the fact that my friend had not written to me for a fortnight suggested to him that he should do so. But occasionally it is not so easy to find such an explanation, and for the following story I can find no explanation at all. It came out of the dark, and into the dark it has gone again.

All my life I have been a habitual dreamer: the nights are few, that is to say, when I do not find on awaking in the morning that some mental experience has been mine, and sometimes, all night long, apparently, a series of the most dazzling adventures befalls me. Almost without exception these adventures are pleasant, though often merely trivial. It is of an exception that I am going to speak.

It was when I was about sixteen that a certain dream first came to me, and this is how it befell. It opened with my being set down at the door of a big red-brick house, where, I understood, I was going to stay. The servant who opened the door told me that tea was being served in the garden, and led me through a low dark-panelled hall with a large open fireplace, on to a cheerful green lawn set round with flower beds. There were grouped about the tea-table a small party of people, but they were all strangers to me except one, who was a schoolfellow called Jack Stone, clearly the son of the house, and he introduced me to his mother and father and a couple of sisters. I was, I remember, somewhat astonished to find myself here, for the boy in question was scarcely known to me, and I rather disliked what I knew of him; moreover, he had left school nearly a year before. The afternoon was very hot, and an intolerable oppression reigned. On the far side of the lawn ran a red-brick wall, with an iron gate in its centre, outside which stood a walnut tree. We sat in the shadow of the house opposite a row of long windows, inside which I could see a table, with cloth laid, glimmering with glass and silver. This garden front of the house was very long, and at one end of it stood a tower of three stories, which looked to me much older than the rest of the building.

Before long, Mrs Stone, who, like the rest of the party, had sat in absolute silence, said to me, "Jack will show you your room: I have given you the room in the tower."

Quite inexplicably my heart sank at her words. I felt as if I had known that I should have the room in the tower, and that it contained something dreadful and significant. Jack instantly got up, and I understood that I had to follow him. In silence we passed through the hall, and mounted a great oak staircase with many corners, and arrived at a small landing with two doors set in it. He pushed one of these open for me to enter, and without coming in himself, closed it after me. Then I knew that my conjecture had been right: there was something awful in the room, and with the terror of nightmare growing swiftly and enveloping me, I awoke in a spasm of terror.

Now that dream or variations on it occurred to me intermittently for fifteen years. Most often it came in exactly this form, the arrival, the tea laid out on the lawn, the deadly silence succeeded by that one deadly sentence, the mounting with Jack Stone up to the room in the tower where horror dwelt, and it always came to a close in the nightmare of terror at that which was in the room, though I never saw what it was. At other times I experienced variations on this same theme. Occasionally, for instance, we would be sitting at dinner in the dining-room, into the windows of which I had looked on the first night when the dream of this house visited me, but wherever we were, there was the same silence, the same sense of dreadful oppression and foreboding. And the silence I knew would always be broken by Mrs Stone saying to me, "Jack will show you your room: I have given you the room in the tower." Upon which (this was invariable) I had to follow him up the oak staircase with many corners, and enter the place that I dreaded more and more each time that I visited it in sleep. Or, again, I would find myself playing cards, still in silence, in a drawing-room lit with immense chandeliers that gave a blinding illumination. What the game was I have no idea; what I remembered, with a sense of miserable anticipation, was that soon Mrs Stone would get up and say to me, "Jack will show you your room: I have given you the room in the tower." This drawing-room where we played cards was next to the dining-room, and, as I have said, was always brilliantly illuminated, whereas the rest of the house was full of dusk and shadows. And yet, how often, in spite of those bouquets of lights, have I not pored over the cards that were dealt me, scarcely able for some reason to see them. Their designs, too, were strange: there were no red suits, but all were black, and among them there were certain cards which were black all over. I hated and dreaded those.

As this dream continued to recur, I got to know the greater part of the house. There was a smoking-room beyond the drawing-room, at the end of a passage with a green-baize door. It was always very dark there, and as often as I went there I passed somebody whom I could not see in the doorway coming out. Curious developments, too, took place in the characters that peopled the dream as might happen to living persons. Mrs Stone, for instance, who, when I first saw her, had been black-haired, became grey, and instead of rising briskly, as she had done at first when she said, "Jack will show you to your room: I have given you the room in the tower," got up very feebly, as if the strength was leaving her limbs. Jack also grew up, and became a rather ill-looking young man, with a brown moustache, while one of the sisters ceased to appear, and I understood she was married.

Then it so happened that I was not visited by this dream for six months or more, and I began to hope, in such inexplicable dread did I hold it, that it had passed away for good. But one night after this interval I again found myself being shown out on to the lawn for tea, and Mrs Stone was not there, while the others were all dressed in black. At once I guessed the reason, and my heart leaped at the thought that perhaps this time I should not have to sleep in the room in the tower, and though we usually all sat in silence, on this occasion the sense of relief made me talk and laugh as I had never yet done. But even then matters were not altogether comfortable, for no one else spoke, but they all looked secretly at each other. And soon the foolish stream of my talk ran dry, and gradually an apprehension worse than anything I had previously known gained on me as the light slowly faded.

Suddenly a voice which I knew well broke the stillness, the voice of Mrs Stone, saying, "Jack will show you your room: I have given you the room in the tower." It seemed to come from near the gate in the red-brick wall that bounded the lawn, and looking up, I saw that the grass outside was sown thick with gravestones. A curious greyish light shone from them, and I could read the lettering on the grave nearest me, and it was, "In evil memory of Julia Stone." And as usual Jack got up, and again I followed him through the hall and up the staircase with many corners. On this occasion it was darker than usual, and when I passed into the room in the tower I could only just see the furniture, the position of which was already familiar to me. Also there was a dreadful odour of decay in the room, and I woke screaming.

The dream, with such variations and developments as I have mentioned, went on at intervals for fifteen years. Sometimes I would dream it two or three nights in succession; once, as I have said, there was an intermission of six months, but taking a reasonable average, I should say that I dreamed it quite as often as once in a month. It had, as is plain, something of nightmare about it, since it always ended in the same appalling terror, which so far from getting less, seemed to me to gather fresh fear every time that I experienced it. There was, too, a strange and dreadful consistency about it. The characters in it, as I have mentioned, got regularly older, death and marriage visited this silent family, and I never in the dream, after Mrs Stone had died, set eyes on her again. But it was always her voice that told me that the room in the tower was prepared for me, and whether we had tea out on the lawn, or the scene was laid in one of the rooms overlooking it, I could always see her gravestone standing just outside the iron gate. It was the same, too, with the married daughter, usually she was not present, but once or twice she returned again, in company with a man, whom I took to be her husband. He, too, like the rest of them, was always silent. But, owing to the constant repetition of the dream, I had ceased to attach, in my waking hours, any significance to it. I never met Jack Stone again during all those years, nor did I ever see a house that resembled this dark house of my dream. And then something happened.

I had been in London in this year, up till the end of the July, and during the first week in August went down to stay with a friend in a house he had taken for the summer months in the Ashdown Forest district of Sussex. I left London early, for John Clinton was to meet me at Forest Row Station and we were going to spend the day golfing and go to his house in the evening. He had his motor with him and we set off, about five of the afternoon, after a thoroughly delightful day, for the drive, the distance being some ten miles. As it was still so early we did not have tea at the clubhouse, but waited till we should get home. As we drove, the weather, which up till then had been, though hot, deliciously fresh, seemed to me to alter in quality, and become very stagnant and oppressive, and I felt that indefinable sense of ominous apprehension that I am accustomed to before thunder. John, however, did not share my views, attributing my loss of lightness to the fact that I had lost both my matches. Events proved, however, that I was right, though I do not think that the thunderstorm that broke that night was the sole cause of my depression.

Our way lay through deep high-banked lanes, and before we had gone very far I fell asleep, and was only awakened by the stopping of the motor. And with a sudden thrill, partly of fear but chiefly of curiosity, I found myself standing in the doorway of my house of dream. We went, I half wondering whether or not I was dreaming still, through a low oak-panelled hall and out on to the lawn, where tea was laid in the shadow of the house. It was set in flower-beds, a red-brick wall, with a gate in it, bounded one side, and out beyond that was a space of rough grass with a walnut tree. The façade of the house was very long, and at one end stood a three-storeyed tower, markedly older than the rest.

Here for the moment all resemblance to the repeated dream ceased. There was no silent and somehow terrible family, but a large assembly of exceedingly cheerful persons, all of whom were known to me. And in spite of the horror with which the dream itself had always filled me, I felt nothing of it now that the scene of it was thus reproduced before me. But I felt intensest curiosity as to what was going to happen.

Tea pursued its cheerful course, and before long Mrs Clinton got up. And at that moment I think I knew what she was going to say. She spoke to me, and what she said was: "Jack will show you your room: I have given you the room in the tower."

At that, for half a second, the horror of the dream took hold of me again. But it quickly passed, and again I felt nothing more than the most intense curiosity. It was not very long before it was amply satisfied.

John turned to me.

"Right up at the top of the house," he said, "but I think you'll be comfortable. We're absolutely full up. Would you like to go and see it now? By Jove, I believe that you are right and that we are going to have a thunderstorm. How dark it has become."

I got up and followed him. We passed through the hall, and up the perfectly familiar staircase. Then he opened the door, and I went in. And at that moment sheer unreasoning terror again possessed me. I did not know what I feared: I simply feared. Then like a sudden recollection, when one remembers a name which has long escaped the memory, I knew what I feared. I feared Mrs Stone, whose grave with the sinister inscription, "In evil memory", I had so often seen in my dream, just beyond the lawn which lay below my window. And then once more the fear passed so completely that I wondered what there was to fear, and I found myself, sober and quiet and sane, in the room in the tower, the name of which I had so often heard in my dream, and the scene of which was so familiar.

I looked around it with a certain sense of proprietorship, and found that nothing had been changed from the dreaming nights in which I knew it so well. Just to the left of the door was the bed, lengthways along the wall, with the head of it in the angle. In a line with it was the fireplace and a small bookcase; opposite the door the outer wall was pierced by two lattice-paned windows, between which stood the dressing-table, while ranged along the fourth wall was the washing-stand and a big cupboard. My luggage had already been unpacked, for the furniture of dressing and undressing lay orderly on the washstand and toilet-table, while my dinner clothes were spread out on the coverlet of the bed. And then, with a sudden start of unexplained dismay, I saw that there were two rather conspicuous objects which I had not seen before in my dreams: one a life-sized oil painting of Mrs Stone, the other a black-and-white sketch of Jack Stone, representing him as he had appeared to me only a week before in the last of the series of these repeated dreams, a rather secret and evil-looking man of about thirty. His picture hung between the windows, looking straight across the room to the other portrait, which hung at the side of the bed. At that I looked next, and as I looked I felt once more the horror of nightmare seize me.

It represented Mrs Stone as I had seen her last in my dreams: old and withered and white-haired. But in spite of the evident feebleness of body, a dreadful exuberance and vitality shone through the envelope of flesh, an exuberance wholly malign, a vitality that foamed and frothed with unimaginable evil. Evil beamed from the narrow, leering eyes; it laughed in the demon-like mouth. The whole face was instinct with some secret and appalling mirth; the hands, clasped together on the knee, seemed shaking with suppressed and nameless glee. Then I saw also that it was signed in the left-hand bottom corner, and wondering who the artist could be, I looked more closely, and read the inscription, "Julia Stone by Julia Stone".

There came a tap at the door, and John Clinton entered.

"Got everything you want?" he asked.

"Rather more than I want," said I pointing to the picture.

He laughed.

"Hard-featured old lady," he said. "By herself, too, I remember. Anyhow she can't have flattered herself much."

"But don't you see?" said I. "It's scarcely a human face at all. It's the face of some witch, of some devil."

He looked at it more closely.

"Yes, it isn't very pleasant," he said. "Scarcely a bedside manner, eh? Yes; I can imagine getting the nightmare if I went to sleep with that close by my bed. I'll have it taken down if you like."

"I really wish you would," I said. He rang the bell, and with the help of a servant we detached the picture and carried it out on to the landing and put it with its face to the wall.

"By Jove, the old lady is a weight," said John, mopping his forehead.

"I wonder if she had something on her mind."

The extraordinary weight of the picture had struck me too. I was about to reply, when I caught sight of my own hand. There was blood on it, in considerable quantities, covering the whole palm.

"I've cut myself somehow," said I.

John gave a little startled exclamation. "Why, I have too," he said.

Simultaneously the footman took out his handkerchief and wiped his hand with it. I saw that there was blood also on his handkerchief.

John and I went back into the tower room and washed the blood off; but neither on his hand nor on mine was there the slightest trace of a scratch or cut. It seemed to me that, having ascertained this, we both, by a sort of tacit consent, did not allude to it again. Something in my case had dimly occurred to me that I did not wish to think about. It was but a conjecture, but I fancied that I knew the same thing had occurred to him.

The heat and oppression of the air, for the storm we had expected was still undischarged, increased very much after dinner, and for some time most of the party, among whom were John Clinton and myself, sat outside on the path bounding the lawn where we had had tea. The night was absolutely dark, and no twinkle of star or moon ray could penetrate the pall of cloud that overset the sky. By degrees our assembly thinned, the women went up to bed, men dispersed to the smoking-or billiard-room, and by eleven o'clock my host and I were the only two left. All the evening I thought that he had something on his mind, and as soon as we were alone he spoke.

"The man who helped us with the picture had blood on his hand too, did you notice?" he said.

"I asked him just now if he had cut himself, and he said he supposed he had, but that he could find no mark of it. Now where did that blood come from?"

By dint of telling myself that I was not going to think about it, I had succeeded in not doing so, and I did not want, especially just at bedtime, to be reminded of it.

"I don't know," said I, "and I don't really care so long as the picture of Mrs Stone is not by my bed."

He got up.

"But it's odd," he said. "Ha! Now you'll see another odd thing."

A dog of his, an Irish terrier by breed, had come out of the house as we talked. The door behind us into the hall was open, and a bright oblong of light shone across the lawn to the iron gate which led on to the rough grass outside, where the walnut tree stood. I saw that the dog had all his hackles up, bristling with rage and fright, his lips were curled back from his teeth, as if he was ready to spring at something, and he was growling to himself. He took not the slightest notice of his master or me, but stiffly and tensely walked across the grass to the iron gate. There he stood for a moment, looking through the bars and still growling. Then of a sudden his courage seemed to desert him: he gave one long howl, and scuttled back to the house with a curious crouching sort of movement.

"He does that half a dozen times a day," said John. "He sees something which he both hates and fears."

I walked to the gate and looked over it. Something was moving on the grass outside, and soon a sound which I could not instantly identify came to my ears. Then I remembered what it was: it was the purring of a cat. I lit a match, and saw the purrer, a big blue Persian, walking round and round in a little circle just outside the gate, stepping high and ecstatically, with tail carried aloft like a banner. Its eyes were bright and shining, and every now and then it put its head down and sniffed at the grass.

I laughed.

"The end of that mystery, I am afraid," I said. "Here's a large cat having Walpurgis Night all alone."

"Yes, that's Darius," said John. "He spends half the day and all night there. But that's not the end of the dog mystery—for Toby and he are the best of friends—but the beginning of the cat mystery. What's the cat doing there? And why is Darius pleased, while Toby is terror-stricken?"

At that moment I remembered the rather horrible detail of my dreams—when I saw through the gate, just where the cat was now, the white tombstone with the sinister inscription. But before I could answer the rain began, as suddenly and heavily as if a tap had been turned on, and simultaneously the big cat squeezed through the bars of the gate and came leaping across the lawn to the house for shelter. Then it sat in the doorway, looking out eagerly into the dark. It spat and struck at John with its paw as he pushed it in in order to close the door.

Somehow, with the portrait of Julia Stone in the passage outside, the room in the tower had absolutely no alarm for me, and as I went to bed, feeling very sleepy and heavy, I had nothing more than interest for the curious incident about our bleeding hands, and the conduct of the cat and dog. The last thing I looked at before I put out my light was the square empty space by my bed where the portrait had been. Here the paper was of its original full tint of dark red: over the rest of the walls it had faded. Then I blew out my candle and instantly fell asleep.

My awakening was equally instantaneous, and I sat bolt upright in bed under the impression that some bright light had been flashed in my face, though it was now absolutely pitch dark. I knew exactly where I was, in the room which I had dreaded in dreams, but no horror that I ever felt when asleep approached the fear that now invaded and froze my brain. Immediately after, a peal of thunder crackled just above the house, but the probability that it was only a flash of lightning which had awoken me gave no reassurance to my galloping heart. Something I knew was in the room with me, and instinctively I put out my right hand, which was nearest the wall, to keep it away. And my hand touched the edge of a picture-frame hanging close to me.

I sprang out of bed, upsetting the small table that stood by it, and I heard my watch, candle and matches clatter on to the floor. But for the moment there was no need of light, for a blinding flash leaped out of the clouds and showed me that by my bed again hung the picture of Mrs Stone. And instantly the room went into blackness again. But in that flash I saw another thing also, namely a figure that leaned over the end of my bed, watching me. It was dressed in some close-clinging white garment, spotted and stained with mould, and the face was that of the portrait.

Overhead the thunder cracked and roared, and when it ceased and the deathly stillness succeeded, I heard the rustle of movement coming nearer me, and, more horrible yet, perceived an odour of corruption and decay. And then a hand was laid on the side of my neck, and close beside my ear I heard quick-taken, eager breathing. Yet I knew that this thing, though it could be perceived by touch, by smell, by eye and by ear, was still not of this earth, but something that had passed out of the body and had power to make itself manifest. Then a voice, already familiar to me, spoke,

"I knew you would come to the room in the tower," it said. "I have been long waiting for you. At last you have come. Tonight I shall feast; before long we will feast together."

And the quick breathing came closer to me; I could feel it on my neck.

At that the terror, which I think had paralysed me for the moment, gave way to the wild instinct of self-preservation. I hit wildly with both arms, kicking out at the same moment, and heard a little animal-squeal, and something soft dropped with a thud beside me. I took a couple of steps forward, nearly tripping up over whatever it was that lay there, and by the merest good-luck found the handle of the door. In another second I ran out on the landing and had banged the door behind me. Almost at the same moment I heard a door open somewhere below, and John Clinton, candle in hand, came running upstairs.

"What is it?" he said. "I sleep just below you, and heard a noise as if—Good heavens, there's blood on your shoulder." I stood there, so he told me afterwards, swaying from side to side, white as a sheet with the mark on my shoulder as if a hand covered with blood had been laid there.

"It's in there," I said, pointing, "She, you know. The portrait is in there, too, hanging up in the place we took it from."

At that he laughed.

"My dear fellow, this is mere nightmare," he said.

He pushed by me, and opened the door, I standing there simply inert with terror, unable to stop him, unable to move.

"Phew! What an awful smell," he said.

Then there was silence; he had passed out of my sight behind the open door. Next moment he came out again, as white as myself, and instantly shut it.

"Yes, the portrait's there," he said, "and on the floor is a thing—a thing spotted with earth, like what they bury people in. Come away, quick, come away."

How I got downstairs I hardly know. An awful shuddering and nausea of the spirit rather than of the flesh had seized me, and more than once he had to place my feet upon the steps, while every now and then he cast glances of terror and apprehension up the stairs. But in time we came to his dressing-room on the floor below, and there I told him what I have here described.

The sequel can be made short; indeed, some of my readers have perhaps already guessed what it was, if they remember that inexplicable affair of the churchyard at West Fawley, some eight years ago where an attempt was made three times to bury the body of a certain woman who had committed suicide. On each occasion the coffin was found in the course of a few days again protruding from the ground. After the third attempt, in order that the thing should not be talked about, the body was buried elsewhere in consecrated ground. Where it was buried was just outside the iron gate of the garden belonging to the house where this woman had lived. She had committed suicide in the room at the top of the tower in that house. Her name was Julia Stone.

Subsequently the body was again secretly dug up, and the coffin was found to be full of blood.

The Beckoning Fair One
Oliver Onions

The three or four "To Let" boards had stood within the low paling as long as the inhabitants of the little triangular "Square" could remember, and if they had ever been vertical it was a very long time ago. They now overhung the palings each at its own angle, and resembled nothing so much as a row of wooden choppers, ever in the act of falling upon some passer-by, yet never cutting off a tenant for the old house from the stream of his fellows. Not that there was ever any great "stream" through the square; the stream passed a furlong and more away, beyond the intricacy of tenements and alleys and byways that had sprung up since the old house had been built, hemming it in completely; and probably the house itself was only suffered to stand pending the falling-in of a lease or two, when doubtless a clearance would be made of the whole neighbourhood.

It was of bloomy old red brick, and built into its walls were the crowns and clasped hands and other insignia of insurance companies long since defunct. The children of the secluded square had swung upon the low gate at the end of the entrance-alley until little more than the solid top bar of it remained, and the alley itself ran past boarded basement windows on which tramps had chalked their cryptic marks. The path was washed and worn uneven by the spilling of water from the eaves of the encroaching next house, and cats and dogs had made the approach their own. The chances of a tenant did not seem such as to warrant the keeping of the "To Let" boards in a state of legibility and repair, and as a matter of fact they were not so kept.

For six months Oleron had passed the old place twice a day or oftener, on his way from his lodgings to the room, ten minutes' walk away, he had taken to work in; and for six months no hatchet-like notice-board had fallen across his path. This might have been due to the fact that he usually took the other side of the square. But he chanced one morning to take the side that ran past the broken gate and the rain-worn entrance alley, and to pause before one of the inclined boards. The board bore, besides the agent's name, the announcement, written apparently about the time of Oleron's own early youth, that the key was to be had at Number Six.

Now Oleron was already paying, for his separate bedroom and workroom, more than an author who, without private means, habitually disregards his public, can afford; and he was paying in addition a small rent for the storage of the greater part of his grandmother's furniture. Moreover, it invariably happened that the book he wished to read in bed was at his working-quarters half a mile or more away, while the note or letter he had sudden need of during the day was as likely as not to be in the pocket of another coat hanging behind his bedroom door. And there were other inconveniences in having a divided domicile. Therefore Oleron, brought suddenly up by the hatchet-like notice-board, looked first down through some scanty privet-bushes at the boarded basement windows, then up at the blank and grimy windows of the first floor, and so up to the second floor and the flat stone coping of the leads. He stood for a minute thumbing his lean and shaven jaw; then, with another glance at the board, he walked slowly across the square to Number Six.

He knocked, and waited for two or three minutes, but, although the door stood open, received no answer. He was knocking again when a long-nosed man in shirt-sleeves appeared.

"I was arsking a blessing on our food," he said in severe explanation.

Oleron asked if he might have the key of the old house; and the long-nosed man withdrew again.

Oleron waited for another five minutes on the step; then the man, appearing again and masticating some of the food of which he had spoken, announced that the key was lost.

"But you won't want it," he said. "The entrance door isn't closed, and a push'll open any of the others. I'm a agent for it, if you're thinking of taking it—"

Oleron recrossed the square, descended the two steps at the broken gate, passed along the alley, and turned in at the old wide doorway. To the right, immediately within the door, steps descended to the roomy cellars, and the staircase before him had a carved rail, and was broad and handsome and filthy. Oleron ascended it, avoiding contact with the rail and wall, and stopped at the first landing. A door facing him had been boarded up, but he pushed at that on his right hand, and an insecure bolt or staple yielded. He entered the empty first floor.

He spent a quarter of an hour in the place, and then came out again. Without mounting higher, he descended and recrossed the square to the house of the man who had lost the key.

"Can you tell me how much the rent is?" he asked.

The man mentioned a figure, the comparative lowness of which seemed accounted for by the character of the neighbourhood and the abominable state of unrepair of the place.

"Would it be possible to rent a single floor?"

The long-nosed man did not know; they might. . .

"Who are they?"

The man gave Oleron the name of a firm of lawyers in Lincoln's Inn.

"You might mention my name—Barrett," he added.

Pressure of work prevented Oleron from going down to Lincoln's Inn that afternoon, but he went on the morrow, and was instantly offered the whole house as a purchase for fifty pounds down, the remainder of the purchase-money to remain on mortgage. It took him half an hour to disabuse the lawyer's mind of the idea that he wished anything more of the place than to rent a single floor of it. This made certain hums and haws of a difference, and the lawyer was by no means certain that it lay within his power to do as Oleron suggested; but it was finally extracted from him that, provided the notice-boards were allowed to remain up, and that, provided it was agreed that in the event of the whole house letting, the arrangement should terminate automatically without further notice, something might be done. That the old place should suddenly let over his head seemed to Oleron the slightest of risks to take, and he promised a decision within a week. On the morrow he visited the house again, went through it from top to bottom, and then went home to his lodgings to take a bath.

He was immensely taken with that portion of the house he had already determined should be his own. Scraped clean and repainted, and with that old furniture of Oleron's grandmother's, it ought to be entirely charming. He went to the storage warehouse to refresh his memory of his half-forgotten belongings, and to take the measurements; and thence he went to a decorator's. He was very busy with his regular work, and could have wished that the notice-board had caught his attention either a few months earlier or else later in the year; but the quickest way would be to suspend work entirely until after his removal...

A fortnight later his first floor was painted throughout in a tender, elderflower white, the paint was dry, and Oleron was in the middle of his installation. He was animated, delighted; and he rubbed his hands as he polished and made disposals of his grandmother's effects—the tall lattice-paned china cupboard with its Derby and Mason and Spode, the large folding Sheraton table, the long, low bookshelves (he had had two of them "copied"), the chairs, the Sheffield candlesticks, the riveted rose-bowls. These things he set against his newly painted elder-white walls—walls of wood panelled in the happiest proportions, and moulded and coffered to the low-seated window-recesses in a mood of gaiety and rest that the builders of rooms no longer know. The ceilings were lofty, and faintly painted with an old pattern of stars; even the tapering mouldings of his iron fireplace were as delicately designed as jewellery; and Oleron walked about rubbing his hands, frequently stopping for the mere pleasure of the glimpses from white room to white room...

"Charming, charming!" he said to himself. "I wonder what Elsie Bengough will think of this!"

He bought a bolt and a Yale lock for his door, and shut off his quarters from the rest of the house. If he now wanted to read in bed, his book could be had for stepping into the next room. All the time, he thought how exceedingly lucky he was to get the place. He put up a hat-rack in the little square hall, and hung up his hats and caps and coats; and passers through the small triangular square late at night, looking up over the little serried row of wooden "To Let" hatchets, could see the light within Oleron's red blinds, or else the sudden darkening of one blind and the illumination of another, as Oleron, candlestick in hand, passed from room to room, making final settlings of his furniture, or preparing to resume the work that his removal had interrupted.

II

As far as the chief business of his life—his writing—was concerned, Paul Oleron treated the world a good deal better than he was treated by it; but he seldom took the trouble to strike a balance, or to compute how far, at forty-four years of age, he was behind his points on the handicap. To have done so wouldn't have altered matters, and it might have depressed Oleron. He had chosen his path, and was committed to it beyond possibility of withdrawal. Perhaps he had chosen it in the days when he had been easily swayed by something a little disinterested, a little generous, a little noble; and had he ever thought of questioning himself he would still have held to it that a life without nobility and generosity and disinterestedness was no life for him. Only quite recently, and rarely, had he even vaguely suspected that there was more in it than this; but it was no good anticipating the day when, he supposed, he would reach that maximum point of his powers beyond which he must inevitably decline, and be left face to face with the question whether it would not have profited him better to have ruled his life by less exigent ideals.

In the meantime, his removal into the old house with the insurance marks built into its brick merely interrupted *Romilly Bishop* at the fifteenth chapter.

As this tall man with the lean, ascetic face moved about his new abode, arranging, changing, altering, hardly yet into his working-stride again, he gave the impression of almost spinster-like precision and nicety. For twenty years past, in a score of lodgings, garrets, flats, and rooms furnished and unfurnished, he had been accustomed to do many things for himself, and he had discovered that it saves time and temper to be methodical. He had arranged with the wife of the long-nosed Barrett, a stout Welsh woman with a falsetto voice, the Merionethshire accent of which long residence in London had not perceptibly modified, to come across the square each morning to prepare his breakfast, and also to "turn the place out" on Saturday mornings; and for the rest, he even welcomed a little housework as a relaxation from the strain of writing.

His kitchen, together with the adjoining strip of an apartment into which a modern bath had been fitted, overlooked the alley at the side of the house; and at one end of it was a large closet with a door, and a square sliding hatch in the upper part of the door. This had been a powder-closet, and through the hatch the elaborately dressed head had been thrust to receive the click and puff of the powder-pistol. Oleron puzzled a little over this closet; then, as its use occurred to him, he smiled faintly, a little moved, he knew not by what... He would have to put it to a very different purpose

from its original one; it would probably have to serve as his larder...
It was in this closet that he made a discovery. The back of it was
shelved, and, rummaging on an upper shelf that ran deeply into the
wall, Oleron found a couple of mushroom-shaped old wooden wig-
stands. He did not know how they had come to be there. Doubtless
the painters had turned them up somewhere or other, and had put
them there. But his five rooms, as a whole, were short of cupboard
and closet-room; and it was only by the exercise of some ingenuity
that he was able to find places for the bestowal of his household
linen, his boxes, and his seldom-used but not-to-be-destroyed
accumulation of papers.

It was in early spring that Oleron entered on his tenancy, and
he was anxious to have *Romilly* ready for publication in the coming
autumn. Nevertheless, he did not intend to force its production.
Should it demand longer in the doing, so much the worse; he realised
its importance, its crucial importance, in his artistic development,
and it must have its own length and time. In the workroom he had
recently left he had been making excellent progress; *Romilly* had
begun, as the saying is, to speak and act of herself; and he did not
doubt she would continue to do so the moment the distraction of his
removal was over. This distraction was almost over; he told himself
it was time he pulled himself together again; and on a March
morning he went out, returned again with two great bunches of
yellow daffodils, placed one bunch on his mantelpiece between the
Sheffield sticks and the other on the table before him, and took out
the half-completed manuscript of *Romilly Bishop*.

But before beginning work he went to a small rosewood
cabinet and took from a drawer his cheque-book and passbook.
He totted them up, and his monk-like face grew thoughtful. His
installation had cost him more than he had intended it should, and
his balance was rather less than fifty pounds, with no immediate
prospect of more.

"Hm! I'd forgotten rugs and chintz curtains and so forth
mounted up so," said Oleron. "But it would have been a pity to spoil

the place for the want of ten pounds or so... Well, *Romilly* simply must be out for the autumn, that's all. So here goes—"

He drew his papers towards him.

But he worked badly; or, rather, he did not work at all. The square outside had its own noises, frequent and new, and Oleron could only hope that he would speedily become accustomed to these. First came hawkers, with their carts and cries; at midday the children, returning from school, trooped into the square and swung on Oleron's gate; and when the children had departed again for afternoon school, an itinerant musician with a mandolin posted himself beneath Oleron's window and began to strum. This was a not unpleasant distraction, and Oleron, pushing up his window, threw the man a penny. Then he returned to his table again...

But it was no good. He came to himself, at long intervals, to find that he had been looking about his room and wondering how it had formerly been furnished—whether a settee in buttercup or petunia satin had stood under the farther window, whether from the centre moulding of the light lofty ceiling had depended a glimmering crystal chandelier, or where the tambour-frame or the picquet-table had stood... No, it was no good; he had far better be frankly doing nothing than getting fruitlessly tired; and he decided that he would take a walk, but, chancing to sit down for a moment, dozed in his chair instead.

"This won't do," he yawned when he awoke at half-past four in the afternoon; "I must do better than this tomorrow—"

And he felt so deliciously lazy that for some minutes he even contemplated the breach of an appointment he had for the evening.

The next morning he sat down to work without even permitting himself to answer one of his three letters—two of them tradesmen's accounts, the third a note from Miss Bengough, forwarded from his old address. It was a jolly day of white and blue, with a gay noisy wind and a subtle turn in the colour of growing things; and over and over again, once or twice a minute, his room became suddenly light and then subdued again, as the shining white clouds rolled northeastwards over the square. The soft fitful illumination was reflected in the polished surface of the table and even in the footworn old floor; and the morning noises had begun again.

Oleron made a pattern of dots on the paper before him, and then broke off to move the jar of daffodils exactly opposite the centre of a creamy panel. Then he wrote a sentence that ran continuously for a couple of lines, after which it broke off into notes and jottings. For a time he succeeded in persuading himself that in making these memoranda he was really working; then he rose and began to pace his room. As he did so, he was struck by an idea. It was that the place might possibly be a little better for more positive colour. It was, perhaps, a thought *too* pale—mild and sweet as a kind old face, but a little devitalised, even wan... Yes, decidedly it would bear a robuster note—more and richer flowers, and possibly some warm and gay stuff for cushions for the window-seats...

"Of course, I really can't afford it," he muttered, as he went for a two-foot and began to measure the width of the window recesses...

In stooping to measure a recess, his attitude suddenly changed to one of interest and attention. Presently he rose again, rubbing his hands with gentle glee.

"Oho, oho!" he said. "These look to me very much like window-boxes, nailed up. We must look into this! Yes, those are boxes, or I'm... oho, this is an adventure!"

On that wall of his sitting-room there were two windows (the third was in another corner), and, beyond the open bedroom door, on the same wall, was another. The seats of all had been painted, repainted, and painted again; and Oleron's investigating finger had barely detected the old nailheads beneath the paint. Under the ledge over which he stooped an old keyhole also had been puttied up. Oleron took out his penknife.

He worked carefully for five minutes, and then went into the kitchen for a hammer and chisel. Driving the chisel cautiously under the seat, he started the whole lid slightly. Again using the penknife, he cut along the hinged edge and outward along the ends; and then he fetched a wedge and a wooden mallet.

"Now for our little mystery—" he said.

The sound of the mallet on the wedge seemed, in that sweet and pale apartment, somehow a little brutal—nay, even shocking. The panelling rang and rattled and vibrated to the blows like a sounding-board. The whole house seemed to echo; from the roomy cellarage to the garrets above a flock of echoes seemed to awake; and the sound got a little on Oleron's nerves. All at once he paused, fetched a duster, and muffled the mallet... When the edge was sufficiently raised he put his fingers under it and lifted. The paint flaked and scarred a little; the rusty old nails squeaked and grunted; and the lid came up, laying open the box beneath. Oleron looked into it. Save for a couple of inches of scurf and mould and old cobwebs it was empty.

"No treasure there," said Oleron, a little amused that he should have fancied there might have been. "*Romilly* will still have to be out by the autumn. Let's have a look at the others."

He turned to the second window.

The raising of the two remaining seats occupied him until well into the afternoon. That of the bedroom like the first, was empty; but from the second seat of his sitting-room he drew out something yielding and folded and furred over an inch thick with dust. He carried the object into the kitchen, and having swept it over a bucket, took a duster to it.

It was some sort of a large bag, of an ancient frieze-like material, and when unfolded it occupied the greater part of the small kitchen floor. In shape it was an irregular, a very irregular, triangle, and it had a couple of wide flaps, with the remains of straps and buckles. The patch that had been uppermost in the folding was of a faded yellowish brown; but the rest of it was of shades of crimson that varied according to the exposure of the parts of it.

"Now whatever can that have been?" Oleron mused as he stood surveying it... "I give it up. Whatever it is, it's settled my work for today, I'm afraid—"

He folded the object up carelessly and thrust it into a corner of the kitchen; then, taking pans and brushes and an old knife, he returned to the sitting-room and began to scrape and to wash and to line with paper his newly discovered receptacles. When he had finished, he put his spare boots and books and papers into them; and he closed the lids again, amused with his little adventure, but also a little anxious for the hour to come when he should settle fairly down to his work again.

III

It piqued Oleron a little that his friend, Miss Bengough, should dismiss with a glance the place he himself had found so singularly winning. Indeed she scarcely lifted her eyes to it. But then she had always been more or less like that—a little indifferent to the graces of life, careless of appearances, and perhaps a shade more herself when she ate biscuits from a paper bag than when she dined with greater observance of the convenances. She was an unattached journalist of thirty-four, large, showy, fair as butter, pink as a dog-rose, reminding one of a florist's picked specimen bloom, and given to sudden and ample movements and moist and explosive utterances. She "pulled a better living out of the pool" (as she expressed it) than Oleron did; and by cunningly disguised puffs of drapers and haberdashers she "pulled" also the greater part of her very varied wardrobe. She left small whirlwinds of air behind her when she moved, in which her veils and scarves fluttered and spun.

Oleron heard the flurry of her skirts on his staircase and her single loud knock at his door when he had been a month in his new abode. Her garments brought in the outer air, and she flung a bundle of ladies' journals down on a chair.

"Don't knock off for me," she said across a mouthful of large-headed hatpins as she removed her hat and veil. "I didn't know whether you were straight yet, so I've brought some sandwiches for lunch. You've got coffee, I suppose?— No, don't get up—I'll find the kitchen—"

"Oh, that's all right, I'll clear these things away. To tell the truth, I'm rather glad to be interrupted," said Oleron.

He gathered his work together and put it away. She was already in the kitchen; he heard the running of water into the kettle. He joined her, and ten minutes later followed her back to the sitting-room with the coffee and sandwiches on a tray. They sat down, with the tray on a small table between them.

"Well, what do you think of the new place?" Oleron asked as she poured out coffee.

"Anybody'd think you were going to get married, Paul."

He laughed.

"Oh no. But it's an improvement on some of them, isn't it?"

"Is it? I suppose it is; I don't know. I liked the last place, in spite of the black ceiling and no watertap. How's *Romilly*?"

Oleron thumbed his chin.

"Hm! I'm rather ashamed to tell you. The fact is, I've not got on very well with it. But it will be all right on the night, as you used to say."

"Stuck?"

"Rather stuck."

"Got any of it you care to read to me?... "

Oleron had long been in the habit of reading portions of his work to Miss Bengough occasionally. Her comments were always quick and practical, sometimes directly useful, sometimes indirectly suggestive. She, in return for his confidence, always kept all mention of her own work sedulously from him. His, she said, was "real work"; hers merely filled space, not always even grammatically.

"I'm afraid there isn't," Oleron replied, still meditatively dry-shaving his chin. Then he added, with a little burst of candour, "The fact is, Elsie, I've not written—not actually written—very much more of it—any more of it, in fact. But, of course, that doesn't mean I haven't progressed. I've progressed, in one sense, rather alarmingly. I'm now thinking of reconstructing the whole thing."

Miss Bengough gave a gasp. "Reconstructing!"

"Making Romilly herself a different type of woman. Somehow, I've begun to feel that I'm not getting the most out of her. As she stands, I've certainly lost interest in her to some extent."

"But—but—" Miss Bengough protested, "you had her so real, so *living*, Paul!"

Oleron smiled faintly. He had been quite prepared for Miss Bengough's disapproval. He wasn't surprised that she liked Romilly as she at present existed; she would. Whether she realised it or not, there was much of herself in his fictitious creation. Naturally Romilly would seem "real," "living," to her...

"But are you really serious, Paul?" Miss Bengough asked presently, with a round-eyed stare.

"Quite serious."

"You're really going to scrap those fifteen chapters?"

"I didn't exactly say that."

"That fine, rich love-scene?"

"I should only do it reluctantly, and for the sake of something I thought better."

"And that beautiful, *beau*tiful description of Romilly on the shore?"

"It wouldn't necessarily be wasted," he said a little uneasily.

But Miss Bengough made a large and windy gesture, and then let him have it.

"Really, you are *too* trying!" she broke out. "I do wish sometimes you'd remember you're human, and live in a world! You know I'd be the *last* to wish you to lower your standard one inch, but it wouldn't be lowering it to bring it within human comprehension. Oh, you're sometimes altogether too godlike!... Why, it would be a wicked, criminal waste of your powers to destroy those fifteen chapters! Look at it reasonably, now. You've been working for nearly twenty years; you've now got what you've been working for almost within your grasp; your affairs are at a most critical stage (oh, don't tell me; I know you're about at the end of your money); and here you are, deliberately proposing to withdraw a thing that will probably make your name, and to substitute for it something that ten to one nobody on earth will ever want to read—and small blame to them! Really, you try my patience!"

Oleron had shaken his head slowly as she had talked. It was an old story between them. The noisy, able, practical journalist was an admirable friend—up to a certain point; beyond that. . . well, each of us knows that point beyond which we stand alone. Elsie Bengough sometimes said that had she had one-tenth part of Oleron's genius there were few things she could not have done—thus making that genius a quantitatively divisible thing, a sort of ingredient, to be added to or to subtracted from in the admixture of his work. That it was a qualitative thing, essential, indivisible, informing, passed her comprehension. Their spirits parted company at that point. Oleron knew it. She did not appear to know it.

"Yes, yes, yes," he said a little wearily, by-and-by, "practically you're quite right, entirely right, and I haven't a word to say. If I could only turn *Romilly* over to you you'd make an enormous success of her. But that can't be, and I, for my part, am seriously doubting whether she's worth my while. You know what that means."

"What does it mean?" she demanded bluntly.

"Well," he said, smiling wanly, "what *does* it mean when you're convinced a thing isn't worth doing? You simply don't do it."

Miss Bengough's eyes swept the ceiling for assistance against this impossible man.

"What utter rubbish!" she broke out at last. "Why, when I saw you last you were simply oozing *Romilly*, you were turning her off at the rate of four chapters a week; if you hadn't moved you'd have had her three-parts done by now. What on earth possessed you to move right in the middle of your most important work?"

Oleron tried to put her off with a recital of inconveniences, but she wouldn't have it. Perhaps in her heart she partly suspected the reason. He was simply mortally weary of the narrow circumstances of his life. He had had twenty years of it—twenty years of garrets and roof-chambers and dingy flats and shabby lodgings, and he was tired of dinginess and shabbiness. The reward was as far off as ever—or if it was not, he no longer cared as once he would have cared to put out his hand and take it. It is all very well to tell a man who is at the point of exhaustion that only another effort is required of him; if he cannot make it he is as far off as ever...

"Anyway," Oleron summed up, "I'm happier here than I've been for a long time. That's some sort of a justification."

"And doing no work," said Miss Bengough pointedly.

At that a trifling petulance that had been gathering in Oleron came to a head.

"And why should I do nothing but work?" he demanded. "How much happier am I for it? I don't say I don't love my work—when it's done; but I hate doing it. Sometimes it's an intolerable burden that I simply long to be rid of. Once in many weeks it has a moment, one moment, of glow and thrill for me; I remember the days when it was all glow and thrill; and now I'm forty-four, and it's becoming drudgery. Nobody wants it; I'm ceasing to want it myself; and if any ordinary sensible man were to ask me whether I didn't think I was a fool to go on, I think I should agree that I was."

Miss Bengough's comely pink face was serious.

"But you knew all that, many, many years ago, Paul—and still you chose it," she said in a low voice.

"Well, and how should I have known?" he demanded. "I didn't know. I was told so. My heart, if you like, told me so, and I thought I knew. Youth always thinks it knows; then one day it discovers that it is nearly fifty—"

"Forty-four, Paul—"

"—forty-four, then—and it finds that the glamour isn't in front, but behind. Yes, I knew and chose, if *that's* knowing and choosing... but it's a costly choice we're called on to make when we're young!"

Miss Bengough's eyes were on the floor. Without moving them she said, "You're not regretting it, Paul?"

"Am I not?" he took her up. "Upon my word, I've lately thought I am! What *do* I get in return for it all?"

"You know what you get," she replied.

He might have known from her tone what else he could have had for the holding up of a finger—herself. She knew, but could not tell him, that he could have done no better thing for himself. Had he, any time these ten years, asked her to marry him, she would have replied quietly, "Very well; when?" He had never thought of it...

"Yours is the real work," she continued quietly. "Without you we jackals couldn't exist. You and a few like you hold everything upon your shoulders."

For a minute there was a silence. Then it occurred to Oleron that this was common vulgar grumbling. It was not his habit. Suddenly he rose and began to stack cups and plates on the tray.

"Sorry you catch me like this, Elsie," he said, with a little laugh... "No, I'll take them out; then we'll go for a walk, if you like..."

He carried out the tray, and then began to show Miss Bengough round his flat. She made few comments. In the kitchen she asked what an old faded square of reddish frieze was, that Mrs Barrett used as a cushion for her wooden chair.

"That? I should be glad if you could tell *me* what it is," Oleron replied as he unfolded the bag and related the story of its finding in the window-seat.

"I think I know what it is," said Miss Bengough. "It's been used to wrap up a harp before putting it into its case."

"By Jove, that's probably just what it was," said Oleron. "I could make neither head nor tail of it..."

They finished the tour of the flat, and returned to the sitting-room.

"And who lives in the rest of the house?" Miss Bengough asked.

"I dare say a tramp sleeps in the cellar occasionally. Nobody else."

"Hm!... Well, I'll tell you what I think about it, if you like."

"I should like."

"You'll never work here."

"Oh?" said Oleron quickly. "Why not?"

"You'll never finish *Romilly* here. Why, I don't know, but you won't. I know it. You'll have to leave before you get on with that book."

He mused for a moment, and then said:

"Isn't that a little—prejudiced, Elsie?"

"Perfectly ridiculous. As an argument it hasn't a leg to stand on. But there it is," she replied, her mouth once more full of the large-headed hat pins.

Oleron was reaching down his hat and coat. He laughed. "I can only hope you're entirely wrong," he said, "for I shall be in a serious mess if *Romilly* isn't out in the autumn."

IV

As Oleron sat by his fire that evening, pondering Miss Bengough's prognostication that difficulties awaited him in his work, he came to the conclusion that it would have been far better had she kept her beliefs to herself. No man does a thing better for having his confidence damped at the outset, and to speak of difficulties is in a sense to make them. Speech itself becomes a deterrent act, to which other discouragements accrete until the very event of which warning is given is as likely as not to come to pass. He heartily confounded her. An influence hostile to the completion of *Romilly* had been born.

And in some illogical, dogmatic way women seem to have, she had attached this antagonistic influence to his new abode. Was ever anything so absurd! "You'll never finish *Romilly* here."... Why not? Was this her idea of the luxury that saps the springs of action and brings a man down to indolence and dropping out of the race? The place was well enough—it was entirely charming, for that matter—but it was not so demoralising as all that! No; Elsie had missed the mark that time...

He moved his chair to look round the room that smiled, positively smiled, in the firelight. He too smiled, as if pity was to be entertained for a maligned apartment. Even that slight lack of robust colour he had remarked was not noticeable in the soft glow. The drawn chintz curtains—they had a flowered and trellised pattern, with baskets and oaten pipes—fell in long quiet folds to the window-seats; the rows of bindings in old bookcases took the light richly; the last trace of sallowness had gone with the daylight; and, if the truth must be told, it had been Elsie herself who had seemed a little out of the picture.

That reflection struck him a little, and presently he returned to it. Yes, the room had, quite accidentally, done Miss Bengough a disservice that afternoon. It had, in some subtle but unmistakable way, placed her, marked a contrast of qualities. Assuming for the sake of argument the slightly ridiculous proposition that the room in which Oleron sat was characterised by a certain sparsity and lack of vigour; so much the worse for Miss Bengough; she certainly erred on the side of redundancy and general muchness. And if one must contrast abstract qualities, Oleron inclined to the austere in taste...

Yes, here Oleron had made a distinct discovery; he wondered he had not made it before. He pictured Miss Bengough again as she had appeared that afternoon—large, showy, moistly pink, with that quality of the prize bloom exuding, as it were from her; and instantly she suffered in his thought. He even recognised now that he had noticed something odd at the time, and that unconsciously his attitude, even while she had been there, had been one of criticism. The mechanism of her was a little obvious; her melting humidity was the result of analysable processes; and behind her there had seemed to lurk some dim shape emblematic of mortality. He had never, during the ten years of their intimacy, dreamed for a moment of asking her to marry him; none the less, he now felt for the first time a thankfulness that he had not done so...

Then, suddenly and swiftly, his face flamed that he should be thinking thus of his friend. What! Elsie Bengough, with whom he had spent weeks and weeks of afternoons—she, the good chum, on whose help he would have counted had all the rest of the world failed him—she, whose loyalty to him would not, he knew, swerve as long as there was breath in her—Elsie to be even in thought dissected thus! He was an ingrate and a cad...

Had she been there in that moment he would have abased himself before her.

For ten minutes and more he sat, still gazing into the fire, with that humiliating red fading slowly from his cheeks. All was still within and without, save for a tiny musical tinkling that came from his kitchen—the dripping of water from an imperfectly turned-off tap into the vessel beneath it. Mechanically he began to beat with his fingers to the faintly heard falling of the drops; the tiny regular movement seemed to hasten that shameful withdrawal from his face. He grew cool once more; and when he resumed his meditation he was all unconscious that he took it up again at the same point...

It was not only her florid superfluity of build that he had approached in the attitude of criticism; he was conscious also of the wide differences between her mind and his own. He felt no thankfulness that up to a certain point their natures had ever run companionably side by side; he was now full of questions beyond that point. Their intellects diverged; there was no denying it; and, looking back, he was inclined to doubt whether there had been any real coincidence. True, he had read his writings to her and she had appeared to speak comprehendingly and to the point; but what can a man do who, having assumed that another sees as he does, is suddenly brought up sharp by something that falsifies and discredits all that has gone before? He doubted all now... It did for a moment occur to him that the man who demands of a friend more than can be given to him is in danger of losing that friend, but he put the thought aside.

Again he ceased to think, and again moved his finger to the distant dripping of the tap...

And now (he resumed by-and-by), if these things were true of Elsie Bengough, they were also true of the creation of which she

197

was the prototype—Romilly Bishop. And since he could say of Romilly what for very shame he could not say of Elsie, he gave his thoughts rein. He did so in that smiling, fire-lighted room, to the accompaniment of the faintly heard tap.

There was no longer any doubt about it; he hated the central character of his novel. Even as he had described her physically she overpowered the senses; she was coarse fibred, over-coloured, rank. It became true the moment he formulated his thought; Gulliver had described the Brobdingnagian maids-of-honour thus: and mentally and spiritually she corresponded—was unsensitive, limited, common. The model (he closed his eyes for a moment)— the model stuck out through fifteen vulgar and blatant chapters to such a pitch that, without seeing the reason, he had been unable to begin the sixteenth. He marvelled that it had only just dawned upon him.

And this was to have been his Beatrice, his vision! As Elsie she was to have gone into the furnace of his art, and she was to have come out the Woman all men desire! Her thoughts were to have been culled from his own finest, her form from his dearest dreams, and her setting wherever he could find one fit for her worth. He had brooded long before making the attempt; then one day he had felt her stir within him as a mother feels a quickening, and he had begun to write; and so he had added chapter to chapter...

And those fifteen sodden chapters were what he had produced!

Again he sat, softly moving his finger...

Then he bestirred himself.

She must go, all fifteen chapters of her. That was settled. For what was to take her place his mind was a blank; but one thing at a time; a man is not excused from taking the wrong course because the right one is not immediately revealed to him. Better would come if it was to come; in the meantime—

He rose, fetched the fifteen chapters, and read them over before he should drop them into the fire.

But instead of putting them into the fire he let them fall from his hand. He became conscious of the dripping of the tap again. It had a tinkling gamut of four or five notes, on which it rang irregular changes, and it was foolishly sweet and dulcimer-like. In his mind Oleron could see the gathering of each drop, its little tremble on the lip of the tap, and the tiny percussion of its fall "Plink—plunk," minimised almost to inaudibility. Following the lowest note there seemed to be a brief phrase, irregularly repeated; and presently Oleron found himself waiting for the recurrence of this phrase. It was quite pretty...

But it did not conduce to wakefulness, and Oleron dozed over his fire.

When he awoke again the fire had burned low and the flames of the candles were licking the rims of the Sheffield sticks. Sluggishly he rose, yawned, went his nightly round of door-locks, and window-fastenings, and passed into his bedroom. Soon, he slept soundly.

But a curious little sequel followed on the morrow. Mrs Barrett usually tapped, not at his door, but at the wooden wall beyond which lay Oleron's bed; and then Oleron rose, put on his dressing-gown, and admitted her. He was not conscious that as he did so that morning he hummed an air; but Mrs Barrett lingered with her hand on the door-knob and her face a little averted and smiling.

"De-ar me!" her soft falsetto rose. "But that will be a very o-ald tune, Mr Oleron! I will not have heard it this for-ty years!"

"What tune?" Oleron asked.

"The tune, indeed, that you was humming, sir."

Oleron had his thumb in the flap of a letter. It remained there.

"*I* was humming?... Sing it, Mrs Barrett."

Mrs Barrett prut-prutted.

"I have no voice for singing, Mr Oleron; it was Ann Pugh was the singer of our family; but the tune will be very o-ald, and it is called 'The Beckoning Fair One'."

"Try to sing it," said Oleron, his thumb still in the envelope; and Mrs Barrett, with much dimpling and confusion, hummed the air.

"They do say it was sung to a harp, Mr Oleron, and it will be very o-ald," she concluded.

"And *I* was singing that?"

"Indeed you was. I would not be likely to tell you lies."

With a "Very well—let me have breakfast," Oleron opened his letter; but the trifling circumstance struck him as more odd than he would have admitted to himself. The phrase he had hummed had been that which he had associated with the falling from the tap on the evening before.

V

Even more curious than that the commonplace dripping of an ordinary water-tap should have tallied so closely with an actually existing air was another result it had, namely, that it awakened, or seemed to awaken, in Oleron an abnormal sensitiveness to other noises of the old house. It has been remarked that silence obtains its fullest and most impressive quality when it is broken by some minute sound; and, truth to tell, the place was never still. Perhaps the mildness of the spring air operated on its torpid old timbers; perhaps Oleron's fires caused it to stretch its old anatomy; and certainly a whole world of insect life bored and burrowed in its baulks and joists. At any rate Oleron had only to sit quiet in his chair and to wait for a minute or two in order to become aware of such a change in the auditory scale as comes upon a man who, conceiving the mid-summer woods to be motionless and still, all at once finds his ear sharpened to the crepitation of a myriad insects.

And he smiled to think of man's arbitrary distinction between that which has life and that which has not. Here, quite apart from such recognisable sounds as the scampering of mice, the falling of plaster behind his panelling, and the popping of purses or coffins from his fire, was a whole house talking to him had he but known its language. Beams settled with a tired sigh into their old mortices; creatures ticked in the walls; joints cracked, boards complained;

with no palpable stirring of the air window-sashes changed their positions with a soft knock in their frames. And whether the place had life in this sense or not, it had at all events a winsome personality. It needed but an hour of musing for Oleron to conceive the idea that, as his own body stood in friendly relation to his soul, so, by an extension and an attenuation, his habitation might fantastically be supposed to stand in some relation to himself. He even amused himself with the far-fetched fancy that he might so identify himself with the place that some future tenant, taking possession, might regard it as in a sense haunted. It would be rather a joke if he, a perfectly harmless author, with nothing on his mind worse than a novel he had discovered he must begin again, should turn out to be laying the foundation of a future ghost!...

In proportion, however, as he felt this growing attachment to the fabric of his abode, Elsie Bengough, from being merely unattracted, began to show a dislike of the place that was more and more marked. And she did not scruple to speak of her aversion.

"It doesn't belong to today at all, and for you especially it's bad," she said with decision. "You're only too ready to let go your hold on actual things and to slip into apathy; you ought to be in a place with concrete floors and a patent gas-meter and a tradesman's lift. And it would do you all the good in the world if you had a job that made you scramble and rub elbows with your fellow-men. Now, if I could get you a job, for, say, two or three days a week, one that would allow you heaps of time for your proper work—would you take it?"

Somehow, Oleron resented a little being diagnosed like this. He thanked Miss Bengough, but without a smile.

"Thank you, but I don't think so. After all each of us has his own life to live," he could not refrain from adding.

"His own life to live!... How long is it since you were out, Paul?"

"About two hours."

"I don't mean to buy stamps or to post a letter. How long is it since you had anything like a stretch?"

"Oh, some little time perhaps. I don't know."

"Since I was here last?"

"I haven't been out much."

"And has Romilly progressed much better for your being cooped up?"

"I think she has. I'm laying the foundations of her. I shall begin the actual writing presently."

It seemed as if Miss Bengough had forgotten their tussle about the first Romilly. She frowned, turned half away, and then quickly turned again.

"Ah!... So you've still got that ridiculous idea in your head?"

"If you mean," said Oleron slowly, "that I've discarded the old Romilly, and am at work on a new one, you're right. I have still got that idea in my head."

Something uncordial in his tone struck her; but she was a fighter. His own absurd sensitiveness hardened her. She gave a "Pshaw!" of impatience.

"Where is the old one?" she demanded abruptly.

"Why?" asked Oleron.

"I want to see it. I want to show some of it to you. I want, if you're not wool-gathering entirely, to bring you back to your senses."

This time it was he who turned his back. But when he turned round again he spoke more gently.

"It's no good, Elsie. I'm responsible for the way I go, and you must allow me to go it—even if it should seem wrong to you. Believe me, I am giving thought to it... The manuscript? I was on the point of burning it, but I didn't. It's in that window-seat, if you must see it."

Miss Bengough crossed quickly to the window-seat, and lifted the lid. Suddenly she gave a little exclamation, and put the back of her hand to her mouth. She spoke over her shoulder:

"You ought to knock those nails in, Paul," she said.

He strode to her side.

"What? What is it? What's the matter?" he asked. "I did knock them in—or, rather, pulled them out."

202

"You left enough to scratch with," she replied, showing her hand. From the upper wrist to the knuckle of the little finger a welling red wound showed.

"Good—Gracious!" Oleron ejaculated... "Here, come to the bathroom and bathe it quickly—"

He hurried her to the bathroom, turned on warm water, and bathed and cleansed the bad gash. Then, still holding the hand, he turned cold water on it, uttering broken phrases of astonishment and concern.

"Good Lord, how did that happen! As far as I knew I'd... is this water too cold? Does that hurt? I can't imagine how on earth... there; that'll do—"

"No—one moment longer—I can bear it," she murmured, her eyes closed.

Presently he led her back to the sitting-room and bound the hand in one of his handkerchiefs; but his face did not lose its expression of perplexity. He had spent half a day in opening and making serviceable the three window-boxes, and he could not conceive how he had come to leave an inch and a half of rusty nail standing in the wood. He himself had opened the lids of each of them a dozen times and had not noticed any nail; but there it was.

"It shall come out now, at all events," he muttered, as he went for a pair of pincers. And he made no mistake about it that time.

Elsie Bengough had sunk into a chair, and her face was rather white; but in her hand was the manuscript of *Romilly*. She had not finished with *Romilly* yet. Presently she returned to the charge.

"Oh, Paul, it will be the greatest mistake you ever, ever made if you do not publish this!" she said.

He hung his head, genuinely distressed. He couldn't get that incident of the nail out of his head, and *Romilly* occupied a second place in his thoughts for the moment. But still she insisted; and when presently he spoke it was almost as if he asked her pardon for something.

"What can I say, Elsie? I can only hope that when you see the new version, you'll see how right I am. And if in spite of all you *don't* like her, well... " he made a hopeless gesture. "Don't you see that I *must* be guided by my own lights?"

She was silent.

"Come, Elsie," he said gently. "We've got along well so far; don't let us split on this."

The last words had hardly passed his lips before he regretted them. She had been nursing her injured hand, with her eyes once more closed; but her lips and lids quivered simultaneously. Her voice shook as she spoke.

"I can't help saying it, Paul, but you are so greatly changed."

"Hush, Elsie," he murmured soothingly; "you've had a shock; rest for a while. How could I change?"

"I don't know, but you are. You've not been yourself ever since you came here. I wish you'd never seen the place. It's stopped your work, it's making you into a person I hardly know, and it's made me horribly anxious about you... Oh, how my hand is beginning to throb!"

"Poor child!" he murmured. "Will you let me take you to a doctor and have it properly dressed?"

"No—I shall be all right presently—I'll keep it raised—" She put her elbow on the back of her chair, and the bandaged hand rested lightly on his shoulder.

At that touch an entirely new anxiety stirred suddenly within him. Hundreds of times previously, on their jaunts and excursions, she had slipped her hand within his arm as she might have slipped it into the arm of a brother, and he had accepted the little affectionate gesture as a brother might have accepted it. But now, for the first time, there rushed into his mind a hundred startling questions. Her eyes were still closed, and her head had fallen pathetically back; and there was a lost and ineffable smile on her parted lips. The truth broke in upon him. Good God!... And he had never divined it!

And stranger than all was that, now that he did see that she was lost in love of him, there came to him, not sorrow and humility and abasement, but something else that he struggled in vain against—something entirely strange and new, that, had he analysed it, he would have found to be petulance and irritation and resentment and ungentleness. The sudden selfish prompting mastered him before he was aware. He all but gave it words. What was she doing there at all? Why was she not getting on with her own work? Why was she here interfering with his? Who had given her this guardianship over him that lately she had put forward so assertively?—"Changed?" It was she, not himself, who had changed...

But by the time she had opened her eyes again he had overcome his resentment sufficiently to speak gently, albeit with reserve.

"I wish you would let me take you to a doctor."

She rose.

"No, thank you, Paul," she said. "I'll go now. If I need a dressing I'll get one; take the other hand, please. Goodbye—"

He did not attempt to detain her. He walked with her to the foot of the stairs. Halfway along the narrow alley she turned.

"It would be a long way to come if you happened not to be in," she said; "I'll send you a postcard the next time."

At the gate she turned again.

"Leave here, Paul," she said, with a mournful look. "Everything's wrong with this house."

Then she was gone.

Oleron returned to his room. He crossed straight to the window-box. He opened the lid and stood long looking at it. Then he closed it again and turned away.

"That's rather frightening," he muttered. "It's simply not possible that I should not have removed that nail..."

VI

Oleron knew very well what Elsie had meant when she had said that her next visit would be preceded by a postcard. She, too, had realised that at last, at last he knew—knew, and didn't want her. It gave him a miserable, pitiful pang, therefore, when she came again within a week, knocking at the door unannounced. She spoke from the landing; she did not intend to stay, she said; and he had to press her before she would so much as enter.

Her excuse for calling was that she had heard of an inquiry for short stories that he might be wise to follow up. He thanked her. Then, her business over, she seemed anxious to get away again. Oleron did not seek to detain her; even he saw through the pretext of the stories; and he accompanied her down the stairs.

But Elsie Bengough had no luck whatever in that house. A second accident befell her. Halfway down the staircase there was the sharp sound of splintering wood, and she checked a loud cry. Oleron knew the woodwork to be old, but he himself had ascended and descended frequently enough without mishap...

Elsie had put her foot through one of the stairs. He sprang to her side in alarm.

"Oh, I say! My poor girl!" She laughed hysterically.

"It's my weight—I know I'm getting fat—"

"Keep still—let me clear these splinters away," he muttered between his teeth.

She continued to laugh and sob that it was her weight—she was getting fat—

He thrust downwards at the broken boards. The extrication was no easy matter, and her torn boot showed him how badly the foot and ankle within it must be abraded.

"Good God—good God!" he muttered over and over again.

"I shall be too heavy for anything soon," she sobbed and laughed.

But she refused to reascend and to examine her hurt.

"No, let me go quickly—let me go quickly," she repeated.

"But it's a frightful gash!"

"No—not so bad—let me get away quickly—I'm—I'm not wanted."

At her words, that she was not wanted, his head dropped as if she had given him a buffet.

"Elsie!" he choked, brokenly and shocked.

But she too made a quick gesture, as if she put something violently aside.

"Oh, Paul, not *that*—not *you*—of course I do mean that too in a sense—oh, you know what I mean!... But if the other can't be, spare me this now! I—I wouldn't have come, but—but oh, I did, I *did* try to keep away!"

It was intolerable, heartbreaking; but what could he do—what could he say? He did not love her...

"Let me go—I'm not wanted—let me take away what's left of me—"

"Dear Elsie—you are very dear to me—"

But again she made the gesture, as of putting something violently aside.

"No, not that—not anything less—don't offer me anything less—leave me a little pride—"

"Let me get my hat and coat—let me take you to a doctor," he muttered.

But she refused. She refused even the support of his arm. She gave another unsteady laugh.

"I'm sorry I broke your stairs, Paul... You will go and see about the short stories, won't you?"

He groaned.

"Then if you won't see a doctor, will you go across the square and let Mrs Barrett look at you? Look, there's Barrett passing now—"

The long-nosed Barrett was looking curiously down the alley, but as Oleron was about to call him he made off without a word. Elsie seemed anxious for nothing so much as to be clear of the place, and finally promised to go straight to a doctor, but insisted on going alone.

"Goodbye," she said.

And Oleron watched her until she was past the hatchet-like "To Let" boards, as if he feared that even they might fall upon her and maim her.

That night Oleron did not dine. He had far too much on his mind. He walked from room to room of his flat, as if he could have walked away from Elsie Bengough's haunting cry that still rang in his ears. "I'm not wanted—don't offer me anything less—let me take away what's left of me—"

Oh, if he could only have persuaded himself that he loved her!

He walked until twilight fell, then, without lighting candles, he stirred up the fire and flung himself into a chair.

Poor, poor Elsie!...

But even while his heart ached for her, it was out of the question. If only he had known! If only he had used common observation! But those walks, those sisterly takings of the arm—what a fool he had been!... Well, it was too late now. It was she, not he, who must now act—act by keeping away. He would help her all he could. He himself would not sit in her presence. If she came, he would hurry her out again as fast as he could... Poor, poor Elsie!

His room grew dark; the fire burned dead; and he continued to sit, wincing from time to time as a fresh tortured phrase rang again in his ears.

Then suddenly, he knew not why, he found himself anxious for her in a new sense—uneasy about her personal safety. A horrible fancy that even then she might be looking over an embankment down into dark water, that she might even now be glancing up at the hook on the door, took him. Women had been known to do those things... Then there would be an inquest, and he himself would be called upon to identify her, and would be asked how she had come by an ill-healed wound on the hand and a bad abrasion of the ankle. Barrett would say that he had seen her leaving his house...

Then he recognised that his thoughts were morbid. By an effort of will he put them aside, and sat for a while listening to the faint creakings and tickings and rappings within his panelling...

If only he could have married her!... But he couldn't. Her face had risen before him again as he had seen it on the stairs, drawn with pain and ugly and swollen with tears. Ugly—yes, positively blubbered; if tears were women's weapons, as they were said to be, such tears were weapons turning against themselves... suicide again...

Then all at once he found himself attentively considering her two accidents.

Extraordinary they had been, both of them. He could not have left that old nail standing in the wood; why, he had fetched tools specially from the kitchen; and he was convinced that that step that had broken beneath her weight had been as sound as the others. It was inexplicable. If these things could happen, anything could happen. There was not a beam nor a jamb in the place that might not fall without warning, not a plank that might not crash inwards, not a nail that might not become a dagger. The whole place was full of life even now; as he sat there in the dark he heard its crowds of noises as if the house had been one great microphone...

Only half conscious that he did so, he had been sitting for some time identifying these noises, attributing to each crack or creak or knock its material cause; but there was one noise which, again not fully conscious of the omission, he had not sought to account for. It had last come some minutes ago; it came again now—a sort of soft sweeping rustle that seemed to hold an almost inaudible minute crackling. For half a minute or so it had Oleron's attention; then his heavy thoughts were of Elsie Bengough again.

He was nearer to loving her in that moment than he had ever been. He thought how to some men their loved ones were but the dearer for those poor mortal blemishes that tell us we are but sojourners on earth, with a common fate not far distant that makes it hardly worth while to do anything but love for the time remaining. Strangling sobs, blearing tears, bodies buffeted by sickness, hearts and mind callous and hard with the rubs of the world—how little love there would be were these things a barrier to love! In that sense he did love Elsie Bengough. What her happiness had never moved in him her sorrow almost awoke...

Suddenly his meditation went. His ear had once more become conscious of that soft and repeated noise—the long sweep with the almost inaudible crackle in it. Again and again it came, with a curious insistence and urgency. It quickened a little as he became increasingly attentive... it seemed to Oleron that it grew louder...

All at once he started bolt upright in his chair, tense and listening. The silky rustle came again; he was trying to attach it to something...

The next moment he had leapt to his feet, unnerved and terrified. His chair hung poised for a moment, and then went over, setting the fire-irons clattering as it fell. There was only one noise in the world like that which had caused him to spring thus to his feet...

The next time it came Oleron felt behind him at the empty air with his hand, and backed slowly until he found himself against the wall.

"God in Heaven!" The ejaculation broke from Oleron's lips. The sound had ceased.

The next moment he had given a high cry.

"What is it? What's there? *Who's* there?"

A sound of scuttling caused his knees to bend under him for a moment; but that, he knew, was a mouse. That was not something that his stomach turned sick and his mind reeled to entertain. That other sound, the like of which was not in the world, had now entirely ceased; and again he called...

He called and continued to call; and then another terror, a terror of the sound of his own voice, seized him. He did not dare to call again. His shaking hand went to his pocket for a match, but found none. He thought there might be matches on the mantelpiece—

He worked his way to the mantelpiece round a little recess, without for a moment leaving the wall. Then his hand encountered the mantelpiece, and groped along it. A box of matches fell to the hearth. He could just see them in the firelight, but his hand could not pick them up until he had cornered them inside the fender.

Then he rose and struck a light.

The room was as usual. He struck a second match. A candle

stood on the table. He lighted it, and the flame sank for a moment and then burned up clear. Again he looked round.

There was nothing.

There was nothing; but there had been something, and might still be something. Formerly, Oleron had smiled at the fantastic thought that, by a merging and interplay of identities between himself and his beautiful room, he might be preparing a ghost for the future; it had not occurred to him *that there might have been a similar merging and coalescence in the past.* Yet with this staggering impossibility he was now face to face. Something did persist in the house; it had a tenant other than himself; and that tenant, whatsoever or whosoever, had appalled Oleron's soul by producing the sound of a woman brushing her hair.

VII

Without quite knowing how he came to be there Oleron found himself striding over the loose board he had temporarily placed on the step broken by Miss Bengough. He was hatless, and descending the stairs. Not until later did there return to him a hazy memory that he had left the candle burning on the table, had opened the door no wider than was necessary to allow the passage of his body, and had sidled out, closing the door softly behind him. At the foot of the stairs another shock awaited him. Something dashed with a flurry up from the disused cellars and disappeared out of the door. It was only a cat, but Oleron gave a childish sob.

He passed out of the gate, and stood for a moment under the "To Let" boards, plucking foolishly at his lip and looking up at the glimmer of light behind one of his red blinds. Then, still looking over his shoulder, he moved stumblingly up the square. There was a small public-house round the corner; Oleron had never entered it; but he entered it now, and put down a shilling that missed the counter by inches.

211

"B—b—bran—brandy," he said, and then stooped to look for the shilling.

He had the little sawdusted bar to himself; what company there was—carters and labourers and the small tradesmen of the neighbourhood—was gathered in the farther compartment, beyond the space where the white-haired landlady moved among her taps and bottles. Oleron sat down on a hardwood settee with a perforated seat, drank half his brandy, and then, thinking he might as well drink it as spill it, finished it.

Then he fell to wondering which of the men whose voices he heard across the public-house would undertake the removal of his effects on the morrow.

In the meantime he ordered more brandy.

For he did not intend to go back to that room where he had left the candle burning. Oh no! He couldn't have faced even the entry and the staircase with the broken step—certainly not that pith-white, fascinating room. He would go back for the present to his old arrangement, of work-room and separate sleeping-quarters; he would go to his old landlady at once—presently—when he had finished his brandy—and see if she could put him up for the night. His glass was empty now...

He rose, had it refilled, and sat down again.

And if anybody asked his reason for removing again? Oh, he had reason enough—reason enough! Nails that put themselves back into wood again and gashed people's hands, steps that broke when you trod on them, and women who came into a man's place and brushed their hair in the dark, were reasons enough! He was querulous and injured about it all. He had taken the place for himself, not for invisible women to brush their hair in; that lawyer fellow in Lincoln's Inn should be told so, too, before many hours were out; it was outrageous, letting people in for agreements like that!

A cut-glass partition divided the compartment where Oleron sat from the space where the white-haired landlady moved; but it stopped seven or eight inches above the level of the counter. There was no partition at the further bar. Presently Oleron, raising his eyes, saw that faces were watching him through the aperture. The faces disappeared when he looked at them.

He moved to a corner where he could not be seen from the other bar; but this brought him into line with the white-haired landlady.

She knew him by sight—had doubtless seen him passing and repassing; and presently she made a remark on the weather. Oleron did not know what he replied, but it sufficed to call forth the further remark that the winter had been a bad one for influenza, but that the spring weather seemed to be coming at last... Even this slight contact with the commonplace steadied Oleron a little; an idle, nascent wonder whether the landlady brushed her hair every night, and, if so, whether it gave out those little electric cracklings, was shut down with a snap; and Oleron was better...

With his next glass of brandy he was all for going back to his flat. Not go back? Indeed, he would go back! They should very soon see whether he was to be turned out of his place like that! He began to wonder why he was doing the rather unusual thing he was doing at that moment, unusual for him—sitting hatless, drinking brandy, in a public-house. Suppose he were to tell the white-haired landlady all about it—to tell her that a caller had scratched her hand on a nail, had later had the bad luck to put her foot through a rotten stair, and that he himself, in an old house full of squeaks and creaks and whispers, had heard a minute noise and had bolted from it in fright—what would she think of him? That he was mad, of course... Pshaw! The real truth of the matter was that he hadn't been doing enough work to occupy him. He had been dreaming his days away, filling his head with a lot of moonshine about a new *Romilly* (as if the old one was not good enough), and now he was surprised that the devil should enter an empty head!

Yes, he would go back. He would take a walk in the air first—he hadn't walked enough lately—and then he would take himself in hand, settle the hash of that sixteenth chapter of *Romilly* (fancy, he had actually been fool enough to think of destroying fifteen chapters!) and thenceforward he would remember that he had obligations to his fellow men and work to do in the world. There was the matter in a nutshell.

He finished his brandy and went out.

He had walked for some time before any other bearing of the matter than that on himself occurred to him. At first, the fresh air had increased the heady effect of the brandy he had drunk; but afterwards his mind grew clearer than it had been since morning. And the clearer it grew, the less final did his boastful self-assurances become, and the firmer his conviction that, when all explanations had been made, there remained something that could not be explained. His hysteria of an hour before had passed; he grew steadily calmer; but the disquieting conviction remained. A deep fear took possession of him. It was a fear for Elsie.

For something in his place was inimical to her safety. Of themselves, her two accidents might not have persuaded him of this; but she herself had said it. *"I'm not wanted here..."* And she had declared that there was something wrong with the place. She had seen it before he had. Well and good. One thing stood out clearly: namely, that if this was so, she must be kept away for quite another reason than that which had so confounded and humiliated Oleron. Luckily she had expressed her intention of staying away; she must be held to that intention. He must see to it.

And he must see to it all the more that he now saw his first impulse, never to set foot in the place again, was absurd. People did not do that kind of thing. With Elsie made secure, he could not with any respect to himself suffer himself to be turned out by a shadow, nor even by a danger merely because it was a danger. He had to live somewhere, and he would live there. He must return.

He mastered the faint chill of fear that came with the decision, and turned in his walk abruptly. Should fear grow on him again he would, perhaps, take one more glass of brandy...

But by the time he reached the short street that led to the square he was too late for more brandy. The little public-house was still lighted, but closed, and one or two men were standing talking on the kerb. Oleron noticed that a sudden silence fell on them as he passed, and he noticed further that the long-nosed Barrett, whom he passed a little lower down, did not return his goodnight. He turned in at the broken gate, hesitated merely an instant in the alley, and then mounted his stairs again.

Only an inch of candle remained in the Sheffield stick, and Oleron did not light another one. Deliberately he forced himself to take it up and to make the tour of his five rooms before retiring. It was as he returned from the kitchen across his little hall that he noticed that a letter lay on the floor. He carried it into his sitting-room, and glanced at the envelope before opening it.

It was unstamped, and had been put into the door by hand. Its handwriting was clumsy, and it ran from beginning to end without comma or period. Oleron read the first line, turned to the signature, and then finished the letter.

It was from the man Barrett, and it informed Oleron that he, Barrett, would be obliged if Mr Oleron would make other arrangements for the preparing of his breakfasts and the cleaning-out of his place. The sting lay in the tail, that is to say, the postscript. This consisted of a text of Scripture. It embodied an allusion that could only be to Elsie Bengough...

A seldom-seen frown had cut deeply into Oleron's brow. So! That was it! Very well; they would see about that on the morrow... For the rest, this seemed merely another reason why Elsie should keep away...

Then his suppressed rage broke out...

The foul-minded lot! The devil himself could not have given a leer at anything that had ever passed between Paul Oleron and Elsie Bengough, yet this nosing rascal must be prying and talking!...

Oleron crumpled the paper up, held it in the candle flame, and then ground the ashes under his heel.

One useful purpose, however, the letter had served: it had created in Oleron a wrathful blaze that effectually banished pale shadows. Nevertheless, one other puzzling circumstance was to close the day. As he undressed, he chanced to glance at his bed. The coverlets bore an impress as if somebody had lain on them. Oleron could not remember that he himself had lain down during the day—off-hand, he would have said that certainly he had not; but after all he could not be positive. His indignation for Elsie, acting possibly with the residue of the brandy in him, excluded all other considerations; and he put out his candle, lay down, and passed immediately into a deep and dreamless sleep, which, in the absence of Mrs Barrett's morning call, lasted almost once round the clock.

VIII

To the man who pays heed to that voice within him which warns him that twilight and danger are settling over his soul, terror is apt to appear an absolute thing, against which his heart must be safeguarded in a twink unless there is to take place an alteration in the whole range and scale of his nature. Mercifully, he has never far to look for safeguards. Of the immediate and small and common and momentary things of life, of usages and observances and modes and conventions, he builds up fortifications against the powers of darkness. He is even content that, not terror only, but joy also, should for working purposes be placed in the category of the absolute things; and the last treason he will commit will be that breaking down of terms and limits that strikes, not at one man, but at the welfare of the souls of all.

In his own person, Oleron began to commit this treason. He began to commit it by admitting the inexplicable and horrible to an increasing familiarity. He did it insensibly, unconsciously, by a neglect of the things that he now regarded it as an impertinence in Elsie Bengough to have prescribed. Two months before, the words "a haunted house," applied to his lovely bemusing dwelling, would have chilled his marrow; now, his scale of sensation becoming depressed, he could ask "Haunted by what?" and remain unconscious that horror, when it can be proved to be relative, by so much loses its proper quality. He was setting aside the landmarks. Mists and confusion had begun to enwrap him.

And he was conscious of nothing so much as of a voracious inquisitiveness. He wanted to *know*. He was resolved to know. Nothing but the knowledge would satisfy him; and craftily he cast about for means whereby he might attain it.

He might have spared his craft. The matter was the easiest imaginable. As in time past he had known, in his writing, moments when his thoughts had seemed to rise of themselves and to embody themselves in words not to be altered afterwards, so now the questions he put himself seemed to be answered even in the moment of their asking. There was exhilaration in the swift, easy processes. He had known no such joy in his own power since the days when his writing had been a daily freshness and a delight to him. It was almost as if the course he must pursue was being dictated to him.

And the first thing he must do, of course, was to define the problem. He defined it in terms of mathematics. Granted that he had not the place to himself; granted that the old house had inexpressibly caught and engaged his spirit; granted that, by virtue of the common denominator of the place, this unknown co-tenant stood in some relation to himself: what next? Clearly, the nature of the other numerator must be ascertained.

And how? Ordinarily this would not have seemed simple, but to Oleron it was now pellucidly clear. The key, *of course*, lay in his half-written novel—or rather, in both *Romilly*s, the old and the proposed new one.

A little while before Oleron would have thought himself mad to have embraced such an opinion; now he accepted the dizzying hypothesis without a quiver.

He began to examine the first and second *Romilly*s.

From the moment of his doing so the thing advanced by leaps and bounds. Swiftly he reviewed the history of the *Romilly* of the fifteen chapters. He remembered clearly now that he had found her insufficient on the very first morning on which he had sat down to work in his new place. Other instances of his aversion leaped up to confirm his obscure investigation. There had come the night when he had hardly forborne to throw the whole thing into the fire; and the next morning he had begun the planning of the new *Romilly*. It had been on that morning that Mrs Barrett, overhearing him humming a brief phrase that the dripping of a tap the night before had suggested, had informed him that he was singing some air he had never in his life heard before, called "The Beckoning Fair One."...

The Beckoning Fair One!...

With scarcely a pause in thought he continued:

The first *Romilly* having been definitely thrown over, the second had instantly fastened herself upon him, clamouring for birth in his brain. He even fancied now, looking back, that there had been something like passion, hate almost, in the supplanting, and that more than once a stray thought given to his discarded creation had—(it was astonishing how credible Oleron found the almost unthinkable idea)—had offended the supplanter.

Yet that a malignancy almost homicidal should be extended to his fiction's poor mortal prototype...

In spite of his inuring to a scale in which the horrible was now a thing to be fingered and turned this way and that, a "Good God!" broke from Oleron.

This intrusion of the first *Romilly*'s prototype into his thought again was a factor that for the moment brought his inquiry into the nature of his problem to a termination; the mere thought of Elsie was fatal to anything abstract. For another thing, he could not yet think of that letter of Barrett's, nor of a little scene that had followed it, without a mounting of colour and a quick contraction of the brow. For, wisely or not, he had had that argument out at once. Striding across the square on the following morning, he had bearded Barrett on his own doorstep. Coming back again a few minutes later, he had been strongly of the opinion that he had only made matters worse. The man had been vagueness itself. He had not been able to be either challenged or browbeaten into anything more definite than a muttered farrago in which the words "Certain things... Mrs Barrett... respectable house... if the cap fits... proceedings that shall be nameless," had been constantly repeated.

"Not that I make any charge—" he had concluded.

"Charge!" Oleron had cried.

"I 'ave my idears of things, as I don't doubt you 'ave yours—"

"Ideas—mine!" Oleron had cried wrathfully, immediately dropping his voice as heads had appeared at windows of the square. "Look you here, my man; you've an unwholesome mind, which probably you can't help, but a tongue which you can help, and shall! If there is a breath of this repeated..."

"I'll not be talked to on my own doorstep like this by anybody..." Barrett had blustered...

"You shall, and I'm doing it..."

"Don't you forget there's a Gawd above all, Who 'as said..."

"You're a low scandalmonger!..."

And so forth, continuing badly what was already badly begun. Oleron had returned wrathfully to his own house, and thenceforward, looking out of his windows, had seen Barrett's face at odd times, lifting blinds or peering round curtains, as if he sought to put himself in possession of Heaven knew what evidence, in case it should be required of him.

The unfortunate occurrence made certain minor differences in Oleron's domestic arrangements. Barrett's tongue, he gathered, had already been busy; he was looked at askance by the dwellers of the square; and he judged it better, until he should be able to obtain other help, to make his purchases of provisions a little farther afield rather than at the small shops of the immediate neighbourhood.

For the rest, housekeeping was no new thing to him, and he would resume his old bachelor habits...

Besides, he was deep in certain rather abstruse investigations, in which it was better that he should not be disturbed.

He was looking out of his window one midday rather tired, not very well, and glad that it was not very likely he would have to stir out of doors, when he saw Elsie Bengough crossing the square towards his house. The weather had broken; it was a raw and gusty day; and she had to force her way against the wind that set her ample skirts bellying about her opulent figure and her veil spinning and streaming behind her.

Oleron acted swiftly and instinctively. Seizing his hat, he sprang to the door and descended the stairs at a run. A sort of panic had seized him. She must be prevented from setting foot in the place. As he ran along the alley he was conscious that his eyes went up to the eaves as if something drew them. He did not know that a slate might not accidentally fall...

He met her at the gate, and spoke with curious volubleness.

"This is really too bad, Elsie! Just as I'm urgently called away! I'm afraid it can't be helped though, and that you'll have to think me an inhospitable beast." He poured it out just as it came into his head.

She asked if he was going to town.

"Yes, yes—to town," he replied. "I've got to call on—on Chambers. You know Chambers, don't you? No, I remember you don't; a big man you once saw me with... I ought to have gone yesterday, and—" this he felt to be a brilliant effort—"and he's going out of town this afternoon. To Brighton. I had a letter from him this morning."

He took her arm and led her up the square. She had to remind him that his way to town lay in the other direction.

"Of course—how stupid of me!" he said, with a little loud laugh. "I'm so used to going the other way with you—of course; it's the other way to the bus. Will you come along with me? I am so awfully sorry it's happened like this..."

They took the street to the bus terminus.

This time Elsie bore no signs of having gone through interior struggles. If she detected anything unusual in his manner she made no comment, and he, seeing her calm, began to talk less recklessly through silences. By the time they reached the bus terminus, nobody, seeing the pallid-faced man without an overcoat and the large ample-skirted girl at his side, would have supposed that one of them was ready to sink on his knees for thankfulness that he had, as he believed, saved the other from a wildly unthinkable danger.

They mounted to the top of the bus, Oleron protesting that he should not miss his overcoat, and that he found the day, if anything, rather oppressively hot. They sat down on a front seat.

Now that this meeting was forced upon him, he had something else to say that would make demands upon his tact. It had been on his mind for some time, and was, indeed, peculiarly difficult to put. He revolved it for some minutes, and then, remembering the success of his story of a sudden call to town, cut the knot of his difficulty with another lie.

"I'm thinking of going away for a little while, Elsie," he said.

She merely said, "Oh?"

"Somewhere for a change. I need a change. I think I shall go tomorrow, or the day after. Yes, tomorrow, I think."

"Yes," she replied.

"I don't quite know how long I shall be," he continued. "I shall have to let you know when I am back."

"Yes, let me know," she replied in an even tone.

The tone was, for her, suspiciously even. He was a little uneasy.

"You don't ask me where I'm going," he said, with a little cumbrous effort to rally her.

She was looking straight before her, past the bus-driver.

"I know," she said.

He was startled. "How do you know?"

"You're not going anywhere," she replied.

He found not a word to say. It was a minute or so before she continued, in the same controlled voice she had employed from the start.

"You're not going anywhere. You weren't going out this morning. You only came out because I appeared; don't behave as if we were strangers, Paul."

A flush of pink had mounted to his cheeks. He noticed that the wind had given her the pink of early rhubarb. Still he found nothing to say.

"Of course, you ought to go away," she continued. "I don't know whether you look at yourself often in the glass, but you're rather noticeable. Several people have turned to look at you this morning. So, of course, you ought to go away. But you won't, and I know why."

He shivered, coughed a little, and then broke silence.

"Then if you know, there's no use in continuing this discussion," he said curtly.

"Not for me, perhaps, but there is for you," she replied. "Shall I tell you what I know?"

"No," he said in a voice slightly raised.

"No?" she asked, her round eyes earnestly on him.

"No."

Again he was getting out of patience with her; again he was conscious of the strain. Her devotion and fidelity and love plagued him; she was only humiliating both herself and him. It would have been bad enough had he ever, by word or deed, given her cause for thus fastening herself on him... but there; that was the worst of that kind of life for a woman. Women such as she, business women, in and out of offices all the time, always, whether they realised it or not, made comradeship a cover for something else. They accepted the unconventional status, came and went freely, as men did, were honestly taken by men at their own valuation—and then it turned out to be the other thing after all, and they went and fell in love. No wonder there was gossip in shops and squares and public houses! In a sense the gossipers were in the right of it. Independent, yet not efficient; with some of womanhood's graces forgone, and yet with all the woman's hunger and need; half sophisticated, yet not wise; Oleron was tired of it all...

And it was time he told her so.

"I suppose," he said tremblingly, looking down between his knees, "I suppose the real trouble is in the life women who earn their own living are obliged to lead."

He could not tell in what sense she took the lame generality; she merely replied, "I suppose so."

"It can't be helped," he continued, "but you do sacrifice a good deal."

She agreed: a good deal; and then she added after a moment, "What, for instance?"

"You may or may not be gradually attaining a new status, but you're in a false position today."

It was very likely, she said; she hadn't thought of it much in that light.

"And," he continued desperately, "you're bound to suffer. Your most innocent acts are misunderstood; motives you never dreamed of are attributed to you; and in the end it comes to"—he hesitated a moment and then took the plunge,"—to the sidelong look and the leer."

She took his meaning with perfect ease. She merely shivered a little as she pronounced the name.

"Barrett?"

His silence told her the rest.

Anything further that was to be said must come from her. It came as the bus stopped at a stage and fresh passengers mounted the stairs.

"You'd better get down here and go back, Paul," she said. "I understand perfectly—perfectly. It isn't Barrett. You'd be able to deal with Barrett. It's merely convenient for you to say it's Barrett. I know what it is... but you said I wasn't to tell you that. Very well. But before you go let me tell you why I came up this morning."

In a dull tone he asked her why. Again she looked straight before her as she replied:

"I came to force your hand. Things couldn't go on as they have been going, you know; and now that's all over."

"All over," he repeated stupidly.

"All over. I want you now to consider yourself, as far as I'm concerned, perfectly free. I make only one reservation."

He hardly had the spirit to ask her what that was.

"If *I* merely need *you*," she said, "please don't give that a thought; that's nothing; I shan't come near for that. But," she dropped her voice, "if *you're* in need of *me*, Paul—I shall know if you are, *and you will be*—then I shall come at no matter what cost. You understand that?"

He could only groan.

"So that's understood," she concluded. "And I think that's all. Now go back. I should advise you to walk back, for you're shivering—goodbye—"

She gave him a cold hand, and he descended. He turned on the edge of the kerb as the bus started again. For the first time in all the years he had known her she parted from him with no smile and no wave of her long arm.

IX

He stood on the kerb plunged in misery, looking after her as long as she remained in sight; but almost instantly with her disappearance he felt the heaviness lift a little from his spirit. She had given him his liberty; true, there was a sense in which he had never parted with it, but now was no time for splitting hairs; he was free to act, and all was clear ahead. Swiftly the sense of lightness grew on him: it became a positive rejoicing in his liberty; and before he was halfway home he had decided what must be done next.

The vicar of the parish in which his dwelling was situated lived within ten minutes of the square. To his house Oleron turned his steps. It was necessary that he should have all the information he could get about this old house with the insurance marks and the sloping "To Let" boards, and the vicar was the person most likely to be able to furnish it. This last preliminary out of the way, and—aha! Oleron chuckled—things might be expected to happen!

But he gained less information than he had hoped for. The house, the vicar said, was old—but there needed no vicar to tell Oleron that; it was reputed (Oleron pricked up his ears) to be haunted—but there were few old houses about which some such rumour did not circulate among the ignorant; and the deplorable lack of Faith of the modern world, the vicar thought, did not tend to dissipate these superstitions. For the rest, his manner was the soothing manner of one who prefers not to make statements without knowing how they will be taken by his hearer. Oleron smiled as he perceived this.

"You may leave my nerves out of the question," he said. "How long has the place been empty?"

"A dozen years, I should say," the vicar replied.

"And the last tenant—did you know him—or her?" Oleron was conscious of a tingling of his nerves as he offered the vicar the alternative of sex.

"Him," said the vicar. "A man. If I remember rightly, his name was Madley; an artist. He was a great recluse; seldom went out of the place, and"—the vicar hesitated and then broke into a little gush of candour—"and since you appear to have come for this information, and since it is better that the truth should be told than that garbled versions should get about, I don't mind saying that this man Madley died there, under somewhat unusual circumstances. It was ascertained at the post-mortem that there was not a particle of food in his stomach, although he was found to be not without money. And his frame was simply worn out. Suicide was spoken of, but you'll agree with me that deliberate starvation is, to say the least, an uncommon form of suicide. An open verdict was returned."

"Ah!" said Oleron... "Does there happen to be any comprehensive history of this parish?"

"No; partial ones only. I myself am not guiltless of having made a number of notes on its purely ecclesiastical history, its registers and so forth, which I shall be happy to show you if you would care to see them; but it is a large parish, I have only one curate, and my leisure, as you will readily understand... "

The extent of the parish and the scantiness of the vicar's leisure occupied the remainder of the interview, and Oleron thanked the vicar, took his leave, and walked slowly home.

He walked slowly for a reason, twice turning away from the house within a stone's-throw of the gate and taking another turn of twenty minutes or so. He had a very ticklish piece of work now before him; it required the greatest mental concentration; it was nothing less than to bring his mind, if he might, into such a state of unpreoccupation and receptivity that he should see the place as he had seen it on that morning when, his removal accomplished, he had sat down to begin the sixteenth chapter of the first *Romilly*.

For, could he recapture that first impression, he now hoped for far more from it. Formerly, he had carried no end of mental lumber. Before the influence of the place had been able to find him out at all, it had had the inertia of those dreary chapters to overcome. No results had shown. The process had been one of slow saturation, charging, filling up to a brim. But now he was light, unburdened, rid at last both of that *Romilly* and of her prototype. Now for the new unknown, coy, jealous, bewitching, Beckoning Fair!...

At half-past two of the afternoon he put his key into the Yale lock, entered, and closed the door behind him...

His fantastic attempt was instantly and astonishingly successful. He could have shouted with triumph as he entered the room; it was as if he had escaped into it. Once more, as in the days when his writing had had a daily freshness and wonder and promise for him, he was conscious of that new ease and mastery and exhilaration and release. The air of the place seemed to hold more oxygen; as if his own specific gravity had changed, his very tread seemed less ponderable. The flowers in the bowls, the fair proportions of the meadowsweet-coloured panels and mouldings, the polished floor, and the lofty and faintly starred ceiling, fairly laughed their welcome. Oleron actually laughed back, and spoke aloud.

"Oh, you're pretty, pretty!" he flattered it.

Then he lay down on his couch.

He spent that afternoon as a convalescent who expected a dear visitor might have spent it—in a delicious vacancy, smiling now and then as if in his sleep, and ever lifting drowsy and contented eyes to his alluring surroundings. He lay thus until darkness came, and, with darkness, the nocturnal noises of the old house...

But if he waited for any specific happening, he waited in vain.

He waited similarly in vain on the morrow, maintaining, though with less ease, that sensitised lake-like condition of his mind. Nothing occurred to give it an impression. Whatever it was which he so patiently wooed, it seemed to be both shy and exacting.

Then on the third day he thought he understood. A look of gentle drollery and cunning came into his eyes, and he chuckled.

"Oho, oho!... Well, if the wind sits in *that* quarter we must see what else there is to be done. What is there, now? No, I won't send for Elsie; we don't need a wheel to break the butterfly on; we won't go to those lengths, my butterfly..."

He was standing musing, thumbing his lean jaw, looking aslant; suddenly he crossed to his hall, took down his hat, and went out.

"My lady is coquettish, is she? Well, we'll see what a little neglect will do," he chuckled as he went down the stairs.

He sought a railway station, got into a train, and spent the rest of the day in the country. Oh, yes: Oleron thought he was the man to deal with Fair Ones who beckoned, and invited, and then took refuge in shyness and hanging back!

He did not return until after eleven that night.

"*Now*, my Fair Beckoner!" he murmured as he walked along the alley and felt in his pocket for his keys...

227

Inside his flat, he was perfectly composed, perfectly deliberate, exceedingly careful not to give himself away. As if to intimate that he intended to retire immediately, he lighted only a single candle; and as he set out with it on his nightly round he affected to yawn. He went first into his kitchen. There was a full moon, and a lozenge of moonlight, almost peacock-blue by contrast with his candle-frame, lay on the floor. The window was uncurtained, and he could see the reflection of the candle, and, faintly, that of his own face, as he moved about. The door of the powder-closet stood a little ajar, and he closed it before sitting down to remove his boots on the chair with the cushion made of the folded harp-bag. From the kitchen he passed to the bathroom. There, another slant of blue moonlight cut the windowsill and lay across the pipes on the wall. He visited his seldom-used study, and stood for a moment gazing at the silvered roofs across the square. Then, walking straight through his sitting-room, his stockinged feet making no noise, he entered his bedroom and put the candle on the chest of drawers. His face all this time wore no expression save that of tiredness. He had never been wilier nor more alert.

His small bedroom fireplace was opposite the chest of drawers on which the mirror stood, and his bed and the window occupied the remaining sides of the room. Oleron drew down his blind, took off his coat, and then stooped to get his slippers from under the bed.

He could have given no reason for the conviction, but that the manifestation that for two days had been withheld was close at hand he never for an instant doubted. Nor, though he could not form the faintest guess of the shape it might take, did he experience fear. Startling or surprising it might be; he was prepared for that; but that was all; his scale of sensation had become depressed. His hand moved this way and that under the bed in search of his slippers...

But for all his caution and method and preparedness, his heart all at once gave a leap and a pause that was almost horrid. His hand had found the slippers, but he was still on his knees; save for this circumstance he would have fallen. The bed was a low one; the groping for the slippers accounted for the turn of his head to one side; and he was careful to keep the attitude until he had partly recovered his self-possession. When presently he rose there was a drop of blood on his lower lip where he had caught at it with his teeth, and his watch had jerked out of the pocket of his waistcoat and was dangling at the end of its short leather guard...

Then, before the watch had ceased its little oscillation, he was himself again.

In the middle of his mantelpiece there stood a picture, a portrait of his grandmother; he placed himself before this picture, so that he could see in the glass of it the steady flame of the candle that burned behind him on the chest of drawers. He could see also in the picture-glass the little glancings of light from the bevels and facets of the objects about the mirror and candle. But he could see more. These twinklings and reflections and re-reflections did not change their position; but there was one gleam that had motion. It was fainter than the rest, and it moved up and down through the air. It was the reflection of the candle on Oleron's black vulcanite comb, and each of its downward movements was accompanied by a silky and crackling rustle.

Oleron, watching what went on in the glass of his grandmother's portrait, continued to play his part. He felt for his dangling watch and began slowly to wind it up. Then, for a moment ceasing to watch, he began to empty his trousers pockets and to place methodically in a little row on the mantelpiece the pennies and halfpennies he took from them. The sweeping, minutely electric noise filled the whole bedroom, and had Oleron altered his point of observation he could have brought the dim gleam of the moving comb so into position that it would almost have outlined his grandmother's head.

Any other head of which it might have been following the outline was invisible.

Oleron finished the emptying of his pockets; then, under cover of another simulated yawn, not so much summoning his resolution as overmastered by an exorbitant curiosity, he swung suddenly round. That which was being combed was still not to be seen, but the comb did not stop. It had altered its angle a little, and had moved a little to the left. It was passing, in fairly regular sweeps, from a point rather more than five feet from the ground, in a direction roughly vertical, to another point a few inches below the level of the chest of drawers.

Oleron continued to act to admiration. He walked to his little washstand in the corner, poured out water, and began to wash his hands. He removed his waistcoat, and continued his preparations for bed. The combing did not cease, and he stood for a moment in thought. Again his eyes twinkled. The next was very cunning—

"Hm!... *I think I'll read for a quarter of an hour*," he said aloud...

He passed out of the room.

He was away a couple of minutes; when he returned again the room was suddenly quiet. He glanced at the chest of drawers; the comb lay still, between the collar he had removed and a pair of gloves. Without hesitation Oleron put out his hand and picked it up. It was an ordinary eighteenpenny comb, taken from a card in a chemist's shop, of a substance of a definite specific gravity, and no more capable of rebellion against the Laws by which it existed than are the worlds that keep their orbits through the void. Oleron put it down again; then he glanced at the bundle of papers he held in his hand. What he had gone to fetch had been the fifteen chapters of the original *Romilly*.

"Hm!" he muttered as he threw the manuscript into a chair... "As I thought... She's just blindly, ragingly, murderously jealous."

CR

On the night after that, and on the following night, and for many nights and days, so many that he began to be uncertain about the count of them, Oleron, courting, cajoling, neglecting, threatening, beseeching, eaten out with unappeased curiosity and regardless that his life was becoming one consuming passion and desire, continued his search for the unknown co-numerator of his abode.

X

As time went on, it came to pass that few except the postman mounted Oleron's stairs; and since men who do not write letters receive few, even the postman's tread became so infrequent that it was not heard more than once or twice a week. There came a letter from Oleron's publishers, asking when they might expect to receive the manuscript of his new book; he delayed for some days to answer it, and finally forgot it. A second letter came, which also he failed to answer. He received no third.

The weather grew bright and warm. The privet bushes among the chopper-like notice-boards flowered, and in the streets where Oleron did his shopping the baskets of flower-women lined the kerbs. Oleron purchased flowers daily; his room clamoured for flowers, fresh and continually renewed; and Oleron did not stint its demands. Nevertheless, the necessity for going out to buy them began to irk him more and more, and it was with a greater and ever greater sense of relief that he returned home again. He began to be conscious that again his scale of sensation had suffered a subtle change—a change that was not restoration to its former capacity, but an extension and enlarging that once more included terror. It admitted it in an entirely new form. *Lux orco, tenebræ Jovi.* The name of this terror was agoraphobia. Oleron had begun to dread air and space and the horror that might pounce upon the unguarded back.

Presently he so contrived it that his food and flowers were delivered daily at his door. He rubbed his hands when he had hit upon this expedient. That was better! Now he could please himself whether he went out or not...

Quickly he was confirmed in his choice. It became his pleasure to remain immured.

But he was not happy—or, if he was, his happiness took an extraordinary turn. He fretted discontentedly, could sometimes have wept for mere weakness and misery; and yet he was dimly conscious that he would not have exchanged his sadness for all the noisy mirth of the world outside. And speaking of noise: noise, much noise, now caused him the acutest discomfort. It was hardly more to be endured than that new-born fear that kept him, on the increasingly rare occasions when he did go out, sidling close to walls and feeling friendly railings with his hand. He moved from room to room softly and in slippers, and sometimes stood for many seconds closing a door so gently that not a sound broke the stillness that was in itself a delight. Sunday now became an intolerable day to him, for, since the coming of the fine weather, there had begun to assemble in the square under his windows each Sunday morning certain members of the sect to which the long-nosed Barrett adhered. These came with a great drum and large brass-bellied instruments; men and women uplifted anguished voices, struggling with their God; and Barrett himself, with upraised face and closed eyes and working brows, prayed that the sound of his voice might penetrate the ears of all unbelievers—as it certainly did Oleron's. One day, in the middle of one of these rhapsodies, Oleron sprang to his blind and pulled it down, and heard as he did so, his own name made the object of a fresh torrent of outpouring.

And sometimes, but not as expecting a reply, Oleron stood still and called softly. Once or twice he called "Romilly!" and then waited; but more often his whispering did not take the shape of a name.

There was one spot in particular of his abode that he began to haunt with increasing persistency. This was just within the opening of his bedroom door. He had discovered one day that by opening every door in his place (always excepting the outer one, which he only opened unwillingly) and by placing himself on this particular spot, he could actually see to a greater or less extent into each of his five rooms without changing his position. He could see the whole of his sitting-room, all of his bedroom except the part hidden by the open door, and glimpses of his kitchen, bathroom, and of his rarely used study. He was often in this place, breathless and with his finger on his lip. One day, as he stood there, he suddenly found himself wondering whether this Madley, of whom the vicar had spoken, had ever discovered the strategic importance of the bedroom entry.

Light, moreover, now caused him greater disquietude than did darkness. Direct sunlight, of which, as the sun passed daily round the house, each of his rooms had now its share, was like a flame in his brain; and even diffused light was a dull and numbing ache. He began, at successive hours of the day, one after another, to lower his crimson blinds. He made short and daring excursions in order to do this; but he was ever careful to leave his retreat open, in case he should have sudden need of it. Presently this lowering of the blinds had become a daily methodical exercise, and his rooms, when he had been his round, had the blood-red half-light of a photographer's dark-room.

One day, as he drew down the blind of his little study and backed in good order out of the room again, he broke into a soft laugh.

"*That* bilks Mr Barrett!" he said; and the baffling of Barrett continued to afford him mirth for an hour.

But on another day, soon after, he had a fright that left him trembling also for an hour. He had seized the cord to darken the window over the seat in which he had found the harp-bag, and was standing with his back well protected in the embrasure, when he thought he saw the tail of a black-and-white check skirt disappear round the corner of the house. He could not be sure—had he run to the window of the other wall, which was blinded, the skirt must have been already past—but he was *almost* sure that it was Elsie. He listened in an agony of suspense for her tread on the stairs...

But no tread came, and after three or four minutes he drew a long breath of relief.

"By Jove, but that would have compromised me horribly!" he muttered... And he continued to mutter from time to time, "Horribly compromising... *no* woman would stand that... not *any* kind of woman... oh, compromising in the extreme!"

Yet he was not happy. He could not have assigned the cause

of the fits of quiet weeping which took him sometimes; they came and went, like the fitful illumination of the clouds that travelled over the square; and perhaps, after all, if he was not happy, he was not unhappy. Before he could be unhappy something must have been withdrawn, and nothing had yet been withdrawn from him, for nothing had been granted. He was waiting for that granting, in that flower-laden, frightfully enticing apartment of his, with the pith-white walls tinged and subdued by the crimson blinds to a blood-like gloom.

He paid no heed to it that his stock of money was running perilously low, nor that he had ceased to work. Ceased to work? He had not ceased to work. They knew very little about it who supposed that Oleron had ceased to work! He was in truth only now beginning to work. He was preparing such a work... such a work... such a Mistress was a-making in the gestation of his Art... let him but get this period of probation and poignant waiting over and men should see... How *should* men know her, this Fair One of Oleron's, until Oleron himself knew her? Lovely radiant creations are not thrown off like How-d'ye-do's. The men to whom it is committed to father them must weep wretched tears, as Oleron did, must swell with vain presumptuous hopes, as Oleron did, must pursue, as Oleron pursued, the capricious, fair, mocking, slippery, eager Spirit that, ever eluding, ever sees to it that the chase does not slacken. Let Oleron but hunt this Huntress a little longer. . . he would have her sparkling and panting in his arms yet... Oh no: they were very far from the truth who supposed that Oleron had ceased to work!

And if all else was falling away from Oleron, gladly he was letting it go. So do we all when our Fair Ones beckon. Quite at the beginning we wink, and promise ourselves that we will put Her Ladyship through her paces, neglect her for a day, turn her own jealous wiles against her, flout and ignore her when she comes wheedling; perhaps there lurks within us all the time a heartless sprite who is never fooled; but in the end all falls away. She beckons, beckons, and all goes.

And so Oleron kept his strategic post within the frame of his bedroom door, and watched, and waited, and smiled, with his finger on his lips... It was his duteous service, his worship, his troth-plighting, all that he had ever known of Love. And when he found himself, as he now and then did, hating the dead man Madley, and wishing that he had never lived, he felt that that, too, was an acceptable service.

But, as he thus prepared himself, as it were, for a Marriage, and moped and chafed more and more that the Bride made no sign, he made a discovery that he ought to have made weeks before.

It was through a thought of the dead Madley that he made it. Since that night when he had thought in his greenness that a little studied neglect would bring the lovely Beckoner to her knees, and had made use of her own jealousy to banish her, he had not set eyes on those fifteen discarded chapters of *Romilly*. He had thrown them back into the window-seat, forgotten their very existence. But his own jealousy of Madley put him in mind of hers, of her jilted rival of flesh and blood, and he remembered them... Fool that he had been! Had he, then, expected his Desire to manifest herself while there still existed the evidence of his divided allegiance? What, and she with a passion so fierce and centred that it had not hesitated at the destruction, twice attempted, of her rival? Fool that he had been!...

But if *that* was all the pledge and sacrifice she required she should have it—ah, yes, and quickly!

He took the manuscript from the window-seat, and brought it to the fire.

He kept his fire always burning now; the warmth brought out the last vestige of odour of the flowers with which his room was banked. He did not know what time it was; long since he had allowed his clock to run down—it had seemed a foolish measurer of time in regard to the stupendous things that were happening to Oleron; but he knew it was late. He took the *Romilly* manuscript and knelt before the fire.

But he had not finished removing the fastening that held the sheets together before he suddenly gave a start, turned his head over his shoulder, and listened intently. The sound he had heard had not been loud—it had been, indeed, no more than a tap, twice or thrice repeated—but it had filled Oleron with alarm. His face grew dark as it came again.

He heard a voice outside on his landing.

"Paul!... Paul!..."

It was Elsie's voice.

"Paul!... I know you're in... I want to see you..."

He cursed her under his breath, but kept perfectly still. He did not intend to admit her.

"Paul!... You're in trouble... I believe you're in danger... at least come to the door!..."

Oleron smothered a low laugh. It somehow amused him that she, in such danger herself, should talk to him of his danger!... Well, if she was, serve her right; she knew, or said she knew, all about it...

"Paul!... Paul! ..."

"*Paul!... Paul!...* " He mimicked her under his breath.

"Oh, Paul, it's *horrible!*..."

Horrible was it? thought Oleron. Then let her get away...

"I only want to help you, Paul... I didn't promise not to come if you needed me..."

He was impervious to the pitiful sob that interrupted the low cry. The devil take the woman! Should he shout to her to go away and not come back? No: let her call and knock and sob. She had a gift for sobbing; she mustn't think her sobs would move him. They irritated him, so that he set his teeth and shook his fist at her, but that was all. Let her sob.

"*Paul!... Paul!...*"

With his teeth hard set, he dropped the first page of *Romilly* into the fire. Then he began to drop the rest in, sheet by sheet.

For many minutes the calling behind his door continued; then suddenly it ceased. He heard the sound of feet slowly descending the stairs. He listened for the noise of a fall or a cry or the crash of a piece of the handrail of the upper landing; but none of these things came. She was spared. Apparently her rival suffered her to crawl abject and beaten away. Oleron heard the passing of her steps under his window; then she was gone.

He dropped the last page into the fire, and then, with a low laugh rose. He looked fondly round his room.

"Lucky to get away like that," he remarked. "She wouldn't have got away if I'd given her as much as a word or a look! What devils these women are!... But no; I oughtn't to say that; one of 'em showed forbearance..."

Who showed forbearance? And what was forborne? Ah, Oleron knew!... Contempt, no doubt, had been at the bottom of it, but that didn't matter: the pestering creature had been allowed to go unharmed. Yes, she was lucky; Oleron hoped she knew it.

And now, now, now for his reward!

Oleron crossed the room. All his doors were open; his eyes shone as he placed himself within that of his bedroom.

Fool that he had been, not to think of destroying the manuscript sooner!

How, in a houseful of shadows, should he know his own Shadow? How, in a houseful of noises, distinguish the summons he felt to be at hand? Ah, trust him! He would know! The place was full of a jugglery of dim lights. The blind at his elbow that allowed the light of a street lamp to struggle vaguely through—the glimpse of greeny blue moonlight seen through the distant kitchen door—the sulky glow of the fire under the black ashes of the burnt manuscript—the glimmering of the tulips and the moon-daisies and narcissi in the bowls and jugs and jars—these did not so trick and bewilder his eyes that he would not know his Own! It was he, not she, who had been delaying the shadowy Bridal; he hung his head for a moment in mute acknowledgment; then he bent his eyes on the deceiving, puzzling gloom again. He would have called her name had he known it—but now he would not ask her to share even a name with the other...

His own face, within the frame of the door, glimmered white as the narcissi in the darkness...

A shadow, light as fleece, seemed to take shape in the kitchen (the time had been when Oleron would have said that a cloud had passed over the unseen moon). The low illumination on the blind at his elbow grew dimmer (the time had been when Oleron would have concluded that the lamplighter going his rounds had turned low the flame of the lamp). The fire settled, letting down the black and charred papers; a flower fell from a bowl, and lay indistinct upon the floor; all was still; and then a stray draught moved through the old house, passing before Oleron's face...

Suddenly, inclining his head, he withdrew a little from the door-jamb. The wandering draught caused the door to move a little on its hinges. Oleron trembled violently, stood for a moment longer, and then, putting his hand out to the knob, softly drew the door to, sat down on the nearest chair, and waited, as a man might await the calling of his name that should summon him to some weighty, high and privy Audience...

XI

One knows not whether there can be human compassion for anæmia of the soul. When the pitch of Life is dropped, and the spirit is so put over and reversed that that only is horrible which before was sweet and worldly and of the day, the human relation disappears. The sane soul turns appalled away, lest not merely itself, but sanity should suffer. We are not gods. We cannot drive out devils. We must see selfishly to it that devils do not enter into ourselves.

And this we must do even though Love so transfuse us that we may well deem our nature to be half divine. We shall but speak of honour and duty in vain. The letter dropped within the dark door will lie unregarded, or, if regarded for a brief instant between two unspeakable lapses, left and forgotten again. The telegram will be undelivered, nor will the whistling messenger (wiselier guided than he knows to whistle) be conscious as he walks away of the drawn blind that is pushed aside an inch by a finger and then fearfully replaced again. No: let the miserable wrestle with his own shadows; let him, if indeed he be so mad, clip and strain and enfold and couch the succubus; but let him do so in a house into which not an air of Heaven penetrates, nor a bright finger of the sun pierces the filthy twilight. The lost must remain lost. Humanity has other business to attend to.

For the handwriting of the two letters that Oleron, stealing noiselessly one June day into his kitchen to rid his sitting-room of an armful of fœtid and decaying flowers, had seen on the floor within his door, had had no more meaning for him than if it had belonged to some dim and far-away dream. And at the beating of the telegraph-boy upon the door, within a few feet of the bed where he lay, he had gnashed his teeth and stopped his ears. He had pictured the lad standing there, just beyond his partition, among packets of provisions and bundles of dead and dying flowers. For his outer landing was littered with these. Oleron had feared to open his door to take them in. After a week, the errand lads had reported that there must be some mistake about the order, and had left no more. Inside, in the red twilight, the old flowers turned brown and fell and decayed where they lay.

Gradually his power was draining away. The Abomination fastened on Oleron's power. The steady sapping sometimes left him for many hours of prostration gazing vacantly up at his red-tinged ceiling, idly suffering such fancies as came of themselves to have their way with him. Even the strongest of his memories had no more than a precarious hold upon his attention. Sometimes a flitting half-memory, of a novel to be written, a novel it was important that he should write, tantalised him for a space before vanishing again; and sometimes whole novels, perfect, splendid, established to endure, rose magically before him. And sometimes the memories were absurdly remote and trivial, of garrets he had inhabited and lodgings that had sheltered him, and so forth. Oleron had known a good deal about such things in his time, but all that was now past. He had at last found a place which he did not intend to leave until they fetched him out—a place that some might have thought a little on the green-sick side, that others might have considered to be a little too redolent of long-dead and morbid things for a living man to be mewed up in, but ah, so irresistible, with such an authority of its own, with such an associate of its own, and a place of such delights when once a man had ceased to struggle against its inexorable will! A novel? Somebody ought to write a novel about a place like that! There must be lots to write about in a place like that if one could but get to the bottom of it! It had probably already been painted, by a man called Madley who had lived there... but Oleron had not known this Madley—had a strong feeling that he wouldn't have liked him—would rather he had lived somewhere else—really couldn't stand the fellow—hated him, Madley, in fact. (Aha! That was a joke!) He seriously doubted whether the man had led the life he ought; Oleron was in two minds sometimes whether he wouldn't tell that long-nosed guardian of the public morals across the way about him; but probably he knew, and had made his praying hullabaloos for him also. That was his line. Why, Oleron himself had had a dust-up with him about something or other... some girl or other... Elsie Bengough her name was, he remembered...

Oleron had moments of deep uneasiness about this Elsie Bengough. Or rather, he was not so much uneasy about her as restless about the things she did. Chief of these was the way in which she persisted in thrusting herself into his thoughts; and, whenever he was quick enough, he sent her packing the moment she made her appearance there. The truth was that she was not merely a bore; she had always been that; it had now come to the pitch when her very presence in his fancy was inimical to the full enjoyment of certain experiences... She had no tact; really ought to have known that people are not at home to the thoughts of everybody all the time; ought in mere politeness to have allowed him certain seasons quite

240

to himself; and was monstrously ignorant of things if she did not know, as she appeared not to know, that there were certain special hours when a man's veins ran with fire and daring and power, in which... well, in which he had a reasonable right to treat folk as he had treated that prying Barrett—to shut them out completely... But no, up she popped: the thought of her, and ruined all. Bright towering fabrics, by the side of which even those perfect, magical novels of which he dreamed were dun and grey, vanished utterly at her intrusion. It was as if a fog should suddenly quench some fair-beaming star, as if at the threshold of some golden portal prepared for Oleron a pit should suddenly gape, as if a bat-like shadow should turn the growing dawn to mirk and darkness again. Therefore, Oleron strove to stifle even the nascent thought of her.

Nevertheless, there came an occasion on which this woman Bengough absolutely refused to be suppressed. Oleron could not have told exactly when this happened; he only knew by the glimmer of the street lamp on his blind that it was some time during the night, and that for some time she had not presented herself.

He had no warning, none, of her coming; she just came—was there. Strive as he would, he could not shake off the thought of her nor the image of her face. She haunted him.

But for her to come at *that* moment of all moments!... Really, it was past belief! How *she* could endure it, Oleron could not conceive! Actually, to look on, as it were, at the triumph of a Rival... Good God! It was monstrous! tact—reticence—he had never credited her with an overwhelming amount of either: but he had never attributed mere—oh, there was no word for it! Monstrous—monstrous! Did she intend thenceforward... Good God! To look on!...

Oleron felt the blood rush up to the roots of his hair with anger against her.

"Damnation take her!" he choked...

But the next moment his heat and resentment had changed to a cold sweat of cowering fear. Panic-stricken, he strove to comprehend what he had done. For though he knew not what, he knew he had done something, something fatal, irreparable, blasting. Anger he had felt, but not *this* blaze of ire that suddenly flooded the twilight of his consciousness with a white infernal light. *That* appalling flash was not his—not his *that* open rift of bright and searing Hell—not his, not his! His had been the hand of a child, preparing a puny blow; but what was *this other* horrific hand that was drawn back to strike in the same place? Had *he* set that in motion? Had *he* provided the spark that had touched off the whole accumulated power of that formidable and relentless place? He did not know. He only knew that that poor igniting particle in himself was blown out, that—Oh, impossible!—a clinging kiss (how else to express it?) had changed on his very lips to a gnashing and a removal, and that for very pity of the awful odds he must cry out to her against whom he had lately raged to guard herself... guard herself...

"*Look out!*" he shrieked aloud...

The revulsion was instant. As if a cold slow billow had broken over him, he came to to find that he was lying in his bed, that the mist and horror that had for so long enwrapped him had departed, that he was Paul Oleron, and that he was sick, naked, helpless, and unutterably abandoned and alone. His faculties, though weak, answered at last to his calls upon them; and he knew that it must have been a hideous nightmare that had left him sweating and shaking thus.

Yes, he was himself, Paul Oleron, a tired novelist, already past the summit of his best work, and slipping downhill again empty-handed from it all. He had struck short in his life's aim. He had tried too much, had over-estimated his strength, and was a failure, a failure...

It all came to him in the single word, enwrapped and complete; it needed no sequential thought; he was a failure. He had missed...

And he had missed not one happiness, but two. He had missed the ease of this world, which men love, and he had missed also that other shining prize for which men forgo ease, the snatching and holding and triumphant bearing up aloft of which is the only justification of the mad adventurer who hazards the enterprise. And there was no second attempt. Fate has no morrow. Oleron's morrow must be to sit down to profitless, ill-done, unrequired work again, and so on the morrow after that, and the morrow after that, and as many morrows as there might be.

He lay there, weakly yet sanely considering it.

And since the whole attempt had failed, it was hardly worth while to consider whether a little might not be saved from the general wreck. No good would ever come of that half-finished novel. He had intended that it should appear in the autumn; was under contract that it should appear; no matter; it was better to pay forfeit to his publishers than to waste what days were left. He was spent; age was not far off; and paths of wisdom and sadness were the properest for the remainder of the journey.

If only he had chosen the wife, the child, the faithful friend at the fireside, and let them follow an *ignis fatuus*—that list!...

In the meantime it began to puzzle him exceedingly why he should be so weak, that his room should smell so overpoweringly of decaying vegetable matter, and that his hand, chancing to stray to his face in the darkness, should encounter a beard.

"Most extraordinary!" he began to mutter to himself. "Have I been ill? Am I ill now? And if so, why have they left me alone?... Extraordinary!..."

He thought he heard a sound from the kitchen or bathroom. He rose a little on his pillow, and listened... Ah! He was not alone, then! It certainly would have been extraordinary if they had left him ill and alone—Alone? Oh no. He would be looked after. He wouldn't be left, ill, to shift for himself. If everybody else had forsaken him, he could trust Elsie Bengough, the dearest chum he had, for that... bless her faithful heart!

But suddenly a short, stifled, spluttering cry rang sharply out:

"*Paul!*"

It came from the kitchen.

And in the same moment it flashed upon Oleron, he knew not how, that two, three, five, he knew not how many minutes before, another sound, unmarked at the time but suddenly transfixing his attention now, had striven to reach his intelligence. This sound had been the slight touch of metal on metal— just such a sound as Oleron made when he put his key into the lock.

"Hallo!... Who's that?" he called sharply from his bed.

He had no answer.

He called again. "Hallo!... Who's there?... Who is it?"

This time he was sure he heard noises, soft and heavy, in the kitchen.

"This is a queer thing altogether," he muttered. "By Jove, I'm as weak as a kitten too... Hallo, there! Somebody called, didn't they?... Elsie! Is that you?..."

Then he began to knock with his hand on the wall at the side of his bed.

"Elsie!... Elsie!... You called, didn't you?... Please come here, whoever it is!..."

There was a sound as of a closing door, and then silence. Oleron began to get rather alarmed.

"It may be a nurse," he muttered; "Elsie'd have to get me a nurse, of course. She'd sit with me as long as she could spare the time, brave lass, and she'd get a nurse for the rest... But it was awfully like her voice... Elsie, or whoever it is!... I can't make this out at all. I must go and see what's the matter..."

He put one leg out of bed. Feeling its feebleness, he reached with his hand for the additional support of the wall...

But before putting out the other leg he stopped and considered, picking at his new-found beard. He was suddenly wondering whether he *dared* go into the kitchen. It was such a frightfully long way; no man knew what horror might not leap and huddle on his shoulders if he went so far; when a man has an over-mastering impulse to get back into bed he ought to take heed of the warning and obey it.

244

Besides, why should he go? What was there to go for? If it was that Bengough creature again, let her look after herself; Oleron was not going to have things cramp themselves on his defenceless back for the sake of such a spoilsport as *she!* If she was in, let her let herself out again, and the sooner the better for her! Oleron simply couldn't be bothered. He had his work to do. On the morrow, he must set about the writing of a novel with a heroine so winsome, capricious, adorable, jealous, wicked, beautiful, inflaming, and altogether evil, that men should stand amazed. She was coming over him now; he knew by the alteration of the very air of the room when she was near him; and that soft thrill of bliss that had begun to stir in him never came unless she was beckoning, beckoning...

He let go the wall and fell back into bed again as—oh, unthinkable!—the other half of that kiss that a gnash had interrupted was placed (how else convey it?) on his lips, robbing him of very breath...

XII

In the bright June sunlight a crowd filled the square, and looked up at the windows of the old house with the antique insurance marks in its walls of red brick and the agents' notice-boards hanging like wooden choppers over the paling. Two constables stood at the broken gate of the narrow entrance-alley, keeping folk back. The women kept to the outskirts of the throng, moving now and then as if to see the drawn red blinds of the old house from a new angle, and talking in whispers. The children were in the houses, behind closed doors.

A long-nosed man had a little group about him, and he was telling some story over and over again; and another man, little and fat and wide-eyed, sought to capture the long-nosed man's audience with some relation in which a key figured.

"...and it was revealed to me that there'd been something that very afternoon," the long-nosed man was saying. "I was standing there, where Constable Saunders is—or rather, I was passing about my business, when they came out. There was no deceiving *me*, oh, no deceiving me! I saw her face..."

"What was it like, Mr Barrett?" a man asked.

"It was like hers whom our Lord said to, 'Woman, doth any man accuse thee?'—white as paper, and no mistake! Don't tell *me*!... And so I walks straight across to Mrs Barrett, and 'Jane,' I says, 'this must stop, and stop at once; we are commanded to avoid evil,' I says, 'and it must come to an end now; let him get help elsewhere.' And she says to me, 'John,' she says, 'it's four-and-sixpence a week'—them was her words. 'Jane,' I says, 'if it was forty-six thousand pounds it should stop'... and from that day to this she hasn't set foot inside that gate."

There was a short silence: then,

"Did Mrs Barrett ever... *see* anythink, like?" somebody vaguely inquired.

Barrett turned austerely on the speaker.

"What Mrs Barrett saw and Mrs Barrett didn't see shall not pass these lips; even as it is written, keep thy tongue from speaking evil," he said.

Another man spoke.

"He was pretty near canned up in the Waggon and Horses that night, weren't he, Jim?"

"Yes, 'e 'adn't 'alf copped it..."

"Not standing treat much, neither; he was in the bar, all on his own..."

"So 'e was, we talked about it..."

The fat, scared-eyed man made another attempt.

"She got the key off of me—she 'ad the number of it—she came into my shop of a Tuesday evening..."

Nobody heeded him.

"Shut your heads," a heavy labourer commented gruffly, "she hasn't been found yet. 'Ere's the inspectors; we shall know more in a bit."

Two inspectors had come up and were talking to the constables who guarded the gate. The little fat man ran eagerly forward, saying that she had bought the key of him. "I remember the number, because of it's being three one's and three three's—111333!" he exclaimed excitedly.

An inspector put him aside.

"Nobody's been in?" he asked of one of the constables.

"No, sir."

"Then you, Brackley, come with us; you, Smith, keep the gate. There's a squad on its way."

The two inspectors and the constable passed down the alley and entered the house. They mounted the wide carved staircase.

"This don't look as if he'd been out much lately," one of the inspectors muttered as he kicked aside a litter of dead leaves and paper that lay outside Oleron's door. "I don't think we need knock—break a pane, Brackley."

The door had two glazed panels; there was a sound of shattered glass; and Brackley put his hand through the hole his elbow had made and drew back the latch.

"Faugh!"... choked one of the inspectors as they entered. "Let some light and air in, quick. It stinks like a hearse—"

The assembly out in the square saw the red blinds go up and the windows of the old house flung open.

"That's better," said one of the inspectors, putting his head out of a window and drawing a deep breath. "That seems to be the bedroom in there; will you go in, Simms, while I go over the rest?... "

They had drawn up the bedroom blind also, and the waxy-white, emaciated man on the bed had made a blinker of his hand against the torturing flood of brightness. Nor could he believe that his hearing was not playing tricks with him, for there were two policemen in his room, bending over him and asking where "she" was. He shook his head.

"This woman Bengough... goes by the name of Miss Elsie Bengough... d'ye hear? Where is she?... No good, Brackley; get him up; be careful with him; I'll just shove *my* head out of the window, I think..."

The other inspector had been through Oleron's study and had found nothing, and was now in the kitchen, kicking aside an ankle-deep mass of vegetable refuse that cumbered the floor. The kitchen window had no blind, and was overshadowed by the blank end of the house across the alley. The kitchen appeared to be empty.

But the inspector, kicking aside the dead flowers, noticed that a shuffling track that was not of his making had been swept to a cupboard in the corner. In the upper part of the door of the cupboard was a square panel that looked as if it slid on runners. The door itself was closed.

The inspector advanced, put out his hand to the little knob, and slid the hatch along its groove.

Then he took an involuntary step back again.

Framed in the aperture, and falling forward a little before it jammed again in its frame, was something that resembled a large lumpy pudding, done up in a pudding-bag of faded browny red frieze.

"Ah!" said the inspector.

To close the hatch again he would have had to thrust that pudding back with his hand; and somehow he did not quite like the idea of touching it. Instead, he turned the handle of the cupboard itself. There was weight behind it, so much weight that, after opening the door three or four inches and peering inside, he had to put his shoulder to it in order to close it again. In closing it he left sticking out, a few inches from the floor, a triangle of black and white check skirt.

He went into the small hall.

"All right!" he called.

They had got Oleron into his clothes. He still used his hands as blinkers, and his brain was very confused. A number of things were happening that he couldn't understand. He couldn't understand the extraordinary mess of dead flowers there seemed to be everywhere; he couldn't understand why there should be police officers in his room; he couldn't understand why one of these should be sent for a four-wheeler and a stretcher; and he couldn't understand what heavy article they seemed to be moving about in the kitchen—his kitchen...

"What's the matter?" he muttered sleepily...

Then he heard a murmur in the square, and the stopping of a four-wheeler outside. A police officer was at his elbow again, and Oleron wondered why, when he whispered something to him, he should run off a string of words— something about "used in evidence against you." They had lifted him to his feet, and were assisting him towards the door...

No, Oleron couldn't understand it at all.

They got him down the stairs and along the alley. Oleron was aware of confused angry shoutings; he gathered that a number of people wanted to lynch somebody or other. Then his attention became fixed on a little fat frightened-eyed man who appeared to be making a statement that an officer was taking down in a notebook.

"I'd seen her with him... they was often together she came into my shop and said it was for him... I thought it was all right... 111333 the number was," the man was saying.

The people seemed to be very angry; many police were keeping them back; but one of the inspectors had a voice that Oleron thought quite kind and friendly. He was telling somebody to get somebody else into the cab before something or other was brought out; and Oleron noticed that a four-wheeler was drawn up at the gate. It appeared that it was himself who was to be put into it; and as they lifted him up he saw that the inspector tried to stand between him and something that stood behind the cab, but was not quick enough to prevent Oleron seeing that this something was a hooded stretcher. The angry voices sounded like a sea; something hard, like a stone, hit the back of the cab; and the inspector followed Oleron in and stood with his back to the window nearer the side where the people were. The door they had put Oleron in at remained open, apparently till the other inspector should come; and through the opening Oleron had a glimpse of the hatchet-like "To Let" boards among the privet-trees. One of them said that the key was at Number Six...

Suddenly the raging of voices was hushed. Along the entrance-alley shuffling steps were heard, and the other inspector appeared at the cab door.

"Right away," he said to the driver.

He entered, fastened the door after him, and blocked up the second window with his back. Between the two inspectors Oleron slept peacefully. The cab moved down the square, the other vehicle went up the hill. The mortuary lay that way.

The Sweeper
AM Burrage

It seemed to Tessa Winyard that Miss Ludgate's strangest characteristic was her kindness to beggars. This was something more than a little peculiar in a nature which, to be sure, presented a surface like a mountain range of unexpected peaks and valleys; for there was a thin streak of meanness in her. One caught glimpses of it here and there, to be traced a little way and lost, like a thin elusive vein in a block of marble. One week she would pay the household bills without a murmur; the next she would simmer over them in a mild rage, questioning the smallest item, and suggesting the most absurd little economies which she would have been the first to condemn later if Mrs. Finch the housekeeper had ever taken her at her word. She was rich enough to be indifferent, but old enough to be crochety.

Miss Ludgate gave very sparsely to local charities, and those good busybodies who went forth at different times with subscription lists and tales of good causes often visited her and came empty away. She had plausible, transparent excuses for keeping her purse-strings tight. Hospitals should be State-aided; schemes for assisting the local poor destroyed thrift; we had heathen of our own to convert, and needed to send no missionaries abroad. Yet she was sometimes overwhelmingly generous in her spasmodic charities to individuals, and her kindness to itinerant beggars was proverbial among their fraternity. Her neighbours were not grateful to her for this, for it was said that she encouraged every doubtful character who came that way.

When she first agreed to come on a month's trial Tessa Winyard had known that she would find Miss Ludgate difficult, doubting whether she would be able to retain the post of companion, and, still more, if she would want to retain it. The thing was not arranged through the reading and answering of an advertisement. Tessa knew a married niece of the old lady, who, while recommending the young girl to her ancient kinswoman, was able to give Tessa hints as to the nature and treatment of the old lady's crochets. So she came to the house well instructed and not quite as a stranger.

Tessa came under the spell of the house from the moment when she entered it for the first time. She had an ingrained romantic love of old country mansions, and Billingdon Abbots, although nothing was left of the original priory after which it was named, was old enough to be worshipped. It was mainly Jacobean, but some eighteenth-century owner, a devotee of the then fashionable cult of Italian architecture, had covered the façade with stucco and added a pillared portico. It was probably the same owner who had erected a summer-house to the design of a Greek temple at the end of a walk between nut bushes, and who was responsible for the imitation ruin—to which Time had since added the authentic touch—beside the reedy fishpond at the rear of the house. Likely enough, thought Tessa, who knew the period, that same romantic squire was wont to engage an imitation "hermit" to meditate beside the spurious ruin on moonlight nights.

The gardens around the house were well wooded, and thus lent the house itself an air of melancholy and the inevitable slight atmosphere of damp and darkness. And here and there, in the most unexpected places, were garden gods, mostly broken and all in need of scouring. Tessa soon discovered these stone ghosts quite unexpectedly, and nearly always with a leap and tingle of surprise. A noseless Hermes confronted one at the turn of a shady walk;

Demeter, minus a hand, stood half hidden by laurels, still keeping vigil for Persephone; a dancing faun stood poised and caught in a frozen caper by the gate of the walled-in kitchen garden; beside a small stone pond a satyr leered from his pedestal, as if waiting for a naiad to break the surface.

The interior of the house was at first a little awe-inspiring to Tessa. She loved pretty things, but she was inclined to be afraid of furniture and pictures which seemed to her to be coldly beautiful and conscious of their own intrinsic values. Everything was highly polished, spotless and speckless, and the reception rooms had an air of state apartments thrown open for the inspection of the public.

The hall was square and galleried, and one could look straight up to the top storey and see the slanting balustrades of three staircases. Two suits of armour faced one across a parquet floor, and on the walls were three or four portraits by Lely and Kneller, those once fashionable painters of Court beauties whose works have lost favour with the collectors of today. The dining-room was long, rectangular, and severe, furnished only with a Cromwellian table and chairs and a great plain sideboard gleaming with silver candelabra. Two large seventeenth-century portraits by unknown members of the Dutch School were the only decorations bestowed on the panelled walls, and the window curtains were brown to match the one strip of carpet which the long table almost exactly covered.

Less monastic, but almost as severe and dignified, was the drawing-room in which Tessa spent most of her time with Miss Ludgate. The boudoir was a homelier room, containing such human things as photographs of living people, work-baskets, friendly arm-chairs, and a cosy, feminine atmosphere; but Miss Ludgate preferred more often to sit in state in her great drawing-room with the "Portrait of Miss Olivia Ludgate", by Gainsborough, the Chippendale furniture, and the cabinet of priceless china. It was as if she realized that she was but the guardian of her treasures, and wanted to have them within sight now that her term of guardianship was drawing to a close.

She must have been well over eighty, Tessa thought; for she was very small and withered and frail, with that almost porcelain delicacy peculiar to certain very old ladies. Winter and summer, she wore a white woollen shawl inside the house, thick or thin according to the season, which matched in colour and to some extent in texture her soft and still plentiful hair. Her face and hands were yellow-brown with the veneer of old age, but her hands were blue-veined, light and delicate, so that her fingers seemed overweighted by the simplest rings. Her eyes were blue and still piercing, and her mouth, once beautiful, was caught up at the corners by puckerings of the upper lip, and looked grim in repose. Her voice had not shrilled and always she spoke very slowly with an unaffected precision, as one who knew that she had only to be understood to be obeyed and therefore took care always to be understood.

Tessa spent her first week with Miss Ludgate without knowing whether or no she liked the old lady, or whether or no she was afraid of her. Nor was she any wiser with regard to Miss Ludgate's sentiments towards herself. Their relations were much as they might have been had Tessa been a child and Miss Ludgate a new governess suspected of severity. Tessa was on her best behaviour, doing as she was told and thinking before she spoke, as children should and generally do not. At times it occurred to her to wonder that Miss Ludgate had not sought to engage an older woman, for in the cold formality of that first week's intercourse she wondered what gap in the household she was supposed to fill, and what return she was making for her wage and board.

Truth to tell, Miss Ludgate wanted to see somebody young about the house, even if she could share with her companion no more than the common factors of their sex and their humanity. The servants were all old retainers kept faithful to her by rumours of legacies. Her relatives were few and immersed in their own affairs. The house and the bulk of the property from which she derived her income were held in trust for an heir appointed by the same will which had given her a life interest in the estate. It saved her from the transparent attentions of any fortune-hunting nephew or niece, but it kept her lonely and starved for young companionship.

It happened that Tessa was able to play the piano quite reasonably well and that she had an educated taste in music. So had Miss Ludgate, who had been a performer of much the same quality until the time came when her rebel fingers stiffened with rheumatism. So the heavy grand piano, which had been scrupulously kept in tune, was silent no longer, and Miss Ludgate regained an old lost pleasure. It should be added that Tessa was twenty-two and, with no pretentions to technical beauty, was rich in commonplace good looks which were enhanced by perfect health and the freshness of her youth. She looked her best in candlelight, with her slim hands—they at least would have pleased an artist—hovering like white moths over the keyboard of the piano.

When she had been with Miss Ludgate a week, the old lady addressed her for the first time as "Tessa". She added: "I hope you intend to stay with me, my dear. It will be dull for you, and I fear you will often find me a bother. But I shan't take up all your time, and I dare say you will be able to find friends and amusements."

So Tessa stayed on, and beyond the probationary month. She was a soft-hearted girl who gave her friendship easily but always sincerely. She tried to like everybody who liked her, and generally succeeded. It would be hard to analyse the quality of the friendship between the two women, but certainly it existed and at times they were able to touch hands over the barrier between youth and age. Miss Ludgate inspired in Tessa a queer tenderness. With all her wealth and despite her domineering manner, she was a pathetic and lonely figure. She reminded Tessa of some poor actress playing the part of Queen, wearing the tawdry crown jewels, uttering commands which the other mummers obeyed like automata; while all the while there awaited her the realities of life at the fall of the curtain—the wet streets, the poor meal, and the cold and comfortless lodging.

It filled Tessa with pity to think that here, close beside her, was a living, breathing creature, still clinging to life, who must, in the course of nature, so soon let go her hold. Tessa could think: "Fifty years hence I shall be seventy-two, and there's no reason why I shouldn't live till then." She wondered painfully how it must feel to be unable to look a month hence with average confidence, and to regard every nightfall as the threshold of a precarious tomorrow.

Tess would have found life very dull but for the complete change in her surroundings. She had been brought up in a country vicarage, one of seven brothers and sisters who had worn one another's clothes, tramped the carpets threadbare, mishandled the cheap furniture, broken everything frangible except their parents' hearts, and had somehow tumbled into adolescence. The unwonted "grandeur" of living with Miss Ludgate flavoured the monotony.

We have her writing home to her "Darling Mother" as follows:

I expect when I get back home again our dear old rooms will look absurdly small. I thought at first that the house was huge, and every room as big as a barrack-room—not that I've ever been in a barrack-room! But I'm getting used to it now, and really it isn't so enormous as I thought. Huge compared with ours, of course, but not so big as Lord Branbourne's house, or even Colonel Exted's.

Really, though, it's a darling old place and might have come out of one of those books in which there's a Mystery, and a Sliding Panel, and the heroine's a nursery governess who marries the Young Baronet. But there's no mystery that I've heard of, although I like to pretend there is, and even if I were the nursery governess there's no young baronet within a radius of miles. But at least it ought to have a traditional ghost, although, since I haven't heard of one, it's probably deficient even in that respect! I don't like to ask Miss Ludgate, because, although she's a dear, there are questions I couldn't ask her. She might believe in ghosts and it might scare her to talk about them; or she mightn't, and then she'd be furious with me for talking rubbish. Of course, I know it's all rubbish, but it would be very nice to know that we were supposed to be haunted by a nice Grey Lady—of, say, about the period of Queen Anne. But if we're haunted by nothing else, we're certainly haunted by tramps.

Her letter went on to describe the numerous daily visits of those nomads of the English countryside, who beg and steal on their way from workhouse to workhouse; those queer, illogical, feckless beings who prefer the most intense miseries and hardships to the comparative comforts attendant on honest work. Three or four was a day's average of such callers, and not one went empty away. Mrs. Finch had very definite orders, and she carried them out with the impassive face of a perfect subject of discipline. When there was no spare food there was the pleasanter alternative of money which could be transformed into liquor at the nearest inn.

Tessa was for ever meeting these vagrants in the drive. Male and female, they differed in a hundred ways; some still trying to cling to the last rags of self-respect, others obscene, leering, furtive, potential criminals who lacked the courage to rise about petty theft. Most faces were either evil or carried the rolling eyes and lewd, loose mouth of the semi-idiot, but they were all alike in their personal uncleanliness and in the insolence of their bearing.

Tessa grew used to receiving from them direct and insolent challenges of the eyes, familiar nods, blatant grins. In their several ways they told her that she was nobody and that, if she hated to see them, so much the better. They knew she was an underling, subject to dismissal, whereas they, for some occult reason, were always the welcome guests. Tessa resented their presence and their dumb insolence, and secretly raged against Miss Ludgate for encouraging them. They were the sewer-rats of society, foul, predatory, and carrying disease from village to village and from town to town.

The girl knew something of the struggles of the decent poor. Her upbringing in a country vicarage had given her intimate knowledge of farm-hands and builders' labourers, the tragic poverty of their homes, their independence and their gallant struggles for existence. On Miss Ludgate's estate there was more than one family living on bread and potatoes and getting not too much of either. Yet the old lady had no sympathy for them, and gave unlimited largess to the underserving. In the ditches outside the park it was always possible to find a loaf or two of bread flung there by some vagrant who had feasted more delicately on the proceeds of a visit to the tradesmen's door.

It was not for Tessa to speak to Miss Ludgate on the subject. Indeed, she knew that—in the phraseology of the servants' hall—it was as much as her place was worth. But she did mention it to Mrs. Finch, whose duty was to provide food and drink, or, failing those, money.

Mrs. Finch, taciturn through her environment but still with an undercurrent of warmth, replied at first with the one pregnant word, "Orders!" After a moment she added: "The mistress has her own good reasons for doing it—or thinks she has."

It was late summer when Tessa first took up her abode at Billingdon Abbots, and sweet lavender, that first herald of the approach of autumn, was already blooming in the gardens. September came and the first warning gleams of yellow showed among the trees. Spiked chestnut husks opened and dropped their polished brown fruit. At evenings the ponds and the trout stream exhaled pale, low-hanging mists. There was a cold snap in the air.

By looking from her window every morning Tessa marked on the trees the inexorable progress of the year. Day by day the green tints lessened as the yellow increased. Then yellow began to give place to gold and brown and red. Only the hollies and the laurels stood fast against the advancing tide.

There came an evening when Miss Ludgate appeared for the first time in her winter shawl. She seemed depressed and said little during dinner, and afterwards in the drawing-room, when she had taken out and arranged a pack of patience cards preparatory to beginning her evening game, she suddenly leaned her elbows on the table and rested her face between her hands.

"Aren't you well, Miss Ludgate?" Tessa asked anxiously.

She removed her hands and showed her withered old face. Her eyes were piteous, fear-haunted, and full of shadows.

"I am very much as usual, my dear," she said. "You must bear with me. My bad time of the year is just approaching. If I can live until the end of November I shall last another year. But I don't know yet—I don't know."

"Of course you're not going to die this year," said Tessa, with a robust note of optimism which she had found useful in soothing frightened children.

"If I don't die this autumn it will be the next, or some other autumn," quavered the old voice. "It will be in the autumn that I shall die. I know that. I know that."

"But how can you know?" Tessa asked, with just the right note of gentle incredulity.

"I know it. What does it matter how I know?... Have many leaves fallen yet?"

"Hardly any as yet," said Tessa. "There has been very little wind."

"They will fall presently," said Miss Ludgate. "Very soon now..."

Her voice trailed away, but presently she rallied, picked up the miniature playing cards, and began her game.

Two days later it rained heavily all the morning and throughout the earlier part of the afternoon. Just as the light was beginning to wane, half a gale of wind sprang up, and showers of yellow leaves, circling and eddying at the wind's will, began to find their way to earth through the level slant of the rain. Miss Ludgate sat watching them, her eyes dull with the suffering of despair, until the lights were turned on and the blinds were drawn.

During dinner the wind dropped again and the rain ceased. Tessa afterwards peeped between the blinds to see still silhouettes of trees against the sky, and a few stars sparkling palely. It promised after all to be a fine night.

As before, Miss Ludgate got out her patience cards, and Tessa picked up a book and waited to be bidden to go to the piano. There was silence in the room save for intermittent sounds of cards being laid with a snap upon the polished surface of the table, and occasional dry rustlings as Tessa turned the pages of her book.

...When she first heard it Tessa could not truthfully have said. It seemed to her that she had gradually become conscious of the sounds in the garden outside, and when at last they had so forced themselves upon her attention as to set her wondering what caused them it was impossible for her to guess how long they had actually been going on.

Tessa closed the book over her fingers and listened. The sounds were crisp, dry, long-drawn-out, and rhythmic. There was an equal pause after each one. It was rather like listening to the leisurely brushing of a woman's long hair. What was it? An uneven surface being scratched by something crisp and pliant? Then Tessa knew. On the long path behind the house which travelled the whole length of the building somebody was sweeping up the fallen leaves with a stable broom. But what a time to sweep up leaves!

She continued to listen. Now that she had identified the sounds they were quite unmistakable. She would not have had to guess twice had it not been dark outside, and the thought of a gardener showing such devotion to duty as to work at that hour had at first been rejected by her subconscious mind. She looked up, with the intention of making some remark to Miss Ludgate— and she said nothing.

Miss Ludgate sat listening intently, her face half turned towards the windows and slightly raised, her eyes upturned. Her whole attitude was one of strained rigidity, expressive of a tension rather dreadful to see in one so old. Tessa not only listened, she now watched.

260

There was a movement in the unnaturally silent room. Miss Ludgate had turned her head, and now showed her companion a white face of woe and doom-ridden eyes. Then, in a flash, her expression changed. Tessa knew that Miss Ludgate had caught her listening to the sounds from the path outside, and that for some reason the old lady was annoyed with her for having heard them. But why? And why that look of terror on the poor, white old face?

"Won't you play something, Tessa?"

Despite the note of interrogation, the words were an abrupt command, and Tessa knew it. She was to drown the noise of sweeping from outside, because, for some queer reason, Miss Ludgate did not want her to hear it. So, tactfully, she played pieces which allowed her to make liberal use of the loud pedal.

After half an hour Miss Ludgate rose, gathered her shawl tighter about her shoulders, and hobbled to the door, pausing on the way to say good night to Tessa.

Tessa lingered in the room alone and reseated herself before the piano. A minute or two elapsed before she began to strum softly and absent-mindedly. Why did Miss Ludgate object to her hearing that sound of sweeping from the path outside? It had ceased now, or she would have peeped out to see who actually was at work. Had Miss Ludgate some queer distaste for seeing fallen leaves lying about, and was she ashamed because she was keeping a gardener at work at that hour? But it was unlike Miss Ludgate to mind what people thought of her; besides, she rose late in the morning, and there would be plenty of time to brush away the leaves before the mistress of the house could set eyes on them. And then, why was Miss Ludgate so terrified? Had it anything to do with her queer belief that she would die in the autumn?

On her way to bed Tessa smiled gently to herself for having tried to penetrate to the secret places of a warped mind which was over eighty years old. She had just seen another queer phase of Miss Ludgate, and all of such seemed inexplicable.

The night was still calm and promised so to remain.

"There won't be many more leaves down tonight," Tessa reflected as she undressed.

But when next morning she sauntered out into the garden before breakfast the long path which skirted the rear of the house was still thickly littered with them, and Toy, the second gardener, was busy among them with a barrow and one of those birch stable brooms which, in mediaeval imaginations, provided steeds for witches.

"Hullo!" exclaimed Tessa. "What a lot of leaves must have come down last night!"

Toy ceased sweeping and shook his head.

"No, miss. This 'ere little lot come down with the wind early part o' the evenin'."

"But surely they were all swept up. I heard somebody at work here after nine o'clock. Wasn't it you?"

The man grinned.

"You catch any of us at work arter nine o'clock, miss!" he said. "No, miss, nobody's touched 'em till now. 'Tes thankless work, too. So soon as you've swept up one lot there's another waitin'. Not a hundred men could keep this 'ere garden tidy this time o' the year."

Tessa said nothing more and went thoughtfully into the house. The sweeping was continued off and on all day, for more leaves descended, and a bonfire built up on the waste ground beyond the kitchen garden wafted its fragrance over to the house.

That evening Miss Ludgate had a fire made up in the boudoir and announced to Tessa that they would sit there before and after dinner. But it happened that the chimney smoked, and, after coughing and grumbling, and rating Mrs. Finch on the dilatoriness and inefficiency of sweeps, the old lady went early to bed.

It was still too early for Tessa to retire. Having been left to herself she remembered a book which she had left in the drawing-room, and with which she purposed sitting over the dining-room fire. Hardly had she taken two steps past the threshold of the drawing-room when she came abruptly to a halt and stood listening. She could not doubt the evidence of her ears. In spite of what Toy had told her, and that it was now after half past nine, somebody was sweeping the path outside.

She tiptoed to the window and peeped out between the blinds. Bright moonlight silvered the garden, but she could see nothing. Now, however, that she was near the window, she could locate the sounds more accurately, and they seemed to proceed from a spot farther down the path which was hidden from her by the angle of the window setting. There was a door just outside the room giving access to the garden, but for no reason that she could name she felt strangely unwilling to go out and look at the mysterious worker. With the strangest little cold thrill she was aware of a distinct preference for seeing him—for the first time, at least—from a distance.

Then Tessa remembered a landing window, and after a little hesitation she went silently and on tiptoe upstairs to the first floor, and down a passage on the left of the stairhead. Here moonlight penetrated a window and threw a pale blue screen upon the opposite wall. Tessa fumbled with the window fastenings, raised the sash softly and silently, and leaned out.

On the path below her, but some yards to her left and close to the angle of the house, a man was slowly and rhythmically sweeping with a stable broom. The broom swung and struck the path time after time with a soft, crisp *swish*, and the strokes were as regular as those of the pendulum of some slow old clock.

From her angle of observation she was unable to see most of the characteristics of the figure underneath. It was that of a working-man, for there was something in the silhouette subtly suggestive of old and baggy clothes. But apart from all else there was something queer, something odd and unnatural, in the scene on which she gazed. She knew that there was something lacking, something that she should have found missing at the first glance, yet for her life she could not have said what it was.

From below some gross omission blazed up at her, and though she was acutely aware that the scene lacked something which she had every right to expect to see, her senses groped for it in vain; although the lack of something which should have been there, and was not, was as obvious as a burning pyre at midnight. She knew that she was watching the gross defiance of some natural law, but what law she did not know. Suddenly sick and dizzy, she withdrew her head.

All the cowardice in Tessa's nature urged her to go to bed, to forget what she had seen and to refrain from trying to remember what she had *not* seen. But the other Tessa, the Tessa who despised cowards, and was herself capable under pressure of rising to great heights of courage, stayed and urged. Under her breath she talked to herself, as she always did when any crisis found her in a state of indecision.

"Tessa, you coward! How dare you be afraid! Go down at once and see who it is and what's queer about him. He can't eat you!"

So the two Tessas imprisoned in the one body stole downstairs again, and the braver Tessa was angry with their common heart for thumping so hard and trying to weaken her. But she unfastened the door and stepped out into the moonlight.

The Sweeper was still at work close to the angle of the house, near by where the path ended and a green door gave entrance to the stable yard. The path was thick with leaves, and the girl, advancing uncertainly with her hands to her breasts, saw that he was making little progress with his work. The broom rose and fell and audibly swept the path, but the dead leaves lay fast and still beneath it. Yet it was not this that she had noticed from above. There was still that unseizable Something missing.

Her footfalls made little noise on the leaf-strewn path, but they became audible to the Sweeper while she was still half a dozen yards from him. He paused in his work and turned and looked at her.

He was a tall, lean man with a white cadaverous face and eyes that bulged like huge rising bubbles as they regarded her. It was a foul, suffering face which he showed to Tessa, a face whose misery could—and did—inspire loathing and a hitherto unimagined horror, but never pity. He was clad in the meanest rags, which seemed to have been cast at random over his emaciated body. The hands grasping the broom seemed no more than bones and skin. He was so thin, thought Tessa, that he was almost—and here she paused in thought, because she found herself hating the word which tried to force itself into her mind. But it had its way, and blew in on a cold wind of terror. Yes, he was almost transparent, she thought, and sickened at the word, which had come to have a new and vile meaning for her.

They faced each other through a fraction of eternity not to be measured by seconds; and then Tessa heard herself scream. It flashed upon her now, the strange, abominable detail of the figure which confronted her—the Something missing which she had noticed, without actually seeing, from above. The path was flooded with moonlight, but the visitant had no shadow. And fast upon this vile discovery she saw dimly *through* it the ivy stirring upon the wall. Then, as unbidden thoughts rushed to tell her that the Thing was not of this world, and that it was not holy, and the sudden knowledge wrung that scream from her, so she was left suddenly and dreadfully alone. The spot where the Thing had stood was empty save for the moonlight and the shallow litter of leaves.

Tessa had no memory of returning to the house. Her next recollection was of finding herself in the hall, faint and gasping and sobbing. Even as she approached the stairs she saw a light dancing on the wall above and wondered what fresh horror was to confront her. But it was only Mrs. Finch coming downstairs in a dressing-gown, candle in hand, and incongruous but a very comforting sight.

"Oh, it's you, Miss Tessa," said Mrs. Finch, reassured. She held the candle lower and peered down at the sobbing girl. "Why, whatever is the matter? Oh, Miss Tessa, Miss Tessa! You haven't never been outside, have you?"

265

Tessa sobbed and choked and tried to speak.

"I've seen—I've seen…"

Mrs. Finch swiftly descended the remaining stairs, and put an arm around the shuddering girl.

"Hush, my dear, my dear! I know what you've seen. You didn't ought never to have gone out. I've seen it too, once—but only once, thank God."

"What is it?" Tessa faltered.

"Never you mind, my dear. Now don't be frightened. It's all over now. He doesn't come here for you. It's the mistress he wants. You've nothing to fear, Miss Tessa. Where was he when you saw him?"

"Close to the end of the path, near the stable gate."

Mrs. Finch threw up her hands.

"Oh, the poor mistress—the poor mistress! Her time's shortening! The end's nigh now!"

"I can't bear any more," Tessa sobbed; and then she contradicted herself, clinging to Mrs. Finch. "I must know. I can't rest until I know. Tell me everything."

"Come into my parlour, my dear, and I'll make a cup of tea. We can both do with it, I think. But you'd best not know. At least not tonight, Miss Tessa—not tonight."

"I must," whispered Tessa, "if I'm ever to have any peace."

The fire was still burning behind a guard in the housekeeper's parlour, for Mrs. Finch had only gone up to bed a few minutes since. There was water still warm in the brass kettle, and in a few minutes the tea was ready. Tessa sipped and felt the first vibrations of her returning courage, and presently looked inquiringly at Mrs. Finch.

"I'll tell you, Miss Tessa," said the old housekeeper, "if it'll make you any easier. But don't let the mistress know as I've ever told you."

Tessa inclined her head and gave the required promise.

"You don't know why," Mrs. Finch began in a low voice, "the mistress gives to every beggar, deserving or otherwise. The reason comes into what I'm going to tell you. Miss Ludgate wasn't always like that—not until up to about fifteen years ago.

"She was old then, but active for her age, and very fond of gardenin'. Late one afternoon in the autumn, while she was cutting some late roses, a beggar came to the tradesmen's door. Sick and ill and starved, he looked—but there, you've seen him. He was a bad lot, we found out afterwards, but I was sorry for him, and I was just going to risk givin' him some food without orders, when up comes Miss Ludgate. 'What's this?' she says.

"He whined something about not being able to get work.

"'Work!' says the mistress. 'You don't want work—you want charity. If you want to eat,' she says, 'you shall, but you shall work first. There's a broom,' she says, ' and there's a path littered with leaves. Start sweeping up at the top, and when you come to the end you can come and see me.'

"Well, he took the broom, and a few minutes later I heard a shout from Miss Ludgate and come hurryin' out. There was the man lyin' at the top of the path where he'd commenced sweeping, and he'd collapsed and fallen down. I didn't know then as he was dying, but he did, and he gave Miss Ludgate a look as I shall never forget.

"'When I've swept to the end of the path,' he says, 'I'll come for you, my lady, and we'll feast together. Only see as you're ready to be fetched when I come.' Those were his last words. He was buried by the parish, and it gave Miss Ludgate such a turn that she ordered something to be given to every beggar who came, and not one of 'em to be asked to do a stroke of work.

"But next autumn, when the leaves began to fall, he came back and started sweeping, right at the top of the path, round about where he died. We've all heard him and most of us have seen him. Year after year he's come back and swept with his broom, which just makes a brushing noise and hardly stirs a leaf. But each year he's been getting nearer and nearer to the end of the path, and when he gets right to the end—well, I wouldn't like to be the mistress, with all her money."

It was three evenings later, just before the hour fixed for dinner, that the Sweeper completed his task. That is to say, if one reposes literal belief in Mrs. Finch's story.

The servants heard somebody burst open the tradesmen's door, and, having rushed out into the passage, two of them saw that the door was open but found no one there. Miss Ludgate was already in the drawing-room, but Tessa was still upstairs, dressing for dinner. Presently Mrs. Finch had occasion to enter the drawing-room a few moments later.

Miss Ludgate was sitting upright in her favourite chair. Her eyes were open, but she was quite dead; and in her eyes there was something that Tessa could not bear to see.

Withdrawing her own gaze from that fixed stare of terror and recognition she saw something on the carpet and presently stooped to pick it up.

It was a little yellow leaf, damp and pinched and frayed, and but for her own experience and Mrs. Finch's tale she might have wondered how it had come to be there. She dropped it, shuddering, for it looked as if it had been picked up by, and had afterwards fallen from, the birch twigs of a stable broom.

Slep Hath His Hous

John Gower

The god of Slep hath mad his hous,
Which of entaille is merveilous.
Under an hell ther is a Cave,
Which of the Sonne mai noght have,
So that noman mai knowe ariht
The point betwen the dai and nyht:
Ther is no fyr, ther is no sparke,
Ther is no dore, which mai charke,
Wherof an yhe scholde unschette,
So that inward ther is no lette.
And forto speke of that withoute,
Ther stant no gret Tree nyh aboute
Wher on ther myhte crowe or pie
Alihte, forto clepe or crie:
Ther is no cok to crowe day,
Ne beste non which noise may
The hell, bot al aboute round
Ther is growende upon the ground
Popi, which berth the sed of slep,
With othre herbes suche an hep.
A stille water for the nones
Rennende upon the smale stones,

Which hihte of Lethes the rivere,
Under that hell in such manere
Ther is, which yifth gret appetit
To slepe. And thus full of delit
Slep hath his hous; and of his couche
Withinne his chambre if I schal touche,
Of hebenus that slepi Tree
The bordes al aboute be,
And for he scholde slepe softe,
Upon a fethrebed alofte
He lith with many a pilwe of doun:
The chambre is strowed up and doun
With swevenes many thousendfold.

The Other Wing
Algernon Blackwood

I

It used to puzzle him that, after dark, someone would look in round the edge of the bedroom door, and withdraw again too rapidly for him to see the face. When the nurse had gone away with the candle this happened: "Good night, Master Tim," she said usually, shading the light with one hand to protect his eyes; "dream of me and I'll dream of you." She went out slowly. The sharp-edged shadow of the door ran across the ceiling like a train. There came a whispered colloquy in the corridor outside, about himself, of course, and—he was alone. He heard her steps going deeper and deeper into the bosom of the old country house; they were audible for a moment on the stone flooring of the hall; and sometimes the dull thump of the baize door into the servants' quarters just reached him, too—then silence. But it was only when the last sound as well as the last sign of her had vanished that the face emerged from its hiding-place and flashed in upon him round the corner. As a rule, too, it came just as he was saying, "Now I'll go to sleep. I won't think any longer. Good night, Master Tim, and happy dreams." He loved to say this to himself; it brought a sense of companionship, as though there were two persons speaking.

The room was on the top of the old house, a big, high-ceilinged room, and his bed against the wall had an iron railing round it; he felt very safe and protected in it. The curtains at the other end of the room were drawn. He lay watching the firelight dancing on the heavy folds, and their pattern, showing a spaniel chasing a long-tailed bird towards a bushy tree, interested and amused him. It was repeated over and over again. He counted the number of dogs, and the number of birds, and the number of trees, but could never make them agree. There was a plan somewhere in that pattern; if only he could discover it, the dogs and birds and trees would "come out right." Hundreds and hundreds of times he had played this game, for the plan in the pattern made it possible to take sides, and the bird and dog were against him. They always won, however; Tim usually fell asleep just when the advantage was on his own side. The curtains hung steadily enough most of the time, but it seemed to him once or twice that they stirred—hiding a dog or bird on purpose to prevent his winning. For instance, he had eleven birds and eleven trees, and, fixing them in his mind by saying, "that's eleven birds and eleven trees, but only ten dogs", his eyes darted back to find the eleventh dog, when—the curtain moved and threw all his calculations into confusion again. The eleventh dog was hidden. He did not quite like the movement; it gave him questionable feelings, rather, for the curtain did not move of itself. Yet, usually, he was too intent upon counting the dogs to feel positive alarm.

Opposite to him was the fireplace, full of red and yellow coals; and, lying with his head sideways on the pillow, he could see directly in between the bars. When the coals settled with a soft and powdery crash, he turned his eyes from the curtains to the grate, trying to discover exactly which bits had fallen. So long as the glow was there the sound seemed pleasant enough, but sometimes he awoke later in the night, the room huge with darkness, the fire almost out—and the sound was not so pleasant then. It startled him. The coals did not fall of themselves. It seemed that someone poked them cautiously. The shadows were very thick before the bars. As with the curtains, moreover, the morning aspect of the extinguished fire, the ice-cold cinders that made a clinking sound like tin, caused no emotion whatever in his soul.

And it was usually while he lay waiting for sleep, tired both of the curtain and the coal games, on the point, indeed, of saying, "I'll go to sleep now," that the puzzling thing took place. He would be staring drowsily at the dying fire, perhaps counting the stockings and flannel garments that hung along the high fender rail when, suddenly, a person looked in with lightning swiftness through the door and vanished again before he could possibly turn his head to see. The appearance and disappearance were accomplished with amazing rapidity always.

It was a head and shoulders that looked in, and the movement combined the speed, the lightness and the silence of a shadow. Only it was not a shadow. A hand held the edge of the door. The face shot round, saw him, and withdrew like lightning. It was utterly beyond him to imagine anything more quick and clever. It darted. He heard no sound. It went. But—it had seen him, looked him all over, examined him, noted what he was doing with that lightning glance. It wanted to know if he were awake still, or asleep. And though it went off, it still watched him from a distance; it waited somewhere; it knew all about him. Where it waited no one could ever guess. It came probably, he felt, from beyond the house, possibly from the roof, but most likely from the garden or the sky. Yet, though strange, it was not terrible. It was a kindly and protective figure, he felt. And when it happened he never called for help, because the occurrence simply took his voice away.

"It comes from the Nightmare Passage," he decided; "but it's not a nightmare." It puzzled him.

Sometimes, moreover, it came more than once in a single night. He was pretty sure—not quite positive—that it occupied his room as soon as he was properly asleep. It took possession, sitting perhaps before the dying fire, standing upright behind the heavy curtains, or even lying down in the empty bed his brother used when he was home from school. Perhaps it played the curtain game, perhaps it poked the coals; it knew, at any rate, where the eleventh dog had lain concealed. It certainly came in and out; certainly, too, it did not wish to be seen. For, more than once, on waking suddenly in the midnight blackness, Tim knew it was standing close beside his bed and bending over him. He felt, rather than heard, its presence. It glided quietly away. It moved with marvellous softness, yet he was positive it moved. He felt the difference, so to speak: it had been near him, now it was gone. It came back, too—just as he was falling into sleep again. Its midnight coming and going, however, stood out sharply different from its first shy, tentative approach. For in the firelight it came alone; whereas in the black and silent hours, it had with it—others.

And it was then he made up his mind that its swift and quiet movements were due to the fact that it had wings. It flew. And the others that came with it in the darkness were "its little ones." He also made up his mind that all were friendly, comforting, protective, and that while positively not a Nightmare, it yet came somehow along the Nightmare Passage before it reached him. "You see, it's like this," he explained to the nurse: "The big one comes to visit me alone, but it only brings its little ones when I'm quite asleep."

"Then the quicker you get to sleep the better, isn't it, Master Tim?"

He replied: "Rather! I always do. Only I wonder where they come from!" He spoke, however, as though he had an inkling.

But the nurse was so dull about it that he gave her up and tried his father. "Of course," replied this busy but affectionate parent, "it's either nobody at all, or else it's Sleep coming to carry you away to the land of dreams." He made the statement kindly but somewhat briskly, for he was worried just then about the extra taxes on his land, and the effort to fix his mind on Tim's fanciful world was beyond him at the moment. He lifted the boy on to his knee, kissed and patted him as though he were a favourite dog, and planted him on the rug again with a flying sweep. "Run and ask your mother," he added; "she knows all that kind of thing. Then come back and tell me all about it—another time."

Tim found his mother in an arm-chair before the fire of another room; she was knitting and reading at the same time—a wonderful thing the boy could never understand. She raised her head as he came in, pushed her glasses on to her forehead, and held her arms out. He told her everything, ending up with what his father said.

"You see, it's not Jackman, or Thompson, or anyone like that," he exclaimed. "It's someone real."

"But nice," she assured him, "someone who comes to take care of you and see that you're all safe and cosy."

"Oh, yes, I know that. But ——"

"I think your father's right," she added quickly. "It's Sleep, I'm sure, who pops in round the door like that. Sleep has got wings, I've always heard."

"Then the other thing—the little ones?" he asked. "Are they just sorts of dozes, you think?"

Mother did not answer for a moment. She turned down the page of her book, closed it slowly, and put it on the table beside her. More slowly still she put her knitting away, arranging the wool and needles with some deliberation.

"Perhaps," she said, drawing the boy closer to her and looking into his big eyes of wonder, "they're dreams!"

Tim felt a thrill run through him as she said it. He stepped back a foot or so and clapped his hands softly. "Dreams!" he whispered with enthusiasm and belief; "of course! I never thought of that."

His mother, having proved her sagacity, then made a mistake. She noted her success, but instead of leaving it there, she elaborated and explained. As Tim expressed it she "went on about it." Therefore he did not listen. He followed his train of thought alone. And presently, he interrupted her long sentences with a conclusion of his own:

"Then I know where She hides," he announced with a touch of awe. "Where She lives, I mean." And without waiting to be asked, he imparted the information: "It's in the Other Wing."

"Ah!" said his mother, taken by surprise. "How clever of you, Tim!"—and thus confirmed it.

Thenceforward this was established in his life—that Sleep and her attendant Dreams hid during the daytime in that unused portion of the great Elizabethan mansion called the Other Wing. This other wing was unoccupied, its corridors untrodden, its windows shuttered and its rooms all closed. At various places green baize doors led into it, but no one ever opened them. For many years this part had been shut up; and for the children, properly speaking, it was out of bounds. They never mentioned it as a possible place, at any rate; in hide-and-seek it was not considered, even; there was a hint of the inaccessible about the Other Wing. Shadows, dust, and silence had it to themselves.

But Tim, having ideas of his own about everything, possessed special information about the Other Wing. He believed it was inhabited. Who occupied the immense series of empty rooms, who trod the spacious corridors, who passed to and fro behind the shuttered windows, he had not known exactly. He had called these occupants, "they", and the most important among them was "The Ruler." The Ruler of the Other Wing was a kind of deity, powerful, far away, ever present yet never seen.

And about this Ruler he had a wonderful conception for a little boy; he connected her, somehow, with deep thoughts of his own, the deepest of all. When he made up adventures to the moon, to the stars, or to the bottom of the sea, adventures that he lived inside himself, as it were—to reach them he must invariably pass through the chambers of the Other Wing. Those corridors and halls, the Nightmare Passage among them, lay along the route; they were the first stage of the journey. Once the green baize doors swung to behind him and the long dim passage stretched ahead, he was well on his way into the adventure of the moment;

the Nightmare Passage once passed, he was safe from capture; but once the shutters of a window had been flung open, he was free of the gigantic world that lay beyond. For then light poured in and he could see his way.

The conception, for a child, was curious. It established a correspondence between the mysterious chambers of the Other Wing and the occupied, but unguessed chambers of his Inner Being. Through these chambers, through these darkened corridors, along a passage, sometimes dangerous, or at least of questionable repute, he must pass to find all adventures that were real. The light—when he pierced far enough to take the shutters down—was discovery. Tim did not actually think, much less say, all this. He was aware of it, however. He felt it. The Other Wing was inside himself as well as through the green baize doors. His inner map of wonder included both of them.

But now, for the first time in his life, he knew who lived there and who the Ruler was. A shutter had fallen of its own accord; light poured in; he made a guess, and Mother had confirmed it. Sleep and her Little Ones, the host of dreams, were the daylight occupants. They stole out when the darkness fell. All adventures in life began and ended by a dream—discoverable by first passing through the Other Wing.

II

And, having settled this, his one desire now was to travel over the map upon journeys of exploration and discovery. The map inside himself he knew already, but the map of the Other Wing he had not seen. His mind knew it, he had a clear mental picture of rooms and halls and passages, but his feet had never trod the silent floors where dust and shadows hid the flock of dreams by day. The mighty chambers where Sleep ruled he longed to stand in, to see the Ruler face to face. He made up his mind to get into the Other Wing.

To accomplish this was difficult; but Tim was a determined youngster, and he meant to try; he meant, also, to succeed. He deliberated. At night he could not possibly manage it; in any case, the Ruler and her host all left it after dark to fly about the world; the Wing would be empty, and the emptiness would frighten him. Therefore he must make a daylight visit; and it was a daylight visit he decided on. He deliberated more. There were rules and risks involved: it meant going out of bounds, the danger of being seen, the certainty of being questioned by some idle and inquisitive grown-up: "Where in the world have you been all this time?"— and so forth. These things he thought out carefully, and though he arrived at no solution, he felt satisfied that it would be all right. That is, he recognised the risks. To be prepared was half the battle, for nothing then could take him by surprise.

The notion that he might slip in from the garden was soon abandoned; the red bricks showed no openings; there was no door; from the courtyard, also, entrance was impracticable: even on tiptoe he could barely reach the broad window-sills of stone. When playing alone, or walking with the French governess, he examined every outside possibility. None offered. The shutters, supposing he could reach them, were thick and solid.

Meanwhile, when opportunity offered, he stood against the tight red bricks; the towers and gables of the Wing rose overhead; he heard the wind go whispering along the eaves; he imagined tiptoe movements and a sound of wings inside. Sleep and her Little Ones were busily preparing for their journeys after dark; they hid, but they did not sleep; in this unused Wing, vaster alone than any other country house he had ever seen, Sleep taught and trained her flock of feathered Dreams. It was very wonderful. They probably supplied the entire County. But more wonderful still was the thought that the Ruler herself should take the trouble to come to his particular room and personally watch over him all night long. That was amazing. And it flashed across his imaginative inquiring mind: "Perhaps they take me with them! The moment I'm asleep! That's why she comes to see me!"

Yet his chief preoccupation was, how Sleep got out. Through the green baize doors, of course! By a process of elimination he arrived at a conclusion: he, too, must enter through a green baize door and risk detection.

Of late, the lightning visits had ceased. The silent, darting figure had not peeped in and vanished as it used to do. He fell asleep too quickly now, almost before Jackman reached the hall, and long before the fire began to die. Also, the dogs and birds upon the curtains always matched the trees exactly, and he won the curtain game quite easily; there was never a dog or bird too many; the curtain never stirred. It had been thus ever since his talk with Mother and Father. And so he came to make a second discovery: His parents did not really believe in his Figure. She kept away on that account. They doubted her; she hid. Here was still another incentive to go and find her out. He ached for her, she was so kind, she gave herself so much trouble—just for his little self in the big and lonely bedroom. Yet his parents spoke of her as though she were of no account. He longed to see her, face to face, and tell her that he believed in her and loved her. For he was positive she would like to hear it. She cared. Though he had fallen asleep of late too quickly for him to see her flash in at the door, he had known nicer dreams than ever in his life before—travelling dreams. And it was she who sent them. More—he was sure she took him out with her.

One evening, in the dusk of a March day, his opportunity came; and only just in time, for his brother, Jack, was expected home from school on the morrow, and with Jack in the other bed, no Figure would ever care to show itself. Also it was Easter, and after Easter, though Tim was not aware of it at the time, he was to say good-bye finally to governesses and become a day-boarder at a preparatory school for Wellington. The opportunity offered itself so naturally, moreover, that Tim took it without hesitation. It never occurred to him to question, much less to refuse it. The thing was obviously meant to be. For he found himself unexpectedly in front of a green baize door; and the green baize door was—swinging! Somebody, therefore, had just passed through it.

It had come about in this wise. Father, away in Scotland, at Inglemuir, the shooting place, was expected back next morning; Mother had driven over to the church upon some Easter business or other; and the governess had been allowed her holiday at home in France. Tim, therefore, had the run of the house, and in the hour between tea and bed-time he made good use of it. Fully able to defy such second-rate obstacles as nurses and butlers, he explored all manner of forbidden places with ardent thoroughness, arriving finally in the sacred precincts of his father's study. This wonderful room was the very heart and centre of the whole big house; he had been birched here long ago; here, too, his father had told him with a grave yet smiling face: "You've got a new companion, Tim, a little sister; you must be very kind to her." Also, it was the place where all the money was kept. What he called "father's jolly smell" was strong in it—papers, tobacco, books, flavoured by hunting crops and gunpowder.

At first he felt awed, standing motionless just inside the door; but presently, recovering equilibrium, he moved cautiously on tiptoe towards the gigantic desk where important papers were piled in untidy patches. These he did not touch; but beside them his quick eye noted the jagged piece of iron shell his father brought home from his Crimean campaign and now used as a letter-weight. It was difficult to lift, however. He climbed into the comfortable chair and swung round and round. It was a swivel-chair, and he sank down among the cushions in it, staring at the strange things on the great desk before him, as if fascinated. Next he turned away and saw the stick-rack in the corner—this, he knew, he was allowed to touch. He had played with these sticks before. There were twenty, perhaps, all told, with curious carved handles, brought from every corner of the world; many of them cut by his father's own hand in queer and distant places. And, among them, Tim fixed his eye upon a cane with an ivory handle, a slender, polished cane that he had always coveted tremendously. It was the kind he meant to use when he became a man. It bent, it quivered, and when he swished it through the air it trembled like a riding-whip, and made a whistling noise. Yet it was very strong in spite of its elastic qualities. A family treasure, it was also an old-fashioned relic; it had been his great-grandfather's walking stick. Something of another century clung visibly about it still. It had dignity and grace and leisure in its very aspect. And it suddenly occurred to him. "How great-grandpapa must miss it! Wouldn't he just love to have it back again!"

How it happened exactly, Tim did not know, but a few minutes later he found himself walking about the deserted halls and passages of the house with the air of an elderly gentleman of a hundred years ago, proud as a courtier, flourishing the stick like an Eighteenth Century dandy in the Mall. That the cane reached to his shoulder made no difference; he held it accordingly, swaggering on his way. He was off upon an adventure. He dived down through the byways of the Other Wing inside himself, as though the stick transported him to the days of the old gentleman who had used it in another century.

It may seem strange to those who dwell in smaller houses, but in this rambling Elizabethan mansion there were whole sections that, even to Tim, were strange and unfamiliar. In his mind the map of the Other Wing was clearer by far than the geography of the part he travelled daily. He came to passages and dim-lit halls, long corridors of stone beyond the Picture Gallery; narrow, wainscoted connecting-channels with four steps down and a little later two steps up; deserted chambers with arches guarding them—all hung with the soft March twilight and all bewilderingly unrecognised. With a sense of adventure born of naughtiness he went carelessly along, farther and farther into the heart of this unfamiliar country, swinging the cane, one thumb stuck into the arm-pit of his blue serge suit, whistling softly to himself, excited yet keenly on the alert—and suddenly found himself opposite a door that checked all further advance. It was a green baize door. And it was swinging.

He stopped abruptly, facing it. He stared, he gripped his cane more tightly, he held his breath. "The Other Wing!" he gasped in a swallowed whisper.

It was an entrance, but an entrance he had never seen before. He thought he knew every door by heart; but this one was new. He stood motionless for several minutes, watching it; the door had two halves, but one half only was swinging, each swing shorter than the one before; he heard the little puffs of air it made; it settled finally, the last movements very short and rapid; it stopped. And the boy's heart, after similar rapid strokes, stopped also—for a moment.

"Someone's just gone through," he gulped. And even as he said it he knew who the someone was. The conviction just dropped into him. "It's great-grandpapa; he knows I've got his stick. He wants it!" On the heels of this flashed instantly another amazing certainty. "He sleeps in there. He's having dreams. That's what being dead means."

His first impulse, then, took the form of, "I must let Father know; it'll make him burst for joy!" but his second was for himself—to finish his adventure. And it was this, naturally enough, that gained the day. He could tell his father later. His first duty was plainly to go through the door into the Other Wing. He must give the stick back to its owner. He must hand it back.

The test of will and character came now. Tim had imagination, and so knew the meaning of fear; but there was nothing craven in him. He could howl and scream and stamp like any other person of his age when the occasion called for such behaviour, but such occasions were due to temper roused by a thwarted will, and the histrionics were half "pretended" to produce a calculated effect. There was no one to thwart his will at present. He also knew how to be afraid of Nothing, to be afraid without ostensible cause that is—which was merely "nerves". He could have "the shudders" with the best of them.

But, when a real thing faced him, Tim's character emerged to meet it. He would clench his hands, brace his muscles, set his teeth—and wish to heaven he was bigger. But he would not flinch. Being imaginative, he lived the worst a dozen times before it happened, yet in the final crash he stood up like a man. He had that highest pluck—the courage of a sensitive temperament. And at this particular juncture, somewhat ticklish for a boy of eight or nine, it did not fail him. He lifted the cane and pushed the swinging door wide open. Then he walked through it—into the Other Wing.

III

The green baize door swung to behind him; he was even sufficiently master of himself to turn and close it with a steady hand, because he did not care to hear the series of muffled thuds its lessening swings would cause. But he realised clearly his position, knew he was doing a tremendous thing.

Holding the cane between fingers very tightly clenched, he advanced bravely along the corridor that stretched before him. And all fear left him from that moment, replaced, it seemed, by a mild and exquisite surprise. His footsteps made no sound, he walked on air; instead of darkness, or the twilight he expected, a diffused and gentle light that seemed like the silver on the lawn when a half-moon sails a cloudless sky, lay everywhere. He knew his way, moreover, knew exactly where he was and whither he was going. The corridor was as familiar to him as the floor of his own bedroom; he recognised the shape and length of it; it agreed exactly with the map he had constructed long ago. Though he had never, to the best of his knowledge, entered it before, he knew with intimacy its every detail.

And thus the surprise he felt was mild and far from disconcerting. "I'm here again!" was the kind of thought he had. It was how he got here that caused the faint surprise, apparently. He no longer swaggered, however, but walked carefully, and half on tiptoe, holding the ivory handle of the cane with a kind of affectionate respect. And as he advanced, the light closed softly up behind him, obliterating the way by which he had come. But this he did not know, because he did not look behind him. He only looked in front, where the corridor stretched its silvery length towards the great chamber where he knew the cane must be surrendered. The person who had preceded him down this ancient corridor, passing through the green baize door just before he reached it, this person, his father's grandfather, now stood in that great chamber, waiting to receive his own. Tim knew it as surely as he knew he breathed. At the far end he even made out the larger patch of silvery light which marked its gaping doorway.

There was another thing he knew as well—that this corridor he moved along between rooms with fast-closed doors, was the Nightmare Corridor; often and often he had traversed it; each room was occupied. "This is the Nightmare Passage," he whispered to himself, "but I know the Ruler—it doesn't matter. None of the Nightmares can get out or do anything." He heard them, none the less, inside, as he passed by; he heard them scratching to get out. The feeling of security made him reckless; he took unnecessary risks; he brushed the panels as he passed. And the love of keen sensation for its own sake, the desire to feel "an awful thrill", temped him once so sharply that he suddenly raised his stick and poked a fast-shut door with it!

He was not prepared for the result, but he gained the sensation and the thrill. For the door opened with instant swiftness half an inch, a hand emerged, caught the stick and tried to draw it in. Tim sprang back as if he had been struck. He pulled at the ivory handle with all his strength, but his strength was less than nothing. He tried to shout, but his voice had gone. A terror of the moon came over him, for he was unable to loosen his hold of the handle; his fingers had become a part of it. An appalling weakness turned him helpless. He was dragged inch by inch towards the fearful door. The end of the stick was already through the narrow crack. He could not see the hand that pulled, but he knew it was gigantic. He understood now why the world was strange, why horses galloped furiously, and why trains whistled as they raced through stations. All the comedy and terror of nightmare gripped his heart with pincers made of ice. The disproportion was abominable. The final collapse rushed over him when, without a sign of warning, the door slammed silently, and between the jamb and the wall the cane was crushed as flat as if it were a bulrush. So irresistible was the force behind the door that the solid stick just went flat as the stalk of a bulrush.

He looked at it. It was a bulrush.

He did not laugh; the absurdity was so distressingly unnatural. The horror of finding a bulrush where he had expected a polished cane—this hideous and appalling detail held the nameless horror of the nightmare. It betrayed him utterly. Why had he not always known really that the stick was not a stick, but a thin and hollow reed...?

Then the cane was safely in his hand, unbroken. He stood looking at it. The Nightmare was in full swing. He heard another door opening behind his back, a door he had not touched. There was just time to see a hand thrusting and waving dreadfully, familiarly, at him through the narrow crack—just time to realise that this was another Nightmare acting in atrocious concert with the first, when he saw closely beside him, towering to the ceiling, the protective, kindly Figure that visited his bedroom. In the turning movement he made to meet the attack, he became aware of her. And his terror passed. It was a nightmare terror merely. The infinite horror vanished. Only the comedy remained. He smiled.

He saw her dimly only, she was so vast, but he saw her, the Ruler of the Other Wing at last, and knew that he was safe again. He gazed with a tremendous love and wonder, trying to see her clearly; but the face was hidden far aloft and seemed to melt into the sky beyond the roof. He discerned that she was larger than the Night, only far, far softer, with wings that folded above him more tenderly even than his mother's arms; that there were points of light like stars among the feathers, and that she was vast enough to cover millions and millions of people all at once. Moreover, she did not fade or go, so far as he could see, but spread herself in such a way that he lost sight of her. She spread over the entire Wing...

And Tim remembered that this was all quite natural really. He had often and often been down this corridor before; the Nightmare Corridor was no new experience; it had to be faced as usual. Once knowing what hid inside the rooms, he was bound to tempt them out. They drew, enticed, attracted him; this was their power. It was their special strength that they could suck him helplessly towards them, and that he was obliged to go. He understood exactly why he was tempted to tap with the cane upon their awful doors, but, having done so, he had accepted the challenge and could now continue his journey quietly and safely. The Ruler of the Other Wing had taken him in charge.

A delicious sense of carelessness came on him. There was softness as of water in the solid things about him, nothing that could hurt or bruise. Holding the cane firmly by its ivory handle, he went forward along the corridor, walking as on air.

The end was quickly reached: He stood upon the threshold of the mighty chamber where he knew the owner of the cane was waiting; the long corridor lay behind him, in front he saw the spacious dimensions of a lofty hall that gave him the feeling of being in the Crystal Palace, Euston Station, or St. Paul's. High, narrow windows, cut deeply into the wall, stood in a row upon the other side; an enormous open fireplace of burning logs was on his right; thick tapestries hung from the ceiling to the floor of stone; and in the centre of the chamber was a massive table of dark, shining wood, great chairs with carved stiff backs set here and there beside it. And in the biggest of these thronelike chairs there sat a figure looking at him gravely—the figure of an old, old man.

Yet there was no surprise in the boy's fast-beating heart; there was a thrill of pleasure and excitement only, a feeling of satisfaction.

He had known quite well the figure would be there, known also it would look like this exactly. He stepped forward on to the floor of stone without a trace of fear or trembling, holding the precious cane in two hands now before him, as though to present it to its owner. He felt proud and pleased. He had run risks for this.

And the figure rose quietly to meet him, advancing in a stately manner over the hard stone floor. The eyes looked gravely, sweetly down at him, the aquiline nose stood out. Tim knew him perfectly: the knee-breeches of shining satin, the gleaming buckles on the shoes, the neat dark stockings, the lace and ruffles about neck and wrists, the coloured waistcoat opening so widely—all the details of the picture over father's mantelpiece, where it hung between two Crimean bayonets, were reproduced in life before his eyes as last. Only the polished cane with the ivory handle was not there.

Tim went three steps nearer to the advancing figure and held out both his hands with the cane laid crosswise on them.

"I've brought it, great-grandpapa," he said, in a faint but clear and steady tone; "here it is."

And the other stooped a little, put out three fingers half concealed by falling lace, and took it by the ivory handle. He made a courtly bow to Tim. He smiled, but though there was pleasure, it was a grave, sad smile. He spoke then: the voice was slow and very deep. There was a delicate softness in it, the suave politeness of an older day.

"Thank you," he said; "I value it. It was given to me by my grandfather. I forgot it when I——" His voice grew indistinct a little.

"Yes?" said Tim.

"When I—left," the old gentleman repeated.

"Oh," said Tim, thinking how beautiful and kind the gracious figure was.

The old man ran his slender fingers carefully along the cane, feeling the polished surface with satisfaction. He lingered specially over the smoothness of the ivory handle. He was evidently very pleased.

"I was not quite myself—er—at the moment," he went on gently; "my memory failed me somewhat." He sighed, as though an immense relief was in him.

"I forget things, too—sometimes," Tim mentioned sympathetically. He simply loved his great-grandfather. He hoped—for a moment—he would be lifted up and kissed. "I'm awfully glad I brought it," he faltered—"that you've got it again."

The other turned his kind grey eyes upon him; the smile on his face was full of gratitude as he looked down.

"Thank you, my boy. I am truly and deeply indebted to you. You courted danger for my sake. Others have tried before, but the Nightmare Passage—er——" He broke off. He tapped the stick firmly on the stone flooring, as though to test it. Bending a trifle, he put his weight upon it. "Ah!" he exclaimed with a short sigh of relief, "I can now——"

His voice again grew indistinct; Tim did not catch the words.

"Yes?" he asked again, aware for the first time that a touch of awe was in his heart.

"—get about again," the other continued very low. "Without my cane," he added, the voice failing with each word the old lips uttered, "I could not...possibly...allow myself...to be seen. It was indeed...deplorable...unpardonable of me...to forget in such a way. Zounds, sir...! I—I..."

His voice sank away suddenly into a sound of wind. He straightened up, tapping the iron ferrule of his cane on the stones in a series of loud knocks. Tim felt a strange sensation creep into his legs. The queer words frightened him a little.

The old man took a step towards him. He still smiled, but there was a new meaning in the smile. A sudden earnestness had replaced the courtly, leisurely manner. The next words seemed to blow down upon the boy from above, as though a cold wind brought them from the sky outside.

Yet the words, he knew, were kindly meant, and very sensible. It was only the abrupt change that startled him. Great-grandpapa, after all, was but a man! This distant sound recalled something in him to that outside world from which the cold wind blew.

"My eternal thanks to you," he heard, while the voice and face and figure seemed to withdraw deeper and deeper into the heart of the mighty chamber. "I shall not forget your kindness and your courage. It is a debt I can, fortunately, one day repay... But now you had best return, and with dispatch. For your head and arm lie heavily on the table, the documents are scattered, there is a cushion fallen... and my son's son is in the house... Farewell! You had best leave me quickly. See! She stands behind you, waiting. Go with her! Go now...!"

The entire scene had vanished even before the final words were uttered. Tim felt empty space about him. A vast, shadowy Figure bore him through it as with mighty wings. He flew, he rushed, he remembered nothing more—until he heard another voice and felt a heavy hand upon his shoulder.

"Tim, you rascal! What are you doing in my study? And in the dark, like this!"

He looked up into his father's face without a word. He felt dazed. The next minute his father had caught him up and kissed him.

"Ragamuffin! How did you guess I was coming back tonight?" He shook him playfully and kissed his tumbling hair. "And you've been asleep, too, into the bargain. Well—how's everything at home—eh? Jack's coming back from school tomorrow, you know, and..."

IV

Jack came home, indeed, the following day, and when the Easter holidays were over, the governess stayed abroad and Tim went off to adventures of another kind in the preparatory school for

289

Wellington. Life slipped rapidly along with him; he grew into a man; his mother and his father died; Jack followed them within a little space; Tim inherited, married, settled down into his great possessions—and opened up the Other Wing. The dreams of imaginative boyhood all had faded; perhaps he had merely put them away, or perhaps he had forgotten them. At any rate, he never spoke of such things now, and when his Irish wife mentioned her belief that the old country house possessed a family ghost, even declaring that she had met an Eighteenth Century figure of a man in the corridors, "an old, old man who bends down upon a stick"—Tim only laughed and said:

"That's as it ought to be! And if these awful land taxes force us to sell some day, a respectable ghost will increase the market value."

But one night he woke and heard a tapping on the floor. He sat up in bed and listened. There was a chilly feeling down his back. Belief had long since gone out of him; he felt uncannily afraid. The sound came nearer and nearer; there were light footsteps with it. The door opened—it opened a little wider, that is, for it already stood ajar—and there upon the threshold stood a figure that it seemed he knew. He saw the face as with all the vivid sharpness of reality. There was a smile upon it, but a smile of warning and alarm. The arm was raised. Tim saw the slender hand, lace falling down upon the long, thin fingers, and in them, tightly gripped, a polished cane. Shaking the cane twice to and fro in the air, the face thrust forward, spoke certain words, and—vanished. But the words were inaudible; for, though the lips distinctly moved, no sound, apparently, came from them.

And Tim sprang out of bed. The room was full of darkness. He turned the light on. The door, he saw, was shut as usual.

He had, of course, been dreaming. But he noticed a curious odour in the air. He sniffed it once or twice—then grasped the truth. It was a smell of burning!

Fortunately, he awoke just in time...

He was acclaimed a hero for his promptitude. After many days, when the damage was repaired, and nerves had settled down once more into the calm routine of country life, he told the story to his wife—the entire story. He told the adventure of his imaginative boyhood with it. She asked to see the old family cane. And it was this request of hers that brought back to memory a detail Tim had entirely forgotten all these years. He remembered it suddenly again—the loss of the cane, the hubbub his father kicked up about it, the endless, futile search. For the stick had never been found, and Tim, who was questioned very closely concerning it, swore with all his might that he had not the smallest notion where it was. Which was, of course, the truth.

Brickett Bottom

Amyas Northcote

The Reverend Arthur Maydew was the hard-working incumbent of a large parish in one of our manufacturing towns. He was also a student and a man of no strong physique, so that when an opportunity was presented to him to take an annual holiday by exchanging parsonages with an elderly clergyman, Mr. Roberts, the Squarson of the Parish of Overbury, and an acquaintance of his own, he was glad to avail himself of it.

Overbury is a small and very remote village in one of our most lovely and rural counties, and Mr. Roberts had long held the living of it.

Without further delay we can transport Mr. Maydew and his family, which consisted only of two daughters, to their temporary home. The two young ladies, Alice and Maggie, the heroines of this narrative, were at that time aged twenty-six and twenty-four years respectively. Both of them were attractive girls, fond of such society as they could find in their own parish and, the former especially, always pleased to extend the circle of their acquaintance. Although the elder in years, Alice in many ways yielded place to her sister, who was the more energetic and practical and upon whose shoulders the bulk of the family cares and responsibilities rested. Alice was inclined to be absent-minded and emotional and to devote more of her thoughts and time to speculations of an abstract nature than her sister.

Both of the girls, however, rejoiced at the prospect of a period of quiet and rest in a pleasant country neighbourhood, and both were gratified at knowing that their father would find in Mr. Roberts' library much that would entertain his mind, and in Mr. Roberts' garden an opportunity to indulge freely in his favourite game of croquet. They would have, no doubt, preferred some cheerful neighbours, but Mr. Roberts was positive in his assurances that there was no one in the neighbourhood whose acquaintance would be of interest to them.

The first few weeks of their new life passed pleasantly for the Maydew family. Mr. Maydew quickly gained renewed vigour in his quiet and congenial surroundings, and in the delightful air, while his daughters spent much of their time in long walks about the country and in exploring its beauties.

One evening late in August the two girls were returning from a long walk along one of their favourite paths, which led along the side of the Downs. On their right, as they walked, the ground fell away sharply to a narrow glen, named Brickett Bottom, about three-quarters of a mile in length, along the bottom of which ran a little-used country road leading to a farm, known as Blaise's Farm, and then onward and upward to lose itself as a sheep track on the higher Downs. On their side of the slope some scattered trees and bushes grew, but beyond the lane and running up over the farther slope of the glen was a thick wood, which extended away to Carew Court, the seat of a neighbouring magnate, Lord Carew. On their left the open Down rose above them and beyond its crest lay Overbury.

The girls were walking hastily, as they were later than they had intended to be and were anxious to reach home. At a certain point at which they had now arrived the path forked, the right hand branch leading down into Brickett Bottom and the left hand turning up over the Down to Overbury.

Just as they were about to turn into the left hand path Alice suddenly stopped and pointing downwards exclaimed:

"How very curious, Maggie! Look, there is a house down there in the Bottom, which we have, or at least I have, never noticed before, often as we have walked up the Bottom."

Maggie followed with her eyes her sister's pointing finger. "I don't see any house," she said.

"Why, Maggie," said her sister, "can't you see it! A quaint-looking, old-fashioned red brick house, there just where the road bends to the right. It seems to be standing in a nice, well-kept garden too."

Maggie looked again, but the light was beginning to fade in the glen and she was short-sighted to boot.

"I certainly don't see anything," she said. "but then I am so blind and the light is getting bad; yes, perhaps I do see a house," she added, straining her eyes.

"Well, it is there," replied her sister, "and to-morrow we will come and explore it." Maggie agreed readily enough, and the sisters went home, still speculating on how they had happened not to notice the house before and resolving firmly on an expedition thither the next day. However, the expedition did not come off as planned, for that evening Maggie slipped on the stairs and fell, spraining her ankle in such a fashion as to preclude walking for some time.

Notwithstanding the accident to her sister, Alice remained possessed by the idea of making further investigations into the house she had looked down upon from the hill the evening before; and the next day, having seen Maggie carefully settled for the afternoon, she started off for Brickett Bottom. She returned in triumph and much intrigued over her discoveries, which she eagerly narrated to her sister.

Yes. There was a nice, old-fashioned red brick house, not very large and set in a charming, old-world garden in the Bottom. It stood on a tongue of land jutting out from the woods, just at the point where the lane, after a fairly straight course from its junction with the main road half a mile away, turned sharply to the right in the direction of Blaise's Farm. More than that, Alice had seen the people of the house, whom she described as an old gentleman and a lady, presumably his wife. She had not clearly made out the gentleman, who was sitting in the porch, but the old lady, who had been in the garden busy with her flowers, had looked up and smiled pleasantly at her as she passed. She was sure, she said, that they were nice people and that it would be pleasant to make their acquaintance.

Maggie was not quite satisfied with Alice's story. She was of a more prudent and retiring nature than her sister; she had an uneasy feeling that, if the old couple had been desirable or attractive neighbours, Mr. Roberts would have mentioned them, and knowing Alice's nature she said what she could to discourage her vague idea of endeavouring to make acquaintance with the owners of the red brick house.

On the following morning, when Alice came to her sister's room to inquire how she did, Maggie noticed that she looked pale and rather absent-minded, and, after a few commonplace remarks had passed, she asked:

"What is the matter, Alice? You don't look yourself this morning." Her sister gave a slightly embarrassed laugh.

"Oh, I am all right," she replied, "only I did not sleep very well. I kept on dreaming about the house. It was such an odd dream too; the house seemed to be home, and yet to be different."

"What, that house in Brickett Bottom?" said Maggie. "Why, what is the matter with you, you seem to be quite crazy about the place?"

"Well, it is curious, isn't it, Maggie, that we should have only just discovered it, and that it looks to be lived in by nice people? I wish we could get to know them."

Maggie did not care to resume the argument of the night before and the subject dropped, nor did Alice again refer to the house or its inhabitants for some little time. In fact, for some days the weather was wet and Alice was forced to abandon her walks, but when the weather once more became fine she resumed them, and Maggie suspected that Brickett Bottom formed one of her sister's favourite expeditions. Maggie became anxious over her sister, who seemed to grow daily more absent-minded and silent, but she refused to be drawn into any confidential talk, and Maggie was nonplussed.

One day, however, Alice returned from her afternoon walk in an unusually excited state of mind, of which Maggie sought an explanation. It came with a rush. Alice said that, that afternoon, as she approached the house in Brickett Bottom, the old lady, who as usual was busy in her garden, had walked down to the gate as she passed and had wished her good day.

Alice had replied and, pausing, a short conversation had followed. Alice could not remember the exact tenor of it, but, after she had paid a compliment to the old lady's flowers, the latter had rather diffidently asked her to enter the garden for a closer view. Alice had hesitated, and the old lady had said "Don't be afraid of me, my dear, I like to see young ladies about me and my husband finds their society quite necessary to him." After a pause she went on: "Of course nobody has told you about us. My husband is Colonel Paxton, late of the Indian Army, and we have been here for many, many years. It's rather lonely, for so few people ever see us. Do come in and meet the Colonel."

"I hope you didn't go in," said Maggie rather sharply.

"Why not?" replied Alice.

"Well, I don't like Mrs. Paxton asking you in that way," answered Maggie.

"I don't see what harm there was in the invitation," said Alice. "I didn't go in because it was getting late and I was anxious to get home; but—"

"But what?" asked Maggie.

Alice shrugged her shoulders. "Well," she said, "I have accepted Mrs. Paxton's invitation to pay her a little visit to-morrow." And she gazed defiantly at Maggie.

Maggie became distinctly uneasy on hearing of this resolution. She did not like the idea of her impulsive sister visiting people on such slight acquaintance, especially as they had never heard them mentioned before. She endeavoured by all means, short of appealing to Mr. Maydew, to dissuade her sister from going, at any rate until there had been time to make some inquiries as to the Paxtons. Alice, however, was obdurate.

What harm could happen to her? she asked. Mrs. Paxton was a charming old lady. She was going early in the afternoon for a short visit. She would be back for tea and croquet with her father and, anyway, now that Maggie was laid up, long solitary walks were unendurable and she was not going to let slip the chance of following up what promised to be a pleasant acquaintance.

Maggie could do nothing more. Her ankle was better and she was able to get down to the garden and sit in a long chair near her father, but walking was still quite out of the question, and it was with some misgivings that on the following day she watched Alice depart gaily for her visit, promising to be back by half-past four at the very latest.

The afternoon passed quietly till nearly five, when Mr. Maydew, looking up from his book, noticed Maggie's uneasy expression and asked:

"Where is Alice?"

"Out for a walk," replied Maggie; and then after a short pause she went on: "And she has also gone to pay a call on some neighbours whom she has recently discovered."

"Neighbours," ejaculated Mr. Maydew, "what neighbours? Mr. Roberts never spoke of any neighbours to me."

"Well, I don't know much about them," answered Maggie. "Only Alice and I were out walking the day of my accident and saw or at least she saw, for I am so blind I could not quite make it out, a house in Brickett Bottom. The next day she went to look at it closer, and yesterday she told me that she had made the acquaintance of the people living in it. She says that they are a retired Indian officer and his wife, a Colonel and Mrs. Paxton, and Alice describes Mrs. Paxton as a charming old lady, who pressed her to come and see them. So she has gone this afternoon, but she promised me she would be back long before this."

Mr. Maydew was silent for a moment and then said:

"I am not well pleased about this. Alice should not be so impulsive and scrape acquaintance with absolutely unknown people. Had there been nice neighbours in Brickett Bottom, I am certain Mr. Roberts would have told us."

The conversation dropped; but both father and daughter were disturbed and uneasy and, tea having been finished and the clock striking half-past five, Mr. Maydew asked Maggie:

"When did you say Alice would be back?"

"Before half-past four at the latest, father."

"Well, what can she be doing? What can have delayed her? You say you did not see the house," he went on.

"No," said Maggie, "I cannot say I did. It was getting dark and you know how short-sighted I am."

"But surely you must have seen it at some other time," said her father.

"That is the strangest part of the whole affair," answered Maggie. "We have often walked up the Bottom, but I never noticed the house, nor had Alice till that evening. I wonder," she went on after a short pause, "if it would not be well to ask Smith to harness the pony and drive over to bring her back. I am not happy about her—I am afraid—"

"Afraid of what?" said her father in the irritated voice of a man who is growing frightened. "What can have gone wrong in this quiet place? Still, I'll send Smith over for her." So saying he rose from his chair and sought out Smith, the rather dull-witted gardener-groom attached to Mr. Roberts' service.

"Smith," he said, "I want you to harness the pony at once and go over to Colonel Paxton's in Brickett Bottom and bring Miss Maydew home."

The man stared at him.

"Go where, sir?" he said.

Mr. Maydew repeated the order and the man, still staring stupidly, answered: "I never heard of Colonel Paxton, sir. I don't know what house you mean." Mr. Maydew was now growing really anxious.

"Well, harness the pony at once," he said; and going back to Maggie he told her of what he called Smith's stupidity, and asked her if she felt that her ankle would be strong enough to permit her to go with him and Smith to the Bottom to point out the house.

Maggie agreed readily and in a few minutes the party started off. Brickett Bottom, although not more than three-quarters of a mile away over the Downs, was at least three miles by road; and as it was nearly six o'clock before Mr. Maydew left the Vicarage, and the pony was old and slow, it was getting late before the entrance to Brickett Bottom was reached. Turning into the lane the cart proceeded slowly up the Bottom, Mr. Maydew and Maggie looking anxiously from side to side, whilst Smith drove stolidly on looking neither to the right nor left.

"Where is the house?" said Mr. Maydew presently.

"At the bend of the road," answered Maggie, her heart sickening as she looked out through the failing light to see the trees stretching their ranks in unbroken formation along it. The cart reached the bend. "It should be here," whispered Maggie.

They pulled up. Just in front of them the road bent to the right round a tongue of land, which, unlike the rest of the right hand side of the road, was free from trees and was covered only by rough grass and stray bushes. A closer inspection disclosed evident signs of terraces having once been formed on it, but of a house there was no trace.

"Is this the place?" said Mr. Maydew in a low voice.

Maggie nodded.

"But there is no house here," said her father. "What does it all mean? Are you sure of yourself, Maggie? Where is Alice?"

Before Maggie could answer a voice was heard calling "Father! Maggie!" The sound of the voice was thin and high and, paradoxically, it sounded both very near and yet as if it came from some infinite distance. The cry was thrice repeated and then silence fell. Mr. Maydew and Maggie stared at each other.

"That was Alice's voice," said Mr. Maydew huskily, "she is near and in trouble, and is calling us. Which way did you think it came from, Smith?" he added, turning to the gardener.

"I didn't hear anybody calling," said the man.

"Nonsense!" answered Mr. Maydew.

And then he and Maggie both began to call "Alice. Alice. Where are you?" There was no reply and Mr. Maydew sprang from the cart, at the same time bidding Smith to hand the reins to Maggie and come and search for the missing girl. Smith obeyed him and both men, scrambling up the turfy bit of ground, began to search and call through the neighbouring wood. They heard and saw nothing, however, and after an agonised search Mr. Maydew ran down to the cart and begged Maggie to drive on to Blaise's Farm for help leaving himself and Smith to continue the search. Maggie followed her father's instructions and was fortunate enough to find Mr. Rumbold, the farmer, his two sons and a couple of labourers just returning from the harvest field. She explained what had happened, and the farmer and his men promptly volunteered to form a search party, though Maggie, in spite of her anxiety, noticed a queer expression on Mr. Rumbold's face as she told him her tale.

The party, provided with lanterns, now went down the Bottom, joined Mr. Maydew and Smith and made an exhaustive but absolutely fruitless search of the woods near the bend of the road. No trace of the missing girl was to be found, and after a long and anxious time the search was abandoned, one of the young Rumbolds volunteering to ride into the nearest town and notify the police.

Maggie, though with little hope in her own heart, endeavoured to cheer her father on their homeward way with the idea that

Alice might have returned to Overbury over the Downs whilst they were going by road to the Bottom, and that she had seen them and called to them in jest when they were opposite the tongue of land.

However, when they reached home there was no Alice and, though the next day the search was resumed and full inquiries were instituted by the police, all was to no purpose. No trace of Alice was ever found, the last human being that saw her having been an old woman, who had met her going down the path into the Bottom on the afternoon of her disappearance, and who described her as smiling but looking "queerlike."

This is the end of the story, but the following may throw some light upon it.

The history of Alice's mysterious disappearance became widely known through the medium of the Press and Mr. Roberts, distressed beyond measure at what had taken place, returned in all haste to Overbury to offer what comfort and help he could give to his afflicted friend and tenant. He called upon the Maydews and, having heard their tale, sat for a short time in silence. Then he said:

"Have you ever heard any local gossip concerning this Colonel and Mrs. Paxton?"

"No," replied Mr. Maydew, "I never heard their names until the day of my poor daughter's fatal visit."

"Well," said Mr. Roberts, "I will tell you all I can about them, which is not very much, I fear." He paused and then went on: "I am now nearly seventy-five years old, and for nearly seventy years no house has stood in Brickett Bottom. But when I was a child of about five there was an old-fashioned, red brick house standing in a garden at the bend of the road, such as you have described. It was owned and lived in by a retired Indian soldier and his wife, a Colonel and Mrs. Paxton. At the time I speak of, certain events having taken place at the house and the old couple having died, it was sold by their heirs to Lord Carew, who shortly after pulled it down on the ground that it interfered with his shooting. Colonel and Mrs. Paxton were well known to my father, who was the clergyman here before me, and to the neighbourhood in general. They lived quietly and were not unpopular, but the Colonel was supposed to possess a violent and vindictive temper. Their family consisted only of themselves, their daughter and a couple of servants, the Colonel's old Army servant and his Eurasian wife. Well, I cannot tell you details of what happened, I was only a child; my father never liked gossip and in later years, when he talked to me on the subject, he always avoided any appearance of exaggeration or sensationalism. However, it is known that Miss Paxton fell in love with and became engaged to a young man to whom her parents took a strong dislike. They used every possible means to break off the match, and many rumours were set on foot as to their conduct—undue influence, even cruelty were charged against them. I do not know the truth, all I can say is that Miss Paxton died and a very bitter feeling against her parents sprang up. My father, however, continued to call, but was rarely admitted. In fact, he never saw Colonel Paxton after his daughter's death and only saw Mrs. Paxton once or twice. He described her as an utterly broken woman, and was not surprised at her following her daughter to the grave in about three months' time. Colonel Paxton became, if possible, more of a recluse than ever after his wife's death and himself died not more than a month after her under circumstances which pointed to suicide. Again a crop of rumours sprang up, but there was no one in particular to take action, the doctor certified Death from Natural Causes, and Colonel Paxton, like his wife and daughter, was buried in this churchyard. The property passed to a distant relative, who came down to it for one night shortly afterwards; he never came again, having apparently conceived a violent dislike to the place, but arranged to pension off the servants and then sold the house to Lord Carew, who was glad to purchase this little island in the middle of his property. He pulled it down soon after he had bought it, and the garden was left to relapse into a wilderness."

Mr. Roberts paused. "Those are all the facts," he added.

"But there is something more," said Maggie.

Mr. Roberts hesitated for a while. "You have a right to know all," he said almost to himself; then louder he continued: "What I am now going to tell you is really rumour, vague and uncertain; I cannot fathom its truth or its meaning. About five years after the house had been pulled down a young maidservant at Carew Court was out walking one afternoon. She was a stranger to the village and a new-comer to the Court. On returning home to tea she told her fellow-servants that as she walked down Brickett Bottom, which place she described clearly, she passed a red brick house at the bend of the road and that a kind-faced old lady had asked her to step in for a while. She did not go in, not because she had any suspicions of there being anything uncanny, but simply because she feared to be late for tea.

"I do not think she ever visited the Bottom again and she had no other similar experience, so far as I am aware.

"Two or three years later, shortly after my father's death, a travelling tinker with his wife and daughter camped for the night at the foot of the Bottom. The girl strolled away up the glen to gather blackberries and was never seen or heard of again. She was searched for in vain—of course, one does not know the truth— and she may have run away voluntarily from her parents, although there was no known cause for her doing so.

"That," concluded Mr. Roberts, "is all I can tell you of either facts or rumours; all that I can now do is to pray for you and for her."

Podolo
LP Hartley

The evening before we made the expedition to Podolo we talked it
over, and I agreed there was nothing against it really.

"But why did you say you'd feel safer if Walter was going too?"
Angela asked me. And Walter said, "What good should I be? I can't
help to row the gondola, you know."

Then I felt rather silly, for everything I had said about Podolo
was merely conversational exaggeration, meant to whet their
curiosity, like a newspaper headline and I knew that when Angela
actually saw the dull little island, its stony and inhospitable shore
littered with broken bottles and empty tins, she would think what
a fool I was, with my romancing. So I took back everything I
said, called my own bluff, as it were, and explained that I avoided
Podolo only because of its exposed position: it was four miles
from Venice, and if a boisterous bora got up (as it sometimes did,
without warning) we should find getting back hard work, and
might be late home. "And what will Walter say," I wound up, "if
he comes back from Trieste" (he was going there for the day on
business) "and finds no wife to welcome him?" Walter said, on
the contrary, he had often wished such a thing might happen.
And so, after some playful recriminations between this lately
married, charming, devoted couple we agreed that Podolo should
be the goal for tomorrow's picnic. "You must curb my wife's

generous impulses," Walter warned me; "she always wants to do something for somebody. It's an expensive habit." I assured him that at Podolo she would find no calls on her heart or her purse. Except perhaps for a rat or two it was quite uninhabited. Next morning in brilliant sunshine Walter gulped down his breakfast and started for the station. It seemed hard that he should have to spend six hours of this divine day in a stuffy train. I stood on the balcony watching his departure.

The sunlight sparkled on the water; the gondola, in its best array, glowed and glittered. "Say goodbye to Angela for me," cried Walter as the gondolier braced himself for the first stroke. "And what is your postal address at Podolo?"

"Full fathom five," I called out, but I don't think my reply reached him.

Until you get right up to Podolo you can form no estimate of its size. There is nothing near by to compare it with. On the horizon it looks like a foot-rule. Even now, though I have been there many times, I cannot say whether it is a hundred yards long or two hundred. But I have no wish to go back and make certain.

We cast anchor a few feet from the stony shore. Podolo, I must say, was looking its best, green, flowery, almost welcoming. One side is rounded to form the shallow arc of a circle: the other is straight. Seen from above, it must look like the moon in its first quarter. Seen as we saw it from the water-line with the grassy rampart behind, it forms a kind of natural amphitheatre. The slim withy-like acacia trees give a certain charm to the foreground, and to the background where they grow in clumps, and cast darker shadows, an air of mystery. As we sat in the gondola we were like theatre-goers in the stalls, staring at an empty stage.

It was nearly two o'clock when we began lunch. I was very hungry, and, charmed by my companion and occupied by my food, I did not let my eyes stray out of the boat. To Angela belonged the honour of discovering the first denizen of Podolo.

"Why," she exclaimed, "there's a cat." Sure enough there was: a little cat, hardly more than a kitten, very thin and scraggy, and mewing with automatic regularity every two or three seconds. Standing on the weedy stones at the water's edge it was a pitiful sight. "It's smelt the food," said Angela. "It's hungry. Probably it's starving."

Mario, the gondolier, had also made the discovery, but he received it in a different spirit. "*Povera bestia,*" he cried in sympathetic accents, but his eyes brightened. "Its owners did not want it. It has been put here on purpose, one sees." The idea that the cat had been left to starve caused him no great concern, but it shocked Angela profoundly.

"How abominable!" she exclaimed. "We must take it something to eat at once."

The suggestion did not recommend itself to Mario, who had to haul up the anchor and see the prospect of his own lunch growing more remote: I too thought we might wait till the meal was over. The cat would not die before our eyes. But Angela could brook no delay. So to the accompaniment of a good deal of stamping and heavy breathing the prow of the gondola was turned to land.

Meanwhile the cat continued to miaow, though it had retreated a little and was almost invisible, a thin wisp of tabby fur, against the parched stems of the outermost grasses.

Angela filled her hand with chicken bones.

"I shall try to win its confidence with these," she said, "and then if I can I shall catch it and put it in the boat and we'll take it to Venice. If it's left here it'll certainly starve."

She climbed along the knife-like gunwale of the gondola and stepped delicately on to the slippery boulders.

Continuing to eat my chicken in comfort, I watched her approach the cat. It ran away, but only a few yards: its hunger was obviously keeping its fear at bay. She threw a bit of food and it came nearer: another, and it came nearer still. Its demeanour grew less suspicious; its tail rose into the air; it came right up to Angela's feet. She pounced. But the cat was too quick for her; it slipped through

307

her hands like water. Again hunger overpowered mistrust. Back it came. Once more Angela made a grab at it; once more it eluded her. But the third time she was successful. She got hold of its leg.

I shall never forget seeing it dangle from Angela's (fortunately) gloved hand. It wriggled and squirmed and fought, and in spite of its tiny size the violence of its struggles made Angela quiver like a twig in a gale. And all the while it made the most extraordinary noise, the angriest, wickedest sound I ever heard. Instead of growing louder as its fury mounted, the sound actually decreased in volume, as though the creature was being choked by its own rage. The spitting died away into the thin ghost of a snarl, infinitely malevolent, but hardly more audible from where I was than the hiss of air from a punctured tyre.

Mario was distressed by what he felt to be Angela's brutality. "Poor beast!" he exclaimed with pitying looks. "She ought not to treat it like that." And his face gleamed with satisfaction when, intimidated by the whirling claws, she let the cat drop. It streaked away into the grass, its belly to the ground.

Angela climbed back into the boat. "I nearly had it," she said, her voice still unsteady from the encounter. "I think I shall get it next time. I shall throw a coat over it." She ate her asparagus in silence, throwing the stalks over the side. I saw that she was preoccupied and couldn't get the cat out of her mind. Any form of suffering in others affected her almost like an illness. I began to wish we hadn't come to Podolo; it was not the first time a picnic there had gone badly.

"I tell you what," Angela said suddenly, "if I can't catch it I'll kill it. It's only a question of dropping one of these boulders on it. I could do it quite easily." She disclosed her plan to Mario, who was horror-struck. His code was different from hers. He did not mind the animal dying of slow starvation; that was in the course of nature. But deliberately to kill it! "*Poveretto*! It has done no one any harm," he exclaimed with indignation. But there was another reason, I suspected, for his attitude. Venice is overrun with cats, chiefly because it is considered unlucky to kill them. If they fall into the water and are drowned, so much the better, but woe betide whoever pushes them in.

I expounded the gondolier's point of view to Angela, but she was not impressed. "Of course I don't expect him to do it," she said, "nor you either, if you'd rather not. It may be a messy business but it will soon be over. Poor little brute, it's in a horrible state. Its life can't be any pleasure to it."

"But we don't know that," I urged, still cravenly averse from the deed of blood. "If it could speak, it might say it preferred to live at all costs." But I couldn't move Angela from her purpose.

"Let's go and explore the island," she said, "until it's time to bathe. The cat will have got over its fright and be hungry again by then, and I'm sure I shall be able to catch it. I promise I won't murder it except as a last resource."

The word "murder" lingered unpleasantly in my mind as we made our survey of the island. You couldn't imagine a better place for one. During the war a battery had been mounted there. The concrete emplacement, about as long as a tennis court, remained: but nature and the weather had conspired to break it up, leaving black holes large enough to admit a man. These holes were like crevasses in a glacier, but masked by vegetation instead of snow. Even in the brilliant afternoon sunlight one had to tread cautiously. "Perhaps the cat has its lair down there," I said, indicating a gloomy cavern with a jagged edge. "I suppose its eyes would shine in the dark." Angela lay down on the pavement and peered in. "I thought I heard something move," she said, "but it might be anywhere in this rabbit-warren."

Our bathe was a great success. The water was so warm one hardly felt the shock of going in. The only drawback was the mud, which clung to Angela's white bathing shoes, nasty sticky stuff. A little wind had got up. But the grassy rampart sheltered us; we leaned against it and smoked. Suddenly I noticed it was past five.

"We ought to go soon," I said. "We promised, do you remember, to send the gondola to meet Walter's train."

"All right," said Angela, "just let me have a go at the cat first. Let's put the food" (we had brought some remnants of lunch with us) "here where we last saw it, and watch."

There was no need to watch, for the cat appeared at once and made for the food. Angela and I stole up behind it, but I inadvertently kicked a stone and the cat was off like a flash. Angela looked at me reproachfully. "Perhaps you could manage better alone," I said. Angela seemed to think she could. I retreated a few yards, but the cat, no doubt scenting a trap, refused to come out.

Angela threw herself on the pavement. "I can see it," she muttered. "I must win its confidence again. Give me three minutes and I'll catch it."

Three minutes passed. I felt concerned for Angela, her lovely hair floating over the dark hole, her face as much as one could see of it, a little red. The air was getting chilly.

"Look here," I said, "I'll wait for you in the gondola. When you've caught it, give a shout and I'll have the boat brought to land." Angela nodded; she dare not speak for fear of scaring her prey.

So I returned to the gondola. I could just see the line of Angela's shoulders; her face, of course, was hidden. Mario stood up, eagerly watching the chase. "She loves it so much," he said, "that she wants to kill it." I remembered Oscar Wilde's epigram, rather uncomfortably; still, nothing could be more disinterested than Angela's attitude to the cat. "We ought to start," the gondolier warned me. "The signore will be waiting at the station and wonder what has happened."

"What about Walter?" I called across the water. "He won't know what to do."

Her mind was clearly on something else as she said: "Oh, he'll find his own way home."

More minutes passed. The gondolier smiled. "One must have patience with ladies," he said; "always patience."

I tried a last appeal. "If we started at once we could just do it."

She didn't answer. Presently I called out again. "What luck, Angela? Any hope of catching him?"

There was a pause: then I heard her say, in a curiously tense voice. "I'm not trying to *catch* him now."

The need for immediate hurry had passed, since we were irrevocably late for Walter. A sense of relaxation stole over me; I wrapped the rug round me to keep off the treacherous cold sirocco and I fell asleep. Almost at once, it seemed, I began to dream. In my dream it was night; we were hurrying across the lagoon trying to be in time for Walter's train. It was so dark I could see nothing but the dim blur of Venice ahead, and the little splash of whitish water where the oar dipped. Suddenly I stopped rowing and looked round. The seat behind me seemed to be empty. "Angela!" I cried; but there was no answer. I grew frightened. "Mario!" I shouted. "Where's the signora? We have left her behind! We must go back at once!" The gondolier, too, stopped rowing and came towards me; I could just distinguish his face; it had a wild look. "She's there, signore," he said. "But where? She's not on the seat." "She wouldn't stay on it," said the gondolier. And then, as is the way in dreams, I knew what his next words would be. "We loved her and so we had to kill her."

An uprush of panic woke me. The feeling of relief at getting back to actuality was piercingly sweet. I was restored to the sunshine. At least I thought so, in the ecstasy of returning consciousness. The next moment I began to doubt, and an uneasiness, not unlike the beginning of nightmare, stirred in me again. I opened my eyes to the daylight but they didn't receive it. I looked out on to darkness. At first I couldn't believe my eyes: I wondered if I was fainting. But a glance at my watch explained everything. It was past seven o'clock. I had slept the brief twilight through and now it was night, though a few gleams lingered in the sky over Fusina.

Mario was not to be seen. I stood up and looked round. There he was on the poop, his knees drawn up, asleep. Before I had time to speak he opened his eyes, like a dog.

"Signore," he said, "you went to sleep, so I did too." To sleep out of hours is considered a joke all the world over; we both laughed.

"But the Signora," he said. "Is *she* asleep? Or is she still trying to catch the cat?"

We strained our eyes towards the island which was much darker than the surrounding sky.

"That's where she was," said Mario, pointing, "but I can't see her now."

"Angela!" I called.

There was no answer, indeed no sound at all but the noise of the waves slapping against the gondola.

We stared at each other.

"Let us hope she has taken no harm," said Mario, a note of anxiety in his voice. "The cat was very fierce, but it wasn't big enough to hurt her, was it?"

"No, no," I said. "It might have scratched her when she was putting her face—you know—into one of those holes."

"She was trying to kill it, wasn't she?" asked Mario. I nodded.

"*Ha fatto male*," said Mario. "In this country we are not accustomed to kill cats."

"*You* call, Mario," I said impatiently. "Your voice is stronger than mine." Mario obeyed with a shout that might have raised the dead. But no answer came.

"Well," I said briskly, trying to conceal my agitation, "we must go and look for her or else we shall be late for dinner, and the signore will be getting worried. She must be a—a heavy sleeper."

Mario didn't answer.

"*Avanti!*" I said. "*Andiamo! Coraggio!*" I could not understand why Mario, usually so quick to execute an order, did not move. He was staring straight in front of him.

"There is someone on the island," he said at last, "but it's not the signora."

I must say, to do us justice, that within a couple of minutes we had beached the boat and landed. To my surprise Mario kept the oar in his hand.

"I have a pocket-knife," he remarked, "but the blade is only so long," indicating the third joint of a stalwart little finger.

"It was a man, then?" said I.

"It looked like a man's head."

"But you're not sure?"

"No, because it didn't walk like a man."

"How then?"

Mario bent forward and touched the ground with his free hand. I couldn't imagine why a man should go on all fours, unless he didn't want to be seen.

"He must have come while we were asleep," I said. "There'll be a boat round the other side. But let's look here first."

We were standing by the place where we had last seen Angela. The grass was broken and bent; she had left a handkerchief as though to mark the spot. Otherwise there was no trace of her.

"Now let's find his boat," I said.

We climbed the grassy rampart and began to walk round the shallow curve, stumbling over concealed brambles.

"Not here, not here," muttered Mario.

From our little eminence we could see clusters of lights twinkling across the lagoon; Fusina three or four miles away on the left, Malamocco the same distance on the right. And straight ahead Venice, floating on the water like a swarm of fire-flies. But no boat. We stared at each other bewildered.

"So he didn't come by water," said Mario at last. "He must have been here all the time."

"But are you quite certain it wasn't the signora you saw?" I asked. "How could you tell in the darkness?"

"Because the signora was wearing a white dress," said Mario. "And this one is all in black—unless he is a Negro."

"That's why it's so difficult to see him."

"Yes, we can't see him, but he can see us all right."

I felt a curious sensation in my spine.

"Mario," I said, "he must have seen her, you know. Do you think he's got anything to do with her not being here?"

Mario didn't answer.

"I don't understand why he doesn't speak to us."

"Perhaps he can't speak."

"But you thought he was a man... Anyhow, we are two against one. Come on. You take the right. I'll go to the left."

We soon lost sight of each other in the darkness, but once or twice I heard Mario swearing as he scratched himself on the thorny acacias. My search was more successful than I expected. Right at the corner of the island, close to the water's edge, I found one of Angela's bathing shoes: she must have taken it off in a hurry for the button was torn away. A little later I made a rather grisly discovery. It was the cat, dead, with its head crushed. The pathetic little heap of fur would never suffer the pangs of hunger again. Angela had been as good as her word.

I was just going to call Mario when the bushes parted and something hurled itself upon me. I was swept off my feet. Alternately dragging and carrying me my captor continued his headlong course. The next thing I knew I was pitched pell-mell into the gondola and felt the boat move under me.

"Mario!" I gasped. And then—absurd question—"What have you done with the oar?"

The gondolier's white face stared down at me.

"The oar? I left it—it wasn't any use, signore. I tried... What it wants is a machine gun."

He was rowing frantically with my oar: the island began to recede.

"But we can't go away!" I cried.

The gondolier said nothing, but rowed with all his strength. Then he began to talk under his breath. "It was a good oar, too," I heard him mutter. Suddenly he left the poop, climbed over the cushions and sat down beside me.

"When I found her," he whispered, "she wasn't quite dead." I began to speak but he held up his hand.

"She asked me to kill her."

"But, Mario!"

"'Before it comes back,' she said. And then she said, 'It's starving, too, and it won't wait...'" Mario bent his head nearer but his voice was almost inaudible.

"Speak up," I cried. The next moment I implored him to stop. Mario clambered on to the poop.

"You don't want to go to the island now, signore?"

"No, no. Straight home."

I looked back. Transparent darkness covered the lagoon save for one shadow that stained the horizon black. Podolo...

Afterward

Edith Wharton

I

"Oh, there *is* one, of course, but you'll never know it."

The assertion, laughingly flung out six months earlier in a bright June garden, came back to Mary Boyne with a sharp perception of its latent significance as she stood, in the December dusk, waiting for the lamps to be brought into the library.

The words had been spoken by their friend Alida Stair, as they sat at tea on her lawn at Pangbourne, in reference to the very house of which the library in question was the central, the pivotal "feature." Mary Boyne and her husband, in quest of a country place in one of the southern or southwestern counties, had, on their arrival in England, carried their problem straight to Alida Stair, who had successfully solved it in her own case; but it was not until they had rejected, almost capriciously, several practical and judicious suggestions that she threw it out: "Well, there's Lyng, in Dorsetshire. It belongs to Hugo's cousins, and you can get it for a song."

The reasons she gave for its being obtainable on these terms— its remoteness from a station, its lack of electric light, hot-water pipes, and other vulgar necessities—were exactly those pleading in its favor with two romantic Americans perversely in search of the economic drawbacks which were associated, in their tradition, with unusual architectural felicities.

"I should never believe I was living in an old house unless I was thoroughly uncomfortable," Ned Boyne, the more extravagant of the two, had jocosely insisted; "the least hint of 'convenience' would make me think it had been bought out of an exhibition, with the pieces numbered, and set up again." And they had proceeded to enumerate, with humorous precision, their various suspicions and exactions, refusing to believe that the house their cousin recommended was *really* Tudor till they learned it had no heating system, or that the village church was literally in the grounds till she assured them of the deplorable uncertainty of the water-supply.

"It's too uncomfortable to be true!" Edward Boyne had continued to exult as the avowal of each disadvantage was successively wrung from her; but he had cut short his rhapsody to ask, with a sudden relapse to distrust: "And the ghost? You've been concealing from us the fact that there is no ghost!"

Mary, at the moment, had laughed with him, yet almost with her laugh, being possessed of several sets of independent perceptions, had noted a sudden flatness of tone in Alida's answering hilarity.

"Oh, Dorsetshire's full of ghosts, you know."

"Yes, yes; but that won't do. I don't want to have to drive ten miles to see somebody else's ghost. I want one of my own on the premises. Is there a ghost at Lyng?"

His rejoinder had made Alida laugh again, and it was then that she had flung back tantalizingly: "Oh, there *is* one, of course, but you'll never know it."

"Never know it?" Boyne pulled her up. "But what in the world constitutes a ghost except the fact of its being known for one?"

"I can't say. But that's the story."

"That there's a ghost, but that nobody knows it's a ghost?"

"Well—not till afterward, at any rate."

"Till afterward?"

"Not till long, long afterward."

"But if it's once been identified as an unearthly visitant, why

318

hasn't its signalement been handed down in the family? How has it managed to preserve its incognito?"

Alida could only shake her head. "Don't ask me. But it has."

"And then suddenly—" Mary spoke up as if from some cavernous depth of divination—"suddenly, long afterward, one says to one's self, '*That was* it?'"

She was oddly startled at the sepulchral sound with which her question fell on the banter of the other two, and she saw the shadow of the same surprise flit across Alida's clear pupils. "I suppose so. One just has to wait."

"Oh, hang waiting!" Ned broke in. "Life's too short for a ghost who can only be enjoyed in retrospect. Can't we do better than that, Mary?"

But it turned out that in the event they were not destined to, for within three months of their conversation with Mrs. Stair they were established at Lyng, and the life they had yearned for to the point of planning it out in all its daily details had actually begun for them.

It was to sit, in the thick December dusk, by just such a wide-hooded fireplace, under just such black oak rafters, with the sense that beyond the mullioned panes the downs were darkening to a deeper solitude: it was for the ultimate indulgence in such sensations that Mary Boyne had endured for nearly fourteen years the soul-deadening ugliness of the Middle West, and that Boyne had ground on doggedly at his engineering till, with a suddenness that still made her blink, the prodigious windfall of the Blue Star Mine had put them at a stroke in possession of life and the leisure to taste it. They had never for a moment meant their new state to be one of idleness; but they meant to give themselves only to harmonious activities. She had her vision of painting and gardening (against a background of gray walls), he dreamed of the production of his long-planned book on the "Economic Basis of Culture"; and with such absorbing work ahead no existence could be too sequestered; they could not get far enough from the world, or plunge deep enough into the past.

Dorsetshire had attracted them from the first by a semblance of remoteness out of all proportion to its geographical position. But to the Boynes it was one of the ever-recurring wonders of the whole incredibly compressed island—a nest of counties, as they put it— that for the production of its effects so little of a given quality went so far: that so few miles made a distance, and so short a distance a difference.

"It's that," Ned had once enthusiastically explained, "that gives such depth to their effects, such relief to their least contrasts. They've been able to lay the butter so thick on every exquisite mouthful."

The butter had certainly been laid on thick at Lyng: the old gray house, hidden under a shoulder of the downs, had almost all the finer marks of commerce with a protracted past. The mere fact that it was neither large nor exceptional made it, to the Boynes, abound the more richly in its special sense—the sense of having been for centuries a deep, dim reservoir of life. The life had probably not been of the most vivid order: for long periods, no doubt, it had fallen as noiselessly into the past as the quiet drizzle of autumn fell, hour after hour, into the green fish-pond between the yews; but these back-waters of existence sometimes breed, in their sluggish depths, strange acuities of emotion, and Mary Boyne had felt from the first the occasional brush of an intenser memory.

The feeling had never been stronger than on the December afternoon when, waiting in the library for the belated lamps, she rose from her seat and stood among the shadows of the hearth. Her husband had gone off, after luncheon, for one of his long tramps on the downs. She had noticed of late that he preferred to be unaccompanied on these occasions; and, in the tried security of their personal relations, had been driven to conclude that his book was bothering him, and that he needed the afternoons to turn over in solitude the problems left from the morning's work. Certainly the book was not going as smoothly as she had imagined it would, and the lines of perplexity between his eyes had never been there in his engineering days. Then he had often looked fagged to the verge of illness, but the native demon of "worry" had never branded his brow. Yet the few pages he had so far read to her—the introduction, and a synopsis of the opening chapter—gave evidences of a firm possession of his subject, and a deepening confidence in his powers.

The fact threw her into deeper perplexity, since, now that he had done with "business" and its disturbing contingencies, the one other possible element of anxiety was eliminated. Unless it were his health, then? But physically he had gained since they had come to Dorsetshire, grown robuster, ruddier, and fresher-eyed. It was only within a week that she had felt in him the undefinable change that made her restless in his absence, and as tongue-tied in his presence as though it were *she* who had a secret to keep from him!

The thought that there *was* a secret somewhere between them struck her with a sudden smart rap of wonder, and she looked about her down the dim, long room.

"Can it be the house?" she mused.

The room itself might have been full of secrets. They seemed to be piling themselves up, as evening fell, like the layers and layers of velvet shadow dropping from the low ceiling, the dusky walls of books, the smoke-blurred sculpture of the hooded hearth.

"Why, of course—the house is haunted!" she reflected.

The ghost—Alida's imperceptible ghost—after figuring largely in the banter of their first month or two at Lyng, had been gradually discarded as too ineffectual for imaginative use. Mary had, indeed, as became the tenant of a haunted house, made the customary inquiries among her few rural neighbors, but, beyond a vague, "They du say so, Ma'am," the villagers had nothing to impart. The elusive specter had apparently never had sufficient identity for a legend to crystallize about it, and after a time the Boynes had laughingly set the matter down to their profit-and-loss account, agreeing that Lyng was one of the few houses good enough in itself to dispense with supernatural enhancements.

"And I suppose, poor, ineffectual demon, that's why it beats its beautiful wings in vain in the void," Mary had laughingly concluded.

"Or, rather," Ned answered, in the same strain, "why, amid so much that's ghostly, it can never affirm its separate existence as *the* ghost." And thereupon their invisible housemate had finally dropped out of their references, which were numerous enough to make them promptly unaware of the loss.

Now, as she stood on the hearth, the subject of their earlier curiosity revived in her with a new sense of its meaning—a sense gradually acquired through close daily contact with the scene of the lurking mystery. It was the house itself, of course, that possessed the ghost-seeing faculty, that communed visually but secretly with its own past; and if one could only get into close enough communion with the house, one might surprise its secret, and acquire the ghost-sight on one's own account. Perhaps, in his long solitary hours in this very room, where she never trespassed till the afternoon, her husband *had* acquired it already, and was silently carrying the dread weight of whatever it had revealed to him. Mary was too well-versed in the code of the spectral world not to know that one could not talk about the ghosts one saw: to do so was almost as great a breach of good-breeding as to name a lady in a club. But this explanation did not really satisfy her. "What, after all, except for the fun of the frisson," she reflected, "would he really care for any of their old ghosts?" And thence she was thrown back once more on the fundamental dilemma: the fact that one's greater or less susceptibility to spectral influences had no particular bearing on the case, since, when one *did* see a ghost at Lyng, one did not know it.

"Not till long afterward," Alida Stair had said. Well, supposing Ned *had* seen one when they first came, and had known only within the last week what had happened to him? More and more under the spell of the hour, she threw back her searching thoughts to the early days of their tenancy, but at first only to recall a gay confusion of unpacking, settling, arranging of books, and calling to each other from remote corners of the house as treasure after treasure of their habitation revealed itself to them. It was in this particular connection that she presently recalled a certain soft afternoon of the previous October, when, passing from the first rapturous flurry of exploration to a detailed inspection of the old house, she had pressed (like a novel heroine) a panel that opened at her touch, on a narrow flight of stairs leading to an unsuspected flat ledge of the roof—the roof which, from below, seemed to slope away on all sides too abruptly for any but practised feet to scale.

The view from this hidden coign was enchanting, and she had flown down to snatch Ned from his papers and give him the freedom of her discovery. She remembered still how, standing on the narrow ledge, he had passed his arm about her while their gaze flew to the long, tossed horizon-line of the downs, and then dropped contentedly back to trace the arabesque of yew hedges about the fish-pond, and the shadow of the cedar on the lawn.

"And now the other way," he had said, gently turning her about within his arm; and closely pressed to him, she had absorbed, like some long, satisfying draft, the picture of the gray-walled court, the squat lions on the gates, and the lime-avenue reaching up to the highroad under the downs.

It was just then, while they gazed and held each other, that she had felt his arm relax, and heard a sharp "Hullo!" that made her turn to glance at him.

Distinctly, yes, she now recalled she had seen, as she glanced, a shadow of anxiety, of perplexity, rather, fall across his face; and, following his eyes, had beheld the figure of a man—a man in loose, grayish clothes, as it appeared to her—who was sauntering down the lime-avenue to the court with the tentative gait of a stranger seeking his way. Her short-sighted eyes had given her but a blurred impression of slightness and grayness, with something foreign, or at least unlocal, in the cut of the figure or its garb; but her husband had apparently seen more—seen enough to make him push past

323

her with a sharp "Wait!" and dash down the twisting stairs without pausing to give her a hand for the descent.

A slight tendency to dizziness obliged her, after a provisional clutch at the chimney against which they had been leaning, to follow him down more cautiously; and when she had reached the attic landing she paused again for a less definite reason, leaning over the oak banister to strain her eyes through the silence of the brown, sun-flecked depths below. She lingered there till, somewhere in those depths, she heard the closing of a door; then, mechanically impelled, she went down the shallow flights of steps till she reached the lower hall.

The front door stood open on the mild sunlight of the court, and hall and court were empty. The library door was open, too, and after listening in vain for any sound of voices within, she quickly crossed the threshold, and found her husband alone, vaguely fingering the papers on his desk.

He looked up, as if surprised at her precipitate entrance, but the shadow of anxiety had passed from his face, leaving it even, as she fancied, a little brighter and clearer than usual.

"What was it? Who was it?" she asked.

"Who?" he repeated, with the surprise still all on his side.

"The man we saw coming toward the house."

He seemed honestly to reflect. "The man? Why, I thought I saw Peters; I dashed after him to say a word about the stable-drains, but he had disappeared before I could get down."

"Disappeared? Why, he seemed to be walking so slowly when we saw him."

Boyne shrugged his shoulders. "So I thought; but he must have got up steam in the interval. What do you say to our trying a scramble up Meldon Steep before sunset?"

That was all. At the time the occurrence had been less than nothing, had, indeed, been immediately obliterated by the magic of their first vision from Meldon Steep, a height which they had dreamed of climbing ever since they had first seen its bare spine heaving itself above the low roof of Lyng. Doubtless it was the mere fact of the other incident's having occurred on the very day of their ascent to Meldon that had kept it stored away in the unconscious fold of association from which it now emerged; for in itself it had no mark of the portentous. At the moment there could have been nothing more natural than that Ned should dash himself from the roof in the pursuit of dilatory tradesmen. It was the period when they were always on the watch for one or the other of the specialists employed about the place; always lying in wait for them, and dashing out at them with questions, reproaches, or reminders. And certainly in the distance the gray figure had looked like Peters.

Yet now, as she reviewed the rapid scene, she felt her husband's explanation of it to have been invalidated by the look of anxiety on his face. Why had the familiar appearance of Peters made him anxious? Why, above all, if it was of such prime necessity to confer with that authority on the subject of the stable-drains, had the failure to find him produced such a look of relief? Mary could not say that any one of these considerations had occurred to her at the time, yet, from the promptness with which they now marshaled themselves at her summons, she had a sudden sense that they must all along have been there, waiting their hour.

II

Weary with her thoughts, she moved toward the window. The library was now completely dark, and she was surprised to see how much faint light the outer world still held.

As she peered out into it across the court, a figure shaped itself in the tapering perspective of bare lines: it looked a mere blot of deeper gray in the grayness, and for an instant, as it moved toward her, her heart thumped to the thought, "It's the ghost!"

She had time, in that long instant, to feel suddenly that the man of whom, two months earlier, she had a brief distant vision from the roof was now, at his predestined hour, about to reveal himself as *not* having been Peters; and her spirit sank under the impending fear of the disclosure. But almost with the next tick of the clock the ambiguous figure, gaining substance and character, showed itself even to her weak sight as her husband's; and she turned away to meet him, as he entered, with the confession of her folly.

"It's really too absurd," she laughed out from the threshold, "but I never *can* remember!"

"Remember what?" Boyne questioned as they drew together.

"That when one sees the Lyng ghost one never knows it."

Her hand was on his sleeve, and he kept it there, but with no response in his gesture or in the lines of his fagged, preoccupied face.

"Did you think you'd seen it?" he asked, after an appreciable interval.

"Why, I actually took *you* for it, my dear, in my mad determination to spot it!"

"Me—just now?" His arm dropped away, and he turned from her with a faint echo of her laugh. "Really, dearest, you'd better give it up, if that's the best you can do."

"Yes, I give it up—I give it up. Have *you*?" she asked, turning round on him abruptly.

The parlor-maid had entered with letters and a lamp, and the light struck up into Boyne's face as he bent above the tray she presented.

"Have *you*?" Mary perversely insisted, when the servant had disappeared on her errand of illumination.

"Have I what?" he rejoined absently, the light bringing out the sharp stamp of worry between his brows as he turned over the letters.

"Given up trying to see the ghost." Her heart beat a little at the experiment she was making.

Her husband, laying his letters aside, moved away into the shadow of the hearth.

"I never tried," he said, tearing open the wrapper of a newspaper.

"Well, of course," Mary persisted, "the exasperating thing is that there's no use trying, since one can't be sure till so long afterward."

He was unfolding the paper as if he had hardly heard her; but after a pause, during which the sheets rustled spasmodically between his hands, he lifted his head to say abruptly, "Have you any idea how long?"

Mary had sunk into a low chair beside the fireplace. From her seat she looked up, startled, at her husband's profile, which was darkly projected against the circle of lamplight.

"No; none. Have *you*?" she retorted, repeating her former phrase with an added keenness of intention.

Boyne crumpled the paper into a bunch, and then inconsequently turned back with it toward the lamp.

"Lord, no! I only meant," he explained, with a faint tinge of impatience, "is there any legend, any tradition, as to that?"

"Not that I know of," she answered; but the impulse to add, "What makes you ask?" was checked by the reappearance of the parlor-maid with tea and a second lamp.

With the dispersal of shadows, and the repetition of the daily domestic office, Mary Boyne felt herself less oppressed by that sense of something mutely imminent which had darkened her solitary afternoon. For a few moments she gave herself silently to the details of her task, and when she looked up from it she was struck to the point of bewilderment by the change in her husband's face. He had seated himself near the farther lamp, and was absorbed in the perusal of his letters; but was it something he had found in them, or merely the shifting of her own point of view, that had restored his features to their normal aspect? The longer she looked, the more definitely the change affirmed itself. The lines of painful tension had vanished, and such traces of fatigue as lingered were of the kind easily attributable to steady mental effort. He glanced up, as if drawn by her gaze, and met her eyes with a smile.

"I'm dying for my tea, you know; and here's a letter for you," he said.

She took the letter he held out in exchange for the cup she proffered him, and, returning to her seat, broke the seal with the languid gesture of the reader whose interests are all inclosed in the circle of one cherished presence.

Her next conscious motion was that of starting to her feet, the letter falling to them as she rose, while she held out to her husband a long newspaper clipping.

"Ned! What's this? What does it mean?"

He had risen at the same instant, almost as if hearing her cry before she uttered it; and for a perceptible space of time he and she studied each other, like adversaries watching for an advantage, across the space between her chair and his desk.

"What's what? You fairly made me jump!" Boyne said at length, moving toward her with a sudden, half-exasperated laugh. The shadow of apprehension was on his face again, not now a look of fixed foreboding, but a shifting vigilance of lips and eyes that gave her the sense of his feeling himself invisibly surrounded.

Her hand shook so that she could hardly give him the clipping.

"This article—from the *Waukesha Sentinel*—that a man named Elwell has brought suit against you—that there was something wrong about the Blue Star Mine. I can't understand more than half."

They continued to face each other as she spoke, and to her astonishment, she saw that her words had the almost immediate effect of dissipating the strained watchfulness of his look.

"Oh, *that!*" He glanced down the printed slip, and then folded it with the gesture of one who handles something harmless and familiar. "What's the matter with you this afternoon, Mary? I thought you'd got bad news."

She stood before him with her undefinable terror subsiding slowly under the reassuring touch of his composure.

"You knew about this, then—it's all right?"

"Certainly I knew about it; and it's all right."

"But what *is* it? I don't understand. What does this man accuse you of?"

"Oh, pretty nearly every crime in the calendar." Boyne had tossed the clipping down, and thrown himself comfortably into an arm-chair near the fire. "Do you want to hear the story? It's not particularly interesting—just a squabble over interests in the Blue Star."

"But who is this Elwell? I don't know the name."

"Oh, he's a fellow I put into it—gave him a hand up. I told you all about him at the time."

"I daresay. I must have forgotten." Vainly she strained back among her memories. "But if you helped him, why does he make this return?"

"Oh, probably some shyster lawyer got hold of him and talked him over. It's all rather technical and complicated. I thought that kind of thing bored you."

His wife felt a sting of compunction. Theoretically, she deprecated the American wife's detachment from her husband's professional interests, but in practice she had always found it difficult to fix her attention on Boyne's report of the transactions in which his varied interests involved him. Besides, she had felt from the first that, in a community where the amenities of living could be obtained only at the cost of efforts as arduous as her husband's professional labors, such brief leisure as they could command should be used as an escape from immediate preoccupations, a flight to the life they always dreamed of living. Once or twice, now that this new life had actually drawn its magic circle about them, she had asked herself if she had done right; but hitherto such conjectures had been no more than the retrospective excursions of an active fancy. Now, for the first time, it startled her a little to find how little she knew of the material foundation on which her happiness was built.

She glanced again at her husband, and was reassured by the composure of his face; yet she felt the need of more definite grounds for her reassurance.

"But doesn't this suit worry you? Why have you never spoken to me about it?"

He answered both questions at once: "I didn't speak of it at first because it *did* worry me—annoyed me, rather. But it's all ancient history now. Your correspondent must have got hold of a back number of the *Sentinel*."

She felt a quick thrill of relief. "You mean it's over? He's lost his case?"

There was a just perceptible delay in Boyne's reply. "The suit's been withdrawn—that's all."

But she persisted, as if to exonerate herself from the inward charge of being too easily put off. "Withdrawn because he saw he had no chance?"

"Oh, he had no chance," Boyne answered.

She was still struggling with a dimly felt perplexity at the back of her thoughts.

"How long ago was it withdrawn?"

He paused, as if with a slight return of his former uncertainty. "I've just had the news now; but I've been expecting it."

"Just now—in one of your letters?"

"Yes; in one of my letters."

She made no answer, and was aware only, after a short interval of waiting, that he had risen, and strolling across the room, had placed himself on the sofa at her side. She felt him, as he did so, pass an arm about her, she felt his hand seek hers and clasp it, and turning slowly, drawn by the warmth of his cheek, she met the smiling clearness of his eyes.

"It's all right—it's all right?" she questioned, through the flood of her dissolving doubts; and "I give you my word it never was righter!" he laughed back at her, holding her close.

III

One of the strangest things she was afterward to recall out of all the next day's incredible strangeness was the sudden and complete recovery of her sense of security.

It was in the air when she woke in her low-ceilinged, dusky room; it accompanied her down-stairs to the breakfast-table, flashed out at her from the fire, and re-duplicated itself brightly from the flanks of the urn and the sturdy flutings of the Georgian teapot. It was as if, in some roundabout way, all her diffused apprehensions of the previous day, with their moment of sharp concentration about the newspaper article,—as if this dim questioning of the future, and startled return upon the past,—had between them liquidated the arrears of some haunting moral obligation. If she had indeed been careless of her husband's affairs, it was, her new state seemed to prove, because her faith in him instinctively justified such carelessness; and his right to her faith had overwhelmingly affirmed itself in the very face of menace and suspicion. She had never seen him more untroubled, more naturally and unconsciously in possession of himself, than after the cross-examination to which she had subjected him: it was almost as if he had been aware of her lurking doubts, and had wanted the air cleared as much as she did.

It was as clear, thank Heaven! as the bright outer light that surprised her almost with a touch of summer when she issued from the house for her daily round of the gardens. She had left Boyne at his desk, indulging herself, as she passed the library door, by a last peep at his quiet face, where he bent, pipe in his mouth, above his papers, and now she had her own morning's task to perform. The task involved on such charmed winter days almost as much delighted loitering about the different quarters of her demesne as if spring were already at work on shrubs and borders. There were such inexhaustible possibilities still before her, such opportunities to bring out the latent graces of the old place, without a single irreverent touch of alteration, that the winter months were all too short to plan what spring and autumn executed. And her recovered sense of safety gave, on this particular morning, a peculiar zest to her progress through the sweet, still place. She went first to the kitchen-garden, where the espaliered pear-trees drew complicated patterns on the walls, and pigeons were fluttering and preening about the silvery-slated roof of their cot. There was something wrong about the piping of the hothouse, and she was expecting an authority from Dorchester, who was to drive out between trains and make a diagnosis of the boiler. But when she dipped into the damp heat of the greenhouses, among the spiced scents and waxy pinks and reds of old-fashioned exotics,—even the flora of Lyng was in the note!—she learned that the great man had not arrived, and the day being too rare to waste in an artificial atmosphere, she came out again and paced slowly along the springy turf of the bowling-green to the gardens behind the house. At their farther end rose a grass terrace, commanding, over the fish-pond and the yew hedges, a view of the long house-front, with its twisted chimney-stacks and the blue shadows of its roof angles, all drenched in the pale gold moisture of the air.

Seen thus, across the level tracery of the yews, under the suffused, mild light, it sent her, from its open windows and hospitably smoking chimneys, the look of some warm human presence, of a mind slowly ripened on a sunny wall of experience. She had never before had so deep a sense of her intimacy with it, such a conviction that its secrets were all beneficent, kept, as they said to children, "for one's good," so complete a trust in its power to gather up her life and Ned's into the harmonious pattern of the long, long story it sat there weaving in the sun.

She heard steps behind her, and turned, expecting to see the gardener, accompanied by the engineer from Dorchester. But only one figure was in sight, that of a youngish, slightly built man, who, for reasons she could not on the spot have specified, did not remotely resemble her preconceived notion of an authority on hot-house boilers. The new-comer, on seeing her, lifted his hat, and paused with the air of a gentleman—perhaps a traveler-desirous of having it immediately known that his intrusion is involuntary. The local fame of Lyng occasionally attracted the more intelligent sight-seer, and Mary half-expected to see the stranger dissemble a camera, or justify his presence by producing it. But he made no gesture of any sort, and after a moment she asked, in a tone responding to the courteous deprecation of his attitude: "Is there any one you wish to see?"

"I came to see Mr. Boyne," he replied. His intonation, rather than his accent, was faintly American, and Mary, at the familiar note, looked at him more closely. The brim of his soft felt hat cast a shade on his face, which, thus obscured, wore to her short-sighted gaze a look of seriousness, as of a person arriving "on business," and civilly but firmly aware of his rights.

Past experience had made Mary equally sensible to such claims; but she was jealous of her husband's morning hours, and doubtful of his having given any one the right to intrude on them.

"Have you an appointment with Mr. Boyne?" she asked.

He hesitated, as if unprepared for the question.

"Not exactly an appointment," he replied.

"Then I'm afraid, this being his working-time, that he can't receive you now. Will you give me a message, or come back later?"

The visitor, again lifting his hat, briefly replied that he would come back later, and walked away, as if to regain the front of the house. As his figure receded down the walk between the yew hedges, Mary saw him pause and look up an instant at the peaceful house-front bathed in faint winter sunshine; and it struck her, with a tardy touch of compunction, that it would have been more humane to ask if he had come from a distance, and to offer, in that case, to inquire if her husband could receive him. But as the thought occurred to her he passed out of sight behind a pyramidal yew, and at the same moment her attention was distracted by the approach of the gardener, attended by the bearded pepper-and-salt figure of the boiler-maker from Dorchester.

The encounter with this authority led to such far-reaching issues that they resulted in his finding it expedient to ignore his train, and beguiled Mary into spending the remainder of the morning in absorbed confabulation among the greenhouses. She was startled to find, when the colloquy ended, that it was nearly luncheon-time, and she half expected, as she hurried back to the house, to see her husband coming out to meet her. But she found no one in the court but an under-gardener raking the gravel, and the hall, when she entered it, was so silent that she guessed Boyne to be still at work behind the closed door of the library.

Not wishing to disturb him, she turned into the drawing-room, and there, at her writing-table, lost herself in renewed calculations of the outlay to which the morning's conference had committed her. The knowledge that she could permit herself such follies had not yet lost its novelty; and somehow, in contrast to the vague apprehensions of the previous days, it now seemed an element of her recovered security, of the sense that, as Ned had said, things in general had never been "righter."

She was still luxuriating in a lavish play of figures when the parlor-maid, from the threshold, roused her with a dubiously worded inquiry as to the expediency of serving luncheon. It was one of their jokes that Trimmle announced luncheon as if she were divulging a state secret, and Mary, intent upon her papers, merely murmured an absent-minded assent.

She felt Trimmle wavering expressively on the threshold as if in rebuke of such offhand acquiescence; then her retreating steps sounded down the passage, and Mary, pushing away her papers, crossed the hall, and went to the library door. It was still closed, and she wavered in her turn, disliking to disturb her husband, yet anxious that he should not exceed his normal measure of work. As she stood there, balancing her impulses, the esoteric Trimmle returned with the announcement of luncheon, and Mary, thus impelled, opened the door and went into the library.

Boyne was not at his desk, and she peered about her, expecting to discover him at the book-shelves, somewhere down the length of the room; but her call brought no response, and gradually it became clear to her that he was not in the library.

She turned back to the parlor-maid.

"Mr. Boyne must be up-stairs. Please tell him that luncheon is ready."

The parlor-maid appeared to hesitate between the obvious duty of obeying orders and an equally obvious conviction of the foolishness of the injunction laid upon her. The struggle resulted in her saying doubtfully, "If you please, Madam, Mr. Boyne's not up-stairs."

"Not in his room? Are you sure?"

"I'm sure, Madam."

Mary consulted the clock. "Where is he, then?"

"He's gone out," Trimmle announced, with the superior air of one who has respectfully waited for the question that a well-ordered mind would have first propounded.

Mary's previous conjecture had been right, then. Boyne must have gone to the gardens to meet her, and since she had missed him, it was clear that he had taken the shorter way by the south door, instead of going round to the court. She crossed the hall to the glass portal opening directly on the yew garden, but the parlor-maid, after another moment of inner conflict, decided to bring out recklessly, "Please, Madam, Mr. Boyne didn't go that way."

Mary turned back. "Where *did* he go? And when?"

"He went out of the front door, up the drive, Madam." It was a matter of principle with Trimmle never to answer more than one question at a time.

"Up the drive? At this hour?" Mary went to the door herself, and glanced across the court through the long tunnel of bare limes. But its perspective was as empty as when she had scanned it on entering the house.

"Did Mr. Boyne leave no message?" she asked.

Trimmle seemed to surrender herself to a last struggle with the forces of chaos.

"No, Madam. He just went out with the gentleman."

"The gentleman? What gentleman?" Mary wheeled about, as if to front this new factor.

"The gentleman who called, Madam," said Trimmle, resignedly.

"When did a gentleman call? Do explain yourself, Trimmle!"

Only the fact that Mary was very hungry, and that she wanted to consult her husband about the greenhouses, would have caused her to lay so unusual an injunction on her attendant; and even now she was detached enough to note in Trimmle's eye the dawning defiance of the respectful subordinate who has been pressed too hard.

"I couldn't exactly say the hour, Madam, because I didn't let the gentleman in," she replied, with the air of magnanimously ignoring the irregularity of her mistress's course.

"You didn't let him in?"

"No, Madam. When the bell rang I was dressing, and Agnes—"

"Go and ask Agnes, then," Mary interjected. Trimmle still wore her look of patient magnanimity. "Agnes would not know, Madam, for she had unfortunately burnt her hand in trying the wick of the new lamp from town—" Trimmle, as Mary was aware, had always been opposed to the new lamp—"and so Mrs. Dockett sent the kitchen-maid instead."

Mary looked again at the clock. "It's after two! Go and ask the kitchen-maid if Mr. Boyne left any word."

She went into luncheon without waiting, and Trimmle presently brought her there the kitchen-maid's statement that the gentleman had called about one o'clock, that Mr. Boyne had gone out with him without leaving any message. The kitchen-maid did not even know the caller's name, for he had written it on a slip of paper, which he had folded and handed to her, with the injunction to deliver it at once to Mr. Boyne.

Mary finished her luncheon, still wondering, and when it was over, and Trimmle had brought the coffee to the drawing-room, her wonder had deepened to a first faint tinge of disquietude. It was unlike Boyne to absent himself without explanation at so unwonted an hour, and the difficulty of identifying the visitor whose summons he had apparently obeyed made his disappearance the more unaccountable. Mary Boyne's experience as the wife of a busy engineer, subject to sudden calls and compelled to keep irregular hours, had trained her to the philosophic acceptance of surprises; but since Boyne's withdrawal from business he had adopted a Benedictine regularity of life. As if to make up for the dispersed and agitated years, with their "stand-up" lunches and dinners rattled down to the joltings of the dining-car, he cultivated the last refinements of punctuality and monotony, discouraging his wife's fancy for the unexpected; and declaring that to a delicate taste there were infinite gradations of pleasure in the fixed recurrences of habit.

Still, since no life can completely defend itself from the unforeseen, it was evident that all Boyne's precautions would sooner or later prove unavailable, and Mary concluded that he had cut short a tiresome visit by walking with his caller to the station, or at least accompanying him for part of the way.

This conclusion relieved her from farther preoccupation, and she went out herself to take up her conference with the gardener. Thence she walked to the village post-office, a mile or so away; and when she turned toward home, the early twilight was setting in.

She had taken a foot-path across the downs, and as Boyne, meanwhile, had probably returned from the station by the highroad, there was little likelihood of their meeting on the way. She felt sure, however, of his having reached the house before her; so sure that, when she entered it herself, without even pausing to inquire of Trimmle, she made directly for the library. But the library was still empty, and with an unwonted precision of visual memory she immediately observed that the papers on her husband's desk lay precisely as they had lain when she had gone in to call him to luncheon.

Then of a sudden she was seized by a vague dread of the unknown. She had closed the door behind her on entering, and as she stood alone in the long, silent, shadowy room, her dread seemed to take shape and sound, to be there audibly breathing and lurking among the shadows. Her short-sighted eyes strained through them, half-discerning an actual presence, something aloof, that watched and knew; and in the recoil from that intangible propinquity she threw herself suddenly on the bell-rope and gave it a desperate pull.

The long, quavering summons brought Trimmle in precipitately with a lamp, and Mary breathed again at this sobering reappearance of the usual.

"You may bring tea if Mr. Boyne is in," she said, to justify her ring.

"Very well, Madam. But Mr. Boyne is not in," said Trimmle, putting down the lamp.

"Not in? You mean he's come back and gone out again?"

"No, Madam. He's never been back."

The dread stirred again, and Mary knew that now it had her fast.

"Not since he went out with—the gentleman?"

"Not since he went out with the gentleman."

"But who *was* the gentleman?" Mary gasped out, with the sharp note of some one trying to be heard through a confusion of meaningless noises.

"That I couldn't say, Madam." Trimmle, standing there by the lamp, seemed suddenly to grow less round and rosy, as though eclipsed by the same creeping shade of apprehension.

"But the kitchen-maid knows—wasn't it the kitchen-maid who let him in?"

"She doesn't know either, Madam, for he wrote his name on a folded paper."

Mary, through her agitation, was aware that they were both

designating the unknown visitor by a vague pronoun, instead of the conventional formula which, till then, had kept their allusions within the bounds of custom. And at the same moment her mind caught at the suggestion of the folded paper.

"But he must have a name! Where is the paper?"

She moved to the desk, and began to turn over the scattered documents that littered it. The first that caught her eye was an unfinished letter in her husband's hand, with his pen lying across it, as though dropped there at a sudden summons.

"My dear Parvis,"—who was Parvis?—"I have just received your letter announcing Elwell's death, and while I suppose there is now no farther risk of trouble, it might be safer—"

She tossed the sheet aside, and continued her search; but no folded paper was discoverable among the letters and pages of manuscript which had been swept together in a promiscuous heap, as if by a hurried or a startled gesture.

"But the kitchen-maid *saw* him. Send her here," she commanded, wondering at her dullness in not thinking sooner of so simple a solution.

Trimmle, at the behest, vanished in a flash, as if thankful to be out of the room, and when she reappeared, conducting the agitated underling, Mary had regained her self-possession, and had her questions pat.

The gentleman was a stranger, yes—that she understood. But what had he said? And, above all, what had he looked like? The first question was easily enough answered, for the disconcerting reason that he had said so little—had merely asked for Mr. Boyne, and, scribbling something on a bit of paper, had requested that it should at once be carried in to him.

"Then you don't know what he wrote? You're not sure it was his name?"

The kitchen-maid was not sure, but supposed it was, since he had written it in answer to her inquiry as to whom she should announce.

"And when you carried the paper in to Mr. Boyne, what did he say?"

The kitchen-maid did not think that Mr. Boyne had said anything, but she could not be sure, for just as she had handed him the paper and he was opening it, she had become aware that the visitor had followed her into the library, and she had slipped out, leaving the two gentlemen together.

"But then, if you left them in the library, how do you know that they went out of the house?"

This question plunged the witness into momentary inarticulateness, from which she was rescued by Trimmle, who, by means of ingenious circumlocutions, elicited the statement that before she could cross the hall to the back passage she had heard the gentlemen behind her, and had seen them go out of the front door together.

"Then, if you saw the gentleman twice, you must be able to tell me what he looked like."

But with this final challenge to her powers of expression it became clear that the limit of the kitchen-maid's endurance had been reached. The obligation of going to the front door to "show in" a visitor was in itself so subversive of the fundamental order of things that it had thrown her faculties into hopeless disarray, and she could only stammer out, after various panting efforts at evocation, "His hat, mum, was different-like, as you might say—"

"Different? How different?" Mary flashed out at her, her own mind, in the same instant, leaping back to an image left on it that morning, but temporarily lost under layers of subsequent impressions.

"His hat had a wide brim, you mean? and his face was pale—a youngish face?" Mary pressed her, with a white-lipped intensity of interrogation. But if the kitchen-maid found any adequate answer to this challenge, it was swept away for her listener down the rushing current of her own convictions. The stranger—the stranger in the garden! Why had Mary not thought of him before?

She needed no one now to tell her that it was he who had called for her husband and gone away with him. But who was he, and why had Boyne obeyed his call?

IV

It leaped out at her suddenly, like a grin out of the dark, that they had often called England so little—"such a confoundedly hard place to get lost in."

A confoundedly hard place to get lost in! That had been her husband's phrase. And now, with the whole machinery of official investigation sweeping its flash-lights from shore to shore, and across the dividing straits; now, with Boyne's name blazing from the walls of every town and village, his portrait (how that wrung her!) hawked up and down the country like the image of a hunted criminal; now the little compact, populous island, so policed, surveyed, and administered, revealed itself as a Sphinx-like guardian of abysmal mysteries, staring back into his wife's anguished eyes as if with the malicious joy of knowing something they would never know!

In the fortnight since Boyne's disappearance there had been no word of him, no trace of his movements. Even the usual misleading reports that raise expectancy in tortured bosoms had been few and fleeting. No one but the bewildered kitchen-maid had seen him leave the house, and no one else had seen "the gentleman" who accompanied him. All inquiries in the neighborhood failed to elicit the memory of a stranger's presence that day in the neighborhood of Lyng. And no one had met Edward Boyne, either alone or in company, in any of the neighboring villages, or on the road across the downs, or at either of the local railway-stations. The sunny English noon had swallowed him as completely as if he had gone out into Cimmerian night.

Mary, while every external means of investigation was working at its highest pressure, had ransacked her husband's papers for any

341

trace of antecedent complications, of entanglements or obligations unknown to her, that might throw a faint ray into the darkness. But if any such had existed in the background of Boyne's life, they had disappeared as completely as the slip of paper on which the visitor had written his name. There remained no possible thread of guidance except—if it were indeed an exception—the letter which Boyne had apparently been in the act of writing when he received his mysterious summons. That letter, read and reread by his wife, and submitted by her to the police, yielded little enough for conjecture to feed on.

"I have just heard of Elwell's death, and while I suppose there is now no farther risk of trouble, it might be safer—" That was all. The "risk of trouble" was easily explained by the newspaper clipping which had apprised Mary of the suit brought against her husband by one of his associates in the Blue Star enterprise. The only new information conveyed in the letter was the fact of its showing Boyne, when he wrote it, to be still apprehensive of the results of the suit, though he had assured his wife that it had been withdrawn, and though the letter itself declared that the plaintiff was dead. It took several weeks of exhaustive cabling to fix the identity of the "Parvis" to whom the fragmentary communication was addressed, but even after these inquiries had shown him to be a Waukesha lawyer, no new facts concerning the Elwell suit were elicited. He appeared to have had no direct concern in it, but to have been conversant with the facts merely as an acquaintance, and possible intermediary; and he declared himself unable to divine with what object Boyne intended to seek his assistance.

This negative information, sole fruit of the first fortnight's feverish search, was not increased by a jot during the slow weeks that followed. Mary knew that the investigations were still being carried on, but she had a vague sense of their gradually slackening, as the actual march of time seemed to slacken. It was as though the days, flying horror-struck from the shrouded image of the one inscrutable day, gained assurance as the distance lengthened, till at last they fell back into their normal gait. And so with the human imaginations at work on the dark event. No doubt it occupied them still, but week by week and hour by hour it grew less absorbing, took up less space, was slowly but inevitably crowded out of the foreground of consciousness by the new problems perpetually bubbling up from the vaporous caldron of human experience.

Even Mary Boyne's consciousness gradually felt the same lowering of velocity. It still swayed with the incessant oscillations of conjecture; but they were slower, more rhythmical in their beat. There were moments of overwhelming lassitude when, like the victim of some poison which leaves the brain clear, but holds the body motionless, she saw herself domesticated with the Horror, accepting its perpetual presence as one of the fixed conditions of life.

These moments lengthened into hours and days, till she passed into a phase of stolid acquiescence. She watched the familiar routine of life with the incurious eye of a savage on whom the meaningless processes of civilization make but the faintest impression. She had come to regard herself as part of the routine, a spoke of the wheel, revolving with its motion; she felt almost like the furniture of the room in which she sat, an insensate object to be dusted and pushed about with the chairs and tables. And this deepening apathy held her fast at Lyng, in spite of the urgent entreaties of friends and the usual medical recommendation of "change." Her friends supposed that her refusal to move was inspired by the belief that her husband would one day return to the spot from which he had vanished, and a beautiful legend grew up about this imaginary state of waiting. But in reality she had no such belief: the depths of anguish inclosing her were no longer lighted by flashes of hope. She was sure that Boyne would never come back, that he had gone out of her sight as completely as if Death itself had waited that day on the threshold. She had even renounced, one by one, the various theories as to his disappearance which had been advanced by the press, the police, and her own agonized imagination. In sheer lassitude her mind turned from these alternatives of horror, and sank back into the blank fact that he was gone.

No, she would never know what had become of him—no one would ever know. But the house *knew*; the library in which she spent her long, lonely evenings knew. For it was here that the last scene had been enacted, here that the stranger had come, and spoken the word which had caused Boyne to rise and follow him. The floor she trod had felt his tread; the books on the shelves had seen his face; and there were moments when the intense consciousness of the old, dusky walls seemed about to break out into some audible revelation of their secret. But the revelation never came, and she knew it would never come. Lyng was not one of the garrulous old houses that betray the secrets intrusted to them. Its very legend proved that it had always been the mute accomplice, the incorruptible custodian of the mysteries it had surprised. And Mary Boyne, sitting face to face with its portentous silence, felt the futility of seeking to break it by any human means.

V

"I don't say it *wasn't* straight, yet don't say it *was* straight. It was business."

Mary, at the words, lifted her head with a start, and looked intently at the speaker.

When, half an hour before, a card with "Mr. Parvis" on it had been brought up to her, she had been immediately aware that the name had been a part of her consciousness ever since she had read it at the head of Boyne's unfinished letter. In the library she had found awaiting her a small neutral-tinted man with a bald head and gold eye-glasses, and it sent a strange tremor through her to know that this was the person to whom her husband's last known thought had been directed.

Parvis, civilly, but without vain preamble,—in the manner of a man who has his watch in his hand,—had set forth the object of his visit. He had "run over" to England on business, and finding himself in the neighborhood of Dorchester, had not wished to leave it without paying his respects to Mrs. Boyne; without asking her, if the occasion offered, what she meant to do about Bob Elwell's family.

The words touched the spring of some obscure dread in Mary's bosom. Did her visitor, after all, know what Boyne had meant by his unfinished phrase? She asked for an elucidation of his question, and noticed at once that he seemed surprised at her continued ignorance of the subject. Was it possible that she really knew as little as she said?

"I know nothing—you must tell me," she faltered out; and her visitor thereupon proceeded to unfold his story. It threw, even to her confused perceptions, and imperfectly initiated vision, a lurid glare on the whole hazy episode of the Blue Star Mine. Her husband had made his money in that brilliant speculation at the cost of "getting ahead" of some one less alert to seize the chance; the victim of his ingenuity was young Robert Elwell, who had "put him on" to the Blue Star scheme.

Parvis, at Mary's first startled cry, had thrown her a sobering glance through his impartial glasses.

"Bob Elwell wasn't smart enough, that's all; if he had been, he might have turned round and served Boyne the same way. It's the kind of thing that happens every day in business. I guess it's what the scientists call the survival of the fittest," said Mr. Parvis, evidently pleased with the aptness of his analogy.

Mary felt a physical shrinking from the next question she tried to frame; it was as though the words on her lips had a taste that nauseated her.

"But then—you accuse my husband of doing something dishonorable?"

Mr. Parvis surveyed the question dispassionately. "Oh, no, I don't. I don't even say it wasn't straight." He glanced up and down the long lines of books, as if one of them might have supplied him with the definition he sought. "I don't say it *wasn't* straight, and yet

345

I don't say it *was* straight. It was business." After all, no definition in his category could be more comprehensive than that.

Mary sat staring at him with a look of terror. He seemed to her like the indifferent, implacable emissary of some dark, formless power.

"But Mr. Elwell's lawyers apparently did not take your view, since I suppose the suit was withdrawn by their advice."

"Oh, yes, they knew he hadn't a leg to stand on, technically. It was when they advised him to withdraw the suit that he got desperate. You see, he'd borrowed most of the money he lost in the Blue Star, and he was up a tree. That's why he shot himself when they told him he had no show."

The horror was sweeping over Mary in great, deafening waves.

"He shot himself? He killed himself because of *that*?"

"Well, he didn't kill himself, exactly. He dragged on two months before he died." Parvis emitted the statement as unemotionally as a gramophone grinding out its "record."

"You mean that he tried to kill himself, and failed? And tried again?"

"Oh, he didn't have to try again," said Parvis, grimly.

They sat opposite each other in silence, he swinging his eye-glass thoughtfully about his finger, she, motionless, her arms stretched along her knees in an attitude of rigid tension.

"But if you knew all this," she began at length, hardly able to force her voice above a whisper, "how is it that when I wrote you at the time of my husband's disappearance you said you didn't understand his letter?"

Parvis received this without perceptible discomfiture. "Why, I didn't understand it—strictly speaking. And it wasn't the time to talk about it, if I had. The Elwell business was settled when the suit was withdrawn. Nothing I could have told you would have helped you to find your husband."

Mary continued to scrutinize him. "Then why are you telling me now?"

Still Parvis did not hesitate. "Well, to begin with, I supposed you knew more than you appear to—I mean about the circumstances of Elwell's death. And then people are talking of it now; the whole matter's been raked up again. And I thought, if you didn't know, you ought to."

She remained silent, and he continued: "You see, it's only come out lately what a bad state Elwell's affairs were in. His wife's a proud woman, and she fought on as long as she could, going out to work, and taking sewing at home, when she got too sick—something with the heart, I believe. But she had his bedridden mother to look after, and the children, and she broke down under it, and finally had to ask for help. That attracted attention to the case, and the papers took it up, and a subscription was started. Everybody out there liked Bob Elwell, and most of the prominent names in the place are down on the list, and people began to wonder why—"

Parvis broke off to fumble in an inner pocket. "Here," he continued, "here's an account of the whole thing from the *Sentinel*—a little sensational, of course. But I guess you'd better look it over."

He held out a newspaper to Mary, who unfolded it slowly, remembering, as she did so, the evening when, in that same room, the perusal of a clipping from the *Sentinel* had first shaken the depths of her security.

As she opened the paper, her eyes, shrinking from the glaring head-lines, "Widow of Boyne's Victim Forced to Appeal for Aid," ran down the column of text to two portraits inserted in it. The first was her husband's, taken from a photograph made the year they had come to England. It was the picture of him that she liked best, the one that stood on the writing-table up-stairs in her bedroom. As the eyes in the photograph met hers, she felt it would be impossible to read what was said of him, and closed her lids with the sharpness of the pain.

"I thought if you felt disposed to put your name down—" she heard Parvis continue.

She opened her eyes with an effort, and they fell on the other portrait. It was that of a youngish man, slightly built, in rough clothes, with features somewhat blurred by the shadow of a projecting hat-brim. Where had she seen that outline before? She stared at it confusedly, her heart hammering in her throat and ears. Then she gave a cry.

"This is the man—the man who came for my husband!"

She heard Parvis start to his feet, and was dimly aware that she had slipped backward into the corner of the sofa, and that he was bending above her in alarm. With an intense effort she straightened herself, and reached out for the paper, which she had dropped.

"It's the man! I should know him anywhere!" she cried in a voice that sounded in her own ears like a scream.

Parvis's voice seemed to come to her from far off, down endless, fog-muffled windings.

"Mrs. Boyne, you're not very well. Shall I call somebody? Shall I get a glass of water?"

"No, no, no!" She threw herself toward him, her hand frantically clenching the newspaper. "I tell you, it's the man! I *know* him! He spoke to me in the garden!"

Parvis took the journal from her, directing his glasses to the portrait. "It can't be, Mrs. Boyne. It's Robert Elwell."

"Robert Elwell?" Her white stare seemed to travel into space. "Then it was Robert Elwell who came for him."

"Came for Boyne? The day he went away?" Parvis's voice dropped as hers rose. He bent over, laying a fraternal hand on her, as if to coax her gently back into her seat. "Why, Elwell was dead! Don't you remember?"

Mary sat with her eyes fixed on the picture, unconscious of what he was saying.

"Don't you remember Boyne's unfinished letter to me—the one you found on his desk that day? It was written just after he'd heard of Elwell's death." She noticed an odd shake in Parvis's unemotional voice. "Surely you remember that!" he urged her.

Yes, she remembered: that was the profoundest horror of it. Elwell had died the day before her husband's disappearance; and this was Elwell's portrait; and it was the portrait of the man who had spoken to her in the garden. She lifted her head and looked slowly about the library. The library could have borne witness that it was also the portrait of the man who had come in that day to call Boyne from his unfinished letter. Through the misty surgings of her brain she heard the faint boom of half-forgotten words—words spoken by Alida Stair on the lawn at Pangbourne before Boyne and his wife had ever seen the house at Lyng, or had imagined that they might one day live there.

"This was the man who spoke to me," she repeated.

She looked again at Parvis. He was trying to conceal his disturbance under what he imagined to be an expression of indulgent commiseration; but the edges of his lips were blue. "He thinks me mad; but I'm not mad," she reflected; and suddenly there flashed upon her a way of justifying her strange affirmation.

She sat quiet, controlling the quiver of her lips, and waiting till she could trust her voice to keep its habitual level; then she said, looking straight at Parvis: "Will you answer me one question, please? When was it that Robert Elwell tried to kill himself?"

"When—when?" Parvis stammered.

"Yes; the date. Please try to remember."

She saw that he was growing still more afraid of her. "I have a reason," she insisted gently.

"Yes, yes. Only I can't remember. About two months before, I should say."

"I want the date," she repeated.

Parvis picked up the newspaper. "We might see here," he said, still humoring her. He ran his eyes down the page. "Here it is. Last October—the—"

She caught the words from him. "The 20th, wasn't it?"

With a sharp look at her, he verified. "Yes, the 20th. Then you *did* know?"

"I know now." Her white stare continued to travel past him. "Sunday, the 20th—that was the day he came first."

Parvis's voice was almost inaudible. "Came *here* first?"

"Yes."

"You saw him twice, then?"

"Yes, twice." She breathed it at him with dilated eyes. "He came first on the 20th of October. I remember the date because it was the day we went up Meldon Steep for the first time." She felt a faint gasp of inward laughter at the thought that but for that she might have forgotten.

Parvis continued to scrutinize her, as if trying to intercept her gaze.

"We saw him from the roof," she went on. "He came down the lime-avenue toward the house. He was dressed just as he is in that picture. My husband saw him first. He was frightened, and ran down ahead of me; but there was no one there. He had vanished."

"Elwell had vanished?" Parvis faltered.

"Yes." Their two whispers seemed to grope for each other. "I couldn't think what had happened. I see now. He *tried* to come then; but he wasn't dead enough—he couldn't reach us. He had to wait for two months; and then he came back again—and Ned went with him."

She nodded at Parvis with the look of triumph of a child who has successfully worked out a difficult puzzle. But suddenly she lifted her hands with a desperate gesture, pressing them to her bursting temples.

"Oh, my God! I sent him to Ned—I told him where to go! I sent him to this room!" she screamed out.

She felt the walls of the room rush toward her, like inward falling ruins; and she heard Parvis, a long way off, as if through the ruins, crying to her, and struggling to get at her. But she was numb to his touch, she did not know what he was saying. Through the tumult she heard but one clear note, the voice of Alida Stair, speaking on the lawn at Pangbourne.

"You won't know till afterward," it said. "You won't know till long, long afterward."

The Watcher

RH Benson

"Il faut d'abord rendre l'organe de la vision analogue et semblable à l'objet qu'il doit contempler."

Maeterlinck

On the following day we went out soon after breakfast and walked up and down a grass path between two yew hedges; the dew was not yet off the grass that lay in shadow; and thin patches of gossamer still hung like torn cambric on the yew shoots on either side. As we passed for the second time up the path, the old man suddenly stooped and pushing aside a dock-leaf at the foot of the hedge lifted a dead mouse, and looked at it as it lay stiffly on the palm of his hand, and I saw that his eyes filled slowly with the ready tears of old age.

"He has chose his own resting-place," he said. "Let him lie there. Why did I disturb him?"—and he laid him gently down again; and then gathering a fragment of wet earth he sprinkled it over the mouse. "Earth to earth, ashes to ashes," he said, "in sure and certain hope"—and then he stopped; and straightening himself with difficulty walked on, and I followed him.

"You seemed interested," he said, "in my story yesterday. Shall I tell you how I saw a very different sight when I was a little older." And when I had told him how strange and attractive his story had been, he began.

"I told you how I found it impossible to see again what I had seen in the glade. For a few weeks, perhaps months, I tried now and then to force myself to feel that Presence, or at least to see that robe but I could not, because it is the gift of God, and can no more be gained by effort than ordinary sight can be won by a sightless man; but I soon ceased to try.

"I reached eighteen years at last, that terrible age when the soul seems to have dwindled to a spark overlaid by a mountain of ashes—when blood and fire and death and loud noises seem the only things of interest, and all tender things shrink back and hide from the dreadful noonday of manhood. Some one gave me one of those shot-pistols that you may have seen, and I loved the sense of power that it gave me, for I had never had a gun. For a week or two in the summer holidays I was content with shooting at a mark, or at the level surface of water, and delighted to see the cardboard shattered, or the quiet pool torn to shreds along its mirror where the sky and green lay sleeping. Then that ceased to interest me, and I longed to see a living thing suddenly stop living at my will. Now," and he held up a deprecating hand, "I think sport is necessary for some natures. After all the killing of creatures is necessary for man's food, and sport as you will tell me is a survival of man's delight in obtaining food, and it requires certain noble qualities of endurance and skill. I know all that, and I know further that for some natures it is a relief—an escape for humours that will otherwise find an evil vent. But I do know this—that for me it was not necessary.

"However, there was every excuse, and I went out in good faith one summer evening intending to shoot some rabbit as he ran to cover from the open field. I walked along the inside of a fence with a wood above me and on my left, and the green meadow on my right. Well, owing probably to my own lack of skill, though I could hear the patter and rush of the rabbits around me, and could see them in the distance sitting up listening with cocked ears, as I stole along the fence, I could not get close enough to fire at them with any hope of what I fancied was success; and by the time that I arrived at the end of the wood I was in an impatient mood.

"I stood for a moment or two leaning on the fence looking out of that pleasant coolness into the open meadow beyond; the sun had at that moment dipped behind the hill before me and all was in shadow except where there hung a glory about the topmost leaves of a beech that still caught the sun. The birds were beginning to come in from the fields, and were settling one by one in the wood behind me, staying here and there to sing one last line of melody. I could hear the quiet rush and then the sudden clap of a pigeon's wings as he came home, and as I listened I heard pealing out above all other sounds the long liquid song of a thrush somewhere above me. I looked up idly and tried to see the bird, and after a moment or two caught sight of him as the leaves of the beech parted in the breeze, his head lifted and his whole body vibrating with the joy of life and music. As some one has said, his body was one beating heart. The last radiance of the sun over the hill reached him and bathed him in golden warmth. Then the leaves closed again as the breeze dropped but still his song rang out.

"Then there came on me a blinding desire to kill him. All the other creatures had mocked me and run home. Here at least was a victim, and I would pour out the sullen anger that had been gathering during my walk, and at least demand this one life as a substitute. Side by side with this I remembered clearly that I had come out to kill for food: that was my one justification. Side by side I saw both these things, and I had no excuse—no excuse.

"I turned my head every way and moved a step or two back to catch sight of him again, and, although this may sound fantastic and overwrought, in my whole being was a struggle between light and darkness. Every fibre of my life told me that the thrush had a right to live. Ah! he had earned it, if labour were wanting, by this very song that was guiding death towards him, but black sullen anger had thrown my conscience, and was now struggling to hold it down till the shot had been fired. Still I waited for the breeze,

355

and then it came, cool and sweet-smelling like the breath of a garden, and the leaves parted. There he sang in the sunshine, and in a moment I lifted the pistol and drew the trigger.

With the crack of the cap came silence overhead, and after what seemed an interminable moment came the soft rush of something falling and the faint thud among last year's leaves. Then I stood half terrified, and stared among the dead leaves. All seemed dim and misty. My eyes were still a little dazzled by the bright background of sunlit air and rosy clouds on which I had looked with such intensity, and the space beneath the branches was a world of shadows. Still I looked a few yards away, trying to make out the body of the thrush, and fearing to hear a struggle of beating wings among the dry leaves.

"And then I lifted my eyes a little, vaguely. A yard or two beyond where the thrush lay was a rhododendron bush. The blossoms had fallen and the outline of dark, heavy leaves was unrelieved by the slightest touch of colour. As I looked at it, I saw a face looking down from the higher branches.

"It was a perfectly hairless head and face, the thin lips were parted in a wide smile of laughter, there were innumerable lines about the corners of the mouth, and the eyes were surrounded by creases of merriment. What was perhaps most terrible about it all was that the eyes were not looking at me, but down among the leaves; the heavy eyelids lay drooping, and the long, narrow, shining slits showed how the eyes laughed beneath them. The forehead sloped quickly back, like a cat's head. The face was the colour of earth, and the outlines of the head faded below the ears and chin into the gloom of the dark bush. There was no throat, or body or limbs so far as I could see. The face just hung there like a down-turned Eastern mask in an old curiosity shop. And it smiled with sheer delight, not at me, but at the thrush's body. There was no change of expression so long as I watched it, just a silent smile of pleasure petrified on the face. I could not move my eyes from it.

"After what I suppose was a minute or so, the face had gone. I did not see it go, but I became aware that I was looking only at leaves.

"No; there was no outline of leaf, or play of shadows that could possibly have taken the form of a face. You can guess how I tried to force myself to believe that that was all; how I turned my head this way and that to catch it again; but there was no hint of a face.

"Now, I cannot tell you how I did it; but although I was half beside myself with fright, I went forward towards the bush and searched furiously among the leaves for the body of the thrush; and at last I found it, and lifted it. It was still limp and warm to the touch. Its breast was a little ruffled, and one tiny drop of blood lay at the root of the beak below the eyes, like a tear of dismay and sorrow at such an unmerited, unexpected death.

"I carried it to the fence and climbed over, and then began to run in great steps, looking now and then awfully at the gathering gloom of the wood behind, where the laughing face had mocked the dead. I think, looking back as I do now, that my chief instinct was that I could not leave the thrush there to be laughed at, and that I must get it out into the clean, airy meadow. When I reached the middle of the meadow I came to a pond which never ran quite dry even in the hottest summer. On the bank I laid the thrush down, and then deliberately but with all my force dashed the pistol into the water; then emptied my pockets of the cartridges and threw them in too.

"Then I turned again to the piteous little body, feeling that at least I had tried to make amends. There was an old rabbit hold near, the grass growing down in its mouth, and a tangle of web and dead leaves behind. I scooped a little space out among the leaves, and then laid the thrush there; gathered a little of the sandy soil and poured it over the body, saying, I remember, half unconsciously, 'Earth to earth, ashes to ashes, in sure and certain hope'—and then I stopped, feeling I had been a little profane, though I do not think so now. And then I went home.

357

"As I dressed for dinner, looking out over the darkening meadow where the thrush lay, I remember feeling happy that no evil thing could mock the defenceless dead out there in the clean meadow where the wind blew and the stars shone down."

We reached in our going to and fro up the yew path a little seat at the end standing back from the path. Opposite us hung a crucifix, with a pent-house over it, that the old man had put up years before. As he did not speak I turned to him, and saw that he was looking steadily at the Figure on the Cross; and I thought how He who bore our griefs and carried our sorrow was one with the heavenly Father, without whom not even a sparrow falls to the ground.

The Yellow Wallpaper
Charlotte Perkins Gilman

It is very seldom that mere ordinary people like John and myself secure ancestral halls for the summer.

A colonial mansion, a hereditary estate, I would say a haunted house, and reach the height of romantic felicity—but that would be asking too much of fate!

Still I will proudly declare that there is something queer about it.

Else, why should it be let so cheaply? And why have stood so long untenanted?

John laughs at me, of course, but one expects that in marriage.

John is practical in the extreme. He has no patience with faith, an intense horror of superstition, and he scoffs openly at any talk of things not to be felt and seen and put down in figures.

John is a physician, and *perhaps*—(I would not say it to a living soul, of course, but this is dead paper and a great relief to my mind)—*perhaps* that is one reason I do not get well faster.

You see he *does* not believe I am sick!

And what can one do?

If a physician of high standing, and one's own husband, assures friends and relatives that there is really nothing the matter with one but temporary nervous depression—a slight hysterical tendency— what is one to do?

My brother is also a physician, and also of high standing, and he says the same thing.

So I take phosphates or phosphites—whichever it is, and tonics, and journeys, and air, and exercise, and am absolutely forbidden to "work" until I am well again.

Personally, I disagree with their ideas.

Personally, I believe that congenial work, with excitement and change, would do me good.

But what is one to do?

I did write for a while in spite of them; but it does exhaust me a good deal—having to be so sly about it, or else meet with heavy opposition.

I sometimes fancy that in my condition if I had less opposition and more society and stimulus—but John says the very worst thing I can do is to think about my condition, and I confess it always makes me feel bad.

So I will let it alone and talk about the house.

The most beautiful place! It is quite alone, standing well back from the road, quite three miles from the village. It makes me think of English places that you read about, for there are hedges and walls and gates that lock, and lots of separate little houses for the gardeners and people.

There is a *delicious* garden! I never saw such a garden—large and shady, full of box-bordered paths, and lined with long grape-covered arbors with seats under them.

There were greenhouses, too, but they are all broken now.

There was some legal trouble, I believe, something about the heirs and coheirs; anyhow, the place has been empty for years.

That spoils my ghostliness, I am afraid, but I don't care—there is something strange about the house—I can feel it.

I even said so to John one moonlight evening, but he said what I felt was a *draught*, and shut the window.

I get unreasonably angry with John sometimes. I'm sure I never used to be so sensitive. I think it is due to this nervous condition.

But John says if I feel so, I shall neglect proper self-control; so I take pains to control myself—before him, at least, and that makes me very tired.

I don't like our room a bit. I wanted one downstairs that opened on the piazza and had roses all over the window, and such pretty old-fashioned chintz hangings! but John would not hear of it.

He said there was only one window and not room for two beds, and no near room for him if he took another.

He is very careful and loving, and hardly lets me stir without special direction.

I have a schedule prescription for each hour in the day; he takes all care from me, and so I feel basely ungrateful not to value it more.

He said we came here solely on my account, that I was to have perfect rest and all the air I could get. "Your exercise depends on your strength, my dear," said he, "and your food somewhat on your appetite; but air you can absorb all the time." So we took the nursery at the top of the house.

It is a big, airy room, the whole floor nearly, with windows that look all ways, and air and sunshine galore. It was a nursery first and then playroom and gymnasium, I should judge; for the windows are barred for little children, and there are rings and things in the walls.

The paint and paper look as if a boys' school had used it. It is stripped off—the paper—in great patches all around the head of my bed, about as far as I can reach, and in a great place on the other side of the room low down. I never saw a worse paper in my life.

One of those sprawling flamboyant patterns committing every artistic sin.

It is dull enough to confuse the eye in following, pronounced enough to constantly irritate and provoke study, and when you follow the lame uncertain curves for a little distance they suddenly commit suicide—plunge off at outrageous angles, destroy themselves in unheard of contradictions.

The color is repellent, almost revolting; a smouldering unclean yellow, strangely faded by the slow-turning sunlight.

It is a dull yet lurid orange in some places, a sickly sulphur tint in others.

No wonder the children hated it! I should hate it myself if I had to live in this room long.

There comes John, and I must put this away,—he hates to have me write a word.

We have been here two weeks, and I haven't felt like writing before, since that first day.

I am sitting by the window now, up in this atrocious nursery, and there is nothing to hinder my writing as much as I please, save lack of strength.

John is away all day, and even some nights when his cases are serious.

I am glad my case is not serious!

But these nervous troubles are dreadfully depressing.

John does not know how much I really suffer. He knows there is no *reason* to suffer, and that satisfies him.

Of course it is only nervousness. It does weigh on me so not to do my duty in any way!

I meant to be such a help to John, such a real rest and comfort, and here I am a comparative burden already!

Nobody would believe what an effort it is to do what little I am able,—to dress and entertain, and order things.

It is fortunate Mary is so good with the baby. Such a dear baby!

And yet I *cannot* be with him, it makes me so nervous.

I suppose John never was nervous in his life. He laughs at me so about this wallpaper!

At first he meant to repaper the room, but afterwards he said that I was letting it get the better of me, and that nothing was worse for a nervous patient than to give way to such fancies.

He said that after the wallpaper was changed it would be the heavy bedstead, and then the barred windows, and then that gate at the head of the stairs, and so on.

"You know the place is doing you good," he said, "and really, dear, I don't care to renovate the house just for a three months' rental."

"Then do let us go downstairs," I said, "there are such pretty rooms there."

Then he took me in his arms and called me a blessed little goose, and said he would go down to the cellar, if I wished, and have it whitewashed into the bargain.

But he is right enough about the beds and windows and things.

It is as airy and comfortable a room as any one need wish, and, of course, I would not be so silly as to make him uncomfortable just for a whim.

I'm really getting quite fond of the big room, all but that horrid paper.

Out of one window I can see the garden, those mysterious deep-shaded arbors, the riotous old-fashioned flowers, and bushes and gnarly trees.

Out of another I get a lovely view of the bay and a little private wharf belonging to the estate. There is a beautiful shaded lane that runs down there from the house. I always fancy I see people walking in these numerous paths and arbors, but John has cautioned me not to give way to fancy in the least. He says that with my imaginative power and habit of story-making, a nervous weakness like mine is sure to lead to all manner of excited fancies, and that I ought to use my will and good sense to check the tendency. So I try.

I think sometimes that if I were only well enough to write a little it would relieve the press of ideas and rest me.

But I find I get pretty tired when I try.

It is so discouraging not to have any advice and companionship about my work. When I get really well, John says we will ask Cousin Henry and Julia down for a long visit; but he says he would as soon put fireworks in my pillowcase as to let me have those stimulating people about now.

I wish I could get well faster.

But I must not think about that. This paper looks to me as if it *knew* what a vicious influence it had!

There is a recurrent spot where the pattern lolls like a broken neck and two bulbous eyes stare at you upside down. I get positively angry with the impertinence of it and the everlastingness. Up and down and sideways they crawl, and those absurd, unblinking eyes are everywhere. There is one place where two breadths didn't match, and the eyes go all up and down the line, one a little higher than the other.

I never saw so much expression in an inanimate thing before, and we all know how much expression they have! I used to lie awake as a child and get more entertainment and terror out of blank walls and plain furniture than most children could find in a toy-store.

I remember what a kindly wink the knobs of our big, old bureau used to have, and there was one chair that always seemed like a strong friend.

I used to feel that if any of the other things looked too fierce I could always hop into that chair and be safe.

The furniture in this room is no worse than inharmonious, however, for we had to bring it all from downstairs. I suppose when this was used as a playroom they had to take the nursery things out, and no wonder! I never saw such ravages as the children have made here.

The wallpaper, as I said before, is torn off in spots, and it sticketh closer than a brother—they must have had perseverance as well as hatred.

Then the floor is scratched and gouged and splintered, the plaster itself is dug out here and there, and this great heavy bed which is all we found in the room, looks as if it had been through the wars.

But I don't mind it a bit—only the paper.

There comes John's sister. Such a dear girl as she is, and so careful of me! I must not let her find me writing.

She is a perfect and enthusiastic housekeeper, and hopes for no better profession. I verily believe she thinks it is the writing which made me sick!

But I can write when she is out, and see her a long way off from these windows.

There is one that commands the road, a lovely shaded winding road, and one that just looks off over the country. A lovely country, too, full of great elms and velvet meadows.

This wallpaper has a kind of sub-pattern in a different shade, a particularly irritating one, for you can only see it in certain lights, and not clearly then.

But in the places where it isn't faded and where the sun is just so—I can see a strange, provoking, formless sort of figure, that seems to skulk about behind that silly and conspicuous front design.

There's sister on the stairs!

Well, the Fourth of July is over! The people are all gone and I am tired out. John thought it might do me good to see a little company, so we just had mother and Nellie and the children down for a week.

Of course I didn't do a thing. Jennie sees to everything now. But it tired me all the same.

John says if I don't pick up faster he shall send me to Weir Mitchell in the fall.

But I don't want to go there at all. I had a friend who was in his hands once, and she says he is just like John and my brother, only more so!

Besides, it is such an undertaking to go so far.

I don't feel as if it was worth while to turn my hand over for anything, and I'm getting dreadfully fretful and querulous.

I cry at nothing, and cry most of the time.

Of course I don't when John is here, or anybody else, but when I am alone.

And I am alone a good deal just now. John is kept in town very often by serious cases, and Jennie is good and lets me alone when I want her to.

So I walk a little in the garden or down that lovely lane, sit on the porch under the roses, and lie down up here a good deal. I'm getting really fond of the room in spite of the wallpaper.

Perhaps *because* of the wallpaper.

It dwells in my mind so!

I lie here on this great immovable bed—it is nailed down, I believe—and follow that pattern about by the hour. It is as good as gymnastics, I assure you. I start, we'll say, at the bottom, down in the corner over there where it has not been touched, and I determine for the thousandth time that I *will* follow that pointless pattern to some sort of a conclusion.

I know a little of the principle of design, and I know this thing was not arranged on any laws of radiation, or alternation, or repetition, or symmetry, or anything else that I ever heard of.

It is repeated, of course, by the breadths, but not otherwise.

Looked at in one way each breadth stands alone, the bloated curves and flourishes—a kind of "debased Romanesque" with *delirium tremens*—go waddling up and down in isolated columns of fatuity.

But, on the other hand, they connect diagonally, and the sprawling outlines run off in great slanting waves of optic horror, like a lot of wallowing seaweeds in full chase.

The whole thing goes horizontally, too, at least it seems so, and I exhaust myself in trying to distinguish the order of its going in that direction.

They have used a horizontal breadth for a frieze, and that adds wonderfully to the confusion.

There is one end of the room where it is almost intact, and there, when the cross-lights fade and the low sun shines directly upon it, I can almost fancy radiation after all,—the interminable grotesques seem to form around a common centre and rush off in headlong plunges of equal distraction.

It makes me tired to follow it. I will take a nap I guess.

I don't know why I should write this.

I don't want to.

I don't feel able.

And I know John would think it absurd. But I *must* say what I feel and think in some way—it is such a relief!

But the effort is getting to be greater than the relief.

Half the time now I am awfully lazy, and lie down ever so much.

John says I mustn't lose my strength, and has me take cod liver oil and lots of tonics and things, to say nothing of ale and wine and rare meat.

Dear John! He loves me very dearly, and hates to have me sick. I tried to have a real earnest reasonable talk with him the other day, and tell him how I wish he would let me go and make a visit to Cousin Henry and Julia.

But he said I wasn't able to go, nor able to stand it after I got there; and I did not make out a very good case for myself, for I was crying before I had finished.

It is getting to be a great effort for me to think straight. Just this nervous weakness I suppose.

And dear John gathered me up in his arms, and just carried me upstairs and laid me on the bed, and sat by me and read to me till it tired my head.

He said I was his darling and his comfort and all he had, and that I must take care of myself for his sake, and keep well.

He says no one but myself can help me out of it, that I must use my will and self-control and not let any silly fancies run away with me.

There's one comfort, the baby is well and happy, and does not have to occupy this nursery with the horrid wallpaper.

If we had not used it, that blessed child would have! What a fortunate escape! Why, I wouldn't have a child of mine, an impressionable little thing, live in such a room for worlds.

I never thought of it before, but it is lucky that John kept me here after all, I can stand it so much easier than a baby, you see.

Of course I never mention it to them any more—I am too wise,—but I keep watch of it all the same.

There are things in that paper that nobody knows but me, or ever will.

Behind that outside pattern the dim shapes get clearer every day.

It is always the same shape, only very numerous.

And it is like a woman stooping down and creeping about behind that pattern. I don't like it a bit. I wonder—I begin to think—I wish John would take me away from here!

It is so hard to talk with John about my case, because he is so wise, and because he loves me so.

But I tried it last night.

It was moonlight. The moon shines in all around just as the sun does.

I hate to see it sometimes, it creeps so slowly, and always comes in by one window or another.

John was asleep and I hated to waken him, so I kept still and watched the moonlight on that undulating wallpaper till I felt creepy.

The faint figure behind seemed to shake the pattern, just as if she wanted to get out.

I got up softly and went to feel and see if the paper *did* move, and when I came back John was awake.

"What is it, little girl?" he said. "Don't go walking about like that—you'll get cold."

I thought it was a good time to talk, so I told him that I really was not gaining here, and that I wished he would take me away.

"Why darling!" said he, "our lease will be up in three weeks, and I can't see how to leave before.

"The repairs are not done at home, and I cannot possibly leave town just now. Of course if you were in any danger, I could and would, but you really are better, dear, whether you can see it or not. I am a doctor, dear, and I know. You are gaining flesh and color, your appetite is better, I feel really much easier about you."

"I don't weigh a bit more," said I, "nor as much; and my appetite may be better in the evening when you are here, but it is worse in the morning when you are away!"

"Bless her little heart!" said he with a big hug, "she shall be as sick as she pleases! But now let's improve the shining hours by going to sleep, and talk about it in the morning!"

"And you won't go away?" I asked gloomily.

"Why, how can I, dear? It is only three weeks more and then we will take a nice little trip of a few days while Jennie is getting the house ready. Really dear you are better!"

"Better in body perhaps—" I began, and stopped short, for he sat up straight and looked at me with such a stern, reproachful look that I could not say another word.

"My darling," said he, "I beg of you, for my sake and for our child's sake, as well as for your own, that you will never for one instant let that idea enter your mind! There is nothing so dangerous, so fascinating, to a temperament like yours. It is a false and foolish fancy. Can you not trust me as a physician when I tell you so?"

So of course I said no more on that score, and we went to sleep before long. He thought I was asleep first, but I wasn't, and lay there for hours trying to decide whether that front pattern and the back pattern really did move together or separately.

On a pattern like this, by daylight, there is a lack of sequence, a defiance of law, that is a constant irritant to a normal mind.

The color is hideous enough, and unreliable enough, and infuriating enough, but the pattern is torturing.

You think you have mastered it, but just as you get well underway in following, it turns a back-somersault and there you are. It slaps you in the face, knocks you down, and tramples upon you. It is like a bad dream.

369

The outside pattern is a florid arabesque, reminding one of a fungus. If you can imagine a toadstool in joints, an interminable string of toadstools, budding and sprouting in endless convolutions—why, that is something like it.

That is, sometimes!

There is one marked peculiarity about this paper, a thing nobody seems to notice but myself, and that is that it changes as the light changes.

When the sun shoots in through the east window—I always watch for that first long, straight ray—it changes so quickly that I never can quite believe it.

That is why I watch it always.

By moonlight—the moon shines in all night when there is a moon—I wouldn't know it was the same paper.

At night in any kind of light, in twilight, candle light, lamplight, and worst of all by moonlight, it becomes bars! The outside pattern I mean, and the woman behind it is as plain as can be.

I didn't realize for a long time what the thing was that showed behind, that dim sub-pattern, but now I am quite sure it is a woman.

By daylight she is subdued, quiet. I fancy it is the pattern that keeps her so still. It is so puzzling. It keeps me quiet by the hour.

I lie down ever so much now. John says it is good for me, and to sleep all I can.

Indeed he started the habit by making me lie down for an hour after each meal.

It is a very bad habit I am convinced, for you see I don't sleep.

And that cultivates deceit, for I don't tell them I'm awake—O no!

The fact is I am getting a little afraid of John.

He seems very queer sometimes, and even Jennie has an inexplicable look.

It strikes me occasionally, just as a scientific hypothesis,—that perhaps it is the paper!

I have watched John when he did not know I was looking, and

come into the room suddenly on the most innocent excuses, and I've caught him several times *looking at the paper*! And Jennie too. I caught Jennie with her hand on it once.

She didn't know I was in the room, and when I asked her in a quiet, a very quiet voice, with the most restrained manner possible, what she was doing with the paper—she turned around as if she had been caught stealing, and looked quite angry—asked me why I should frighten her so!

Then she said that the paper stained everything it touched, that she had found yellow smooches on all my clothes and John's, and she wished we would be more careful!

Did not that sound innocent? But I know she was studying that pattern, and I am determined that nobody shall find it out but myself!

Life is very much more exciting now than it used to be. You see I have something more to expect, to look forward to, to watch. I really do eat better, and am more quiet than I was.

John is so pleased to see me improve! He laughed a little the other day, and said I seemed to be flourishing in spite of my wallpaper.

I turned it off with a laugh. I had no intention of telling him it was *because* of the wallpaper—he would make fun of me. He might even want to take me away.

I don't want to leave now until I have found it out. There is a week more, and I think that will be enough.

I'm feeling ever so much better! I don't sleep much at night, for it is so interesting to watch developments; but I sleep a good deal in the daytime.

In the daytime it is tiresome and perplexing.

There are always new shoots on the fungus, and new shades of yellow all over it. I cannot keep count of them, though I have tried conscientiously.

It is the strangest yellow, that wallpaper! It makes me think of all the yellow things I ever saw—not beautiful ones like buttercups, but old foul, bad yellow things.

But there is something else about that paper—the smell! I noticed it the moment we came into the room, but with so much air and sun it was not bad. Now we have had a week of fog and rain, and whether the windows are open or not, the smell is here.

It creeps all over the house.

I find it hovering in the dining-room, skulking in the parlor, hiding in the hall, lying in wait for me on the stairs.

It gets into my hair.

Even when I go to ride, if I turn my head suddenly and surprise it—there is that smell!

Such a peculiar odor, too! I have spent hours in trying to analyze it, to find what it smelled like.

It is not bad—at first, and very gentle, but quite the subtlest, most enduring odor I ever met.

In this damp weather it is awful, I wake up in the night and find it hanging over me.

It used to disturb me at first. I thought seriously of burning the house—to reach the smell.

But now I am used to it. The only thing I can think of that it is like is the *color* of the paper! A yellow smell.

There is a very funny mark on this wall, low down, near the mopboard. A streak that runs round the room. It goes behind every piece of furniture, except the bed, a long, straight, even *smooch*, as if it had been rubbed over and over.

I wonder how it was done and who did it, and what they did it for. Round and round and round—round and round and round—it makes me dizzy!

I really have discovered something at last.

Through watching so much at night, when it changes so, I have finally found out.

The front pattern *does* move—and no wonder! The woman behind shakes it!

Sometimes I think there are a great many women behind, and sometimes only one, and she crawls around fast, and her crawling shakes it all over.

Then in the very bright spots she keeps still, and in the very shady spots she just takes hold of the bars and shakes them hard.

And she is all the time trying to climb through. But nobody could climb through that pattern—it strangles so; I think that is why it has so many heads.

They get through, and then the pattern strangles them off and turns them upside down, and makes their eyes white!

If those heads were covered or taken off it would not be half so bad.

I think that woman gets out in the daytime!

And I'll tell you why—privately—I've seen her!

I can see her out of every one of my windows!

It is the same woman, I know, for she is always creeping, and most women do not creep by daylight.

I see her on that long shaded lane, creeping up and down. I see her in those dark grape arbors, creeping all around the garden.

I see her on that long road under the trees, creeping along, and when a carriage comes she hides under the blackberry vines.

I don't blame her a bit. It must be very humiliating to be caught creeping by daylight!

I always lock the door when I creep by daylight. I can't do it at night, for I know John would suspect something at once.

And John is so queer now, that I don't want to irritate him. I wish he would take another room! Besides, I don't want anybody to get that woman out at night but myself.

I often wonder if I could see her out of all the windows at once.

But, turn as fast as I can, I can only see out of one at one time.

And though I always see her, she *may* be able to creep faster than I can turn!

I have watched her sometimes away off in the open country, creeping as fast as a cloud shadow in a high wind.

If only that top pattern could be gotten off from the under one! I mean to try it, little by little.

I have found out another funny thing, but I shan't tell it this time! It does not do to trust people too much.

There are only two more days to get this paper off, and I believe John is beginning to notice. I don't like the look in his eyes.

And I heard him ask Jennie a lot of professional questions about me. She had a very good report to give.

She said I slept a good deal in the daytime.

John knows I don't sleep very well at night, for all I'm so quiet!

He asked me all sorts of questions, too, and pretended to be very loving and kind.

As if I couldn't see through him!

Still, I don't wonder he acts so, sleeping under this paper for three months.

It only interests me, but I feel sure John and Jennie are secretly affected by it.

Hurrah! This is the last day, but it is enough. John is to stay in town over night, and won't be out until this evening.

Jennie wanted to sleep with me—the sly thing! but I told her I should undoubtedly rest better for a night all alone.

That was clever, for really I wasn't alone a bit! As soon as it was moonlight and that poor thing began to crawl and shake the pattern, I got up and ran to help her.

I pulled and she shook, I shook and she pulled, and before morning we had peeled off yards of that paper.

A strip about as high as my head and half around the room.

And then when the sun came and that awful pattern began to laugh at me, I declared I would finish it today!

We go away tomorrow, and they are moving all my furniture down again to leave things as they were before.

Jennie looked at the wall in amazement, but I told her merrily that I did it out of pure spite at the vicious thing.

She laughed and said she wouldn't mind doing it herself, but I must not get tired.

How she betrayed herself that time!

But I am here, and no person touches this paper but me,— not *alive*!

She tried to get me out of the room—it was too patent! But I said it was so quiet and empty and clean now that I believed I would lie down again and sleep all I could; and not to wake me even for dinner—I would call when I woke.

So now she is gone, and the servants are gone, and the things are gone, and there is nothing left but that great bedstead nailed down, with the canvas mattress we found on it.

We shall sleep downstairs tonight, and take the boat home tomorrow.

I quite enjoy the room, now it is bare again.

How those children did tear about here!

This bedstead is fairly gnawed!

But I must get to work.

I have locked the door and thrown the key down into the front path.

I don't want to go out, and I don't want to have anybody come in, till John comes.

I want to astonish him.

I've got a rope up here that even Jennie did not find. If that woman does get out, and tries to get away, I can tie her!

But I forgot I could not reach far without anything to stand on!

This bed will *not* move!

I tried to lift and push it until I was lame, and then I got so angry I bit off a little piece at one corner—but it hurt my teeth.

Then I peeled off all the paper I could reach standing on the floor. It sticks horribly and the pattern just enjoys it! All those strangled heads and bulbous eyes and waddling fungus growths just shriek with derision!

I am getting angry enough to do something desperate. To jump out of the window would be admirable exercise, but the bars are too strong even to try.

Besides I wouldn't do it. Of course not. I know well enough that a step like that is improper and might be misconstrued.

I don't like to *look* out of the windows even—there are so many of those creeping women, and they creep so fast.

I wonder if they all come out of that wallpaper as I did?

But I am securely fastened now by my well-hidden rope—you don't get *me* out in the road there!

I suppose I shall have to get back behind the pattern when it comes night, and that is hard!

It is so pleasant to be out in this great room and creep around as I please!

I don't want to go outside. I won't, even if Jennie asks me to.

For outside you have to creep on the ground, and everything is green instead of yellow.

But here I can creep smoothly on the floor, and my shoulder just fits in that long smooch around the wall, so I cannot lose my way.

Why there's John at the door!

It is no use, young man, you can't open it!

How he does call and pound!

Now he's crying for an axe.

It would be a shame to break down that beautiful door! "John dear!" said I in the gentlest voice, "the key is down by the front steps, under a plantain leaf!"

That silenced him for a few moments.

Then he said—very quietly indeed, "Open the door, my darling!"

"I can't," said I. "The key is down by the front door under a plantain leaf!" And then I said it again, several times, very gently and slowly, and said it so often that he had to go and see, and he got it of course, and came in. He stopped short by the door.

"What is the matter?" he cried. "For God's sake, what are you doing!"

I kept on creeping just the same, but I looked at him over my shoulder.

"I've got out at last," said I, "in spite of you and Jane. And I've pulled off most of the paper, so you can't put me back!"

Now why should that man have fainted? But he did, and right across my path by the wall, so that I had to creep over him every time!

The Bird in the Garden
Richard Middleton

The room in which the Burchell family lived in Love Street, SE, was underground and depended for light and air on a grating let into the pavement above.

Uncle John, who was a queer one, had filled the area with green plants and creepers in boxes and tins hanging from the grating, so that the room itself obtained very little light indeed, but there was always a nice bright green place for the people sitting in it to look at. Toby, who had peeped into the areas of other little boys, knew that his was of quite exceptional beauty, and it was with a certain awe that he helped Uncle John to tend the plants in the morning, watering them and taking the pieces of paper and straws that had fallen through the grating from their hair. "It is a great mistake to have straws in one's hair," Uncle John would say gravely; and Toby knew that it was true.

It was in the morning after they had just been watered that the plants looked and smelt best, and when the sun shone through the grating and the diamonds were shining and falling through the forest, Toby would tell the baby about the great bird who would one day come flying through the trees—a bird of all colours, ugly and beautiful, with a harsh sweet voice. "And that will be the end of everything," said Toby, though of course he was only repeating a story his Uncle John had told him.

There were other people in the big, dark room besides Toby and Uncle John and the baby; dark people who flitted to and fro about secret matters, people called father and mother and Mr Hearn, who were apt to kick if they found you in their way, and who never laughed except at nights, and then they laughed too loudly.

"They will frighten the bird," thought Toby; but they were kind to Uncle John because he had a pension. Toby slept in a corner on the ground beside the baby, and when father and Mr Hearn fought at nights he would wake up and watch and shiver; but when this happened it seemed to him that the baby was laughing at him, and he would pinch her to make her stop. One night, when the men were fighting very fiercely and mother had fallen asleep on the table, Uncle John rose from his bed and began singing in a great voice. It was a song Toby knew very well about Trafalgar's Bay, but it frightened the two men a great deal because they thought Uncle John would be too mad to fetch the pension any more. Next day he was quite well, however, and he and Toby found a large green caterpillar in the garden among the plants.

"This is a fact of great importance," said Uncle John, stroking it with a little stick. "It is a sign!"

Toby used to lie awake at nights after that and listen for the bird, but he only heard the clatter of feet on the pavement and the screaming of engines far away.

Later there came a new young woman to live in the cellar—not a dark person, but a person you could see and speak to. She patted Toby on the head; but when she saw the baby she caught it to her breast and cried over it, calling it pretty names.

At first father and Mr Hearn were both very kind to her, and mother used to sit all day in the corner with burning eyes, but after a time the three used to laugh together at nights as before, and the woman would sit with her wet face and wait for the coming of the bird, with Toby and the baby and Uncle John, who was a queer one.

"All we have to do," Uncle John would say, "is to keep the garden clean and tidy, and to water the plants every morning so that they may be very green." And Toby would go and whisper this to the baby, and she would stare at the ceiling with large, stupid eyes.

There came a time when Toby was very sick, and he lay all day in his corner wondering about wonder. Sometimes the room in which he lay became so small that he was choked for lack of air, sometimes it was so large that he screamed out because he felt lonely. He could not see the dark people then at all, but only Uncle John and the woman, who told him in whispers that her name was "Mummie". She called him Sonny, which is a very pretty name, and when Toby heard it he felt a tickling in his sides which he knew to be gladness. Mummie's face was wet and warm and soft, and she was very fond of kissing. Every morning Uncle John would lift Toby up and show him the garden, and Toby would slip out of his arms and walk among the trees and plants. And the place would grow bigger and bigger until it was all the world, and Toby would lose himself amongst the tangle of trees and flowers and creepers. He would see butterflies there and tame animals, and the sky was full of birds of all colours, ugly and beautiful, but he knew that none of these was the bird, because their voices were only sweet. Sometimes he showed these wonders to a little boy called Toby, who held his hand and called him Uncle John, sometimes he showed them to his mummie and he himself was Toby; but always when he came back he found himself lying in Uncle John's arms, and, weary from his walk, would fall into a pleasant dreamless sleep.

It seemed to Toby at this time that a veil hung about him, which, dim and unreal in itself, served to make all things dim and unreal. He did not know whether he was asleep or awake, so strange was life, so vivid were his dreams. Mummie, Uncle John, the baby, Toby himself came with a flicker of the veil and disappeared vaguely without cause. It would happen that Toby would be speaking to Uncle John, and suddenly he would find himself looking into the large eyes of the baby, turned stupidly towards the ceiling, and again the baby would be Toby himself, a hot, dry little body without legs or arms, that swayed suspended as if by magic a foot above the bed.

Then there was the vision of two small feet that moved a long way off, and Toby would watch them curiously, as kittens do their tails, without knowing the cause of their motion.

It was all very wonderful and very strange, and day by day the veil grew thicker; there was no need to wake when the sleeptime was so pleasant; there were no dark people to kick you in that dreamy place.

And yet Toby woke—woke to a life and in a place which he had never known before.

He found himself on a heap of rags in a large cellar which depended for its light on a grating let into the pavement of the street above. On the stone floor of the area and swinging from the grating were a few sickly, grimy plants in pots. There must have been a fine sunset up above, for a faint red glow came through the bars and touched the leaves of the plants.

There was a lighted candle standing in a bottle on the table, and the cellar seemed full of people. At the table itself two men and a woman were drinking, though they were already drunk, and beyond in a corner Toby could see the head and shoulders of a tall old man. Beside him there crouched a woman with a faded, pretty face, and between Toby and the rest of the room there stood a box in which lay a baby with large, wakeful eyes.

Toby's body tingled with excitement, for this was a new thing; he had never seen it before, he had never seen anything before.

The voice of the woman at the table rose and fell steadily without a pause; she was abusing the other woman, and the two drunken men were laughing at her and shouting her on; Toby thought the other woman lacked spirit because she stayed crouching on the floor and said nothing.

At last the woman stopped her abuse, and one of the men turned and shouted an order to the woman on the floor. She stood up and came towards him, hesitating; this annoyed the man and he swore at her brutally; when she came near enough he knocked her down with his fist, and all the three burst out laughing.

Toby was so excited that he knelt up in his corner and clapped his hands, but the others did not notice because the old man was up and swaying wildly over the woman. He seemed to be threatening the man who had struck her, and that one was evidently afraid of him, for he rose unsteadily and lifted the chair on which he had been sitting above his head to use as a weapon.

The old man raised his fist and the chair fell heavily on to his wrinkled forehead and he dropped to the ground.

The woman at the table cried out, "The pension!" in her shrill voice, and then they were all quiet, looking.

Then it seemed to Toby that through the forest there came flying, with a harsh sweet voice and tumult of wings, a bird of all colours, ugly and beautiful, and he knew, though later there might be people to tell him otherwise, that that was the end of everything.

Seaton's Aunt
Walter De La Mare

I had heard rumours of Seaton's Aunt long before I actually encountered her. Seaton, in the hush of confidence, or at any little show of toleration on our part, would remark, "My aunt," or "My old aunt, you know," as if his relative might be a kind of cement to an *entente cordiale*.

He had an unusual quantity of pocket-money; or, at any rate, it was bestowed on him in unusually large amounts; and he spent it freely, though none of us would have described him as an "awfully generous chap." "Hullo, Seaton," he would say, "the old Begum?" At the beginning of term, too, he used to bring back surprising and exotic dainties in a box with a trick padlock that accompanied him from his first appearance at Gummidge's in a billycock hat to the rather abrupt conclusion of his school-days.

From a boy's point of view he looked distastefully foreign, with his yellow skin, and slow chocolate-coloured eyes, and lean weak figure. Merely for his looks he was treated by most of us true-blue Englishmen with condescension, hostility, or contempt. We used to call him "Pongo," but without any better excuse for the nickname than his skin. He was, that is, in one sense of the term what he assuredly was not in the other sense, a sport.

Seaton and I were never in any sense intimate at school, our orbits only intersected in class. I kept instinctively aloof from him.

I felt vaguely he was a sneak, and remained quite unmollified by advances on his side, which, in a boy's barbarous fashion, unless it suited me to be magnanimous, I haughtily ignored.

We were both of us quick-footed, and at Prisoner's Base used occasionally to hide together. And so I best remember Seaton— his narrow watchful face in the dusk of summer evening; his peculiar crouch, and his inarticulate whisperings and mumblings. Otherwise he played all games slackly and limply; used to stand and feed at his locker with a crony or two until his "tuck" gave out; or waste his money on some outlandish fancy or other. He bought, for instance, a silver bangle, which he wore above his left elbow, until some of the fellows showed their masterly contempt of the practice by dropping it nearly red-hot down his neck.

It needed, therefore, a rather peculiar taste, a rather rare kind of schoolboy courage and indifference to criticism, to be much associated with him. And I had neither the taste nor the courage. None the less, he did make advances, and on one memorable occasion went to the length of bestowing on me a whole pot of some outlandish mulberry-coloured jelly that had been duplicated in his term's supplies. In the exuberance of my gratitude I promised to spend the next half-term holiday with him at his aunt's house.

I had clean forgotten my promise when, two or three days before the holiday, he came up and triumphantly reminded me of it.

"Well, to tell you the honest truth, Seaton, old chap——" I began graciously; but he cut me short.

"My aunt expects you," he said; "she is very glad you are coming. She's sure to be quite decent to *you*, Withers."

I looked at him in some astonishment; the emphasis was unexpected. It seemed to suggest an aunt not hitherto hinted at, and a friendly feeling on Seaton's side that was more disconcerting than welcome.

We reached his home partly by train, partly by a lift in an empty farm-cart, and partly by walking. It was a whole-day holiday, and we were to sleep the night; he lent me extraordinary night-gear, I remember. The village street was unusually wide, and was fed from a green by two converging roads, with an inn, and a high green sign at the corner. About a hundred yards down the street was a chemist's shop—Mr. Tanner's. We descended the two steps into his dusky and odorous interior to buy, I remember, some rat poison. A little beyond the chemist's was the forge. You then walked along a very narrow path, under a fairly high wall, nodding here and there with weeds and tufts of grass, and so came to the iron garden-gates, and saw the high flat house behind its huge sycamore. A coach-house stood on the left of the house, and on the right a gate led into a kind of rambling orchard. The lawn lay away over to the left again, and at the bottom (for the whole garden sloped gently to a sluggish and rushy pond-like stream) was a meadow.

We arrived at noon, and entered the gates out of the hot dust beneath the glitter of the dark-curtained windows. Seaton led me at once through the little garden-gate to show me his tadpole pond, swarming with what, being myself not the least bit of a naturalist, I considered the most horrible creatures—of all shapes, consistencies, and sizes, but with whom Seaton seemed to be on the most intimate of terms. I can see his absorbed face now as he sat on his heels and fished the slimy things out in his sallow palms. Wearying at last of his pets, we loitered about awhile in an aimless fashion. Seaton seemed to be listening, or at any rate waiting, for something to happen or for some one to come. But nothing did happen and no one came.

That was just like Seaton. Anyhow, the first view I got of his aunt was when, at the summons of a distant gong, we turned from the garden, very hungry and thirsty, to go into luncheon. We were approaching the house when Seaton suddenly came to a standstill. Indeed, I have always had the impression that he plucked at my sleeve. Something, at least, seemed to catch me back, as it were, as he cried, "Look out, there she is!"

She was standing in an upper window which opened wide on a hinge, and at first sight she looked an excessively tall and overwhelming figure. This, however, was mainly because the window reached all but to the floor of her bedroom. She was in reality rather an under-sized woman, in spite of her long face and big head. She must have stood, I think, unusually still, with eyes fixed on us, though this impression may be due to Seaton's sudden warning and to my consciousness of the cautious and subdued air that had fallen on him at sight of her. I know that without the least reason in the world I felt a kind of guiltiness, as if I had been "caught." There was a silvery star pattern sprinkled on her black silk dress, and even from the ground I could see the immense coils of her hair and the rings on her left hand which was held fingering the small jet buttons of her bodice. She watched our united advance without stirring, until, imperceptibly, her eyes raised and lost themselves in the distance, so that it was out of an assumed reverie that she appeared suddenly to awaken to our presence beneath her when we drew close to the house.

"So this is your friend, Mr. Smithers, I suppose?" she said, bobbing to me.

"Withers, aunt," said Seaton.

"It's much the same," she said, with eyes fixed on me. "Come in, Mr. Withers, and bring him along with you."

She continued to gaze at me—at least, I think she did so. I know that the fixity of her scrutiny and her ironical "Mr." made me feel peculiarly uncomfortable. But she was extremely kind and attentive to me, though perhaps her kindness and attention showed up more vividly against her complete neglect of Seaton. Only one remark that I have any recollection of she made to him: "When I look on my nephew, Mr. Smithers, I realise that dust we are, and dust shall become. You are hot, dirty, and incorrigible, Arthur."

She sat at the head of the table, Seaton at the foot, and I, before a wide waste of damask tablecloth, between them. It was an old and rather close dining-room, with windows thrown wide to the green garden and a wonderful cascade of fading roses. Miss Seaton's great chair faced this window, so that its rose-reflected light shone full on her yellowish face, and on just such chocolate eyes as my schoolfellow's, except that hers were more than half-covered by unusually long and heavy lids.

There she sat, eating, with those sluggish eyes fixed for the most part on my face; above them stood the deep-lined fork between her eyebrows; and above that the wide expanse of a remarkable brow beneath its strange steep bank of hair. The lunch was copious, and consisted, I remember, of all such dishes as are generally considered mischievous and too good for the schoolboy digestion—lobster mayonnaise, cold game sausages, an immense veal and ham pie farced with eggs and numberless delicious flavours; besides sauces, kickshaws, creams, and sweetmeats. We even had wine, a half-glass of old darkish sherry each.

Miss Seaton enjoyed and indulged an enormous appetite. Her example and a natural schoolboy voracity soon overcame my nervousness of her, even to the extent of allowing me to enjoy to the best of my bent so rare a "spread." Seaton was singularly modest; the greater part of his meal consisted of almonds and raisins, which he nibbled surreptitiously and as if he found difficulty in swallowing them.

I don't mean that Miss Seaton "conversed" with me. She merely scattered trenchant remarks and now and then twinkled a baited question over my head. But her face was like a dense and involved accompaniment to her talk. She presently dropped the "Mr.," to my intense relief, and called me now Withers, or Wither, now Smithers, and even once towards the close of the meal distinctly Johnson, though how on earth my name suggested it, or whose face mine had reanimated in memory, I cannot conceive.

"And is Arthur a good boy at school, Mr. Wither?" was one of her many questions. "Does he please his masters? Is he first in his class? What does the reverend Dr. Gummidge think of him, eh?"

I knew she was jeering at him, but her face was adamant against the least flicker of sarcasm or facetiousness. I gazed fixedly at a blushing crescent of lobster.

"I think you're eighth, aren't you, Seaton?"

Seaton moved his small pupils towards his aunt. But she continued to gaze with a kind of concentrated detachment at me.

"Arthur will never make a brilliant scholar, I fear," she said, lifting a dexterously-burdened fork to her wide mouth...

After luncheon she preceded me up to my bedroom. It was a jolly little bedroom, with a brass fender and rugs and a polished floor, on which it was possible, I afterwards found, to play "snow-shoes." Over the washstand was a little black-framed water-colour drawing, depicting a large eye with an extremely fishlike intensity in the spark of light on the dark pupil; and in "illuminated" lettering beneath was printed very minutely, "Thou God Seest ME," followed by a long looped monogram, "S.S.," in the corner. The other pictures were all of the sea: brigs on blue water; a schooner overtopping chalk cliffs; a rocky island of prodigious steepness, with two tiny sailors dragging a monstrous boat up a shelf of beach.

"This is the room, Withers, my brother William died in when a boy. Admire the view!"

I looked out of the window across the tree-tops. It was a day hot with sunshine over the green fields, and the cattle were standing swishing their tails in the shallow water. But the view at the moment was only exaggeratedly vivid because I was horribly dreading that she would presently enquire after my luggage, and I had not brought even a toothbrush. I need have had no fear. Hers was not that highly-civilised type of mind that is stuffed with sharp material details. Nor could her ample presence be described as in the least motherly.

"I would never consent to question a schoolfellow behind my nephew's back," she said, standing in the middle of the room, "but tell me, Smithers, why is Arthur so unpopular? You, I understand, are his only close friend." She stood in a dazzle of sun, and out of it her eyes regarded me with such leaden penetration beneath their thick lids that I doubt if my face concealed the least thought from her. "But there, there," she added very suavely, stooping her head a little, "don't trouble to answer me. I never extort an answer. Boys are queer fish. Brains might perhaps have suggested his washing his hands before luncheon; but—not my choice, Smithers. God forbid! And now, perhaps, you would like to go into the garden again. I cannot actually see from here, but I should not be surprised if Arthur is now skulking behind that hedge."

He was. I saw his head come out and take a rapid glance at the windows.

"Join him, Mr. Smithers; we shall meet again, I hope, at the tea-table. The afternoon I spend in retirement."

Whether or not, Seaton and I had not been long engaged with the aid of two green switches in riding round and round a lumbering old gray horse we found in the meadow, before a rather bunched-up figure appeared, walking along the field-path on the other side of the water, with a magenta parasol studiously lowered in our direction throughout her slow progress, as if that were the magnetic needle and we the fixed pole. Seaton at once lost all nerve in his riding. At the next lurch of the old mare's heels he toppled over into the grass, and I slid off the sleek broad back to join him where he stood, rubbing his shoulder and sourly watching the rather pompous figure till it was out of sight.

"Was that your aunt, Seaton?" I enquired; but not till then.

He nodded.

"Why didn't she take any notice of us, then?"

"She never does."

"Why not?"

"Oh, she knows all right, without; that's the dam awful part of it." Seaton was about the only fellow at Gummidge's who ever had the ostentation to use bad language. He had suffered for it, too. But it wasn't, I think, bravado. I believe he really felt certain things more intensely than most of the other fellows, and they were generally things that fortunate and average people do not feel at all—the peculiar quality, for instance, of the British schoolboy's imagination.

"I tell you, Withers," he went on moodily, slinking across the meadow with his hands covered up in his pockets, "she sees everything. And what she doesn't see she knows without."

"But how?" I said, not because I was much interested, but because the afternoon was so hot and tiresome and purposeless, and it seemed more of a bore to remain silent. Seaton turned gloomily and spoke in a very low voice.

"Don't appear to be talking of her, if you wouldn't mind. It's— because she's in league with the devil." He nodded his head and stooped to pick up a round flat pebble. "I tell you," he said, still stooping, "you fellows don't realise what it is. I know I'm a bit close and all that. But so would you be if you had that old hag listening to every thought you think."

I looked at him, then turned and surveyed one by one the windows of the house.

"Where's your *pater*?" I said awkwardly.

"Dead, ages and ages ago, and my mother too. She's not my aunt by rights."

"What is she, then?"

"I mean she's not my mother's sister, because my grandmother married twice; and she's one of the first lot. I don't know what you call her, but anyhow she's not my real aunt."

"She gives you plenty of pocket-money."

Seaton looked steadfastly at me out of his flat eyes. "She can't give me what's mine. When I come of age half of the whole lot will be mine; and what's more"—he turned his back on the house— "I'll make her hand over every blessed shilling of it."

I put my hands in my pockets and stared at Seaton. "Is it much?" He nodded.

"Who told you?" He got suddenly very angry; a darkish red came into his cheeks, his eyes glistened, but he made no answer, and we loitered listlessly about the garden until it was time for tea...

Seaton's aunt was wearing an extraordinary kind of lace jacket when we sidled sheepishly into the drawing-room together. She greeted me with a heavy and protracted smile, and bade me bring a chair close to the little table.

"I hope Arthur has made you feel at home," she said as she handed me my cup in her crooked hand. "He don't talk much to me; but then I'm an old woman. You must come again, Wither, and draw him out of his shell. You old snail!" She wagged her head at Seaton, who sat munching cake and watching her intently.

"And we must correspond, perhaps." She nearly shut her eyes at me. "You must write and tell me everything behind the creature's back." I confess I found her rather disquieting company. The evening drew on. Lamps were brought by a man with a nondescript face and very quiet footsteps. Seaton was told to bring out the chess-men. And we played a game, she and I, with her big chin thrust over the board at every move as she gloated over the pieces and occasionally croaked "Check!" after which she would sit back inscrutably staring at me. But the game was never finished. She simply hemmed me defencelessly in with a cloud of men that held me impotent, and yet one and all refused to administer to my poor flustered old king a merciful *coup de grâce*.

"There," she said, as the clock struck ten—"a drawn game, Withers. We are very evenly matched. A very creditable defence, Withers. You know your room. There's supper on a tray in the dining-room. Don't let the creature over-eat himself. The gong will sound three-quarters of an hour before a punctual breakfast." She held out her cheek to Seaton, and he kissed it with obvious perfunctoriness. With me she shook hands.

"An excellent game," she said cordially, "but my memory is poor, and"—she swept the pieces helter-skelter into the box— "the result will never be known." She raised her great head far back. "Eh?"

It was a kind of challenge, and I could only murmur: "Oh, I was absolutely in a hole, you know!" when she burst out laughing and waved us both out of the room.

Seaton and I stood and ate our supper, with one candlestick to light us, in a corner of the dining-room. "Well, and how would you like it?" he said very softly, after cautiously poking his head round the doorway.

"Like what?"

"Being spied on—every blessed thing you do and think?"

"I shouldn't like it at all," I said, "if she does."

"And yet you let her smash you up at chess!"

"I didn't let her!" I said indignantly.

"Well, you funked it, then."

"And I didn't funk it either," I said; "she's so jolly clever with her knights." Seaton stared fixedly at the candle. "You wait, that's all," he said slowly. And we went upstairs to bed.

I had not been long in bed, I think, when I was cautiously awakened by a touch on my shoulder. And there was Seaton's face in the candlelight and his eyes looking into mine.

"What's up?" I said, rising quickly to my elbow.

"Don't scurry," he whispered, "or she'll hear. I'm sorry for waking you, but I didn't think you'd be asleep so soon."

"Why, what's the time, then?" Seaton wore, what was then rather unusual, a night-suit, and he hauled his big silver watch out of the pocket in his jacket.

"It's a quarter to twelve. I never get to sleep before twelve— not here."

"What do you do, then?"

"Oh, I read and listen."

"Listen?"

Seaton stared into his candle-flame as if he were listening even then. "You can't guess what it is. All you read in ghost stories, that's all rot. You can't see much, Withers, but you know all the same."

"Know what?"

"Why, that they're there."

"Who's there?" I asked fretfully, glancing at the door.

"Why, in the house. It swarms with 'em. Just you stand still and listen outside my bedroom door in the middle of the night. I have, dozens of times; they're all over the place."

"Look here, Seaton," I said, "you asked me to come here, and I didn't mind chucking up a leave just to oblige you and because I'd promised; but don't get talking a lot of rot, that's all, or you'll know the difference when we get back."

"Don't fret," he said coldly, turning away. "I shan't be at school long. And what's more, you're here now, and there isn't anybody else to talk to. I'll chance the other."

"Look here, Seaton," I said, "you may think you're going to scare me with a lot of stuff about voices and all that. But I'll just thank you to clear out; and you may please yourself about pottering about all night."

He made no answer; he was standing by the dressing-table looking across his candle into the looking-glass; he turned and stared slowly round the walls.

"Even this room's nothing more than a coffin. I suppose she told you—'It's all exactly the same as when my brother William died'—trust her for that! And good luck to him, say I. Look at that." He raised his candle close to the little water-colour I have mentioned. "There's hundreds of eyes like that in the house; and even if God does see you, he takes precious good care you don't see Him. And it's just the same with them. I tell you what, Withers, I'm getting sick of all this. I shan't stand it much longer."

The house was silent within and without, and even in the yellowish radiance of the candle a faint silver showed through the open window on my blind. I slipped off the bedclothes, wide awake, and sat irresolute on the bedside.

"I know you're only guying me," I said angrily, "but why is the house full of—what you say? Why do you hear—what you *do* hear?

Tell me that, you silly foal!"

Seaton sat down on a chair and rested his candlestick on his knee. He blinked at me calmly. "She brings them," he said, with lifted eyebrows.

"Who? Your aunt?"

He nodded.

"How?"

"I told you," he answered pettishly. "She's in league. You don't know. She as good as killed my mother; I know that. But it's not only her by a long chalk. She just sucks you dry. I know. And that's what she'll do for me; because I'm like her—like my mother, I mean. She simply hates to see me alive. I wouldn't be like that old she-wolf for a million pounds. And so"—he broke off, with a comprehensive wave of his candlestick—"they're always here. Ah, my boy, wait till she's dead! She'll hear something then, I can tell you. It's all very well now, but wait till then! I wouldn't be in her shoes when she has to clear out—for something. Don't you go and believe I care for ghosts, or whatever you like to call them. We're all in the same box. We're all under her thumb."

He was looking almost nonchalantly at the ceiling at the moment, when I saw his face change, saw his eyes suddenly drop like shot birds and fix themselves on the cranny of the door he had just left ajar. Even from where I sat I could see his colour change; he went greenish. He crouched without stirring, simply fixed. And I, scarcely daring to breathe, sat with creeping skin, simply watching him. His hands relaxed, and he gave a kind of sigh.

"Was that one?" I whispered, with a timid show of jauntiness. He looked round, opened his mouth, and nodded. "What?" I said. He jerked his thumb with meaningful eyes, and I knew that he meant that his aunt had been there listening at our door cranny.

"Look here, Seaton," I said once more, wriggling to my feet. "You may think I'm a jolly noodle; just as you please. But your aunt has been civil to me and all that, and I don't believe a word you say about her, that's all, and never did. Every fellow's a bit off his pluck at night, and you may think it a fine sport to try your rubbish on me. I heard your aunt come upstairs before I fell asleep. And I'll bet you a level tanner she's in bed now. What's more, you can keep your blessed ghosts to yourself. It's a guilty conscience, I should think."

Seaton looked at me curiously, without answering for a moment. "I'm not a liar, Withers; but I'm not going to quarrel either. You're the only chap I care a button for; or, at any rate, you're the only chap that's ever come here; and it's something to tell a fellow what you feel. I don't care a fig for fifty thousand ghosts, although I swear on my solemn oath that I know they're here. But she"—he turned deliberately—"you laid a tanner she's in bed, Withers; well, I know different. She's never in bed much of the night, and I'll prove it, too, just to show you I'm not such a nolly as you think I am. Come on!"

"Come on where?"

"Why, to see."

I hesitated. He opened a large cupboard and took out a small dark dressing-gown and a kind of shawl-jacket. He threw the jacket on the bed and put on the gown. His dusky face was colourless, and I could see by the way he fumbled at the sleeves he was shivering. But it was no good showing the white feather now. So I threw the tasselled shawl over my shoulders and, leaving our candle brightly burning on the chair, we went out together and stood in the corridor. "Now then, listen!" Seaton whispered.

We stood leaning over the staircase. It was like leaning over a well, so still and chill the air was all around us. But presently, as I suppose happens in most old houses, began to echo and answer in my ears a medley of infinite small stirrings and whisperings. Now out of the distance an old timber would relax its fibers, or a scurry die away behind the perishing wainscot. But amid and behind such sounds as these I seemed to begin to be conscious, as it were, of the lightest of footfalls, sounds as faint as the vanishing remembrance of voices in a dream. Seaton was all in obscurity except his face; out of that his eyes gleamed darkly, watching me.

"You'd hear, too, in time, my fine soldier," he muttered. "Come on!"

He descended the stairs, slipping his lean fingers lightly along the balusters. He turned to the right at the loop, and I followed him barefooted along a thickly-carpeted corridor. At the end stood a door ajar. And from here we very stealthily and in complete blackness ascended five narrow stairs. Seaton, with immense caution, slowly pushed open a door and we stood together looking into a great pool of duskiness, out of which, lit by the feeble clearness of a night-light, rose a vast bed. A heap of clothes lay on the floor; beside them two slippers dozed, with noses each to each, two yards apart. Somewhere a little clock ticked huskily. There was a rather close smell of lavender and eau de Cologne, mingled with the fragrance of ancient sachets, soap, and drugs. Yet it was a scent even more peculiarly commingled than that.

And the bed! I stared warily in; it was mounded gigantically, and it was empty.

Seaton turned a vague pale face, all shadows: "What did I say?" he muttered. "Who's—who's the fool now, I say? How are we going to get back without meeting her, I say? Answer me that! Oh, I wish to goodness you hadn't come here, Withers."

He stood visibly shivering in his skimpy gown, and could hardly speak for his teeth chattering. And very distinctly, in the hush that followed his whisper, I heard approaching a faint unhurried voluminous rustle. Seaton clutched my arm, dragged me to the right across the room to a large cupboard, and drew the door close to on us. And, presently, as with bursting lungs I peeped out into the long, low, curtained bedroom, waddled in that wonderful great head and body. I can see her now, all patched and lined with shadow, her tied-up hair (she must have had enormous quantities of it for so old a woman), her heavy lids above those flat, slow, vigilant eyes. She just passed across my ken in the vague dusk; but the bed was out of sight.

We waited on and on, listening to the clock's muffled ticking. Not the ghost of a sound rose up from the great bed. Either she lay archly listening or slept a sleep serener than an infant's. And when, it seemed, we had been hours in hiding and were cramped, chilled, and half suffocated, we crept out on all fours, with terror knocking at our ribs, and so down the five narrow stairs and back to the little candle-lit blue-and-gold bedroom.

Once there, Seaton gave in. He sat livid on a chair with closed eyes.

"Here," I said, shaking his arm, "I'm going to bed; I've had enough of this foolery; I'm going to bed." His lids quivered, but he made no answer. I poured out some water into my basin and, with that cold pictured azure eye fixed on us, bespattered Seaton's sallow face and forehead and dabbled his hair. He presently sighed and opened fish-like eyes.

"Come on!" I said. "Don't get shamming, there's a good chap. Get on my back, if you like, and I'll carry you into your bedroom."

He waved me away and stood up. So, with my candle in one hand, I took him under the arm and walked him along according to his direction down the corridor. His was a much dingier room than mine, and littered with boxes, paper, cages, and clothes. I huddled him into bed and turned to go. And suddenly, I can hardly explain it now, a kind of cold and deadly terror swept over me. I almost ran out of the room, with eyes fixed rigidly in front of me, blew out my candle, and buried my head under the bedclothes.

When I awoke, roused by a long-continued tapping at my door, sunlight was raying in on cornice and bedpost, and birds were singing in the garden. I got up, ashamed of the night's folly, dressed quickly, and went downstairs. The breakfast-room was sweet with flowers and fruit and honey. Seaton's aunt was standing in the garden beside the open French window, feeding a great flutter of birds. I watched her for a moment, unseen. Her face was set in a deep reverie beneath the shadow of a big loose sunhat. It was deeply lined, crooked, and, in a way I can't describe, fixedly vacant and strange. I coughed, and she turned at once with a prodigious smile to inquire how I had slept. And in that mysterious way by which we learn each other's secret thoughts without a sentence spoken I knew that she had followed every word and movement of the night before, and was triumphing over my affected innocence and ridiculing my friendly and too easy advances.

We returned to school, Seaton and I, lavishly laden, and by rail all the way. I made no reference to the obscure talk we had had, and resolutely refused to meet his eyes or to take up the hints he let fall. I was relieved—and yet I was sorry—to be going back, and strode on as fast as I could from the station, with Seaton almost trotting at my heels. But he insisted on buying more fruit and sweets—my share of which I accepted with a very bad grace. It was uncomfortably like a bribe; and, after all, I had no quarrel with his rum old aunt, and hadn't really believed half the stuff he had told me.

I saw as little of him as I could after that. He never referred to our visit or resumed his confidences, though in class I would sometimes catch his eye fixed on mine, full of a mute understanding, which I easily affected not to understand. He left Gummidge's, as I have said, rather abruptly, though I never heard of anything to his discredit. And I did not see him or have any news of him again till by chance we met one summer's afternoon in the Strand.

He was dressed rather oddly in a coat too large for him and a bright silky tie. But we instantly recognised one another under the awning of a cheap jeweler's shop. He immediately attached himself to me and dragged me off, not too cheerfully, to lunch with him at an Italian restaurant near by. He chattered about our old school, which he remembered only with dislike and disgust; told me cold-bloodedly of the disastrous fate of one or two of the old fellows who had been among his chief tormentors; insisted on an expensive wine and the whole gamut of the "rich" menu; and finally informed me, with a good deal of niggling, that he had come up to town to buy an engagement-ring.

And of course: "How is your aunt?" I enquired at last.

He seemed to have been awaiting the question. It fell like a stone into a deep pool, so many expressions flitted across his long un-English face.

"She's aged a good deal," he said softly, and broke off.

"She's been very decent," he continued presently after, and paused again. "In a way." He eyed me fleetingly. "I dare say you heard that she—that is, that we—had lost a good deal of money."

"No," I said.

"Oh, yes!" said Seaton, and paused again.

And somehow, poor fellow, I knew in the clink and clatter of glass and voices that he had lied to me; that he did not possess, and never had possessed, a penny beyond what his aunt had squandered on his too ample allowance of pocket-money.

"And the ghosts?" I enquired quizzically. He grew instantly solemn, and, though it may have been my fancy, slightly yellowed. But "You are making game of me, Withers," was all he said.

He asked for my address, and I rather reluctantly gave him my card.

"Look here, Withers," he said, as we stood in the sunlight on the thronging kerb, saying good-bye, "here I am, and it's all very well; I'm not perhaps as fanciful as I was. But you are practically the only friend I have on earth—except Alice... And there—to make a clean breast of it, I'm not sure that my aunt cares much about my getting married. She doesn't say so, of course. You know her well enough for that." He looked sidelong at the rattling gaudy traffic.

"What I was going to say is this. Would you mind coming down? You needn't stay the night unless you please, though, of course, you know you would be awfully welcome. But I should like you to meet my—to meet Alice; and then, perhaps, you might tell me your honest opinion of—of the other too."

I vaguely demurred. He pressed me. And we parted with a half promise that I would come. He waved his ball-topped cane at me and ran off in his long jacket after a 'bus.

A letter arrived soon after, in his small weak handwriting, giving me full particulars regarding route and trains. And without the least curiosity, even, perhaps with some little annoyance that chance should have thrown us together again, I accepted his invitation and arrived one hazy midday at his out-of-the-way station to find him sitting on a low seat under a clump of double hollyhocks, awaiting me.

His face looked absent and singularly listless; but he seemed, none the less, pleased to see me.

We walked up the village street, past the little dingy apothecary's and the empty forge, and, as on my first visit, skirted the house together, and, instead of entering by the front door, made our way down the green path into the garden at the back. A pale haze of cloud muffled the sun; the garden lay in a grey shimmer—its old trees, its snap-dragoned faintly glittering walls. But there seemed now an air of neglect where before all had been neat and methodical. There was a patch of shallowly-dug soil and a worn-down spade leaning against a tree. There was an old broken wheelbarrow. The goddess of neglect was there.

"You ain't much of a gardener, Seaton," I said, with a sigh of ease.

"I think, do you know, I like it best like this," said Seaton. "We haven't any gardener now, of course. Can't afford it." He stood staring at his little dark square of freshly-turned earth. "And it always seems to me," he went on ruminatingly, "that, after all, we are nothing better than interlopers on the earth, disfiguring and staining wherever we go. I know it's shocking blasphemy to say so, but then it's different here, you see. We are farther away."

"To tell you the truth, Seaton, I don't quite see," I said; "but it isn't a new philosophy, is it? Anyhow, it's a precious beastly one."

"It's only what I think," he replied, with all his odd old stubborn meekness.

We wandered on together, talking little, and still with that expression of uneasy vigilance on Seaton's face. He pulled out his watch as we stood gazing idly over the green meadow and the dark motionless bulrushes.

"I think, perhaps, it's nearly time for lunch," he said. "Would you like to come in?"

We turned and walked slowly towards the house, across whose windows I confess my own eyes, too, went restlessly wandering in search of its rather disconcerting inmate. There was a pathetic look of draggledness, of want of means and care, rust and overgrowth and faded paint. Seaton's aunt, a little to my relief, did not share our meal. Seaton carved the cold meat, and dispatched a heaped-up plate by the elderly servant for his aunt's private consumption. We talked little and in half-suppressed tones, and sipped a bottle of Madeira which Seaton had rather heedfully fetched out of the great mahogany sideboard.

I played him a dull and effortless game of chess, yawning between the moves he generally made almost at haphazard, and with attention elsewhere engaged. About five o'clock came the sound of a distant ring, and Seaton jumped up, overturning the board, and so ending a game that else might have fatuously continued to this day. He effusively excused himself, and after some little while returned with a slim, dark, rather sallow girl of about nineteen, in a white gown and hat, to whom I was presented with some little nervousness as "his dear old friend and schoolfellow."

We talked on in the pale afternoon light, still, as it seemed to me, and even in spite of real effort to be clear and gay, in a half-suppressed, lack-lustre fashion. We all seemed, if it were not my fancy, to be expectant, to be rather anxiously awaiting an arrival, the appearance of someone who all but filled our collective consciousness. Seaton talked least of all, and in a restless interjectory way, as he continually fidgeted from chair to chair. At last he proposed a stroll in the garden before the sun should have quite gone down.

Alice walked between us. Her hair and eyes were conspicuously dark against the whiteness of her gown. She carried herself not ungracefully, and yet without the least movement of her arms or body, and answered us both without turning her head. There was a curious provocative reserve in that impassive and rather long face, a half-unconscious strength of character.

And yet somehow I knew—I believe we all knew—that this walk, this discussion of their future plans was a futility. I had nothing to base such a cynicism on, except only a vague sense of oppression, the foreboding remembrance of the inert invincible power in the background, to whom optimistic plans and love-making and youth are as chaff and thistledown. We came back, silent, in the last light. Seaton's aunt was there—under an old brass lamp. Her hair was as barbarously massed and curled as ever. Her eye-lids, I think, hung even a little heavier in age over their slow-moving inscrutable pupils. We filed in softly out of the evening, and I made my bow.

"In this short interval, Mr. Withers," she remarked amiably, "you have put off youth, put on the man. Dear me, how sad it is to see the young days vanishing! Sit down. My nephew tells me you met by chance—or act of Providence, shall we call it?—and in my beloved Strand! You, I understand, are to be best man—yes, best man, or am I divulging secrets?" She surveyed Arthur and Alice with overwhelming graciousness. They sat apart on two low chairs and smiled in return.

"And Arthur—how do you think Arthur is looking?"

"I think he looks very much in need of a change," I said deliberately.

"A change! Indeed?" She all but shut her eyes at me and with an exaggerated sentimentality shook her head. "My dear Mr. Withers! Are we not all in need of a change in this fleeting, fleeting world?" She mused over the remark like a connoisseur. "And you," she continued, turning abruptly to Alice, "I hope you pointed out to Mr. Withers all my pretty bits?"

"We walked round the garden," said Alice, looking out of the window. "It's a very beautiful evening."

"Is it?" said the old lady, starting up violently. "Then on this very beautiful evening we will go in to supper. Mr. Withers, your arm; Arthur, bring your bride."

I can scarcely describe with what curious ruminations I led the way into the faded, heavy-aired dining-room, with this indefinable old creature leaning weightily on my arm—the large flat bracelet on the yellow-laced wrist. She fumed a little, breathed rather heavily, as if with an effort of mind rather than of body; for she had grown much stouter and yet little more proportionate. And to talk into that great white face, so close to mine, was a queer experience in the dim light of the corridor, and even in the twinkling crystal of the candles. She was naïve—appallingly naïve; she was sudden and superficial; she was even arch; and all these in the brief, rather puffy passage from one room to the other, with these two tongue-tied children bringing up the rear. The meal was tremendous. I have never seen such a monstrous salad. But the dishes were greasy and over-spiced, and were indifferently cooked. One thing only was quite unchanged—my hostess's appetite was as Gargantuan as ever. The old solid candelabra that lighted us stood before her high-backed chair. Seaton sat a little removed, with his plate almost in darkness.

And throughout this prodigious meal his aunt talked, mainly to me, mainly at Seaton, with an occasional satirical courtesy to Alice and muttered explosions of directions to the servant. She had aged, and yet, if it be not nonsense to say so, seemed no older. I suppose to the Pyramids a decade is but as the rustling down of a handful of dust. And she reminded me of some such unshakable prehistoricism. She certainly was an amazing talker—racy, extravagant, with a delivery that was perfectly overwhelming. As for Seaton—her flashes of silence were for him. On her enormous volubility would suddenly fall a hush: acid sarcasm would be left implied; and she would sit softly moving her great head, with eyes fixed full in a dreamy smile; but with her whole attention, one could see, slowly, joyously absorbing his mute discomfiture.

She confided in us her views on a theme vaguely occupying at the moment, I suppose, all our minds. "We have barbarous institutions, and so must put up, I suppose, with a never-ending procession of fools—of fools *ad infinitum*. Marriage, Mr. Withers, was instituted in the privacy of a garden; *sub rosa*, as it were. Civilization flaunts it in the glare of day. The dull marry the poor; the rich the effete; and so our New Jerusalem is peopled with naturals, plain and coloured, at either end. I detest folly; I detest still more (if I must be frank, dear Arthur) mere cleverness. Mankind has simply become a tailless host of uninstinctive animals. We should never have taken to Evolution, Mr. Withers. 'Natural Selection!'—little gods and fishes!—the deaf for the dumb. We should have used our brains— intellectual pride, the ecclesiastics call it. And by brains I mean— what do I mean, Alice?—I mean, my dear child," and she laid two gross fingers on Alice's narrow sleeve. "I mean courage. Consider it, Arthur. I read that the scientific world is once more beginning to be afraid of spiritual agencies. Spiritual agencies that tap, and actually float, bless their hearts! I think just one more of those mulberries—thank you.

"They talk about 'blind Love,'" she ran inconsequently on as she helped herself, with eyes fixed on the dish, "but why blind? I think, do you know, from weeping over its rickets. After all, it is we plain women that triumph, Mr. Withers, beyond the mockery of time. Alice, now! Fleeting, fleeting is youth, my child! What's that you were confiding to your plate, Arthur? Satirical boy! He laughs at his old aunt: nay, but thou didst laugh. He detests all sentiment. He whispers the most acid asides. Come, my love, we will leave these cynics; we will go and commiserate with each other on our sex. The choice of two evils, Mr. Smithers!" I opened the door, and she swept out as if borne on a torrent of unintelligible indignation; and Arthur and I were left in the clear four-flamed light alone.

For a while we sat in silence. He shook his head at my cigarette-case, and I lit a cigarette. Presently he fidgeted in his chair and poked his head forward into the light. He paused to rise and shut again the shut door.

406

"How long will you be?" he said, standing by the table.

I laughed.

"Oh, it's not that!" he said, in some confusion. "Of course, I like to be with her. But it's not that only. The truth is, Withers, I don't care about leaving her too long with my aunt."

I hesitated. He looked at me questioningly.

"Look here, Seaton," I said, "you know well enough that I don't want to interfere in your affairs, or to offer advice where it is not wanted. But don't you think perhaps you may not treat your aunt quite in the right way? As one gets old, you know, a little give and take. I have an old godmother, or something. She talks, too... A little allowance: it does no harm. But, hang it all, I'm no talker."

He sat down with his hands in his pockets and still with his eyes fixed almost incredulously on mine. "How?" he said.

"Well, my dear fellow, if I'm any judge—mind, I don't say that I am—but I can't help thinking she thinks you don't care for her; and perhaps takes your silence for—for bad temper. She has been very decent to you, hasn't she?"

"'Decent'? My God!" said Seaton.

I smoked on in silence; but he still continued to look at me with that peculiar concentration I remembered of old.

"I don't think, perhaps, Withers," he began presently, "I don't think you quite understand. Perhaps you are not quite our kind. You always did, just like the other fellows, guy me at school. You laughed at me that night you came to stay here—about the voices and all that. But I don't mind being laughed at—because I know."

"Know what?" It was the same old system of dull question and evasive answer.

"I mean I know that what we see and hear is only the smallest fraction of what is. I know she lives quite out of this. She *talks* to you; but it's all make-believe. It's all a 'parlour game.' She's not really with you; only pitting her outside wits against yours and enjoying the fooling. She's living on inside, on what you're rotten without. That's what it is—a cannibal feast. She's a spider.

It doesn't much matter what you call it. It means the same kind of thing. I tell you, Withers, she hates me; and you can scarcely dream what that hatred means. I used to think I had an inkling of the reason. It's oceans deeper than that. It just lies behind: herself against myself. Why, after all, how much do we really understand of anything? We don't even know our own histories, and not a tenth, not a tenth of the reasons. What has life been to me?— nothing but a trap. And when one is set free, it only begins again. I thought you might understand; but you are on a different level: that's all."

"What on earth are you talking about?" I said, half contemptuously, in spite of myself.

"I mean what I say," he said gutturally. "All this outside's only make-believe—but there! what's the good of talking? So far as this is concerned I'm as good as done. You wait."

Seaton blew out three of the candles and, leaving the vacant room in semi-darkness, we groped our way along the corridor to the drawing-room. There a full moon stood shining in at the long garden windows. Alice sat stooping at the door, with her hands clasped, looking out, alone.

"Where is she?" Seaton asked in a low tone.

Alice looked up; their eyes met in a kind of instantaneous understanding, and the door immediately afterwards opened behind us.

"*Such* a moon!" said a voice that, once heard, remained unforgettably on the ear. "A night for lovers, Mr. Withers, if ever there was one. Get a shawl, my dear Arthur, and take Alice for a little promenade. I dare say we old cronies will manage to keep awake. Hasten, hasten, Romeo! My poor, poor Alice, how laggard a lover!"

Seaton returned with a shawl. They drifted out into the moonlight. My companion gazed after them till they were out of hearing, turned to me gravely, and suddenly twisted her white face into such a convulsion of contemptuous amusement that I could only stare blankly in reply.

"Dear innocent children!" she said, with inimitable unctuousness. "Well, well, Mr. Withers, we poor seasoned old creatures must move with the times. Do you sing?"

I scouted the idea.

"Then you must listen to my playing. Chess"—she clasped her forehead with both cramped hands—"chess is now completely beyond my poor wits."

She sat down at the piano and ran her fingers in a flourish over the keys. "What shall it be? How shall we capture them, those passionate hearts? That first fine careless rapture? Poetry itself." She gazed softly into the garden a moment, and presently, with a shake of her body, began to play the opening bars of Beethoven's "Moonlight" Sonata. The piano was old and woolly. She played without music. The lamplight was rather dim. The moonbeams from the window lay across the keys. Her head was in shadow. And whether it was simply due to her personality or to some really occult skill in her playing I cannot say: I only know that she gravely and deliberately set herself to satirise the beautiful music. It brooded on the air, disillusioned, charged with mockery and bitterness. I stood at the window; far down the path I could see the white figure glimmering in that pool of colourless light. A few faint stars shone; and still that amazing woman behind me dragged out of the unwilling keys her wonderful grotesquerie of youth and love and beauty. It came to an end. I knew the player was watching me. "Please, please, go on!" I murmured, without turning. "Please go on playing, Miss Seaton."

No answer was returned to my rather fluttering sarcasm, but I knew in some indefinite way that I was being acutely scrutinised, when suddenly there followed a procession of quiet, plaintive chords which broke at last softly into the hymn, 'A Few More Years Shall Roll'.

I confess it held me spellbound. There is a wistful strained, plangent pathos in the tune; but beneath those masterly old hands it cried softly and bitterly the solitude and desperate estrangement of the world. Arthur and his lady-love vanished from my thoughts. No one could put into a rather hackneyed old hymn-tune such an appeal who had never known the meaning of the words. Their meaning, anyhow, isn't commonplace. I turned very cautiously and glanced at the musician. She was leaning forward a little over the keys, so that at the approach of my cautious glance she had but to turn her face into the thin flood of moonlight for every feature to become distinctly visible. And so, with the tune abruptly terminated, we steadfastly regarded one another, and she broke into a chuckle of laughter.

"Not quite so seasoned as I supposed, Mr. Withers. I see you are a real lover of music. To me it is too painful. It evokes too much thought..."

I could scarcely see her little glittering eyes under their penthouse lids.

"And now," she broke off crisply, "tell me, as a man of the world, what do you think of my new niece?"

I was not a man of the world, nor was I much flattered in my stiff and dullish way of looking at things by being called one; and I could answer her without the least hesitation.

"I don't think, Miss Seaton, I'm much of a judge of character. She's very charming."

"A brunette?"

"I think I prefer dark women."

"And why? Consider, Mr. Withers; dark hair, dark eyes, dark cloud, dark night, dark vision, dark death, dark grave, dark DARK!"

Perhaps the climax would have rather thrilled Seaton, but I was too thick-skinned. "I don't know much about all that," I answered rather pompously. "Broad daylight's difficult enough for most of us."

"Ah," she said, with a sly inward burst of satirical laughter.

"And I suppose," I went on, perhaps a little nettled, "it isn't the actual darkness one admires, its the contrast of the skin, and the colour of the eyes, and—and their shining. Just as," I went blundering on, too late to turn back, "just as you only see the stars in the dark. It would be a long day without any evening. As for death and the grave, I don't suppose we shall much notice that." Arthur and his sweetheart were slowly returning along the dewy path. "I believe in making the best of things."

"How very interesting!" came the smooth answer. "I see you are a philosopher, Mr. Withers. H'm! 'As for death and the grave, I don't suppose we shall much notice that.' Very interesting... And I'm sure," she added in a particularly suave voice, "I profoundly hope so." She rose slowly from her stool. "You will take pity on me again, I hope. You and I would get on famously—kindred spirits—elective affinities. And, of course, now that my nephew's going to leave me, now that his affections are centred on another, I shall be a very lonely old woman... Shall I not, Arthur?"

Seaton blinked stupidly. "I didn't hear what you said, Aunt."

"I was telling our old friend, Arthur, that when you are gone I shall be a very lonely old woman."

"Oh, I don't think so;" he said in a strange voice.

"He means, Mr. Withers, he means, my dear child," she said, sweeping her eyes over Alice, "he means that I shall have memory for company—heavenly memory—the ghosts of other days. Sentimental boy! And did you enjoy our music, Alice? Did I really stir that youthful heart?... O, O, O," continued the horrible old creature, "you billers and cooers, I have been listening to such flatteries, such confessions! Beware, beware, Arthur, there's many a slip." She rolled her little eyes at me, she shrugged her shoulders at Alice, and gazed an instant stonily into her nephew's face.

I held out my hand. "Good night, good night!" she cried. "'He that fights and runs away.' Ah, good night, Mr. Withers; come again soon!" She thrust out her cheek at Alice, and we all three filed slowly out of the room.

Black shadow darkened the porch and half the spreading sycamore. We walked without speaking up the dusty village street. Here and there a crimson window glowed. At the fork of the high-road I said good-bye. But I had taken hardly more than a dozen paces when a sudden impulse seized me.

"Seaton!" I called.

He turned in the moonlight.

"You have my address; if by any chance, you know, you should care to spend a week or two in town between this and the—the Day, we should be delighted to see you."

"Thank you, Withers, thank you," he said in a low voice.

"I dare say"—I waved my stick gallantly to Alice—"I dare say you will be doing some shopping; we could all meet," I added, laughing.

"Thank you, thank you, Withers—immensely;" he repeated.

And so we parted.

But they were out of the jog-trot of my prosaic life. And being of a stolid and incurious nature, I left Seaton and his marriage, and even his aunt, to themselves in my memory, and scarcely gave a thought to them until one day I was walking up the Strand again, and passed the flashing gloaming of the covered-in jeweller's shop where I had accidentally encountered my old schoolfellow in the summer. It was one of those still close autumnal days after a rainy night. I cannot say why, but a vivid recollection returned to my mind of our meeting and of how suppressed Seaton had seemed, and of how vainly he had endeavoured to appear assured and eager. He must be married by now, and had doubtless returned from his honeymoon. And I had clean forgotten my manners, had sent not a word of congratulation, nor—as I might very well have done, and as I knew he would have been immensely pleased at my doing—the ghost of a wedding-present.

On the other hand, I pleaded with myself, I had had no invitation. I paused at the corner of Trafalgar Square, and at the bidding of one of those caprices that seize occasionally on even an unimaginative mind, I suddenly ran after a green 'bus that was passing, and found myself bound on a visit I had not in the least foreseen.

All the colours of autumn were over the village when I arrived. A beautiful late afternoon sunlight bathed thatch and meadow. But it was close and hot. A child, two dogs, a very old woman with a heavy basket I encountered. One or two incurious tradesmen looked idly up as I passed by. It was all so rural and so still, my whimsical impulse had so much flagged, that for a while I hesitated to venture under the shadow of the sycamore-tree to enquire after the happy pair. I deliberately passed by the faint-blue gates and continued my walk under the high green and tufted wall. Hollyhocks had attained their topmost bud and seeded in the little cottage gardens beyond; the Michaelmas daisies were in flower; a sweet warm aromatic smell of fading leaves was in the air. Beyond the cottages lay a field where cattle were grazing, and beyond that I came to a little churchyard. Then the road wound on, pathless and houseless, among gorse and bracken. I turned impatiently and walked quickly back to the house and rang the bell.

The rather colourless elderly woman who answered my enquiry informed me that Miss Seaton was at home, as if only taciturnity forbade her adding, "But she doesn't want to see *you*."

"Might I, do you think, have Mr. Arthur's address?" I said.

She looked at me with quiet astonishment, as if waiting for an explanation. Not the faintest of smiles came into her thin face.

"I will tell Miss Seaton," she said after a pause. "Please walk in."

She showed me into the dingy undusted drawing-room, filled with evening sunshine and the green-dyed light that penetrated the leaves overhanging the long French windows. I sat down and waited on and on, occasionally aware of a creaking footfall overhead. At last the door opened a little, and the great face I had once known peered round at me. For it was enormously changed; mainly, I think, because the old eyes had rather suddenly failed, and so a kind of stillness and darkness lay over its calm and wrinkled pallor.

"Who is it?" she asked.

I explained myself and told her the occasion of my visit.

She came in and shut the door carefully after her and, though the fumbling was scarcely perceptible, groped her way to a chair. She had on an old dressing-gown, like a cassock, of a patterned cinnamon colour.

"What is it you want?" she said, seating herself and lifting her blank face to mine.

"Might I just have Arthur's address?" I said deferentially. "I am so sorry to have disturbed you."

"H'm. You have come to see my nephew?"

"Not necessarily to see him, only to hear how he is, and, of course, Mrs. Seaton too. I am afraid my silence must have appeared..."

"He hasn't noticed your silence," croaked the old voice out of the great mask; "besides, there isn't any Mrs. Seaton."

"Ah, then," I answered, after a momentary pause, "I have not seemed so black as I painted myself! And how is Miss Outram?"

"She's gone into Yorkshire," answered Seaton's aunt.

"And Arthur too?"

She did not reply, but simply sat blinking at me with lifted chin, as if listening, but certainly not for what I might have to say. I began to feel rather at a loss.

"You were no close friend of my nephew's, Mr. Smithers?" she said presently.

"No," I answered, welcoming the cue, "and yet, do you know, Miss Seaton, he is one of the very few of my old schoolfellows I have come across in the last few years, and I suppose as one gets older one begins to value old associations..." My voice seemed to trail off into a vacuum. "I thought Miss Outram," I hastily began again, "a particularly charming girl. I hope they are both quite well."

Still the old face solemnly blinked at me in silence.

"You must find it very lonely, Miss Seaton, with Arthur away?"

"I was never lonely in my life," she said sourly. "I don't look to flesh and blood for my company. When you've got to be my age, Mr. Smithers (which God forbid), you'll find life a very different affair from what you seem to think it is now. You won't seek company then, I'll be bound. It's thrust on you." Her face edged round into the clear green light, and her eyes, as it were, groped over my vacant, disconcerted face. "I dare say, now," she said, composing her mouth, "I dare say my nephew told you a good many tarradiddles in his time. Oh, yes, a good many, eh? He was always a liar. What, now, did he say of me? Tell me, now." She leant forward as far as she could, trembling, with an ingratiating smile.

"I think he is rather superstitious," I said coldly, "but, honestly, I have a very poor memory, Miss Seaton."

"Why?" she said. "*I* haven't."

"The engagement hasn't been broken off, I hope."

"Well, between you and me," she said, shrinking up and with an immensely confidential grimace, "it has."

"I'm sure I'm very sorry to hear it. And where is Arthur?"

"Eh?"

"Where is Arthur?"

We faced each other mutely among the dead old bygone furniture. Past all my scrutiny was that large, flat, grey, cryptic countenance. And then, suddenly, our eyes for the first time, really met. In some indescribable way out of that thick-lidded obscurity a far small something stooped and looked out at me for a mere instant of time that seemed of almost intolerable protraction. Involuntarily I blinked and shook my head. She muttered something with great rapidity, but quite inarticulately; rose and hobbled to the door. I thought I heard, mingled in broken mutterings, something about tea.

"Please, please, don't trouble," I began, but could say no more, for the door was already shut between us. I stood and looked out on the long-neglected garden. I could just see the bright greenness of Seaton's old tadpole pond. I wandered about the room. Dusk began to gather, the last birds in that dense shadowiness of trees had ceased to sing. And not a sound was to be heard in the house. I waited on and on, vainly speculating. I even attempted to ring the bell; but the wire was broken, and only jangled loosely at my efforts.

I hesitated, unwilling to call or to venture out, and yet more unwilling to linger on, waiting for a tea that promised to be an exceedingly comfortless supper. And as darkness drew down, a feeling of the utmost unease and disquietude came over me. All my talks with Seaton returned on me with a suddenly enriched meaning. I recalled again his face as we had stood hanging over the staircase, listening in the small hours to the inexplicable stirrings of the night. There were no candles in the room; every minute the autumnal darkness deepened. I cautiously opened the door and listened, and with some little dismay withdrew, for I was uncertain of my way out. I even tried the garden, but was confronted under a veritable thicket of foliage by a padlocked gate. It would be a little too ignominious to be caught scaling a friend's garden fence!

Cautiously returning into the still and musty drawing-room, I took out my watch and gave the incredible old woman ten minutes in which to reappear. And when that tedious ten minutes had ticked by I could scarcely distinguish its hands. I determined to wait no longer, drew open the door, and, trusting to my sense of direction, groped my way through the corridor that I vaguely remembered led to the front of the house.

I mounted three or four stairs and, lifting a heavy curtain, found myself facing the starry fanlight of the porch. Hence I glanced into the gloom of the dining-room. My fingers were on the latch of the outer door when I heard a faint stirring in the darkness above the hall. I looked up and became conscious of, rather than saw, the huddled old figure looking down on me.

There was an immense hushed pause. Then, "Arthur, Arthur," whispered an inexpressively peevish, rasping voice, "is that you? Is that you, Arthur?"

I can scarcely say why, but the question horribly startled me. No conceivable answer occurred to me. With head craned back, hand clenched on my umbrella, I continued to stare up into the gloom, in this fatuous confrontation.

"Oh, oh;" the voice croaked. "It is you, is it? *That* disgusting man!... Go away out. Go away out."

Hesitating no longer, I caught open the door and, slamming it behind me, ran out into the garden, under the gigantic old sycamore, and so out at the open gate.

I found myself half up the village street before I stopped running. The local butcher was sitting in his shop reading a piece of newspaper by the light of a small oil-lamp. I crossed the road and enquired the way to the station. And after he had with minute and needless care directed me, I asked casually if Mr. Arthur Seaton still lived with his aunt at the big house just beyond the village. He poked his head in at the little parlour door.

"Here's a gentleman enquiring after young Mr. Seaton, Millie," he said. "He's dead, ain't he?"

"Why, yes, bless you," replied a cheerful voice from within. "Dead and buried these three months or more—young Mr. Seaton. And just before he was to be married, don't you remember, Bob?"

I saw a fair young woman's face peer over the muslin of the little door at me.

"Thank you," I replied, "then I go straight on?"

"That's it, sir; past the pond, bear up the hill a bit to the left, and then there's the station lights before your eyes."

We looked intelligently into each other's faces in the beam of the smoky lamp. But not one of the many questions in my mind could I put into words.

And again I paused irresolutely a few paces further on. It was not, I fancy, merely a foolish apprehension of what the raw-boned butcher might "think" that prevented my going back to see if I could find Seaton's grave in the benighted churchyard. There was precious little use in pottering about in the muddy dark merely to find where he was buried. And yet I felt a little uneasy. My rather horrible thought was that, so far as I was concerned—one of his esteemed few friends—he had never been much better than "buried" in my mind.

Present at the End
HR Wakefield

When Mr. Benchley noticed the rabbit he was for the moment out of sight of the other guns. The rabbit crouched and stared at him for a second or two, and then started to run past him across the ride. Mr. Benchley swung his gun ahead of it and fired. The rabbit somersaulted and then lay kicking. Mr. Benchley went up to it. Some of its fur, cut by the pellets, was shaken on to the pine needles as it kicked. One shot had struck its left eye, which was broken and bleeding. When it saw Mr. Benchley looking hugely over it, it ceased to struggle for a moment, and with its uninjured eye it stared at the other animal who had done this to it. And then it kicked out convulsively once more, trembled through its length, and was dead. Mr. Benchley picked it up by the hind legs and walked on. Before he rejoined the other guns at the edge of the wood he had three other opportunities of making the fur fly, but he did not take them. He could hear the other guns taking theirs to right and left of him. It was a very quiet and coldly radiant October morning. As Mr. Benchley strode along, the rabbit swung as it dangled from his hand, and he saw there was a thin trickle of blood pouring down the white patch below its left eye and dripping to the ground. This somewhat distracted his attention from the beauty of the day. As he came out from the wood, an under-keeper took the rabbit from him and flung it down on a rapidly growing pile of its fellows, many of which had rosy cheeks also. One by one the other guns arrived, refilled their pipes and sat down to rest. After a short consultation between Mr. Benchley's host and his head-keeper it was decided to send the beaters round by the road and into the big field of roots facing them, for the purpose of driving the animal inhabitants of that field towards the guns. Those that were edible would be bombarded, and in certain cases the non-edible—stoats, poaching-cats, owls and so on. The guns spread themselves out, lightly concealed by the hedge bordering the wood. The beaters trudged off and Mr. Benchley lit a cigarette. After ten minutes or so he could see the beaters in the distance forming into line and beginning to move forward. Soon he could hear the tapping of their sticks, and almost immediately a big covey rose and flew hard and low towards the wood. As they neared it they rose to clear it.

"Bang-bang. Bang-bang-bang. Bang-bang-bang!"

Mr. Benchley got a beautiful right and left and he could hear the birds' bodies crash into the trees behind him. The root field was well stocked and he was kept very busy for the next quarter of an hour. And he was so occupied with events over-head that he had no time to attend to two hares, which, dazed by the din ahead of them, hesitated for a moment at the edge of the roots, and then with their ears back dashed wildly past him. When it was all over and the beaters were mopping their brows, the attention of Mr. Benchley was attracted by a fluttering sound just behind him. This he discovered was being made by a hen partridge with a broken wing and leg, which was attempting unsuccessfully to adjust itself to its altered circumstances. When Mr. Benchley went up to it, it paid little attention to the person who had necessitated this adjustment, but continued to flutter and roll itself over on to its side, and, when this hurt, roll back again. Mr. Benchley picked it up and struck its head twice against his right boot. Not hard enough, obviously, for it continued to writhe in his hand.

"Not often you have to do that, Mr. Benchley,' said a voice. He looked up and there was his host's rather pretty flapper daughter. He smiled back at her rather uncertainly, and again struck the bird's head against his toe. It became inert in his hand. The girl took it from him, and he wiped the blood from his boot with a handful of grass. It was then time for lunch, which was eaten in a barn near by. A rough count proved that the morning's work had been reasonably successful. The number of hares seen and shot surprised his host. "Too damned many of 'em," he declared. Mr. Benchley agreed with him, but remarked very emphatically that he derived little amusement from killing them.

"No more do I," agreed someone. "Too much target. All right for anyone who can shoot, but the bad shots are always back-ending them, and even if they're stopped, they scream, and I don't like that sound a little bit." And he patted his retriever's rump affectionately.

"All the same," said the host, "there are too many of 'em. So shoot all you can."

Presently they moved off to Pearson's spinney, one of the finest pheasant shoots in the country. Mr. Benchley spent the next half-hour dexterously picking those gloriously high birds out of the sky, and hearing the pleasant plump with which they met the ground. His mind was disconnectedly busy with a certain problem, but he continued to load and fire with the virtuosity born of forty years' practice and training. The flapper, who had heard many tales of his prowess, watched him with bright-eyed enthusiasm, and she never forgot having seen him kill fifty-eight pheasants stone dead with his first seventy cartridges. Mr. Benchley was only vaguely aware of her presence, and it was a sudden sight of her dark blue jumper which made him a shade late on a hare which dashed out straight in front of him and swung left for cover. It began to drag its hind legs and scream. It managed to pull itself into the heart of a thick thorn bush, and, though Mr. Benchley could hear it well enough, he could not at first catch sight of it. Presently, however, he saw it move and gave it the left barrel. It died at once and he left it there. He jerked out the empty cases, but did not reload. It was near the end of the drive, and when the beaters came up he went to his host and told him he had gun-headache and wouldn't shoot any more.

"All right," said his host; "give your gun to someone to carry back, and if you want tea or a drink, Jenkins will get it for you. There are some aspirins in my medicine chest if you want them. We'll knock off in about another hour."

Mr. Benchley was rather silent during dinner, and pleading a violent headache, went early to bed. He left for London the next morning.

A month later the organising secretary of a certain society for protecting the interests of animals was going through his letters. Eventually he opened one, the contents of which seemed to cause him surprise. He got up and went to the next room, which was occupied by the publicity manager.

"Dick," he said, "I've got a note here from a bloke named Mr. Benchley. I seem to have heard of him. Who is he?"

"A famous Mass Murderer," replied the person addressed. "He's put an end to nearly everything which flies, swims and runs, and in most cases in vast quantities. He once killed a thousand grouse in a day—or a million—some charming record or other— one of the five best shots in England, in every sense of the word—a Bloody Man, I imagine. What the devil does he want with us?"

The publicity manager was a person of intolerant views and intemperate utterance.

"He says he would like to see someone connected with this outfit," replied the secretary. "Let's look him up in *Who's Who.*" He fetched that encyclopaedia of mediocrity and read out:

"Benchley, Robert Aloysius. Born in 1870. Eldest son of (We'll skip that). Educated at Eton and New College, Oxford. He took a first in Greats, by Jove! Founded firm of R. A. Benchley & Co., Limited. Recreations: shooting, fishing, golf. Address: 43 Brook Crescent, W.1.—Well, he's less verbose and full of himself than most of them."

"Does he mention how many grouse he once killed in a day?" asked the manager. "Recreations: mangling birds, beasts, fishes and golf balls. Imagine confessing to it! What he wants to bother with us for I cannot conceive, said the duchess. But go and see him."

The secretary thereupon rang up 43 Brook Crescent, and was told that Mr. Benchley would be glad to see him at half-past three that afternoon.

Precisely at that hour the secretary was shown into a large, quietly furnished, sedately appointed room, and Mr. Benchley got up to greet him.

"It's very good of you to come," he said.

The secretary found himself not quite at his ease. For one thing he was somewhat taken aback by Mr. Benchley's appearance. He had expected to find a hearty, rubicund, confident Mass Murderer; instead he saw before him a pale, soft-voiced neurasthenic. Well, perhaps not so bad as that, but he looked ill and strained about the eyes, and he had some nervous tricks—staring so hard at his boot—and then that occasional and discomforting sudden throwing up of his hands towards his head, a very noticeable and obviously involuntary trick, though he half controlled it.

"I imagine," said Mr. Benchley, "that you are very curious as to my reasons for asking you to come to-day. You probably know me, if you know me at all, as the incarnation of a kind of cruelty; that is badly phrased, but you know what I mean, a blood-sportsman to adapt an epithet of Shaw's. So I have been, but the past tense is appropriate, for I do not intend to merit that epithet ever again."

As he said this his hands once again jumped towards his head, were controlled and brought down again. He wiped his forehead with his handkerchief.

"Officially at least, we do not attack or concern ourselves with fishing, shooting or hunting." Replied the secretary guardedly. "Many of our members shoot, fish and hunt."

"I know that," said Mr. Benchley, staring fixedly at the toe of his shoe. "All the same I have fired my last shot exactly a month ago. Do you have many cases of so sudden a conversion?"

"I've known quite a few," answered the secretary. "In fact in a little way I am such a case myself; I shot when I was young and enjoyed it."

"Have you ever in a sense enjoyed anything more?"

"In a limited sense, no."

"Then why did you give it up?"

"Well," said the secretary, "I found that the memory of the movements and sounds made by the animals I had wounded remained with me. I used to dream of them. But besides that, I suppose I grew up sensitively as it were." He would have expanded this remark slightly if it had not been for the fact that Mr. Benchley threw his hands up again, which distracted him.

"I believe," said Mr. Benchley, " that the sensitiveness to which you refer is an unchallengeable symptom of intellectual, and to some extent, moral superiority. Highly sensitive people are ahead of their time. A general quickening of sensitiveness in a race is equivalent to a general refinement of its civilisation. One day, it may be, to kill an animal for amusement will be considered an act of flagrant indecency, as serious an offence as wearing a white tie with a dinner jacket. As a matter of fact my conversion was not quite as abrupt as it seems. My father shot all his life, and I killed my first rabbit when I was twelve. It seemed a perfectly natural thing to do. But I can recall certain more or less short-lived premonitions that it wouldn't always seem so natural. Every now and again I felt disgusted and uncertain, and these occasions became more and more frequent until that day a month ago. On that day I had certain experiences, experiences I had had before, but they suddenly seemed vile and harrowing, unendurable, intolerable. As a result of them I had a mild form of nervous breakdown. I have been in the doctor's hands for the last month—I am better now, but not entirely cured, I'm afraid. It sounds an absurd question, but can you see any mark, any stain of any kind on the toe of my right shoe?" He pushed it forward.

The secretary made rather a business of deciding this point, for he was not feeling too comfortable. "None whatever," he replied with great emphasis, after a close scrutiny.

"I thought not," replied Mr. Benchley; "it is simply that I have been a little worried about my eyesight since that trouble a month ago. I quite realise," he continued, "that it would probably split your society from top to bottom if it attempted to tackle the shooting-hunting problem, and the money I am going to give it will be given unconditionally. At the same time I should prefer that some of it at least was expended in furthering the following causes. I will put all this in writing, of course.

"Firstly: To put pressure on the Government to bring in a Bill making it compulsory for all drivers of horse vehicles to pass an examination in horse-mastership before they are allowed to drive.

"Secondly: I should like a certain percentage of this money devoted to the discovery of a humane trap for rabbits.

"Thirdly: To inquire temperately and impartially into the vivisection question.

"Fourthly: To put pressure on the Government, by arousing public opinion, concerning the export overseas of old horses. Any money within reason you want for rest-homes for such horses will be forthcoming.

"That will do for a start, and now I will give you a cheque." He went to his bureau and fetched it.

When the secretary saw the figures his eyes grew wide and he began to utter fervent expressions of gratitude, to which Mr. Benchley put, almost rudely, an immediate stop.

When the secretary was out in the street again, he set off whistling and swinging his cane. "That old bird gave me the 'willies' for some reason or other," he said to himself. "There's something slightly 'dunno-what' about him. Who cares! It's his money we want! He seems extremely tame. I can imagine him allowing a really fierce snipe to bite his ear. Who cares! It's his money we want!"

After he had left, Mr. Benchley opened and shut his right hand many times, and he did this to convince himself that he no longer had the sensation that he was gripping something warm and feathered which writhed slightly whenever his nails met his palm.

A few days later his drawing-room was transformed into a highly efficient office, with a secretary and three plain but serviceable typists, all of whom were kept exceedingly busy. After they had been at it for three weeks the first-fruits of their labours were seen in the shape of a column long letter to *The Times* signed by their employer. In this he had the cool nerve to suggest that, as a result of many years' desultory, and a few weeks concentrated, examination of the subject, he had come to the conclusion that the utilitarian arguments for hunting and shooting were completely fallacious. He himself had shot all his life, though he had not given up doing so, but he realised he had shot simply and solely because he had found killing animals amusing; obeying a potent, savage impulse. Many people, he believed, salved their consciences when they inflicted gross pain on animals by reflecting that, "someone had got to do it." In his opinion no one had got to do it. And an elaborately documented argument followed.

This bombshell started one of the most heated and copious controversies in the history of Press debate, for this discordant chatter spread from *The Times* and ripped out over the length and breadth of the British Isles, and wherever two or three were gathered together, the introduction of this tinder topic made for fiery dissension. Mr. Benchley's former friends shook compassionate fists in protest. "The poor old dotard! Incipient senile decay! Nervous breakdown! Blood pressure! Piffling sentimentality! Hopeless bunk!" Such were the exclamatory refutations with which they repudiated such sloppy heresy. Yet he did not lack adherents, and the skirmish swirled into a battle, and the battle surged into a campaign. Mr. Benchley's post-bag was worthy of a film-star's, though he had few requests for signed photographs; but every communication which deserved one received a courteous, if usually and necessarily a controversial, reply. He had always had the capacity to write concisely; now controlled passion lent him a style, so that his short contributions to sympathetic weekly papers were well worthy of their polished company. These little papers usually took the form of impressionist sketches of incidents he had witnessed during his sporting career; vignettes of animals' terror and pain, very often. Sometimes they were dispassionate little studies of the psychology of those responsible for that terror and pain. One and all made a curious impression of authenticity, and many of great horror and distress.

Throughout all this time Mr. Benchley kept himself entirely aloof from his fellow-men. His former friends had no more wish to meet him than he had to meet them. And he was in no mood to make new friends. He worked ten hours a day, making up for much lost time. He left his business to his partner. The secretary dined with him once a week to report progress and plan schemes for the future. He became gradually acclimatised to his host's eccentricities, for which he made St. Vitus responsible. Mr. Benchley still continued at intervals most fixedly and urgently to regard certain apparently blank spots on the wall of the table-cloth, and once in a while he flung his hands up to his head, but he no longer seemed so unnecessarily preoccupied with the toe of his shoe. St. Vitus had yielded a point. He had observed correctly, the explanation being that Mr. Benchley no longer was compelled to accept the fact that he could see a small splashed globe of blood on the toe of his shoe. This visual relief coincided with the patenting of an efficient humane rabbit trap and the initiation of a campaign to make its use compulsory. The bitter controversy started by Mr. Benchley's letters gradually died down as he had realised it would, but it left, nevertheless, certain permanent results, revealed, not so much by a perceptible but probably temporary decrease in the number of those who hunted and shot, as in a general intensification

427

of that uncertainty and unease which had always troubled humane persons at the thought of at what expense they took their pleasure, a slight moving of the waters of sensitive perception. He was ahead of his time, but his teaching was not merely ridiculed. It was frantically assailed by some, its sincerity was grudgingly conceded by others, it was fervently welcomed as a potent aperient for the bowels of compassion by those who had long laboured in the same cause against apparently hopeless odds.

It was on the day that *The Times* announced it could no longer extend the hospitality of its columns to the debate that Mr. Benchley found himself most blessedly free from another ocular bother. That swollen, red blob which always reminded him so horribly of the pulped eye of a rabbit no longer imprinted itself on flat surfaces, and remained there as it were staring aloofly at him. This, he had hoped subjective appearance, had been both frequent and regular, but like shell-fire its effect on his mind increased rather than diminished with repetition.

The day after he was freed from this eccentricity, all the windows on the ground-floor of his house were broken by persons unknown, and some abusive phrases were painted on his front door, a gesture charitably attributed to medical students. This was quite probable, for the society's inquiry into the pros and cons of vivisection had brought some uncomfortable facts to the light, and it was generally known that Mr. Benchley had been at the back of this inquest. He heard the succession of crashes just as he was reading a report from the secretary stating that, since the date when he had first interested himself in its affairs, the subscriptions and donations received by the society had increased four hundred per cent, that a grant of £10,000 had been made to the affiliated society in Spain, and that the long over-due fight against the torture of the Indian Water Buffalo was about to be begun with adequate financial support. Mr. Benchley felt that those crashes rather appropriately signalled these announcements. A little later the society announced that a certain person, who desired to remain anonymous, had subscribed £5,000 to it to form the nucleus of a special Benchley Fund to be devoted to the further education of the public in regard to Blood Sports.

The fund reached £20,000 in a week. On the last day of that week, Mr. Benchley ceased to fling his hands up towards his ears at regular intervals, for he no longer felt that agonised scream suddenly shake on their drums. Nevertheless he went to bed that night feeling utterly exhausted and ill. The next morning he couldn't get up, and when the doctor came he diagnosed pulmonary pneumonia and engaged day and night nurses.

Up to the crisis, Mr. Benchley fought for his life, for he had much still to do, but he had undermined his powers of resistance by insensate over-work, and presently he knew he could fight no more. After that he relapsed into gradually lengthening periods of unconsciousness. When he realised he was dying he sent for the secretary, to whom he gave certain instructions regarding the use of the fortune he was leaving to the society. The secretary had come to regard Mr. Benchley as a very great man, and when he had shaken hands with him, and said good-bye and left him, there were tears in his eyes as he swung his cane jauntily.

The doctor came about four o'clock and made his examination. He took the nurse out from the sick-room with him, and shrugging his shoulders said "There is nothing more to be done. He may last one hour or twelve."

"I'm wanted for another case to-morrow," said the nurse. "Will it be safe for me to accept it?"

"Oh, yes, he can't possibly last through the night. He refuses to have any more oxygen. I can't help respecting him, though I know he financed that damn-fool inquiry."

During his periods of unconsciousness Mr. Benchley had dreams. In one of them he seemed to be watching a small excited boy who was staring across a surging field of corn over which a windhover was poised against the gale. And suddenly it lifted and soared over the bordering trees, a dark speck against the green, and disappeared. This dream recurred three times. And then he awoke full of a great weakness and a certain sense of peace. The nurse had gone out to pack her bag. The fire was alive but dying, just one still pregnant coal was thrusting forth lazy, lolling flames which slightly darkened the shadows. Mr. Benchley was just about to surrender again to that overmastering weariness when it seemed to him that something leapt lightly on to the bed beside him, something which turned and faced him. And at first one of its eyes was clear, and the other bleeding and broken. With an effort he turned his head towards it, and then he saw that both its eyes were bright and whole again. And it nestled to his side. And after a little while something else fluttered up on to the blanket, something which for a moment trailed a wing and writhed, and then settled itself down beside him, trimly and stealthily. The flames died down, but there was just enough light left to enable Mr. Benchley to catch the outline of something big and brown which dragged its hind legs towards him. Mr. Benchley tried with all his might to get his hands to his ears, and he shut his eyes. But the silence was unbroken and he opened them again, and that big, brown shadow moved easily towards him and tucked itself down beside his arm. And then the fire shook itself slightly and the room was dark. And Mr. Benchley, feeling three little pressures against him, rallied his failing strength, and just succeeded in moving his right hand over and down, and it closed over two long, soft ears, which twitched gently, as if with pleasure. And a moment later Mr. Benchley fell asleep.

Biographical Notes

Compiled by Mark Valentine

Nugent Barker (1888-1955) was the author of only one book, *Written With My Left Hand* (1951), a collection of original, exuberant macabre stories. Very little is known about him. The only known biographical notice briefly states that he came from an old Irish family, the Nugents of Westmeath, and was educated at Cheltenham. It explains that poor eyesight prevented him joining up in the First World War: and that he began work as a black-and-white illustrator but "has recently devoted himself entirely to literature." In his introduction to the 2002 Tartarus Press reprint, Douglas Anderson notes that in the 1920s Barker lived at 16, Tite Street, Chelsea, where Oscar Wilde resided just before his trials, and it was still Barker's address at the time of his death.

Arthur Christopher Benson (1862-1925) was born into scholarly and ecclesiastical circles, since his father was in turn Chancellor of Lincoln and Bishop of Truro, then appointed Archbishop of Canterbury in 1882. AC Benson was a contemporary of MR James at Cambridge, successively a Fellow, then President, then Master of Magdalene College. A prolific essayist, mellow and ruminatory in style, his voluminous diaries reveal a sharper tongue. His ghost stories may be found in *The Hill of Trouble and Other Stories* (1903) and *The Isles of Sunset* (1904), among other volumes.

BIOGRAPHICAL NOTES

Edward Frederic Benson (1867-1940), brother of AC and RH Benson, was a highly prolific and versatile writer who first had success with the light comedy *Dodo, A Detail of the Day* (1893), and showed a flair for the macabre with his *The Luck of the Vails* (1901), about an ancient family legend, a taste which continued throughout his career right up to his last novel, *Ravens' Brood* (1934). He settled in the picturesque Sussex town of Rye, and his gentle social satires set there featuring two rival grand dames, Mapp and Lucia, won appreciation. He was a dedicated exponent of the ghost story and may be seen as one of the most accomplished contemporaries of MR James. His work here can be found in *The Room in the Tower and Other Stories* (1912), *Spook Stories* (1928), *More Spook Stories* (1934) and others.

Robert Hugh Benson (1871-1914), third of the literary Benson brothers, caused a stir by converting to Roman Catholicism in his early thirties. He then wrote numerous often rather lurid novels in which heroes of his faith battle against sin and villainy: some of these are apocalyptic in range and vision, most notably *Lord of the World* (1907). He was an enthusiast of the work of Frederick Rolfe, 'Baron Corvo', and they planned a book on Thomas Becket in collaboration, but inevitably the Baron fell out with him. Benson's ghost stories were gathered in *The Light Invisible* (1903) and *A Mirror of Shalott* (1907).

Algernon Blackwood (1869-1951) was born in Kent, the son of a senior civil servant with rigid religious views. As a youth, Blackwood became interested in Eastern religions and later extolled in his stories a form of pantheistic nature worship. He travelled in the USA and Canada in his twenties, taking casual jobs and often in poverty. From his earliest writing, *The Empty House and Other Ghost Stories* (1906), he excelled at the supernatural tale, and later, when he broadcast these on BBC wireless, was so identified with the form that he was known simply as 'the Ghost Man'. His approach is the opposite of that of MR James – he is fervent, lyrical, interested in the meaning of the otherworldly. He also wrote mystical novels concerned with reincarnation and cosmic forces, such as

The Centaur (1911) and *Julius LeVallon* (1916). His 'The Willows' is often cited as one of the finest-ever supernatural stories.

Alfred McClelland Burrage (1889-1956) was a versatile professional writer who wrote *War is War* (1930), a noted memoir of the First World War, under the pseudonym 'Ex-Private X'. He wrote widely for Fleet Street newspapers and magazines and a 1920 biographical note described him as "one of the most popular of magazine writers. Everything he does has charm and reflects his own romantic spirit." He evidently enjoyed writing ghost stories, returning to the form often, and these may be found in *Some Ghost Stories* (1927), *Someone in the Room* (as 'Ex-Private X', 1931), *Don't Break the Seal* (1946) and others.

Colette de Curzon (1927-2018) was the daughter of the French Consul-General in Portsmouth and wrote 'Payman's Trio' at the age of 22, but did not know how to go about getting it published. Preserved for some sixty-seven years, it was rediscovered by one of her daughters, the novelist Gabrielle Kimm, and published as a chapbook by Nicholas Royle's Nightjar Press. This fine tale of haunted music, in the tradition of J Meade Falkner's *The Lost Stradivarius* (1895), was soon warmly acclaimed.

Walter De La Mare (1873-1956) was as a young man attracted to the Aesthetical movement and briefly published a magazine, *The Basilisk*, printed in purple ink. He worked as a clerk for an oil company but his poetry attracted admiration, and friends secured him a government pension so he could escape drudgery and devote himself to writing. Some of his poems are still anthology favourites, and his enigmatic short stories, with their dream-like qualities, helped suggest a different direction for the ghostly tale. His best collections include *The Riddle and Other Stories* (1923) and *The Connoisseur and Other Stories* (1926).

Emilia Francis Dilke (1840-1904) was an art historian and progressive campaigner who became Lady Dilke when she married the baronet and Radical politician Sir Charles Dilke in 1884. After attending art school, she was art critic and then art editor for *The Academy* for some years, and published several studies of the fine and applied arts in eighteenth-century France. She was also active in women's and trade union causes. Her ghost stories, aesthetical in style and decadent in theme, were published as *The Shrine of Death and Other Stories* (1886) and *The Shrine of Love and Other Stories* (1891).

Henrietta Dorothy Everett (1851-1923), who mostly wrote under the pseudonym 'Theo Douglas', attracted attention with her dramatic Egyptian revivification fantasy *Iras: A Mystery* (1896), in which the mummy of a princess is restored to life. She went on to publish over a dozen further novels as Douglas, some also with macabre and fantastical elements, but never quite captured the same success. From at least 1910 she published under her own name, as 'Mrs HD Everett', and late in life issued a collection of weird stories, *The Death-Mask and Other Ghosts* (1920). Her work in the form is often sad, gentle, even sentimental, her spirits lovelorn or lost.

Charlotte Perkins Gilman (1860-1935), from Connecticut, was a novelist, dramatist, poet, short story writer, lecturer, early feminist and social reformer, a woman of formidable energy and determination. But she is known today mainly for the story 'The Yellow Wallpaper' (1892). This concerns a young woman, diagnosed as depressive, who becomes morbidly obsessed with the décor in a sinister upper room in the house where she is convalescing. The story had strong autobiographical elements. Its Decadent patina and terse cumulative tension have won the tale high praise. Her other work, like her character, has tended to be absorbed by that dominating wallpaper, but she is also known for *Herland* (1915), a feminist utopia.

John Gower (about 1325-1408) was a squire and medieval poet of genteel birth but his exact origins, despite scholarly speculation, remain unknown. Links to families in Wales, Yorkshire or Suffolk have been suggested. He was in later life involved as a lay member with a priory in Southwark, which he generously supported. His chief literary work, *Confessio Amantis*, was published by Caxton in 1483. It mingles classical deities and imagery with Christian morality, and discourses in verse on the seven deadly sins. The numerous contemporary manuscript copies may attest to its popularity in its time.

Leslie Poles Hartley (1895-1972) was born in Whittlesey, Cambridgeshire. His father was a solicitor, later the director of a brickworks, and Hartley grew up in a turreted Victorian Gothic edifice. He was educated at Eton and Balliol, enlisted in the First World War and was commissioned, but because of his weak health was confined to the home front and eventually invalided out. He is best known today as the author of *The Go-Between* (1953), a smouldering recollection of an Edwardian childhood, with its memorable opening line, 'The past is a foreign country; they do things differently there.' He was also a keen writer of highly effective macabre tales, some gathered in *The Travelling Grave and Other Stories* (1948).

Leslie Allin Lewis (1899-1961) was the author of only one book, *Tales of the Grotesque* (1934). Little was known about him until the eminent ghost story anthologist Richard Dalby contacted his estate and was able to bring his work back into print: US scholar Douglas Anderson later added further details about him. Lewis was born in Sheffield, educated at a private school in Abingdon, enlisted in the Artists' Rifles in the First World War and later trained as a pilot. He apparently suffered from hallucinations and episodes of mental illness in later life. Richard Dalby noted: "Lewis never doubted the existence of demonic creatures and elements on the other side... which continually strive to break through into our world."

Thomas Ligotti (born Detroit, USA, 1953) was recognised as a distinctive voice in the weird fiction field with the publication of his *Songs of A Dead Dreamer* (1986) and *Grimscribe: His Lives and Works* (1991), collections of macabre stories and vignettes replete with images of dolls, puppets, mannequins and other simulacra of the human form. His work introduces Middle-European melancholia and arcane imagery to small-town Middle America. Further collections followed, enhancing his reputation as a poet of pessimism and chronicler of decay. His *The Conspiracy Against the Human*

Race (2010) is a philosophical work which argues that 'behind the scenes of life lurks something pernicious that makes a nightmare of our world.'

Arthur Machen (1863-1947) was born in the old Roman town of Caerleon in the Welsh border county of Gwent but went to London as a young man to make his way in literature. He worked in poverty as a book cataloguer, tutor, and translator from the French, before finding success in the decadent 'Yellow Nineties' with two novellas, *The Great God Pan and The Inmost Light* (1894), and with *The Three Impostors* (1895). His mystical and semi-autobiographical *The Hill of Dreams* (1907) had to wait ten years for book publication. His tales of horror and the supernatural, some collected in *The House of Souls* (1906), place him among the highest regarded writers in this field. His 'The White People' is often seen as one of the greatest horror stories.

Richard Barham Middleton (1882-1911) was primarily a poet who tried and failed to make a living from his verses and took his own life in despair in Brussels at the age of 29. At the New Bohemians literary and drinking society he was a friend of Arthur Machen, who wrote the introduction to a posthumous collection of supernatural tales, *The Ghost Ship and Other Stories* (1912): other volumes of poems, tales, sketches and essays followed. The title story, in which a spectral buccaneering galleon descends on a cabbage field near a quiet English village, is regarded as one of the best humorous ghost stories, while his 'On the Brighton Road' is one of the most effective involving gentle pathos.

Amyas Northcote (1864-1923) was the youngest son of the 1st Earl of Iddesleigh, a leading Victorian Conservative statesman who served as Chancellor of the Exchequer and Foreign Secretary. He grew up in the ancestral family home near Exeter, Devon and attended Eton, where he would have been a contemporary of MR James. He emigrated to the USA, praising the kindness and hospitality of the people, and was in business in Chicago. He returned to England around the turn of the century, where he seems to have settled into life as a country squire

MARK VALENTINE

in Buckinghamshire. He was the author of only one book, the well-regarded *In Ghostly Company* (1922).

Oliver Onions (1873-1961), born in Bradford in the West Riding of Yorkshire, began his working life as a commercial artist but switched to journalism and then became a versatile author of novels in several different fields, embracing comedy, romance, bohemian life, political satire and crime fiction. He earned late recognition for a brooding and powerful historical novel, *The Story of Ragged Robyn* (1945), about the inexorable working-out of a curse, and a further historical novel, *Poor Man's Tapestry* (1946) won the prestigious James Tait Black Prize for Fiction. *The Hand of Kornelius Voyt* (1939), set in Bradford, has uncanny elements, and he is now respected also for his subtle, reflective ghost stories, some published in *Widdershins* (1911), and gathered in a *Collected Ghost Stories* (1935).

Edna Worthley Underwood (1873-1961) was born in Maine, USA, but lived mostly in Kansas and New York. She pursued a determined course of self-education and wrote and published widely. As an anthologist and translator, she introduced writing from Haiti, Mexico and elsewhere to American audiences. She also wrote historical novels and poetry, and one collection of macabre stories, *A Book of Dear Dead Women* (1911), which was compared to the work of Hawthorne. In his introduction to the 2010 Tartarus Press reprint, ST Joshi noted the "distinctive atmosphere of horror in which beauty is inextricably mingled" in her stories.

Herbert Russell Wakefield (1888-1964), like so many other ghost story writers, was the son of a clergyman: his father became the Bishop of Birmingham. He was educated at Marlborough and Oxford, served at the front in the First World War, and later worked for a while in publishing. He wrote some crime novels and an efficient and nuanced study of a noted murder trial acquittal, *The Green Bicycle Case* (1930), but he is remembered now for his several volumes of assured, crisply-told ghost stories. These are found in *They Return At Evening* (1928), *Old Man's Beard* (1929), *The Clock Strikes Twelve* (1940) and other selections. Wakefield is regarded as one of the

437

most impressive contributors to the supernatural fiction field in the period after MR James. 'Present At the End' reflects his humanitarian opposition to blood sports.

Edith Newbold Wharton (1862-1937) was born into prosperous New York society but spent much of her later life in Europe, particularly in Paris, reflecting her cosmopolitan outlook. Choosing to remain in France during the First World War, she did tireless work for refugees and the destitute and in 1916 was made a Chevalier of the Legion D'Honneur for her war work. She wrote about France and Italy in sympathetic and well-received studies, but achieved eminence for her society novels, particularly *The House of Mirth* (1905), *Ethan Frome* (1911) and *The Age of Innocence* (1920). Her work in the uncanny is sophisticated, measured and subtle and she was one of the first to see the opportunity for literary distinction in this field.

On And Over Grave Cartoons

All artwork for, and in, this volume is by David Tibet.

Front cover: *The Children In The Midst Of The Graveyard At The End Of Their World*; front endpaper: *The Children Dance Around The Grave In Their Midst*; rear endpaper: *The Children Ascend From The Grave In Their Midst*; frontispiece: *The Children Lament Over The Grave In Their Midst; back cover: Bella Beyond The Midst Of The Mist.* Front cover, back cover, frontispiece, and endpapers rendered into darkness and larkness and nightness by Ania Goszczyńska.

The title font used in this book's design was created by Ania Goszczyńska as an expansion of the font used on the boards of the first edition of *Studies of Death* by Count Stanislaus Eric Stenbock (David Nutt, London, 1894), designed by Aymer Vallance. Photograph of David Tibet in Heptonstall, West Yorkshire, January 2019 by Ania Goszczyńska.

Grateful Moons
David Tibet

If A City Is Set Upon A Grave...

A thousand thanks and singing flowers, numberless and free, to all of those who have helped me, in ways known and unknown, as I built and tended this Graveyard:

Mark Pilkington and Jamie Sutcliffe, Supreme and Strangest of Attractors, whose Energized Enthusiasm for Moons and Graveyards brought this book to both you and me; Mark Valentine for laying so many trails for me to chase, and for the perfect biographies he supplied for this volume; Ossian Brown for his Touches of Pan, his Love and Inspiration, and his Kitten Paws and Claws; Ray Russell of Tartarus Press, for helps beyond the Calls of the Æthyrs and books beyond compare; Keith Richmond who has not only sent me a *Magus* or two, but more importantly gave me his friendship as well as a message directly from Bournemouth, or at least from *The Spirit Of Irene*; Henry Boxer for his lucid Channellings from the pellucid planets, and for the kittens, and for Madge too; Martin Worthington for his Assyriological advice, and the inspiration and knowledge he so readily gives me from his ᴴᵀhood; Ola Wikander for Biblical Hebrew and for singing me sweet ⵁⴹⵁ from Ugarit since the beginning, or at least *a* beginning—בְּרֵאשִׁית;Seth Sanders for his uniqueness and his utter Ugariticity and books and 𐎘𐎗𐎅 too; Hugo Lundhaug for shared Coptic obsessions and magic bowls—ïⲁ︧ⲱ ⲁⲃⲣⲁⲭⲁ ⲁⲃⲣⲁⲥⲁⲕ; Sam Goodman for more Borley than my heart—and our house—could hold; Douglas Anderson for werewolves and moonshines and Housmans too; Robert Eldridge who *Swept And Garnished* my bookcase, and who perhaps one day will even deliver *Mists* to *Our Lady*; Daniel Wilson for Zodiacs, Gefs, and the Pseudo-Occult; Timothy Mark Lewis for farsight and friendship and for looking after me and my unruly Family and Friends; and Jake Gill for lovelily looking after those things that don't look after me.

And I too shall not forget, and I am OverMoon too to thank: Anohni, Nina Antonia, Phil Baker, George Barnett, Jack Barnett, Ruth Bayer, Aloma Ruiz Boada, Mark Bourdeau, William Breeze, Jacqueline Bunge, Dylan Burns, Nick Cave, Ben Chasny, Shirley Collins, Kat Cormie, Geoff Cox, Jennifer Cromwell, Baby Dee, Rosie Evans, Stewart Evans, Michel Faber, Bill Fay, Reinier van Houdt, Christopher Josiffe, Michael Lawrence, Andrew Liles, Melon Liles, Thomas Ligotti, Mark Logan, Giulio Di Mauro, Rose McDowall, Tony (TS) McPhee, Chris Mikul, Rita Knuistingh Neven, José Pacheco, Jim Pascoe, Charles Peltz, Davide Pepe, Steven Pittis, Edwin Pouncey, Shaun Richards, Alasdair Roberts, Steven Stapleton, Stephen Thrower, Alexandra Waliszewska, Patrick Wells, Boyd White, Lauren Winton, Michael J. York, and Paschalis Zervas.

The brief translation from the Akkadian text of *Maqlû* is by me. I used Tzvi Abusch's edition of the text, published in 2015 in Volume XI of the Neo-Assyrian Text Corpus Project's series of the *State Archives of Assyria Cuneiform Texts*. The Assurbanipal font was used for the Neo-Assyrian cuneiform text in this volume.

Thank you to everyone and everything and All Shall Be Well—one day we shall all meet again on the Dear Old BattleField, under soft black stars.

David, ŠapšuDay, the 5th of Hare, Hastings 2020.

David Tibet was born in Batu Gajah in 1960 and is the founder and Ba'al of the PickNick Cartoon Chariot Family Current 93. He lives in Hastings with Ania St. Polka, their 3 cats, Fairy, Gef!, and Voirrey, all the ghosts of all their past and coming Cats, and the fetch of Sunex Amures who communicates with him by means of skittles.

Strange Attractor Press 2020